DEAD WOMAN WALKING

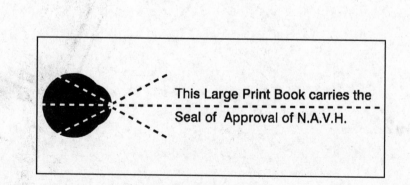

This Large Print Book carries the
Seal of Approval of N.A.V.H.

DEAD WOMAN WALKING

SHARON BOLTON

THORNDIKE PRESS
A part of Gale, a Cengage Company

GALE
A Cengage Company

Farmington Hills, Mich • San Francisco • New York • Waterville, Maine
Meriden, Conn • Mason, Ohio • Chicago

Copyright © 2017 by Sharon Bolton.
Thorndike Press, a part of Gale, a Cengage Company.

ALL RIGHTS RESERVED
This is a work of fiction. All of the characters, organizations, and events portrayed in this novel are either products of the author's imagination or are used fictitiously.
Thorndike Press® Large Print Core.
The text of this Large Print edition is unabridged.
Other aspects of the book may vary from the original edition.
Set in 16 pt. Plantin.

**LIBRARY OF CONGRESS CIP DATA ON FILE.
CATALOGUING IN PUBLICATION FOR THIS BOOK
IS AVAILABLE FROM THE LIBRARY OF CONGRESS**

ISBN-13: 978-1-4328-4578-0 (hardcover)
ISBN-10: 1-4328-4578-0 (hardcover)

Published in 2018 by arrangement with Macmillan Publishing Group, LLC/St. Martin's Press

Printed in the United States of America
1 2 3 4 5 6 7 22 21 20 19 18

For my friends in Ealing,
who have been wonderful.

1

'This woman — Jessica Lane — should have died. Eleven people were killed in that crash. Not only did Lane survive, she walked away. She's still walking.

'So, I want to know where she's going. I want to know why she hasn't been in touch. Why she isn't seeking help. Why she's deliberately avoiding the police.

'I want to know who she's running from.

'Most of all, I want her found.'

■ ■ ■ ■

PART ONE

■ ■ ■ ■

2

Wednesday, 20 September

The balloon hung in the air like an inverted Christmas bauble, its voluptuous, candy-striped sphere reflected perfectly in the lake. In the early light, the water glowed with the colours of a ripe peach, pale gold towards its edges, a deeper, richer pink at its heart. There was no wind. No sound. The trees along the shoreline had ceased their pre-dawn rustling and none of the balloon's thirteen passengers was either moving or speaking. The world seemed to be holding its breath.

Below, as far as the passengers could see in every direction, lay the heather-swept moorland of the Northumberland National Park. Acres of grasses rippled like the pelt of a huge waking animal, streams shimmered like silver snakes and the burning sunrise set the hilltops on fire. The landscape was vast, wild, unchanged in hundreds of years, as though the balloon had become a time machine, floating them back to when the far north of England was home to even fewer people than it is now. They could see no roads, no train lines, no towns or villages.

But for the thirteen of them, the world seemed empty.

The basket was large and rectangular, as is common with pleasure flights, and subdivided into four sections to restrict on-board movement of the passengers. The pilot had his own space in the centre of the rectangle. In one of the compartments were two women in their mid to late thirties. One wearing black, the other green, the two were not quite alike enough to be twins, but obviously sisters. The one in black breathed out a soft bubble of sound, too audible to be a sigh, too happy to be a moan.

'You're welcome.' The sister in green smiled.

The sisters were sharing their compartment with an accountant from Dunstable. His wife and two teenage children were in the one adjacent. On the other side of the pilot were three men on a hiking holiday, dressed like traffic lights in red, orange and green anoraks, a middle-aged couple from Scotland and a retired journalist.

12

The basket continued its slow, lazy spiral as they drifted above the lake. The constant movement had been one of the biggest surprises of the experience, as had the feel of the air at altitude. It was sharper, somehow, and fresher than it ever felt on the ground. Cool, but not uncomfortably so in the way that frosty mornings are. This air tingled against the skin, fizzed its way down to the lungs.

The woman in green, Jessica, edged closer to her sister, whose face had grown pale and whose hands were clutching the rim of the basket. Her eyes, staring directly down at the water's surface, were wide with wonder. Jessica was suddenly disturbed by the most alarming thought. That her sister might be about to jump out.

A short while later, she was to think it might have been better if both of them had jumped, that one or two petrifying seconds and a painful encounter with the water's surface wouldn't have been so bad. The cool, choking blackness might have finished them off, but equally might have buoyed them up and carried them to shore. Had they leapt at that point they might both have lived.

'Isn't it fabulous?' she said, because she'd learned a long time ago that distraction could sometimes halt a reckless course of action on her sister's part. 'Are you enjoying it? I can't believe we never did this before.'

Isabel smiled but said nothing, because a reply would have been pointless. She was clearly besotted with the whole experience.

'It's gorgeous, isn't it? Look at those colours.'

Still no reply, but Jessica had the satisfaction of seeing her sister lift her head and beam at the trees growing right to the edge of the water. They were like ladies at a ball, jostling for space, their floating gowns trailing down, twisting together, until it was impossible to tell where one ended and another began. Beyond the trees the hills, glowing like precious metals, went on for ever.

'We're now above the Harcourt Estate.' From take-off the pilot had been the only one to speak above a whisper. 'The original house was built on the rise directly ahead, but destroyed by fire in the late nineteenth century.'

'Do we need a bit more height?' The retired journalist with the thinning hair and thickening waistline was frowning at the rapidly approaching trees.

'Don't worry, folks, I've done this before.'

14

The six-foot, red-haired Geordie pilot tickled the air above the burner with a short burst of flame and those closest to him felt the oven-blast of hot air on their heads. 'I like to stay low at this point because these woods are one of the best places in Northumberland to see red squirrels. Also, whilst it's a bit late in the year, ospreys.'

There was a sudden flurry of camera activity, and a pressing towards the side of the basket closest to the woods. Neither of the sisters had brought a camera, so they were the first to see the ruined upper sections of the house come into view, rising from the tree canopy like badly stained teeth. The sister in black shuddered.

'The sixteenth-century house was built here for defensive purposes,' said the pilot as the balloon rose a little to skirt the treetops. 'Back then, you'd get an uninterrupted view of nearly fifty miles of countryside. Fifteen minutes from landing, folks.'

'Is that one? Top of the wide tree with yellow leaves? Greyish-brown feathers.' One of the hikers was pointing back towards the treetops and the focus of attention shifted away from the house.

'Could be.' The pilot raised his binoculars, turning his back on the direction of travel.

'There's someone down there.'

15

'Where? In the woods?' Jessica followed her sister's gaze, but her own eyesight had never been as good. Isabel's hearing was better too, and she had always been the first to pick up scents, to detect the strange flavours in food. As though she were the sharper, clearer-forged of the two.

'Behind the house.'

Jessica stood on tiptoe. Over her sister's shoulder she could see the great gaping holes in the roof, the collapsing walls.

'A girl. Running.'

Low enough to make out tiny pillows of moss and broken roof slates, the balloon passed over the house. The pilot, distracted by his attempt to spot an osprey, had allowed them to fall lower still.

'There.'

A darting figure — a young woman, slim and dark-haired, wearing blue clothes that had an eastern look about them — had reached the far wall of the garden.

'What's she doing?'

Behind them, others were trying to photograph the osprey and the journalist was advising on how best to capture wildlife. Only the two sisters were watching the girl on the ground. Jessica glanced round, unsure whether to alert the others or not. Reaching into the pocket of her jacket she

16

found her phone.

Down in the garden, from around a line of bushes, a man came walking slowly, but purposefully. From above, the two sisters could only make out his build, short but stocky. He wore an oversized leather jacket and a dark trilby. White shirt. His dark hair curled down below the rim of the hat.

Trotting along by his side was a large German shepherd.

'Oh!' Jessica pressed even closer to her sister. 'Bella, hold still, let me just —'

At the sight of the man, the girl cowered down, her hands clasped tight above her head.

'What?' said Isabel.

'I don't believe it! It is him.'

'Who? Jess, do you know that man?'

'Sean!' Jessica reached back, touched the pilot's arm. 'You need to see this.'

'What is it?' He turned their way, so did the accountant.

'He's got a gun.' The accountant's teenage son had spotted the pair on the ground, was pointing to what appeared to be a rifle or shotgun in the man's left hand. In his right, he had a large stone.

'Oh my God, he has,' said the teenager's mother. 'What do we do?'

They were still talking in shrill whispers.

Others in the basket had lost interest in the osprey and more heads were turning their way. The girl on the ground looked up, saw the balloon, and began to scream. The man, who hadn't seen them or heard them yet, raised the stone high. The girl seemed to be trying to press herself into the ground. The man brought the stone down.

The girl didn't scream again. The strangled cry, perfectly audible in the dawn air, came from someone in the balloon. It was the only sound they made. Shock held them tight. The man on the ground turned and looked up. His dog did the same. The dog began to bark. The passengers in the balloon saw the man drop the rock and lift a hand to his head, holding his hat in place as he craned his neck and stared upwards.

'Oh Christ,' said Jessica.

The air around them roared as Sean opened the valve and released the flame, but he'd told them in the briefing that up to ten seconds' delay would follow any action on his part. It could be ten seconds before the balloon was rising properly. Isabel, probably remembering the same thing, was counting softly. 'Ten, nine . . .'

Jessica brought her phone up, flicked to camera mode and took the man's picture. He saw her do it. For a second he stared directly into her eyes.

'Eight, seven . . .'

The man on the ground passed the gun into his right hand.

'Get down! Everyone down!' Jessica pushed her sister below the rim of the basket and dropped down herself, reaching back to tug on the accountant's arm. Unable to duck completely, there simply wasn't room for all of them to kneel in the basket. She left her eyes pinned on the man below, the top of her head dangerously exposed.

His dog was running in excited circles now, barking up at the strange thing in the sky.

'Six, five . . .' counted Isabel.

Jessica thought perhaps they were rising, but slowly. People were still on their feet. 'Get down,' she tried again.

Another flame burst upwards, just as the man on the ground raised his gun. The sounds of terror erupted into the still dawn air. Passengers began to scream, to shout to each other, to the pilot. As the accountant reached across, pushing his family below its brim, the basket began to turn, taking the two sisters further away from the drama on the ground.

'Four, three . . .' They were definitely going up, faster now.

'Hold tight!' Sean burned a third time.

'Two, one.' In her head, Jessica counted another second, then another. Yes, they were climbing quickly now. The balloon passed beyond the walled perimeter of the garden, gaining height with every second.

'Oh thank God! — Quick, take us up — Oh my God! Everyone, keep your heads down.'

The basket swung back and she could see the garden again. Through an archway, where a sturdy wooden door would once have hung, the man on the ground had stepped out into the open space behind the house. Jessica brought her phone up and took his picture again. A clear shot this time. Unfortunately, he had the same.

'Heads down! Heads down!'

She had no idea who was shouting, she thought it was probably the pilot, but she couldn't move, couldn't duck completely below the basket rim. She continued to stare at the man who was holding the rifle, had the butt tucked against his shoulder, was steadying himself against the wall.

He was aiming at her. She was sure of it.

The shot — so loud, so clear, and so very, very close — was followed by several seconds of shocked silence. Then low mutterings and a stifled moan. The teenage girl began to sob.

The balloon was rising very fast now, the ground shrinking away. Already the two figures, one coiled like a felled snake, the other striding fast along the rise of land as though it might catch him, were becoming indistinct. In the corner of her eye, Jessica saw another head appear over the rim. She could hear movement, scrabbling against the rattan framework of the basket. The other passengers were getting to their feet. Her sister pushed and she leaned back, allowing her to rise.

'Did that really happen?' 'I can't believe that just happened!' 'Is everyone all right?' 'Helen? Poppy? Nathan? Talk to me.'

The man on the ground raised his rifle again and the basket swung as people ducked for cover. This time, the two sisters stayed where they were. They were very high now, probably as high as they'd been since the trip started, and several hundred metres away. They must be safe.

'Is there a signal up here?' The journalist was still below the rim of the basket. 'We need to call the police.'

Jessica had already checked her phone. Nothing. There was little or no signal in the Northumberland National Park. It remained one of the most remote, sparsely populated, least accessible regions of the country.

Heads began appearing again. The accountant, who'd introduced himself earlier as Harry, reached out for his wife, who had one arm around each of her children. People, visibly shaken, were looking down at the rise of land, the ruined house, the autumn patchwork of woodland. The lake was still shining in the dawn light like a discarded penny. It seemed a long way away.

'It's OK. Everybody be calm. Nat, are you all right? It's over. We're too far away now. I can't even see him any more. Jesus wept, did I really see that?'

Jessica could feel tension settling as terror gave way to relief. She checked her phone again. Down on the ground was a woman who couldn't get away. Someone with a different network might have more luck. She opened her mouth to ask them all to check their phones —

The screaming thumped against the side of her head like a hammer blow.

As one, the passengers turned towards the sound. On the other side of the basket stood a middle-aged schoolteacher called Natalie. Her screaming continued, her hands clamped tight to her face. Her husband clutched her shoulders, trying to turn her face towards himself.

The other passengers looked at her, followed her eyeline and saw immediately that something was missing. And that its absence spelled disaster.

Sean, the big, red-haired pilot, was no longer standing upright in his separate compartment in the middle of the basket, one hand on the burner valve, the other clutching his binoculars. Those closest to him craned forward, as though he too might be cowering out of sight. The teenage boy was pulled back by his father. A male hiker turned away, revulsion on his face.

'What?' 'Where is he?' 'Where's he gone?'

Jessica pressed closer and stood on tiptoe to see over the accountant's shoulder, then raised her phone again and began taking photographs.

The interior of the pilot's compartment looked as though someone had shaken a lidless can of red paint around. Blood and a glutinous grey slime dripped down the rattan sides. In the bottom of the basket was slumped a tangle of limbs and torso.

The pilot's head had been shot clean from his body.

3

Taking out the pilot with a single shot had been one of the most satisfying experiences of his life. Patrick felt his entire body tingling with excitement, energy coursing through his veins as though it had been Tasered into him. Now, though, he had his sight upon the dark-haired woman in the green jacket. He took a breath, held it, and felt his trigger finger glow. She was staring straight at him, dumb as a rabbit, and in a split second her brains would be spraying through the air like a firework. He felt the familiar stirring in his groin at knowing the hunt was coming to an end and, in the middle of his chest, the outline of the crucifix burned through his shirt and into his skin.

But the freaking basket was spinning again, taking the woman's head out of the sight, partially obscuring it behind one of the balloon's strong supporting wires, and with every passing second they were getting higher in the sky. Other heads began to appear, darting below the rim again when they caught sight of him. He counted six, eight, maybe more. Very little time left now.

'Shut it, Shinto.' He aimed a kick at the dog. It dodged him with the skill of long practice.

He could shoot the basket. The woven material wouldn't hold back bullets. He could take out most of them simply by peppering it. There, the cleanest, tidiest shot he'd ever get. She was looking directly at him again, had even raised herself up, was staring down at him, almost as though she knew him — he pulled gently on the trigger.

And stopped. He could not shoot any more of them. Even one might have been too many. This had to look like an accident. The rest would have to die on impact.

No problem. Actually, a lot more fun.

Patrick lowered the gun, watched as the balloon sailed out of reach and then pulled out his phone. No signal. There never was a signal out here. None of them would be calling for help or reporting the incident any time soon.

From close behind, a low moan reminded him he wasn't done here yet. He walked back into the garden, the dog at his heels.

The girl on the ground still had a pulse, but it was faint. She was bleeding from the cut on her head and possibly also from one ear. He lifted a strand of black hair, leaned low and pressed it to his face. It smelled of oil and sweat and when he let it fall in disgust, her eyes opened. She couldn't focus. Her eyes were black but there was no gleam in them any more. She moaned, but made no attempt to move.

He watched her for three minutes that he couldn't spare. He arranged her long hair until it covered her face but didn't bring his fingers up to his nose again. The colour was right, the colour was what he liked, but the smell was wrong. He stepped back, looking at the outline of her thin body beneath the dirty clothes, and had thoughts that according to his ma would send him straight to hell.

Time was running on. Shouldering his gun, he ran across the garden, through the ruined house and back out the front. His quad bike was waiting. He tucked his hat into a pocket, turned on the ignition and steered around the front of the house. Shinto followed. He could keep up with the bike all day if he had to.

4

Shock had wrapped itself around the balloon like a chill wind. The hiker in the far corner of the basket was shouting instructions that nobody could properly hear. The teenage boy, using his phone to take pictures of the dead pilot, was a mass of jumpy, nervous movement. His father, by contrast, seemed frozen in place. The mother and daughter were locked tight together as far from the dead man as they could get.

Natalie was clinging to her husband and yelling that she had to get down, they had to get her down, that she really couldn't cope with any more and could they please get her down now.

Below them, the earth had lost most of its colour, all of its shine. Almost from nowhere, heavy clouds had massed in the sky, draining the park of its beauty. Now it looked desolate and empty. A place from which no help could come.

The balloon was still rising, picking up speed, its shadow racing along the ground. The air around them was colder too. The gentle tingling against the skin of the first part of the flight had given way to the harsh nip of almost-winter mornings. For the first time since they'd taken off, Jessica experienced the dull ache of nausea.

A cold hand closed gently around hers. 'What do we do?' Isabel asked.

On the other side of the pilot's compartment, the three hikers were on their feet, pale but composed. The journalist too.

'We need a new pilot.' Jessica willed her voice not to show the terror she was feeling. 'It's not a fighter jet. We go up, we go down. How hard can it be?'

One of the hikers, a man called Nigel, said, 'I'm a mechanical engineer. Anyone think they're better qualified?'

'Somebody do something now,' wailed Natalie. 'I don't want to die.'

'Nobody's going to die.' The hiker in red, Walter, was a loud man, a man who spoke and laughed noisily. Being scared was making him louder.

'We have plenty of time,' the journalist, Martyn, said. 'We can get up to something like ten thousand feet before we need oxygen. The important thing is not to panic.'

28

Such wise words. So hard to obey. Panic had swooped down from above like a giant bird of prey. Jessica didn't want to look up in case she saw it, perched on the supporting framework above their heads, leering down, waiting for their control to break. She glanced over the side instead. The landscape below didn't seem to be getting smaller.

'Give me a leg up, Walt.' Nigel reached up to grasp the leather-covered uprights.

Natalie broke away from her husband and began screaming, hurling her terror out into the thinning air.

'Shut up!' The last of the three hikers — Bob — pointed at Natalie's husband. 'You, shut her up. All of you, shut up now or I will throw you overboard myself.'

An angry red face looked back at him. 'There's no need for that.'

'We should all try to be calm,' Jessica heard her sister say. 'I know we're frightened but there are lots of things we can do.'

They listened to Isabel. Screams were stifled, sobs held back. The new calm was fragile, though, like a bubble made from soap. It could burst at any second.

Nigel, dangerously exposed, wobbled on the brink of the pilot's compartment. His face was ashen as he dropped down. 'Shit.'

He turned back to his two mates. 'I can't see a bloody thing in here. We have to get rid of Sean.'

Walter stared. 'What do you mean, get rid of him?'

'Look at him.'

As those closest pressed forward, Bob did something that seemed stupidly daring. He took hold of the uprights that held the basket to the balloon and jumped up so that he was sitting on the basket's rim. Everyone looked down. The space in the centre of the basket was tiny, built for one person to stand upright. The pilot had been a big man. Slumped in death, he took up the entire floor space.

'We have to throw him over.'

'We can't do that. Lie him down.'

'It won't work, we won't be able to move.'

Martyn said, 'Get him into this basket.'

A fresh wail from Natalie. 'Don't bring him in with us. I couldn't bear it.'

The journalist turned on her. 'We can't just drop him.'

'For God's sake, he's dead, he couldn't be more dead.'

Jessica had to say something. 'We're not rising any more,' she called. 'In fact, we've lost quite a bit of height. Whatever we do, we have to do it quickly.'

Bob jumped down from the rim. 'Natalie has a point. This is no time for sentiment. We have to get rid of him.'

Walter said, 'I'll climb over, Nigel, give you a hand.'

Nigel nodded. 'Martyn, are you OK to help? Ladies, I'm sorry to ask, but I might need you to shove his legs and feet.'

'No problem,' said Jessica.

As Walter began to climb over to join Nigel, Jessica couldn't help glancing over the side again. The ground was an awful lot closer. Was that a good thing, or . . . ?

'Don't look,' said her sister, quietly in her ear. 'We've got time.'

'He's a big bloke.' Nigel and Walter were bent over in the pilot's compartment. 'Martyn, grab an arm and pull when I say. OK, guys, and lift.'

The three men heaved. The pilot was heavy in death, but they got his torso over the rim and then gravity took over.

'Wait!' Jessica yelled. Too late. One final heave and the pilot's legs scraped over the rattan and he slid out of sight.

The balloon responded immediately to the lost weight. It went up, faster than it had previously, swimming up towards the thickening cloud.

Fresh wails broke out from all sides. Up

they went.

'What's happening?' someone shouted.

'We've lost the pilot's weight,' Jessica yelled. 'He was a big man, the balloon was bound to react. It will sort itself out. Hold on and don't panic.'

Easy to say, when the seaside-rock colours of the balloon seemed to be growing bigger and brighter above them.

In the pilot's space, Nigel was looking at the variometer, the one instrument in the basket that was clipped to an upright. He stared as though willing it to stop showing ever-higher numbers. 'Christ, I should have thought of that.' He ran a hand over his face, leaving behind red smudges from the pilot's blood. 'We're nearly at two thousand feet,' he said.

'It's not a problem,' Jessica shouted. 'We were very low over the house. There's a lot of sky above us. It will sort itself out.' She turned to look at the scared faces. 'We're getting an unexpected lesson in physics. I think it's slowing already.'

It wasn't. They were still rising quickly, but the filthy black bird above them had spread its wings. She could feel its shadow cloaking them, its vile stench settling.

'She's right,' the journalist yelled. 'We can't go up indefinitely. I did some reading before I booked this trip. Also, the terminal velocity of a balloon like this is roughly eight hundred feet per minute.'

'What the hell's that got to do with anything?' said Bob.

'That's about the same as an old-fashioned parachute.' The journalist looked across at the sisters. 'It means we won't die, ladies. We might break a few bones, but even if all we do now is drift back to earth, we should be OK. There really is no need to panic. And no jumping out, at any point, or the balloon will fly up again.'

Around the basket, faces creased in concentration as people processed his words and tried to understand them.

'Thanks, Martyn,' said Nigel. 'Walt, you use a radio on the boat, see if you can figure out how to work this one. We need to let people on the ground know what's happening and get some help. They can talk us down. It can't be that hard.'

'Does anyone have a signal?' Jessica was holding up her phone, trying to catch the attention of the others. 'We still need to get help for the woman on the ground, if we can. We need to get the police looking for that guy. Phones will be quicker than waiting for Walter to work the radio. Can you all check, please?'

Nigel dug into his pocket and handed over a slim phone. Jessica shook her head in frustration. 'Same as mine. Anyone on anything other than Orange?'

People were taking out their phones, holding them up, waving them around, tapping them against the side of the basket.

'Keep trying, please. We have to get in range sometime.'

Nigel, still staring at the variometer, was breathing heavily, as though he'd just run a race. 'OK,' he said, 'one of the last things Sean told us was that we were fifteen minutes from landing, so we must be close.' He glanced over the side. 'What I need you to do, ladies and gents, is be my lookouts. Look for the ground crew, for a suitable landing site, somewhere big and flat. Most importantly, look for obstacles. We don't want to go flying into a big tree or a mountain.'

'I can't actually see a radio at the moment,' Walter muttered. 'Anyone know what it should look like?'

Jessica glanced up from her phone. 'The old house will be our best landmark. The old Harcourt Estate. There's nothing else in view. We just need to work out how far we've travelled.' She checked her watch. 'Twelve minutes since we passed over the house. I'd

34

say we've gone about two miles.'

Nigel had one hand on a red-painted metal valve. 'If I'm right, this will release the gas and send us up.' When no one objected, he turned the valve. A burst of flame shot into the air.

'No! Don't take us up. We need to go down.'

'I need to figure out how it works.' Nigel fired the burner again.

'Stop it! Take us down.'

'Am I going blind?' Walter was on his knees and only the two sisters heard him. They looked at each other.

'Hush, love, he knows what he's doing,' said Natalie's husband.

'No, he doesn't. He hasn't a clue. None of us have.'

There is no radio in this balloon. Jessica mouthed the words, making no sound, but feeling them echo around her head all the same. Above her, the bird with its rotting black feathers opened its beak and screeched down at them.

The balloon responded to the hot air and began rising.

'There is no radio in this balloon.' Walt repeated her words quietly, glancing up at the two sisters.

'There must be,' Jessica said. 'We all heard

Sean using it.'

'I've got a signal.' The teenage boy was holding his phone up high, twisting it around in the air, as though trying to capture the elusive signal. 'It's faint though. Only one bar.'

'Call 999,' Jessica snapped at him. 'Tell them what's happening. They'll know what to do. Give it to me if you have any problems. Walter, what's that over there? Behind that canvas?'

Nigel spoke to the journalist. 'Martyn, the fire extinguisher's next to you. When we land, one of the biggest dangers is going to be fire, so I want you to figure out how to use it. Don't set it off too soon.'

'Right you are,' replied the journalist.

'Oh my God, we're not going to burn, are we? I can't burn.'

'Someone please shut her up.'

Natalie's husband had one hand wrapped tight around the uprights. 'She's scared, OK? We all are.'

'Yeah, well some of us are trying to be constructive.'

'I've lost the signal again,' the teenage boy said. 'Sorry, guys.'

'Keep trying.' Jessica was intent on her own phone. 'Everyone keep trying. We have to get a signal sometime.'

'We're too high.' The mother and the teenage girl were locked together. 'Don't send us any higher.'

'OK, I won't.' Nigel gave them a nervous smile. 'I think I've figured out how the vent works — we pull on this coloured line here — so I'm going to let us drift lower now. I'll only use the burner if I think we're descending too quickly.'

He wrapped his hand around a coloured cord, hesitated for a second, and then pulled. There was an audible intake of breath and then everyone looked up to see that the central circle of the balloon had collapsed down, revealing a ring of daylight in the top. As Nigel released the cord it vanished. Jessica started to count to ten in her head. At eight, the balloon began to sink.

In the pilot's space, Nigel gave a little grunt of satisfaction. 'Everyone, I want you to keep looking round. Don't look at me. Don't look at the balloon. We need to spot that ground crew. If you have phones, I want you using them. Nathan, is it? Any luck yet?'

'Not yet.' The teenager looked up briefly. 'It keeps cutting out. I'm going to try a text.'

'How we doing with the radio, Walt? I could really use some advice from the ground.'

'Dad?' said the teenage girl.

'Keep trying, Nathan. Did anyone get photographs of that bastard back at the house?'

'Dad?' said the girl, a bit louder this time.

'I did.' Martyn held his phone aloft.

'Good. Post them on Twitter, Instagram or something. People need to know what happened.'

'What are you doing?' Jessica heard her sister's voice in her ear.

'Sending Neil the password for my laptop,' she replied. 'Lot of important stuff on it.' She looked up and forced a smile at her sister's worried face. 'Just being cautious, you know me.'

'Nige, I really don't think there's a radio in this basket.'

'Dad! Everyone!'

This time they gave the girl their attention. She was pointing back the way they'd travelled.

'That guy with the gun is following us!'

5

The balloon was already some distance away. Getting a quick fix from the sun and checking the wind by breathing in deeply and processing the various scents, Patrick set off easterly along the treeless, wind-scorched, tundra-like landscape. Few people knew these four hundred square miles of nothing better than he did, and if the wind held he had a pretty good idea where they were going to come down.

The heather, just starting to glow purple in the early sun, grew thickly on the downward slope but his large bike wheels travelled over it easily. The hidden stones, hard and sharp as knives, were more of a problem. He was leaving tracks but the grey clouds on the horizon would be here in less than an hour. The bright day was turning dark. Rain would piss right down and his tracks, if not obliterated, would be indistinguishable from those made by farmers and park rangers.

He lost sight of the balloon as he steered down through a patch of scrubland but found it again when he came out the other side. It was much lower in the sky now. He began counting again, starting with the woman in the green jacket. Six, nine, ten, eleven. Twelve, he thought. Yes, he was sure, definitely twelve.

His attention in the sky, he steered too close to an outcrop of rocks. His front left wheel struck a stone, sending him lurching forwards and he had to stop, reverse and find his way around the rock pile. The ground here was rough, the steep hills of the Cheviots giving way to bogs and hidden rocks, and he couldn't get the bike up to its top speed. On the other hand, the wind wasn't strong and he was gaining on them.

He figured another ten minutes, fifteen at most. He shifted on the seat. One day. Two hunts. He'd had worse mornings.

6

'No, no, no, guys, you can't all look back. I need you looking where we're going. And keep still. Stop jumping around.'

Ignoring Nigel, the passengers pressed towards what had become the rear of the basket, facing the way they'd travelled. On the ground, far below them, a male figure riding a quad bike appeared to be following their course.

'I'm taking us up.' Nigel burned as he spoke. 'Until we know for sure.'

'He can't catch us, can he?' asked the teenage boy.

Another blast of flame. The balloon began to rise. Nigel said, 'Has anyone made contact with the ground yet? Any phone signals? Walt, any luck with that radio?'

'I've posted a tweet,' said the teenage boy. 'I'm not sure anyone's spotted it yet. I've only got forty-three followers.'

His father said, 'My emergency call was

answered but I lost the connection.'

Jessica checked her phone again. Still no signal. The photographs she'd taken of the man on the ground and the dead pilot were safely stored, though. The message to Neil would go through as soon as she had a signal.

'He can't follow us for long,' said Nigel. 'There'll be rivers in his way. Walls, all sorts of things. Guys, I need you to look forward not back. I can't do it all myself. Walt, talk to me.'

'There are woods ahead,' Jessica heard her sister call out. 'We need to avoid those. And some electricity pylons to the south.'

'He's gone. I can't see him any more.'

Jessica turned to see the bike and its rider had indeed disappeared.

'He's in a small valley,' said the journalist. 'Going up and down steep slopes will slow him down. Keep trying the phones, everyone.'

Walter was back on his feet, his face drawn and pale. 'Nige, there's no radio in this basket.'

'There has to be. We heard Sean using it.'

'I've looked everywhere. I've looked in every pocket, every bag, everywhere. It isn't here.'

'I know where it is.'

Jessica turned to see tears gleaming in her sister's eyes. 'Sean was wearing the radio around his neck, on a strap,' Isabel said. 'When he wasn't using it, he must have tucked it into a pocket.'

'What are you saying?' one of the men asked.

'You wouldn't have seen it. Wouldn't have known. It wasn't your fault.'

Every other passenger was staring at her calm-faced sister in dismay. 'We threw it overboard? We threw it overboard when we threw Sean?'

'I told you,' wailed Natalie. 'I told you not to do it.'

'No, you fucking didn't,' yelled Walter. 'You told us not to put him in with you.'

'There's no need for language like that,' snapped her husband.

'Jesus, are you a moron? Look at us. Can you suggest when bad language might be appropriate?'

Frightened eyes glared across the basket. 'You should have some respect.'

'Enough! Quiet.'

They obeyed Nigel, thank God. He was in charge now.

'We have no means of contacting the ground?' Nigel asked.

'We've got phones,' said Bob. 'Sooner or

43

later, we'll get a signal. We'll have to stay up a bit longer, that's all.'

'I've sent another tweet,' said the teenager. 'And my first one's been retweeted. And I might have got a text through to Gran.'

Thank God for the young, Jessica thought. 'What's happening with the guy on the quad bike?' she said. 'Have we lost him?'

'No. He's fallen back but he's still following us,' the journalist said. 'We should definitely stay up.'

'OK, staying up seems sensible right now.' Nigel was looking from one gas cylinder to the next. 'Trouble is, this tank's getting low,' he said. 'We need to figure out how to switch them over.'

'I'll have a look,' Walt said.

Nigel burned. The balloon rose again. As a wail of protest began he said, 'We have to be quite high before I risk disconnecting the tank. And, guys, keep looking round. Can anyone see a road? A vehicle? Keep trying your phones.'

Nigel burned again. The variometer said 4,000 feet . . . 4,200 . . . 4,500 . . . The balloon speed picked up. It was noticeably colder now.

'I think I know how to do it, but I'd like someone else to check,' said Walt.

'We're leaving him behind.'

'Well, that's something.'

Suddenly, the world darkened. A shadow had fallen over them. Above, the balloon swung sharply round and its perfect shape began to billow and twist.

'This can't be good,' said Martyn, looking up.

'We've hit a squall,' said Nigel. 'We probably should go down now, see if we can get out of it. Walt, let me have a look at that.' He moved to Walter's side of the balloon. 'You give the vent a quick pull.'

The two men swapped places.

'This?' Walt said, taking hold of a thin, coloured line.

Nigel didn't look round. 'I've got it. We need to unscrew this valve and swap the pipe over. Yeah, mate. Coloured cord. Give it a gentle tug.'

Walter pulled on the line and the world fell away.

Jessica felt a second of weightlessness akin to being in a rapidly descending lift. Her stomach lurched and she realized the basket was falling.

'What's happening?'

'Jesus, what's going on?'

The basket continued to fall. They were picking up speed. She was on her knees, hurtling towards the earth, her hair flying up around her head. A great weight was pushing her down, squeezing the bones of her skull.

Up. Up. Get up!

She reached out, clutching for something, anything, to give her a purchase on the world and her hands found the basket side. As though she was pulling herself out of water, she dragged herself upright.

The basket was tilting as it fell, the heavier passengers taking their side down faster. Over the rim she could see the grey, green, brown patterns of the earth spinning up towards her.

Everyone in the basket was screaming. Maybe she was too.

'Let it go! Walt, let it go!' Nigel had one arm wrapped around the support wires, his feet braced against something on the basket floor. 'Let it go!'

Somehow Jessica's eyes fixed on the variometer: 4,000 feet . . . 3,500 . . . The distance to the ground was melting away.

Walter was slumped in the bottom of the basket, his hands empty. 'I have.'

'What the hell did you pull?' Nigel screamed at him.

Walter, his face ashen, pointed to the thin red line.

. . . 3,000 feet . . . 2,500 . . .

Panic rippled across Nigel's face as though an invisible hand had struck him. 'That's not it. That's not the one I've been pulling.'

Above their heads, the balloon had lost all shape, had collapsed in on itself, was almost close enough to touch.

. . . 2,000 . . . 1,800 . . . 1,500 . . .

'No, no, no.' Natalie, out of sight on the other side of the basket, was wailing.

'Use the burner!' Jessica heard the words in her head, wasn't sure whether they were audible above the rushing wind and the screams. 'I can't reach it. Nigel, use the burner.'

Keeping one hand on the burner frame, Nigel reached out and released the flame. It shot up high. Ten seconds. She wasn't sure they had ten seconds. The ground was flying up to meet them now, was getting ready to swallow them whole. Nigel burned again but the giant flame, so hot and so bright, was making no difference. The balloon was limp and dead, kept above them only by the speed of descent.

. . . 900 . . . 550 . . .

She was staring at the red line that had deflated the balloon. A short distance away was the candy-striped one that Nigel had been pulling. 'There are two lines,' she shouted up at him. 'Pull the other one.'

. . . 300 . . . 250 . . .

'We could make things worse.'

'How can they get worse?' Jessica leaned over, thought for a split second that she was going to leave the basket, took hold of the candy-striped cord and tugged.

Their descent continued. Silence fell, as though people around her were too terrified to scream. She looked up.

The balloon billowed and swayed, then burst into its former shape. The basket bounced once and then seemed to hang in the air, as though giant hands had caught it. The sensation of falling had stopped.

. . . 200 feet . . . 180 feet . . . 150 feet . . . They were still going down but more slowly now. Nigel burned again . . . 140 feet . . . 120 . . .

She started counting. Seven, eight, nine, ten.

. . . 70 feet . . . 50 feet . . . 55 feet . . . 60 feet. They'd stabilized. Someone threw up, noisily.

'Thank God.' Beads of sweat had broken out on Nigel's face. 'Nobody touch the red line again.' He was breathing heavily as he turned to Walter. 'Keep burning. I'm going to switch tanks.'

They seemed tantalizingly close to the ground now. They could make out detail in the trees again. In the distance, a cluster of buildings was visible, and the gunmetal gleam of a road.

'Can anyone see that bloke?' Bob had climbed up on to the basket rim again. 'We must be in range at this height.'

'We have to go up,' Isabel yelled. 'We're going to hit the pylon. Now!'

All heads turned. They were dangerously close to a string of electric wires, crossing the park at height.

Walter fired the burner. Then a second time. The pylon was getting closer with every second. Still too many seconds before they started to rise. The balloon began to lift, slowly, sluggishly.

'Hold on,' yelled Martyn. 'Hold on to something.'

They flew past the tip of the pylon, close enough so that Jessica could have leaned out to touch it. The occupants of the balloon breathed a collective sigh of relief, just as the bottom of the basket crashed into the wires.

The bang seemed deafening. Sparks littered the air around them. The basket bounced and tipped, tossing out Natalie and her husband as though they'd been emptied from a refuse bin. They sailed through the air, still clinging together, leaving a smell of

49

burning in their wake. There was a sound like a siren going off as the teenage girl began to scream.

The basket hit the wires again. Bob, still perilously high on the rim, overbalanced, clutched at the air around him, then he too toppled. Fewer than ten feet below the basket, he landed on the wires. He was close enough to the pylon for the power to leap across, run through him and complete the circuit. His body started to shake and jitter and smoke crept out of his clothes like escaping snakes. Screams leapt from his mouth like the bolts of electricity that were causing them.

Below him, Natalie and her husband had hit the ground.

'Oh my God, oh my God, oh my God.' The mother's fingers were white on her children's shoulders.

'Fasten your harnesses.' The accountant leaned over to reach his family. 'All of you, clip yourselves on.'

Nigel tried to burn but the flame was too small to make any real difference. 'Guys, we're coming down. I've got no more control. Fasten yourselves on.'

'We're going to hit those trees.'

'Bella, I'm clipping you on. Shit, stop moving.'

Jessica had been expecting the impact. She'd seen the rush of golden foliage as the trees raced towards them. Still, the force of the crash took her by surprise, sending her hurtling to the floor of the basket, banging her head hard against the solid metal of a loose harness. A second before the world slipped away, she saw her sister, whose harness she hadn't managed to fasten, thrown from the basket. Her black dress trailing behind, Bella soared into the air and out of sight.

Bella was flying.

7

Twenty-eight years earlier
Three children sat cross-legged on the sand, some distance from the sea, around a half-finished sandcastle. The bubble of youthful enthusiasm for the task had burst when they'd realized that, without buckets or spades, working only with hands, the shapes they could create fell a long way short of the turreted, crenellated parapets they'd seen in books.

The youngest child, a mere eight years old but still the most patient of the three, thought they could probably improve their lump of sand with decorations of shells, pebbles and seaweed, but her siblings had lost interest.

'Time travel,' said the eldest, a boy of around fourteen. Like his sisters, he was tall for his age, with dark hair and brown eyes, heavy eyebrows and plump, red lips. When he smiled his teeth seemed large and very white. 'So that I can go back to the time of great crimes, and stop them happening.'

'Yeah, that'd be good,' said the middle child.

The youngest thought that, yes, it might be good, but on the other hand could cause problems that went way beyond the impact of the original crime. She was smart for an eight-year-old.

'Mine would be flight.' The middle child thrust back her arms to simulate wings. 'To be able to take off and soar up into the clouds. To see everything and go anywhere.'

The youngest child thought that sounded amazing. And also very scary.

'How about you, Jessie?' said the boy. 'What would your superpower be?'

Jessica thought for a moment longer. It was hard sometimes — most of the time, actually — keeping up with these two.

'I'd like to be invisible,' she said, and then, because that didn't sound quite impressive enough, 'To have the power of invisibility. You know, to be able to turn it on and off. Not be invisible all the time.'

There was a moment's silence, and Jessica wondered if she'd said the wrong, or even a stupid, thing.

'Jessie, you're such a mouse, half the time you're invisible anyway,' said her brother.

'Don't tease her.' Bella smiled at her sister. 'Invisibility is a great superpower.'

'Let's go to the rock pools.' Ned jumped to his feet and started running along the beach. Bella sprang up too.

'What about the shoes?' Jessica looked back towards the sand dunes, to the pile of shoes and socks they'd left there.

'They'll be fine.' Bella was bouncing, eager to be off after Ned. 'The tide won't come this high. And who'd steal Ned's trainers?'

She set off, at a speed Jessica knew she could never keep up with. She started trotting along behind anyway. Bella would wait for her. She always did.

8

Wednesday, 20 September

The woman he'd watched spiral out of the balloon towards the ground had landed on top of the man who'd preceded her. Her head was facing away from his, her legs sprawled across his upper body. As Patrick drew closer, they looked more like puppets than people, dropped into a box that was too small. Their loose, bendable limbs had landed in strange positions and at odd angles.

They weren't moving.

He stopped the quad bike twenty metres away and climbed down. He left the gun on the seat so he wouldn't be tempted to use it and moved towards them, keeping an eye out for loose rocks, deep puddles, or the sudden appearance of a witness. Shinto got to them first and bent down, his nose close.

The woman wasn't the one he was hoping to see. Not the one in the green jacket who'd stared at him as though she were memorizing every line and curve of his face. Or as though she knew him already. He shook his head, dismissing the thought. This woman was older, in her late fifties, with dyed brown hair and grey roots. This woman was plump, her skin grey and loose on her bones.

The woman in the green jacket had been slim, had looked fit. She looked as though she could run, even fight. He pushed down a wave of excitement.

He could no longer see the balloon, but it couldn't have gone far. Not after hitting the power lines the way it had. He looked up. A man still dangled in the air above him. More than one of the wires had broken. One was dancing around, sparks flying off it. The smell reminded him of nights his family had cook-outs.

No need to worry about him, at least. Three down, another nine to go, if he'd been right about there being twelve people on board. He bent and searched the dead pair, finding a mobile phone in the inside pocket of the bloke. Directly beneath the twitching man on the wires, he found another phone in a conveniently bright red case. He took them both.

Calling to his dog, he walked back to the

bike, treading on the more solid bits of ground, or the springier patches of heather, taking care not to leave footprints. He fired it up again and set off, his mind's eye fixed on a dark-haired woman in a green jacket. He hoped she wasn't dead. Not yet.

9

Pain was everywhere, rushing through her like a blood transfusion. Jessica could hear it loud in her head, and in the cries of those around her. As the basket hit trees for a second and then a third time, she could hear the crack of skulls colliding against hard surfaces, of bones breaking. Metal scraped against metal. Wires went singing into the air like crazed snakes. The wicker in front of her eyes was torn away and the jagged branch of a tree stabbed in towards her. It missed her by inches.

The basket hit the ground hard and bounced back up. It did the same thing again. Each impact felt as though she were being thrown against a stone wall. She could no longer see Nigel at the controls. They were completely pilotless now.

She'd fallen into the bottom of the basket. She was staring directly up at the balloon but its beautiful sphere had twisted into something misshapen and ugly. It seemed to leer down towards her and she cringed away instinctively. She tried to curl up, to keep her limbs close to her body, but she was being thrown about so much. Only the harness that she was clinging to kept her within the confines of the basket and yet her shoulder muscles felt stretched and torn with the effort. The jarring and banging stopped as they were swooped up one more time.

She had a moment of wondering if she were alone in the basket, the only one not to have been thrown overboard, but then the screaming made its way into her head. There were others, still clinging to this flimsy piece of wickerwork, clinging and screaming.

She had no idea where her sister was.

The basket flew into something and tipped. She fell against its side, the jagged edge of the torn wicker scraping her face. A scream burst nearby and faded as it fell towards the ground. Then the basket seemed to settle.

'Bella!'

There was an answering cry. It didn't sound like her sister but she couldn't be sure.

'Bella, I can't see you.'

59

The balloon soared up into the sky again and, for a split second, the basket was surrounded by the purest, clearest blue.

10

Twenty-two years earlier

Jessica had never seen sky such a consistent shade of blue before.

A blue that was pure, clear and rich, too soft to be sapphire, too deep to be corn-flower. There was simply no other shade to which it could be compared. It was the colour of for ever, of timelessness, a colour one could lose oneself in.

She knew that, for her, it would always be the colour of sadness.

The ocean was blue too, and calmer than Jessica had ever seen it. When a gull flew low, following the line of the sand, its streamlined white shape was reflected perfectly in the water.

Her sister was a metre or two ahead. Jessica had dropped back when she'd started to cry.

'I don't get it, Bella,' she called out.

Isabel stopped walking, but didn't turn,

and she didn't plant her weight evenly on both feet. She was pausing, not stopping. This wasn't going to be a conversation, merely a repetition of the point she'd already made.

'I don't expect you to understand, Jess. Not yet.'

Jessica had run out of arguments. All she could do now was cry and complain like a child. 'First Mum, then Ned, then Dad. Now you. I'm losing everyone!'

In her head, she stamped her foot on the sand. Her misery was becoming rage. Also, she was afraid. Fourteen years old, but still with a child's natural fear of abandonment.

Bella turned then, stepped back and put her arms around Jessica. She was still taller. All these years, Jessica had been waiting to catch up. Now she was wondering if she ever would.

'You'll be fine, Jess. Auntie Brenda and Uncle Rob love you. They will take very good care of you. In four more years, you'll go to university. You'll do brilliantly and make me so proud. And then you'll get married and you'll have children. You'll be happy and this sadness will be something that was with you once but passed.'

'What about Ned? Why can't he come

home so we can live together? You, me and Ned?'

Bella stiffened in her sister's arms. 'That can't happen, Jess. You mustn't ask me that again.'

'Why? What has he done? Why did he have to go away? Where has he even gone?'

Bella began pulling away. Jessica held on, but Bella was stronger. She always had been. She pulled out of her sister's reach.

'I'll tell you more in time, Jess,' she said. 'When you're older. For now, you just have to accept that this is how it has to be.'

'Everyone is leaving me.'

'Jess, I can't live with you right now, but I will never leave you. I promise you. Never.'

11

Wednesday, 20 September

The other passengers were dead. They had to be. She could sense a great silence closing in, creeping into her mouth and spreading downwards, like dark slime, filling every hollow in her body.

It wasn't so bad, actually, just a quiet slipping away.

The explosion flung her through the air. There was a burning heat on her face, then tiny wounds jabbed at her on all sides. She thought of the fires of hell, and of a thousand little devils prodding her with pitchforks. She felt heavy. There was a crippling pain in her body, as though she were being hung from a great height.

Then nothing.

12

Twenty-one years earlier

Candles flickered as people started to move. The service was drawing to a close. Several women had handkerchiefs to their faces. Jessica had heard sniffing throughout, even the occasional sob.

'Lovely service,' said someone behind.

In her new red coat and hat, Jessica felt as cold and unmoved as the stone pillars.

To the glorious crescendo of organ music, the procession made its way down the aisle. It seemed to Jessica as though all eyes were on her sister. The lace of her long white dress gleamed in the candlelight and her face could have been carved from marble. Her new wedding ring shone on her left hand.

Bella had never looked more beautiful. She seemed to smile at something in the distance as heads turned to watch the lovely girl in her bridal gown glide down the aisle and out of the chapel doors. Jessica felt a hand on her shoulder.

'Come on, love,' said Aunt Brenda, who had also bought a new coat and hat for the occasion.

The congregation was leaving too, following the procession. Jessica, who had been sitting on one of the aisle seats, picked up her bag and joined them. Her aunt and uncle followed behind.

In the lobby of the chapel, out on the steps, spilling down into the garden, people gathered, chattering sombrely, congratulating each other, pretending to be happy.

Nobody here was happy. It was a ridiculous farce. And that her clever, strong, wise sister should be a part of it.

Jessica edged her way through the crowd and out of the main door. There were six steps and she ran down them. She'd seen peacocks in the grounds, and although she'd always been slightly afraid of them, she thought she might hunt them down now.

Maybe she'd wring one of their necks.

'Jess!'

She turned. Bella was at the top of the steps. Lifting the lace of her gown with one hand, she made her way carefully down towards her sister. She looked so beautiful. And so very, very sad.

'You look pathetic,' Jessica said. 'It's a travesty. Worse, it's disgusting.'

Bella sighed. 'This is something I need to do. You have to accept that. You have your own life to lead. Why can't you let me lead mine?'

Jessica stepped closer, so that she could hiss in her sister's face. 'Because this isn't you. Look at you, all decked up a like a bride in a cheap, second-hand, nylon dress. Where's your groom, Isabel? A married woman with no man? It's a joke.'

'I'm sorry you feel that way. I have to go now. I have to change.'

The gravel crunched as Isabel stepped away. She looked impossibly slim in the tight bodice, her long skirts trailing behind her. Jessica knew it would be the last time she saw her sister looking this way. When she and the others came back down from their rooms and rejoined the congregation in chapel, they would all be shrouded in black.

'You will not stay here,' Jessica shouted. 'I don't know what you're running from and I don't care what you're afraid of, but this is monstrous.'

Isabel didn't turn.

'Do you hear me, Bella? You will never be a nun.'

People on the steps, other postulants who'd just formalized their vows, their families, several of the black-clad sisters of the Carmelite order, were watching the two of them.

Jessica turned and walked away from the priory. She hadn't known it was possible to hurt this much.

13

Wednesday, 20 September

Where was she? Where was this place of darkness and pain? She hadn't known it was possible to hurt so much. It was tearing her apart from the inside and crushing her into dust. Her body was broken. There was no way out of this agony, it was consuming her whole.

She wasn't breathing, she was panting, gasping for each breath. She lay bewildered, frightened, unable to move. She had a sense, too, that she'd been hurting for a long time, slipping in and out of consciousness.

The air around her was crackling and rustling, like the inside of a faulty radio. Radio. Walter was looking for a radio. But Walt had leapt out of the basket after the second time it hit the trees. He'd thrown himself over the side and disappeared.

What on earth had happened to her?

She remembered driving through the dark

pre-dawn. Being surrounded by pale, excited faces.

Nigel — brave, clever Nigel — yelling at them to fasten themselves in, even as they fell, at impossible speed, through the last bit of sky.

The balloon. They'd crashed.

She opened her mouth. Nothing came out. So she tried her eyes and they, at least, still worked. After a few seconds of blinking away tears, she was able to focus.

She was in a tree, surrounded by dry, yellow leaves. Sharp twigs pressed into her. There was something hard in the small of her back and something else digging into her neck. As she lay there, staring up into the tangle of branches and foliage, she became aware that the pain surrounding her was changing, focusing. She was able to say now which parts of her hurt and which didn't. Most did. Also, that she was lying on her side, one leg caught higher in the tree, the other hanging loose.

A loud flapping sounded just out of view and she turned her head, even though her neck felt as if it could barely hold it up. The balloon. It was close, less than three metres away, hanging empty and spent from the tree branches. It jumped and stretched in the wind, desperate to be free again, to fly one last time but the branches held it tight. Then she was distracted again, by a voice from directly below.

'Help! Help! Can anyone hear me?'

Someone else was alive. She began feeling around, knowing she was some way off the ground, dreading the cracking sound that would be the branch beneath her breaking. Her arms, at least, did what she told them to. She could move her head. Looking up, she could see a vertical trail of broken branches. Also, several feet above her head, too high to reach, and almost invisible amongst the yellow leaves, was the turquoise case of a mobile phone.

There was something very, very important about that phone.

14

Patrick drove the quad bike up the last rise and smiled. The balloon was draped around a tree like a clumsily wrapped Christmas parcel, its basket hanging lopsided just a few feet from the ground. He freed one hand to pull out his phone. Still no signal, but it told him that nearly thirty minutes had passed since the balloon had flown over the old house. If the pilot had been in radio contact with his ground crew, they might not be far away. He had very little time.

Bouncing over the moor, he almost missed the man lying face down in the heather. At its highest before the winter frost struck, the vegetation hid much of his body and had it not been for the bright-coloured anorak he would have driven straight past him. He cut the bike's engine, again some distance away, and ran over.

He was trying not to give in to a sense of panic, but the ground crews always followed hot on the trail of these balloons.

This guy had leapt out. He couldn't be this distance away otherwise. His right leg was broken, bent at an angle. He'd put a horse down with an injury that bad, no question. Not to mention a dog.

He was still alive. From several feet away, it was possible to see the rapid panting, hear the breath hissing in and out through damaged lungs. Blood had gathered in his mouth and slipped out on to the heather.

Patrick stood above the injured man for a second, having no sense of whether or not the guy knew he was there. Then he dropped down heavily, kneeling on the man's back, driving his face into the ground. He grasped his head, took a deep breath and then pulled up and round.

The neck broke with a satisfying snap.

He had to reach in three pockets before he found the guy's mobile phone. He slipped it into his own pocket, along with the one he'd taken from the dead couple and the one he'd found beneath the man hanging from the electricity wires. That was four passengers taken care of, another eight to go. A mother and two teenage kids, he thought. A few more blokes.

And the woman in the green jacket. He was saving her till last.

He got back on the bike and drove closer to the balloon. There'd been an explosion of some sort. Only a small one, there were no flames left, but he could see where part of the wicker was charred and black. Thin spirals of smoke reached up towards the branches of the tree.

On foot again, he approached carefully. If people were still alive and able to fight back, they were more likely to be in the basket. He heard someone shouting when he was several metres away.

'Is someone there? Help!'

So much for being quiet. She must have heard the bike.

'My son's badly injured. And I think my leg's broken. I have no idea where my husband and daughter are. Can you help, please?'

Yes, he could help. He had a pretty good idea where her husband was. There was a body five feet from the basket, lying sprawled over a crop of jagged rocks. Five down. This guy had taken the brunt of the explosion. He moved in closer and looked down at the reddened, scorched skin of the dead man.

'Your husband lost his face,' he called. 'He stinks like burned meat. And one of his ribs seems to be sticking out through his shirt.'

A moment of silence, then, 'Who are you?'

'Don't worry. I'm here to help. I'll make it all better.'

The woman didn't reply.

He stepped towards the basket and heard her whimper.

'Hi.' He peered over the rim.

She looked up before reaching across the basket, as though to shield her son who was by her side. Her twisted legs didn't move.

'My son's only fifteen,' she said. 'Please don't hurt us.'

Her son was dead. His skin was already turning a sickly pale white.

'Give me his phone.'

She stared dumbly back at him. 'I don't know where it is.'

He grabbed her hair and pulled her upwards, hearing the sickening crunch of broken bones rubbing together. She let out a strangled cry.

He turned round, saw a rock the right size and bent to pick it up.

She was tougher than she looked. It took three good strikes to finish her off. Seven down. Five remaining.

A bloke who'd obviously fancied himself as a pilot was still strapped into a harness in the centre of the basket. His head had been sliced nearly clean from his body by the metal frame that had once held the burners in place. Blood was still pumping out, but feebly. He too had taken some of the explosion's blast.

Four still missing. One of them a teenage girl. And the woman in green.

Keeping an eye on the horizon, his ears alert, he walked round to check the other basket compartments. Just one man, huddled down in the corner of the balloon. Blood surrounded him. As he drew closer he saw the white gleam of bone sticking out of the man's neck, found a phone in a top jacket pocket. It was all going well. But he was probably running out of time.

He caught sight of dark brown hair just as he was thinking he was going to have to leave it at that, trust to luck that no one else had survived. A woman was lying at the base of a large beech tree.

He stood perfectly still, watching, savouring the moment. He really didn't want her to be dead. Then he heard something. A rustling sound. Coming from directly above.

15

Clinging to the tree trunk, breathing in its damp-sawdust smell, terrified of missing her footing, she inched herself down until she could make out the moorland grass and a corner of the tilted basket through a latticework of branches.

Below, a quad bike was drawing close. It seemed to be directly beneath her when the engine stopped. The excited barking of a dog rang out and the woman below called again.

'Hello, can you help me, please?'

A dark shadow moved across the ground, a man came into view, and terror grabbed her by the throat. No, no. This man was not here to help. She had no idea how she knew this, she just knew. Closing her eyes tight, she heard the crash of a rock slamming down again and again on a human skull and the strangled, inhuman cries that left the dying woman's mouth.

Then silence.

Only for a second. His shadow approached the trunk, his feet crunched over the scattering of beechnuts at its base. She drew back her head a second before he looked up.

She could hear his breathing, feel his eyes roving through the leaves and branches.

'Anyone up there?' he called.

Pressing her face into the bark she closed her eyes, the temptation to speak, to end the torturous suspense almost overwhelming. A rush of wind tore through the tree, she heard it shake the surrounding leaves, lift the ripped silk of the balloon, as though the wind were on his side, trying to pull her from the tree, lift the covering of balloon fabric and expose her.

'Hello?' he called again.

He was toying with her. He could see her. He could almost reach her if he stood on tiptoe. She waited, panting, for the feel of his hand gripping her ankle.

'This is the police,' he said. 'An ambulance is on its way. Anyone up there need help?'

He was not the police. The wind ran cold fingers through the branches, as though the man had sent his dark thoughts into the tree to search her out. She had a sense of small, evil creatures, scurrying along, lifting foliage, searching out her scent. Then she heard the twist of dried grass as he turned and left the shade of the tree.

Still playing with her. He wanted to lure her out. Or, maybe —

She held on tight and let her weight slide lower until she found another branch. Dangerously exposed now, she could see the man walking away. She knew this man. Images flashed through her head, of him raising a gun, bringing a rock down on a young woman's head. Chasing them.

His hair was long, curling beneath his hat to the nape of his neck. He was broad in the shoulder, strong in the legs. He was heading for a figure on the ground. A figure she recognized instantly. She saw him stop when he was close enough. He nudged her sister's body with his foot.

Why was her sister lying over there, not moving?

She had to do something. Her body wouldn't obey her. Terror held her frozen.

He seemed to spend a long time looking down. She let out the breath and drew another. Then another. She watched him kneel, lean forward and — he seemed to be smelling her sister's hair.

He moved his head backwards and forwards, like an animal nuzzling for food. She saw the rise of his shoulders as he inhaled. Finally, he pulled a mobile phone out of his pocket and stared at the screen. He made a gesture with his other hand, a clenching of the fist, then began punching at the keyboard. As he did so, he jumped up and strode back to his bike. He fired the engine, turned it around and drove away, the phone pressed to his face. The dog followed behind.

When she could no longer see the bike, she dropped to the ground, one thought clear in her bemused, befuddled brain. He hadn't killed her sister. He hadn't even tried. That meant she was already dead.

16

It was shortly after nine o'clock when Patrick got back to the ruins of the Harcourt Manor. His mother's steel-grey Land Rover Defender was parked at the front, next to his brother's Mercedes. As he cut the engine, he realized he was holding his breath. His two older brothers climbed down out of the car and leaned against its side.

The stout woman with the bright red hair struggled down from the Defender, her wellingtons making deep imprints in the mud. Her skirt was tight around her broad hips and it had ridden up in the car, exposing fat legs in thick black tights. She wore a silver quilted jacket with gold zips and giant hooped earrings bounced against her sagging jawline. She walked over, cigarette clamped between her teeth. When she was close enough to swing for him, she did exactly that. A short, hard slap across his left cheek nearly knocked his nose off his face.

'Get off, Ma.' At least he was breathing again. Waiting for it was always the worst.

'How can you not hear a fucking hot-air balloon? Where is she?'

He pointed back, through the house, towards the garden. His mother marched ahead, her wellingtons squelching with every step. His brothers followed. He brought up the rear, as Shinto leapt into his mother's vehicle and settled down on the back seat.

The girl was where he'd left her. His mother strode up, squatted down and put her plump fingers on the girl's neck. Her other hand went to the rosary around her own neck.

'Is she alive?' asked William.

'Just.' She straightened up. His brothers bent down and lifted the girl's unconscious body. The four of them set off back towards the front of the house.

'Talk to me, idiot,' his ma said.

'I shot the man on the burner thing,' Patrick said. 'The rest of them died when the balloon crashed.' He kept his gaze down and out of the corner of his eye saw his mother cross herself, the gold crucifix on the end of her rosary clutched in her right hand. 'God bless us and save us,' she muttered.

'They threw him out of the balloon,' he said. 'I know where he is. We find him, hide the body, and no one will ever know it wasn't a bad accident.'

'Do you think they didn't have phones with them, you numbskull? They'll have been taking pictures, sending messages.'

'There's no signal here. And I picked up all the phones I could find.' He pulled open his coat pocket to reveal the collection of mobile phones that had been weighing him down all the way back. He'd found eight.

'Well, that in itself will make them curious. Umpteen people in a balloon and none of them had their phones with them?'

'Loads of stuff on Twitter,' said Charles as William held open the rear door of the Mercedes and the girl was pushed inside. 'But just retweets and comments. Nothing from the balloon itself apart from that first couple. And they didn't mention you.'

'We'll be bloody lucky if no one sent a text, if no one took your photo. And how do you know you found them all?'

'I counted them, didn't I, when I was following it. Twelve passengers. I found ten. All dead.'

'You found ten?'

'I ran out of time. Don't worry, Ma, they have to be dead.'

'We need to find the pilot,' Charles said.

'I know,' their mother said. 'Before the whole fucking moor is swarming with filth. Jesus love us, we do not need this. Not this week.'

17

Twelve years earlier

Two women, one wearing an oversized green sweater, the other in the flowing black robes of a Carmelite nun, kicked their way through a shallow drift of leaves. Autumn had come late to Northumberland, the Indian summer had lasted well into October and only towards the end of the month had the leaves started to turn and fall. Now, the first week in November, the weather was unseasonably mild, with apples still clinging to branches in the priory's orchard.

'Bella,' said Jessica, as she held up the willow basket.

'Hmmn?' her sister replied. The apple she was stretching for fell into her hand and went in the basket.

'Whenever I have something I need to work out, some problem I'm grappling with, do you know how I do it?'

Isabel walked around the tree to reach the

other side. 'I have a feeling you want to tell me. Pass me the step, will you?'

Jessica positioned the small, plastic step against the trunk, checking it was stable before stepping back and letting her sister use it. 'I have an imaginary conversation with you in my head,' she said. 'I put my arguments to you and you respond.'

Isabel, a good head higher on the step, thought about this for a second. 'Do I give good advice?' she asked.

'Mainly you tell me what I want to hear.'

'Doesn't sound much like me.' With three apples in her hands, Isabel jumped down. 'I like your sweater. Is it new?'

'Yes, it's from Hobbs. How do you do it?'

Isabel set off towards the next tree. 'Sorry?'

'How do you work out problems? Do you have imaginary conversations with me? Or with Hildegard? Or with, I don't know, with —'

'God?' suggested Isabel. 'What colour would you call it?'

'Green,' said Jessica. 'Do you?'

'If I'd known how interrogative taking your detective exams would make you, I'm not sure I'd have suggested it.'

'I'm serious, Bella.'

Isabel was silent for a while. Then, 'I have

very few problems that merit that amount of effort,' she said. 'And green doesn't do it justice. That sweater's the colour of a shamrock. Or an emerald. I'd try it on but . . .' She nodded towards the other side of the orchard, to where several of the nuns were working in the vegetable garden. 'You know.'

Jessica could feel her stomach tightening. Isabel always did this. She would listen, patiently, for hours, while Jessica talked about her own life, but ask her a question about her own . . .

'When I'm doing well,' she tried again. 'When I'm doing something impressive at work, or when I won that commendation last year, I always imagine you watching me on a hidden CCTV camera, silently cheering me on.'

'Which I am, of course, always. Even if there is no hidden CCTV. What's this about, Jess?'

'I'm nothing to you, am I?'

Her sister stopped dead. If the look on her face could be trusted, she was genuinely shocked. 'Jess!'

Jessica gestured that they should carry on fruit picking. 'Oh, I know you love me, of course you do, but I make no difference to your life. You'd get on perfectly well with or without me.'

Isabel's voice was low and thoughtful when she spoke again, finally taking her younger sister seriously. 'That's completely untrue.'

'I don't blame you, really I don't. We both made our choices, but I can't help thinking about the difference. If you lost me, you'd cope fine. Whereas, if I lost you, I think it would be the end of me.'

18

Wednesday, 20 September
Her sister's body was feet away. Impossible to mistake that wide-eyed stare, that lifeless pallor. The person she loved most in the world had been taken. Was this, then, the end of her?

19

When the pilot's body had fallen to the ground, Patrick had made a point of fixing the location in his mind. Gently rising land, narrow stream to the south-west, a small copse of evergreen trees to the north. Even so, it took the better part of an hour to find it again.

The pilot had landed on scrubland. Giant spires of cow parsley and burdock reached higher than any man fighting his way through them. Nettles spread across the ground and the thick stems of ground elder clutched at his bike's wheels. As he approached the spot, he could hear his mother's Land Rover close behind, then his brother's Mercedes.

He thought for a second, then veered left. The ground was softer here, and getting stuck could be the last straw for his short-tempered mother. He steered around a cluster of stones and saw him. The high-visibility waterproof jacket, gleaming white, blue and yellow on the hillside, made it easy. The pilot was lying face up, or would have been, if he'd had any face left. He drove over and cut his engine. Behind him, his mother and brother did the same.

Mary crossed herself as she approached the body. Charles and William copied her instantly. After a moment, he did too. Sometimes, it was easier to go along with it. They stared down at the headless corpse.

'Bless us, his own mother wouldn't know him,' Mary said.

'Police will know him,' said Charles. 'Fingerprints. Dental records. DNA.'

'Chop his fingers off?' suggested William.

'Don't be a fucking fool. They'll still know it's him. We have to get rid of him. Pat, check his pockets.'

Patrick did as he was told, finding the pilot's phone and wallet in one inside pocket. His name had been Sean Allan.

William, his shaved head pink and sore from a summer of sunburn, was looking down at the dead man with an expression like someone had pissed on his shoes. 'What I don't get, like, is where's his fucking head?'

Patrick didn't have to turn round to know the look on his mother's face. She loved all her sons but, as she often said, some made it easier than others.

'I shot it,' he said, moving on to the outside pockets of the pilot's coat.

'Yeah, but it should still be somewhere. It's bone and blood and — what are brains made out of?'

'Brains,' said Charles.

'Yeah, but what I'm saying is, they don't just vanish because they've been shot.'

'Even a stopped clock is right twice a day,' muttered Mary. 'There'll be traces of this man in the balloon. The police will find them. Even if they never find this.' She nudged the pilot with her foot. 'They'll know something went down.'

'Maybe.' Patrick continued looking through pockets. There were a lot of them. 'But they won't know what. And by the time they're sure there's something to investigate, there won't be anything left to see. And I am a lucky man.' He held up what he'd found: the balloon's radio.

'They couldn't call for help,' he said. 'The daft twats threw the radio overboard. And there's no phone signal here. They couldn't tell anyone what happened.'

Charles, who had the sharpest ears, had stepped away from the group. 'Can anyone else hear that?'

They listened for a second.

'Helicopter,' said Mary. 'Fuck's sake, get him in the car.'

She strode back to the Defender and pulled open the rear doors. Her sons scooped up the body and carried him over. They bundled him into the rear of the vehicle, threw a groundsheet over him and closed the doors.

'Home?' Mary said.

'I'll see you there,' Patrick said. 'Got something to do.'

20

She had no idea how long she'd been sitting beside her sister's body. She wasn't even sure she'd been conscious for all of it. All she knew was that the pain in her head was sending waves of nausea through her, that her clothes were cold and clinging, and that her legs didn't feel as though they'd ever be able to unfold and get her back to her feet.

The sky overhead was darker now. On the horizon she could see grey streaks running in sharp diagonal lines from the heavens to the ground. That was a very heavy storm coming.

The woodland they'd crashed into was on one of the lower crests of the park and she could see for some distance in every direction except through the trees. There were no buildings, no roads. The only sign that others still shared the planet were the power lines.

There were dead people everywhere. The mother and son, the father a little distance from the basket. The journalist, the hiker in the red coat. So many dead people. Maybe she was one of them. Maybe all around her were ghosts of these other people, just sitting and wondering what on earth had happened.

Somewhere out of sight, a dog began barking. Then, through the sound of the approaching storm, she heard the engine of a quad bike. Distant, but getting louder. Heading this way. Panic coursed like red-hot liquid through her body once more. He was coming back.

21

'Ajax! Over here! Ajax, lad!'

Superintendent Ajax Maldonado stopped in his tracks, sighed and turned a hundred and eighty degrees. The tiny, deeply wrinkled West Indian woman was heading towards him across the reception area at a speed that shouldn't have been possible, given her age, her size, and the zimmer frame she tossed out in front of her before every step.

'Teresa, how did you get here?' She lived miles away, and as far as he knew, she'd never owned a car.

'Number seventeen,' she told him. 'Them buggers have been at it again. Swear words on my back fence. Red paint this time.'

'Teresa, why didn't you go to Clifford Street like I told you? Or phone? This is headquarters. We don't deal with —' He'd been about to say minor complaints, but that was not a phrase you used with Teresa when she was off on one.

She pulled a face. 'Them idiots! They don't know their backsides from their elbows, pardon my Jamaican. I told them I know the boss, I told them you went to school with my Clark and they said they'd never heard of you, that the new boss was some fella called Jones. Chief Constable John Jones. Why'd you tell me you're the boss?'

There was no point asking her to lower her voice, it would only make her worse. 'I never said I was the boss, Teresa.'

She stepped right up close. It would hurt her neck to look up at him for long, but she didn't seem to care. She brushed a few drops of rain off his coat. Any second now she'd have her hanky out, be spitting on it, rubbing a smudge off his nose. 'How many buttons and baubles does that Jones fella have then?' she said.

'More than me.' He lifted her zimmer and turned her gently back towards reception. 'Now, I'm going to have someone drive you home. A nice young lady, how about that?'

'Nice young man,' she told him, her lips pressing tight together.

'And I'm going to come round to see you this evening.'

She darted a sideways glance. 'What time?'

'We'll have a cup of tea and I'll try to get the paint off.'

'You'll do that?' Her round, wrinkled face lit up. 'Tonight?'

'Yeah, I don't have much on,' he said, hoping he hadn't jinxed the entire day. 'But only if you promise me that you won't come here again.'

'Why?' She raised her voice again. 'You worried they'll think I'm your mam?' She threw back her head and cackled like the Witch of Endor. 'Lad, you'd be a lot better looking if you were my boy.'

Five minutes later, after waving Teresa out of the building, Ajax reached the second floor.

'Morning, sir.' Stacey, who he swore bribed the reception staff to let her know when he arrived every morning, was waiting at the top of the stairs. 'I wanted to catch you before you get stuck into something.'

'I'm all yours, Stace.' He walked down the corridor, past the glass-fronted offices, towards his own room at the far end.

'Sir!' The door to the main office opened and a constable in shirtsleeves leaned out.

'Two minutes, Chappers,' Ajax told him. 'Stacey has the comms.'

He carried on, conscious that DC Steve

98

Chapman was following him as well now.

'The bottom line from Cheltenham,' said Stacey, hurrying to keep pace, 'I was on to them first thing, is that the email they've intercepted came from a server with no history of interacting with any known persons of interest and is probably not to be taken seriously.'

'Hoax?' Ajax pushed open his door and spun his hat towards the coat stand. It missed.

Stacey bent to pick it up. 'On the other hand, given a match of this prominence, given Britain's recent engagement in the Middle East, just the existence of the threat bumps the match up to Category C-plus.'

'Sir.' DC Chapman was hovering in the doorway. 'This is really —'

Ajax held up a finger. The following evening, Newcastle were playing AC Milan in a friendly at St James's Park and GCHQ had picked up traffic about a possible terrorist incident. It wasn't considered high priority, but the constabulary was to be on maximum alert all the same.

'A hot-air balloon crashed in the National Park,' Chapman almost shouted at him. 'Thirteen people on board. All believed dead.'

Ajax gave the news the second of silence

it seemed to demand, then dropped his head into his hands. When he looked up, it was to see a small crowd gathering in the doorway. For an instant, he let his eyes rest on the one photograph on his desk. A young woman with a wide grin and dark curly hair.

'OK, people.' He raised his head. 'Room 201 becomes the incident room. We need an op name and as many free lines as we've got diverting to it. Chappers, get on the phone to Alan in IT.'

'It's Operation Wildfire, sir. I already checked. And the lines are in hand.'

'Good lad. I want you, Stacey, Becks and George to make your way to 201. I need all the computers switched on, the whiteboards clearing and maps of the National Park. Stacey, you're in charge of initial comms. As soon as we have a statement, get it on the home page, along with an emergency phone number. We'll need a press statement ASAP. See if you can draft something for me.'

George was holding up a phone. 'Owner of the balloon company,' he told his boss. 'Richard Allan.'

Ajax un-muted the handset. 'Richard, I'm on my way out to you. Stay in the office, please, and by the phone. I'll be there within the hour.'

22

A second before Ajax released the hand-brake, MoJo joined him. Her perfume filled the car, making him think of pine forests and sweet woodsmoke. He smiled, and the grip on his chest relaxed a fraction.

'Good morning.' He paused, just for a second, just to look at her.

She smiled back, said, 'I was first with my hand up.'

Northumberland Constabulary emergency protocols dictated that a senior officer attend each major or potentially major incident, until an appropriate line of command could be established. It also recommended that the senior officer take an experienced detective constable to assist. Ajax and MoJo had worked together many times.

'You up to speed?' he asked her, raising his voice above the clatter of the rain on the car roof. The outside world was barely visible beyond the grey streaks. The northern edge of the National Park was about sixty miles distant. He had to hope the weather was better there.

'Not really.'

'The balloon company is based in Kelso,' he told her. 'The balloon itself took off from a site about ten miles south-west of there, shortly before six this morning. It was expected to come down up to an hour later somewhere in the National Park. It didn't, but that's not so very unusual, apparently, they often drift slightly off course, so no one at the company was worried at first.'

MoJo looked at her watch, although she probably already knew it was going up for ten o'clock. Good police officers were always aware of the time.

'Experienced pilot?' she asked.

'According to the company's owner, one of the best. But he would say that, he's the guy's dad.'

'Ouch.'

'Shortly before nine, Northern Area took a call from a local farmer,' Ajax continued. 'He'd seen the balloon flying very low over his land and wasn't happy. Scares his sheep, or something. So he gave chase on his quad bike, meaning to give the pilot what for, and after quite a bit of driving around he found it hanging from some trees. Believed to be multiple casualties.'

'OK, let's panic check. Incident room set up?'

Ajax pulled out on to the main road. 'Done.' He put his foot down to catch the lights. Already puddles were forming at the side of the road.

'Uniform on site?'

'Three patrol cars. One ambulance with a couple of paramedics is on its way and I've requested air ambulance. And three appliances from Fire and Rescue.'

'Hospital and morgue informed?' She dropped her head forward to fluff the rainwater out of her long dark hair. It was currently tinted purple, not his favourite.

'Berwick Infirmary and Borders General are on standby. I've also let Newcastle General know. We're talking a maximum body count of thirteen.'

'Park authorities notified?' MoJo folded down the passenger mirror and leaned towards it.

'Done. They're putting out a call to their search teams. I've also requested assistance from the dogs unit. It'll take them at least an hour to mobilize. And why don't you get ready in the station toilets like all the other girls?'

The car phone was ringing. MoJo pulled a

face when she saw who was calling. She and Stacey had never seen eye to eye.

'Go ahead, Stacey,' he said.

'Sir, it's on Twitter. Low key at the moment, but you know how these things can go viral. From what we can gather, one of the passengers tweeted while they were still in the air and it's been retweeted a few times.'

'What?' said Ajax. 'What did it say?'

'Hold on. Got it. *Hot-air balloon out of control over Northumberland National Park. Red, yellow, blue spiral. Pl call 999. #SOS #help!* The National Park picked up on it and started asking their staff and visitors to look out for a stray hot-air balloon. Any minute now they're going to catch on that it's crashed. You might have a crowd to deal with when you get there. Oh, and we're getting quite a few people phoning in.'

'Relatives or journalists?'

'Journos for now, and we can put them off, but it won't be long.'

He'd no sooner disconnected Stacey than another call came in.

'We've had final numbers from Milan, Ajax. They've sold ten thousand tickets, expecting another two thousand to travel on spec. Fifty officers, best they can do.'

'Great. Do me a favour, Gaz. Let the boss

know we will need to deploy the full two hundred of ours and keep our fingers crossed nothing else happens tomorrow night, because the good citizens of Northumbria will be on their own.'

Another call. Stacey again.

'Sir, we have a passenger list,' she said. 'Thirteen people, including the pilot, as we thought.'

'Any kids on board?' he asked, with a sideways glance at MoJo.

'The company don't take anyone up under the age of fourteen,' Stacey told him. 'But there were a couple of older teenagers. Nathan and Poppy Carlton, with their parents Harry and Helen.'

'Bad enough. Anyone else I need to know about?'

'A few hikers, middle-aged couple, bloke on his own. Oh, and there was a nun,' Stacey said. 'Sister Maria Magdalena. She went up with her sister. A fortieth birthday present, apparently. For the nun, not the sister.'

'I can see it.' MoJo leaned forward in her seat, wiping condensation off the passenger window. Ten minutes earlier, they'd left the road behind and followed open moorland to the GPS reference of the crash site. As he turned the car, Ajax, too, could see the balloon, collapsed over trees, its bright colours incongruous in the autumn rainstorm. A little further and he could see the emergency vehicles. Several police Land Rovers. An ambulance. Lots of people milling around, several of them civilians. Police tape in a wide circle around the copse of trees. The basket, burned and torn. He pulled up a few metres short of the tape and he and MoJo climbed down. A uniformed officer came to meet them.

'It isn't good, sir,' the constable said as they all walked back towards the tape. 'No survivors that we've found.'

Twenty metres in front of the trees sat a man on a quad bike, wearing heavy-duty clothes and a tweed cap. Two collie dogs huddled, shivering, at his side.

'Chuff Reynolds,' the constable told Ajax. 'Local farmer. He came across the crash. Seems to be in shock. Probably needs medical attention but not a priority right now.'

Ajax strode ahead as uniformed officers continued to hammer stakes into the ground and unroll extra police tape, to erect tents over bodies. He saw the first of them when he was still thirty metres away. A bloke, wearing a blue oilskin jacket, face down.

He crouched beside him, put a finger to his neck. The skin was cold and damp,

106

already turning the colour of church candles. No pulse that he could feel. He lifted the jacket and pulled a wallet out of the pocket.

'Superintendent Maldonado?'

Ajax got to his feet to see a man wearing the logo of the balloon company on his jacket. His face was the colour of ash and his jaw set tight.

'I'm Richard Allan,' he said. 'We spoke on the phone. I own the company.'

'Any idea what happened here, Mr Allan?'

Allan stared at the garishly clothed tree and let his eyes drop. 'It didn't come down naturally, that's for sure. Not with this amount of mayhem.'

'You mean a crash landing?'

Allan shook his head. 'A crash landing wouldn't be this bad. People would have survived a crash landing. That thing plummeted.'

They took a few steps closer. Allan seemed to be hanging back.

'Only thing I can think of is that someone accidentally pulled the RDL,' Allan said.

'The what?'

'Rapid deceleration line. It's a red cord in the pilot's compartment. It's meant to empty the envelope quickly once the basket's on the ground. If you pull it at altitude,

107

the envelope collapses completely and the whole thing goes down like a brick.'

'Why on earth would anyone do that?'

'The pilot wouldn't,' Allan said. 'Someone with a death wish might have leaned across and done it, but Sean would simply have pulled another line, a candy-striped one, that would reinflate the balloon. Even if the red cord was pulled, if Sean was on board, he could have rescued the situation.'

They were very close to the basket now.

'But I think something else has gone on here. See these scorch marks?' He indicated blackened lines on the wicker. 'This looks to me like the basket hit a power line at some point. And one of the tanks exploded.'

They turned and fixed on the distant pylons. Something about them didn't look quite right.

'I'll have someone drive over there,' said Ajax. 'I'm going to check the basket now. You might want to stay here.'

Ajax stepped forward. He'd been first on scene to many disasters. It never got easier. He could feel MoJo's breathing on the back of his neck, felt her hand brush briefly against his.

'Thirteen people in this balloon,' he muttered. 'How come I can only see one of them?'

'Most of them would have been harnessed,' she replied. 'They'll still be in the basket. It isn't going to be pretty in there, AJ.'

He stopped just shy of the basket and peered over the brim. Two bodies directly beneath him. The teenage boy whose name he couldn't remember and a woman who was probably his mother.

The pilot was still in his compartment. Still in his harness. His head was practically hanging off. If the pilot was still in position, what the hell had gone wrong here?

'That isn't Sean,' said a voice behind him. Without being heard, Allan had followed him.

Ajax looked from the dead pilot to the man he'd understood was his father. 'Are you sure?'

'Sean was a big guy. Six two, fifteen stone. And he had red hair. This will be one of the passengers, but what he's doing in the pilot's compartment, in the pilot's harness, is beyond me.'

There was one more passenger, also dead, in the basket. A middle-aged, portly man.

'Where are the others?' MoJo asked.

Allan looked up into the tree. So did Ajax.

'There is something up there.'

'I see it,' Allan said. 'Not a body, though.

109

A piece of cloth.'

'Lots of broken branches. I'd say someone fell through the tree.'

They stepped away from the basket to see that CSIs were climbing the rise towards them.

'That's five people accounted for,' Ajax said. 'Eight still to find.'

A uniform was waiting to talk to him. 'Sir, there's another body. Twenty metres in that direction.'

The woman on the ground looked asleep, not dead. She lay on her back, her eyes closed, arms at her sides. Her body barely seemed broken at all, until you got very close and saw the line of her neck didn't quite run true.

Her black dress was torn and filthy but the cross around her neck lay perfectly between her small breasts. Her hair would perhaps have reached her chin if she'd been upright; it was very curly, with a few strands of silver breaking up its deep brown. There was no sign of her veil.

'Sister Maria Magdalena,' said MoJo. 'She was so pretty.'

Ajax walked up to the dead nun and stood looking down. One side of her face was perfect, a high cheekbone, a half-moon of dark eyelashes below an arched brow. A full, plump mouth. The other side was barely recognizable as a face. Sister Maria had been caught in the explosion.

'Six dead,' he said. 'It's not looking good, is it?'

'Nine,' said the constable. 'We've found another three.'

23

Fifteen minutes later, Ajax felt his neck aching from looking up at the charred body on the power lines. 'We need to get that poor bastard down from there. How long before the power company can get here?'

'Another hour, sir.'

Ajax cursed. 'We do not want pictures of this on the Internet.'

'There'll be power out somewhere.' MoJo, too, was staring up at the broken lines and at the man who'd broken them. Middle-aged, dressed in hiking clothes. His face like a tasteless Hallowe'en mask.

'How close is the nearest town, village, hamlet?' Ajax asked.

One of his constables had a map of the National Park. 'Town Yetholm is about three miles south-west,' he said. 'All the other places round here are tiny. One-street villages. These remote places are used to regular power cuts. Give it a couple of hours, though, and we'll hear about it.'

Another officer was approaching. Ajax looked beyond him to where a white tent was being erected.

'Natalie and Raymond Hastings, sir.' The constable carried a clipboard. His job was to match bodies to passengers on the balloon company's list. 'They both had ID on them. I tell you what is starting to puzzle me, though.'

'What's that?'

'I just checked with Rob, who's doing the non-organic inventory. We haven't found a single mobile phone yet.'

'Superintendent Maldonado!'

Ajax turned. A constable was running towards him from the patrol car at the top of the field. He was panting when he arrived. 'The woman in the basket,' he gasped. 'Helen Carlton. She's not dead.'

'How in Christ's name did we miss that?' Ajax jumped down from the car as the paramedics were carrying the stretchered body of Helen Carlton towards the air ambulance. 'I've rarely seen anyone look more dead.'

The doctor who'd attended the scene was accompanying the paramedics to the helicopter. 'I made the same assumption myself.

But she seemed warmer than her son, and I got an ocular reflex.'

'Where are they taking her? Newcastle?'

'I believe so.'

Ajax stepped back to let the paramedics load their patient into the ambulance. Then the whole group backed away further as the blades started to spin.

'She won't live, AJ,' said MoJo. 'Not with injuries like that.'

Ajax turned to the constable beside him. 'Any sign of her daughter?'

'Nothing yet,' the constable replied. 'Jane would like a quick word though.' He indicated the young CSI who was hovering by his side.

'I may be getting a bit ahead of myself,' the CSI said, as Ajax followed her back towards the crash tree. 'But I've been having a close look at the inside of the basket and I'm not sure we've got the full story yet.'

'How do you mean?' Ajax stopped a metre short of the basket.

She pointed to the middle of the wicker structure where the pilot had stood. 'There's blood there,' she said, 'which isn't unexpected, given the ferocity of the crash, but there's other organic material as well. Can you see, under the leather strap?'

Ajax looked at the glistening, greyish-pink stain. 'What is it?'

The CSI looked unsure of herself. 'I'm far from certain, you understand, but it's not impossible it's brain tissue, and none of the passengers we've recovered had head injuries severe enough to spatter brain tissue around.'

'None that we've found so far,' Ajax said.

'But anyone with a head injury that serious couldn't have walked away,' she said. 'Or jumped out of their own accord.'

'You wouldn't think so,' Ajax agreed. 'Keep me posted, won't you?' He set off back towards his car. 'OK, that leaves three missing now, including the pilot. And Poppy, the youngster. It's becoming increasingly urgent that we find them. I want people working with the balloon's ground crew, following the likely course that thing took through the park. If these people jumped out, fell out or were thrown out, I want *us* to find them, not a family of picnickers.'

He'd reached the car and turned back. 'What was the name of the woman again? The nun's sister?'

'Jessica Lane, sir.'

24

Ten years earlier

'Bella?'

'Hmmn?'

'Do you remember, when I was small, I used to creep into your room at night, after I'd had a nightmare?'

'Only too well.' Isabel's tone suggested it might not be the happiest of memories, but she'd always liked teasing her sister.

'I'd lie beside you, listening to your breathing, see that little smile on your face.'

'You were dreaming that bit. My bedroom was too dark to see anything.'

Jessica thought for a second. 'No, I think there must have been a lamp outside. Do you know, you're still the only person I've ever known who smiles while she's asleep?'

'I have to hope your experience of such matters is limited.'

'I used to pretend that if I hugged you for long enough, you'd allow me into those happy dreams of yours.'

'The happy dreams were yours, my dear, never mine. And that street lamp was broken. Our — someone smashed the bulb and it was never repaired.'

'Oh, I remember now, it was Ned.'

Isabel stood up. 'We should go. They'll be serving tea.'

Jessica watched her sister move to the door of the library and pull it open. When they stepped out into the corridor, Isabel strode ahead. She was still so very fit, moved so fast when she wanted to. In her heels and tight skirt, Jessica struggled to keep up.

'When Mum died, I was sad, but never afraid,' she said. 'I still had Dad, who would always make sure I had enough to eat and a warm house to come home to. Hold up, Bella, what's the hurry?'

Isabel slowed a fraction. 'Hilda hates us being late. Jess, is this going somewhere?'

'Yes, I'm making a point here. Can you not wait a sec?'

Isabel kept walking.

'Most of all, I had you,' Jessica said. 'Overnight, you turned into Mum. I remember you getting up early to pour milk into that tiny bottle for my breakfast. I remember you drawing smiley faces on my Weetabix with raisins, always making sure I went to school with a chocolate biscuit in my bag.'

They'd reached the door of the recreation room. Isabel turned, her fist clasped tight on the handle.

'Are you done?'

'Almost. One last question. When you answer it, I'm done. When did it all go wrong, Bella? Why did Dad do what he did? Why did Ned vanish? When are you going to tell me what happened to us?'

Isabel pulled open the door and let it swing shut. Had Jessica not stuck out her foot in time, it would have slammed in her face.

'Bella!' she snapped, in annoyance.

25

Wednesday, 20 September
She woke herself up, shouting something, maybe her sister's name. She was lying on the earth, overhanging and protruding rocks sheltering her on three sides. Not in a cave exactly, but the approximation of one. She had no idea how she came to be there.

Then the jumble of noise and images came back, and the crash replayed in her head as a nauseating mix of violence, blistering heat and screaming. She remembered, or thought she did, hanging in the tree for what felt like hours, listening to the leaves whisper and the wind moan.

Maybe it hadn't been the wind moaning.

She remembered scrambling and falling through branches, with torn clothes and bleeding fingers. And people. Faces swimming in front of her barely conscious mind. A sweet, teenage boy, hikers in brightly coloured anoraks, a terrified woman who

119

couldn't stop screaming. Who were all these people, and why did she feel so certain they were all dead?

She sat up, nausea and pain battling for attention. She'd banged her head in the crash. A dull ache had spread over most of her skull and somewhere behind her left temple she could feel a sickening pounding. People weren't supposed to sleep after head injuries, tiredness was often a sign of internal damage. Maybe the crash had killed her too. Maybe she was on borrowed time, a dead woman walking, oblivious to the clock relentlessly ticking away her last remaining minutes.

She remembered finding her sister, her lovely face burned, her slender neck broken.

And the barking of a dog, feeling sure the man on the quad bike was coming back. She'd fled, into the woods, over a rise, then along what looked like an animal track. She'd walked for hours. Or maybe it had only been a few minutes. She held her breath, listening for the sound of the quad bike, or the dog, but the world beyond her cave was silent.

By her side was a rucksack that she had never seen before. Had she brought it with her from the crash site? Had she found it here? Blue, with black zips. It wasn't hers.

And yet, she realized, she knew what was inside. A bottle of water. Peanut butter chocolate. A sweater — green. She could put it on now, she was so cold. She drew the zip and pulled it open. She was right. Everything she'd expected to find was there. Also a wallet with money. And keys. Did she have a car? She remembered, or thought she did, driving a small silver one. She had no idea where it was.

Driving through the pre-dawn darkness, seeing fire on the horizon. Exceptional excitement. Had that been today?

She crawled out of her shelter. A mist had formed while she'd been sleeping and visibility had reduced to a few metres in each direction. The ground at her feet, though, told her she was on the steeply sloping side of a hill. It was still daytime, but the light beyond the mist was dull and flat. She had no idea which direction was north, south, east or west, whether she should turn right, left or go straight on.

'Don't be dead,' she murmured, not entirely sure to whom she was speaking. No one answered.

Loneliness hit her like a burden she'd have to carry for the rest of her days. She set off walking. Downhill, because it was easier.

121

26

Officially, the Faa family lived in Castle Faa, a stone-built, rendered house in the hamlet of Kirk Yetholm in the Scottish Borders. Unofficially, none of the family slept in any of the house's four bedrooms. The bedrooms were kept for another purpose entirely and the family lived in caravans parked around the yard at the back.

A high steel fence encircled the house, the caravans and the yard. Dogs slunk around the perimeter, night and day, stealing through the shadows, always on the watch for a stray fox, a sly rabbit or a stupid human.

Beyond the fence lay a thin strip of woodland. Beyond that, the ground had been quarried in the past. Now, it lay in odd hillocks and hollows, grass-covered, like a weird, alien landscape. The family's collection of piebald and skewbald ponies grazed here. They weren't supposed to, but the owner had given up objecting. It wasn't as though he had any other use for the land and no sensible man got on the wrong side of the Faas.

A boy spotted the quad bike and pulled the gates open. Patrick drove through and steered round the campfire to the biggest caravan at the back of the house. His mother's.

The cloying smell of Calor-gas heating, mingled with the rich rose-oil perfume she used, hit him the moment he opened the door. Directly ahead, at eye level on the caravan wall, was a black-and-white photograph of a horse-drawn caravan with a black-eyed gypsy woman in the driving seat. His great-grandmother, his ma always claimed, although Charles swore he could remember her buying the picture in a junk shop.

His mother's caravan held as much furniture as the floor space allowed. Some of it was fitted, much of it just squeezed in anyhow. Her favourite floral fabrics, none of which matched, were everywhere.

She, his brothers and two uncles were drinking tea. She didn't allow alcohol before the sun went down, although there were many times he'd smelled it on her breath. She was playing an odd game with six dice that she'd never agreed to explain to any of her sons. 'Tell me,' she said, without looking up.

'Two bodies still missing. Three, including the one in the back of your car.'

'Two people still missing.' She slammed the dice down hard on the table. 'We don't know they're dead. Men or women?'

'Women. One in her thirties. The other just a kid.'

'Names?'

'Jessica Lane, Poppy Carlton.'

'Do we know what they look like?'

'Not yet. Working on it.'

Mary reached across the stained wood-veneer of the table for a dog-eared road atlas and opened it at a pre-marked page. Patrick drew closer and saw the National Park. She'd drawn a bull's-eye around the spot where the balloon came down.

'We need to get out there.' She turned to her brothers. 'Take everyone. If these two lasses are alive, they're lost or injured, or they would have got to help by now. Someone should follow the valley. People head for running water when they're lost. Take the dogs.'

'Ma, the place will be crawling with police,' Charles said.

'Dress like walkers. The park's always full

of them daft fuckers. And someone needs to stay on the road, drive up and down, keep a lookout.'

'What are you going to do?' William asked, the only one brave enough. Or stupid enough.

She raised her eyebrows. 'I'm going to stay here, make myself a light lunch and co-ordinate operations. Is there a reason you lot are still here?'

The other men got up. 'How d'you get on?' Patrick said to his uncle. 'Is she —'

Tommy, together with Uncle Jeremy, had been tasked with getting the unconscious girl from that morning to hospital. 'Died an hour after we got there,' he said. 'In theatre now. You were fucking lucky.'

'Fucking psycho, more like,' said William, as he pushed his way out.

When the caravan door closed, Mary stared at her youngest son. 'Right, what are you not telling me?'

He sighed. 'Someone was taken to hospital.'

She put her hands on the table. Her fingernails were dirty. Every finger held at least one silver ring. 'Someone you missed?'

He shook his head. 'Ma, she looked dead. She should have been dead.'

'Where have they taken her?'

'Newcastle General. Went by helicopter.'

'Pity you couldn't bring that down as well.'

He said nothing.

She closed her eyes and sighed heavily. 'You'd better get over there.'

'No point, she'll be in surgery. I'll go later. If need be. She's not expected to come through it.'

She swiped at him again, but he was too far away. 'Better pray she doesn't, you fucking fool.'

27

A shape emerged from the fog, too straight to be a tree, too thin to be human. She stumbled over the rough ground towards it, not allowing herself to hope. She'd lost track of time, as though the day itself, shrouded in thick mist and misery, had given up on the concept. It seemed so long ago that she and her sister had driven through the pre-dawn darkness, seen the balloon's fire glow against the black sky, climbed aboard as the night had given way to silver light, then to the rosy dawn. So long ago since the world had been as it should be. Now the world was about sorrow, and soggy, grey twilight. Now it was about weariness and a thick, gloopy mass in her head that was stopping her thinking properly.

She'd drunk the water and eaten the peanut butter chocolate from her backpack and promptly thrown up both. She needed to drink again and was close to exhaustion. And for all she knew she'd been going round in circles since she left the cave. The mist had stolen any sense of direction she might have had if the world had been visible.

The shadowy form ahead was taking substance. It was a path sign, pointing in two opposite directions. She couldn't read the writing until she was almost upon it.

Welcome to England, said the arrow pointing one way. *Welcome to Scotland,* said the other. The spongy mass in her head lightened a little as she realized where she was. By chance, she'd stumbled across an ancient pilgrims' trail, one that led some sixty miles from Melrose in the Scottish Borders to Lindisfarne off the Northumbrian coast. She was on St Cuthbert's Way.

England or Scotland?

She lived in England. Home was in England. It wasn't a question, really.

28

Eight years earlier

Jessica reached out to brush her fingers against the last of the crossing posts and a fraction of it crumbled away beneath her touch. When she brought her hand to her face, she could smell brine and the long, green tendrils the tide had left behind. She opened her mouth to speak, and felt a completely unexpected tightness in her throat.

'And so St Cuthbert arrived upon Holy Island and blessed it,' said Isabel, who'd been walking at her side, whistling and humming, for most of the last few miles of their three-day hike. 'And when he rose from his knees, he said no way am I doing that God-awful walk again, I'm staying put. You fuckers can build me an abbey.'

'That's a lovely story,' said Jessica.

The damp, puddle-strewn, densely packed sand they'd walked over was gaining substance as they neared land. Rocks were appearing, becoming more frequent, then clumps of dry, sharp grass. They were almost there. Jessica glanced back at the seven other women, all of them dressed in black like Isabel, who were walking with them. It was lucky, given her sister's language, that they were all still some distance back across the sand.

They reached the line of rocks that edged the road and Jessica stepped over them on to the tarmac. 'Lindisfarne.' She tried the beautiful word out on her tongue and repeated it for good measure. 'I'm actually quite moved.'

A mile or so away, over the low rise of the island, she could see the tip of the hilltop castle; just around a bend or two along this narrow road would be the abbey. Isabel, meanwhile, was sitting on a rock, emptying the sand out of one stout, black shoe and banging it down hard.

'In spite of the company I find myself in,' Jessica added.

Isabel raised her face to catch the wind. 'I'm kidding,' she said, taking several deep breaths. 'I love this trip. If only for the chance to get out for a few days.'

Jessica looked across the sand to where the sea was a gleam on the horizon. 'And is it your job to know the tide times? Because, you know, those photographs of submerged cars were scary. How long have we got?'

Lindisfarne, or Holy Island, wasn't a true island as such, but formed by tides. At low water, it could be reached across a mile-long stretch of sand marked by tall posts. Visitors were warned against crossing the sand unless in the company of an experienced guide, because when the tide returned, the path quickly became submerged. Most pedestrian visitors to Lindisfarne took the safer, causeway route, although even on the road cars were regularly stranded, and sometimes swept away.

Isabel was pulling her shoelace tight. 'Loads of time,' she said. 'Reg will be here already with the bus. And Hilda will be waiting in St Aidan's to give thanks for our safe crossing. Half an hour on our knees, a quick bowl of soup in the village hall and we'll have you back before dusk.'

They had to be about fifteen minutes ahead of the rest of the party. Taking advantage of the privacy, Jessica sat down beside her sister. She said, 'Bella, do you ever think about Ned?'

For the longest time, Isabel didn't reply and the other nuns drew nearer.

'I left that life behind a long time ago,'

Isabel said at last. 'I have a new family now. A family in God. And you really should call me Sister Maria Magdalena. You might slip up sometime and call me Bella in front of Mother Hildegard.'

'Brenda told me he left the army and that she lost track of him after that,' Jessica said. 'I was just wondering if you'd ever heard from him.'

Isabel's face had clenched tight. 'No. How could I? No one knows where I am. Apart from you, Aunt Brenda and Uncle Rob. No one.'

'Take it easy, what does it matter? You're in a convent, not a satanic cult.'

Unusually clumsy, getting tangled in her habit, Isabel scrambled to her feet. 'I don't want to talk about this again,' she said.

She waved at the others still crossing the sand and raised her arm, waggling her thumb this way and that. *Everyone OK?* When she had an answering gesture from the woman at the head of the line, she turned again and set off along the damp coastal road towards the town. As always, Jessica had to walk slightly faster than she was comfortable with, to keep up.

29

Wednesday, 20 September

'So what are you saying, the pilot committed suicide? He jumped out?'

John Jones, acting chief constable of Northumbria Police and Ajax's immediate boss, pushed his chair back, away from the desk.

'It's one possibility, sir,' Ajax said. 'No sign of his body anywhere near the balloon. Evidence that one of the other passengers took over the job of trying to fly it and made some serious errors. The ground crew are adamant the crash probably wouldn't have happened, and certainly wouldn't have been as bad as it was, if Sean Allan had been on board and functioning.'

Ajax wondered, again, whether he really should share CSI Jane's theory about the brain tissue.

'But no sign of his body?' the chief asked.

Jane hadn't been certain. Better to wait a

while. 'The search-and-rescue helicopter has flown over the likely route of the balloon a couple of times and found nothing,' he said instead. 'We've also got a team on the ground, and dogs.'

'Presumably we've got people going to his home, looking for notes?'

Ajax glanced at the clock. Gone two o'clock and he was starving. 'Mr and Mrs Allan, the pilot's parents, insist he was fine. In good health, in a good frame of mind. But when I pushed them a bit harder, I found out that he and his wife divorced a year ago and that it hadn't exactly been amicable. There may have been undiagnosed depression. Feelings of anger.'

The chief turned towards the window. 'Are they still looking? It's vile out there.'

'They called back the helicopter when the mist came down, but they hope to go out again as soon as it clears.'

'Well, if he did jump out, they'll find him.'

Sighing deeply, Ajax stepped further into the room. 'Thing is though, sir, they may not. Not immediately. The balloons tend to fly over Harcourt Lake, and it's a bit of a thing with the pilots to fly as low as they can over water. Not strictly legal, from what I understand, but they do it all the same. Well, I'm thinking, what if he leapt out as they went over the lake?'

The chief's dark eyebrows crept closer together. 'He wouldn't die.'

'What if he had some weights in his pockets? That lake is deep. I wouldn't put money on our dredging something out of it any time soon.'

'I heard something about no mobile phones being found. Isn't that odd?'

Giving in, Ajax pulled out a chair and sat down. 'I've been thinking about that, and I'm not so sure. Once those people knew the balloon was in trouble, their first instinct would have been to pull out their phones and try to summon help. The signal is bad in the park, so they'd have to keep trying. If their phones were in their hands when the crash happened, they could have flown some distance. I'm sure we'll find most of them in the next few hours.'

The chief said, 'And two bodies still missing?'

Ajax glanced down at his notes. 'Two females. Fifteen-year-old Poppy Carlton and a woman called Jessica Lane. Probably dead, given the state the others were in, but I suppose we can't rule anything out. Helen Carlton's still hanging on, or was, thirty minutes ago.' He suddenly realized how still the chief had become. 'You all right, sir?'

135

The boss dropped his eyes. 'Run those names by me again.'

'Poppy Carlton. Jessica Lane.'

Another silence. Longer this time. Ajax looked towards the door. Then the boss mumbled something.

'Sorry, sir?' Ajax said.

'I knew a Jessica Lane.' The boss was talking to his desk. 'Long time ago.' He looked up. 'What else do we know about her?'

Ajax opened his notebook. 'Mid to late thirties, five sixish, slim, dark shoulder-length hair, wearing a bright green jacket. This is all from the staff at the balloon company. Gave her address as York and her next of kin as Sister Maria Magdalena of Wynding Priory just outside Fenham on the coast.'

The chief got up and turned to the window. He stood, his back to Ajax, staring at the rain-streaked glass. 'What relation was the nun to Jessica, do we know?' he asked.

'Her sister, I think.' Ajax watched his boss's shoulders stiffen.

'And the sister is at this priory? Fenham's not far, is it? Opposite Holy Island, if I'm right. Has someone been out to inform her?'

'The sister was in the balloon too. The trip was a present for her fortieth birthday. We found her body quickly. Sir, is it the same Jessica Lane, do you think? Did you know her?'

The chief spun round. 'Nah.' He pulled his chair out again. 'Mine would be much older than late thirties. She was older than me. Common name, I guess. OK, what else you got?'

'The bodies have all been taken to Newcastle General. The postmortems will start tomorrow but may take a couple of days to complete. The basket is on its way to the lab.'

'If these two females survived, we really need to find them quickly,' said the chief. 'They'll definitely know what happened, and they could be in a very vulnerable state. What do you need to keep the search going overnight?'

'I've spoken to air rescue but they don't recommend flying at night in these circumstances. Visibility can be zero and the heat-detecting equipment is of limited use with so many sheep around.'

The chief nodded, but reluctantly, it seemed. 'First light then. What about the dog teams?'

'As I said, still out there. The park authorities have people looking too.'

'We should do what we can to find these people.'

'We'll do our best, although . . .' Ajax didn't finish the thought. There was no need. 'If that's everything, sir, I really should see how the team is getting on with alerting next of kin. And I need to get out to Wynding Priory before too much longer.'

The boss was staring at him in a vacant manner.

'They haven't been answering the phone,' Ajax went on. 'Closed order, from what I can gather. And silent. They don't speak from one day to the next. But someone has to tell them Sister Maria won't be home for evening prayers.'

'Wynding? Out by Fenham.'

'That's right. So, can I —'

'Of course. Off you go.'

Ajax turned.

'Wait a minute, Ajax.'

His hand had been on the door. 'Sir?' He turned back slowly.

'Are you OK? I keep meaning to ask how you're doing. But you always seem so together, not to mention busy. This has bothered you, though, hasn't it?'

Ajax picked his words carefully. 'Not what I was expecting this morning, sir. But I think that's the nature of disasters.'

'Quite. So, you're off to see the nuns. Right. Thanks, Ajax. Keep me posted.'

Ajax looked round as the door closed. The boss was back at the window, staring at a rain-streaked, opaque sheet of glass.

30

On she walked, through long grass that soaked her shoes, then her socks. She walked when all feeling in her feet seemed to evaporate, when her mud-clogged footwear became nothing more than burdens to be dragged along with each step. She walked as the damp air seeped through the thin fabric of her clothes and the curls in her hair became limp and heavy, clinging to her neck like seaweed to a rock.

For a while she tried to keep track of distance and time, counting steps, looking out for any sign of the sun, but at some point she gave up doing both and when she cast her mind back, she couldn't remember when or why but thought probably it was when the voices began.

They'd started quietly. A low cry from behind, a whispered curse just beyond her left shoulder. She'd ignored them, telling herself they were nothing more than temporary manifestations of shock and a blow to the head, but still they clamoured for her attention. Voices of the hungry, the footsore, the weary, all of those who'd walked the path before her. Some sang, some prayed, some muttered confessions in low, angry voices. Sometimes the voices were in old dialects that she couldn't understand, other times they spoke of TV programmes that had been aired within the last year.

For a while, her dead sister kept pace alongside, telling her stories of when the two of them were young and then, when the waves of nausea in her stomach had finally ceded ground to pangs of hunger, she heard singing.

'Shall make him once relent,
His first avowed intent,
To be a pilgrim.'

More phantom voices? She looked to both sides, down the hill. It was still raining. Cloud cover was low and the day was overcast. The mist of earlier, though, had faded as the day had worn on.

There was a burst of laughter. Then the choir, real or imaginary, began the second verse, one strong tenor voice taking the lead.

141

'Whoso beset him round,
With dismal stories.'

The singers were getting closer, had been following her along the path. Then a head wrapped in the hood of a yellow coat appeared, climbing the hill towards her. Another coloured hood joined it, then a third. At least two of them were men.

The man. There was a man looking for her. This was a big group. Was he among them? She hadn't heard a bike engine, but maybe he was craftier than that.

Why did he want her, exactly?

The man in front, the lead tenor, was in his early sixties. He carried a walking stick fashioned from a long branch that had the look of a wizard's staff. The man to his left was older, smaller and thinner, the woman on his right portly and red-faced. Ten people in the group. None looked like him, but —

The man in front saw her and held up his hand for silence as they drew close. His face was large and all the lines on it curved upwards.

'Greetings. Good afternoon to you, fellow pilgrim.' He was Welsh.

'Hello,' she croaked back, her eyes going from one face to the next. If he were here, she couldn't run away. She wasn't sure how much further she could walk.

'You don't look dressed for the weather, if you don't mind my saying so. And you've ripped that lovely jacket of yours.'

She followed his eyeline and saw that the sleeve of her jacket was badly torn.

'Did you take a tumble?' one of the women asked. 'You're covered in cuts and bruises. And wet through.'

They were crowding her, circling her like a pack of wolves. They meant to be kind, at least she thought they did, but she wished they'd just —

'Well, we can do something about that.' Another of the women stepped forward, pulling her rucksack off her shoulders.

'OK, everyone,' said the Welshman. 'Take a breather. Nick, do we have any coffee left for this young lady, who looks frozen to death?'

'Here.' The woman in the red anorak was holding out a waterproof jacket. 'It's a spare,' she said. 'Go on, it won't get you dry, but it will keep some heat in.'

'Oh no, I couldn't.'

'Course you could.' The tenor was handing her coffee in a thin plastic cup. 'We're probably staying at the same place tonight, aren't we? The Youth Hostel in Wooler? You can give it back then.'

'That's a nasty tear.' The woman in the red anorak seemed fixated on her jacket. 'Did you catch it on something?'

She closed her eyes, had a sudden flash-back of crashing through trees, of branches scratching and clawing.

'Steady on.' A hand gripped her arm. 'Have some coffee. And get this coat on. Warm up a bit.'

The anorak on offer was thin but large. It would cover her head, come down almost to her thighs, would keep her dry for the rest of the day.

'Thank you,' she said. She raised the coffee to her lips, found it exactly the right temperature to drink and practically poured it down her throat.

'Now, do you need some help?' the tenor said. 'More than we can give you, I mean? We're in the middle of nowhere here, but we all have phones. I'm sure we can contact the authorities if you need us to.'

Authorities? What did that even mean? Who were the authorities? She had to go home, let her sister know she was all right. Home was this way, wasn't it? She looked beyond the tenor to the slope of the hill and the trees in the distance.

Trees. A terrible crash. Torn fabric of the

balloon. People screaming.

Her sister was dead. Everyone was dead. Maybe she was too. Maybe she was nothing but a ghost, and even that shadowy image was slipping away now, fading before their eyes, and that was the reason they were looking at her in alarm.

'I think she needs to sit down.'

'Get on the phone, Jeff, see if we can get someone out here.'

Someone? Who? Who were they phoning? They looked kind but how could she know for sure?

'I'm fine,' she said, surprised at how loud and clear she sounded. 'Really, I'm OK now. Thank you.'

They weren't convinced, she could tell from their puzzled frowns and sneaky little glances at each other. She couldn't let them phone. They might phone him.

'You're so kind,' she said, handing the cup back. 'God bless you.'

The tenor beamed. 'My name's Jeff and this is my wife, Hannah. I'd tell you the names of the rest of this bunch of reprobates but I don't want to overload you. We're from the Baptist Church in Little Crinton in Buckinghamshire, and I know that's already far more information than you looked for.'

He wanted a smile from her, she could

tell from the expectant way he was staring at her. She pressed the corners of her mouth outwards in response.

'And you would be . . . ?'

He wanted her name. Why did he need to know her name?

'Maria,' she said, the first thing that came into her head. Why had she said that? Maria was not her name.

'Now, don't take this wrong, but are you going all the way?'

'Oh, for goodness' sake, Jeff!' His wife poked him in the arm.

She'd walked this way before. Where did the path lead to again?

'I'm going to Lindisfarne,' she said. 'Holy Island.'

'Splendid. We'll see you along the way, no doubt. Although we have some very elderly folk in this group, don't we, Steve, and we might not be able to keep up with a young-ster like yourself. But we'd welcome your company at any time.' He half turned away and seemed to think again. 'Come to think of it, I think you'd better stay with us for a while. Till you feel a bit more sprightly.'

The man's wife, Hannah, was pressing another cup of coffee on her. By the time she'd finished it, the group were ready to move on and determined to take her with them.

They set off, the downhill slope making the going easier, the hot coffee she'd drunk helping. She walked at the back of the group, reluctant to intrude, but two of the ladies in the rear attached themselves to either side of her.

'Were you at Town Yetholm last night?' one of them asked. 'I don't remember seeing you at The Plough. Humbug?'

She took the sweet gratefully. 'I was. But I stayed with a friend. Someone I went on a retreat with last year.' She felt a moment of surprise. Who'd have thought she'd prove such a good liar? And why was she lying anyway? Why did she not just tell them what had happened?

What had happened, exactly?

'They told us it was haunted,' said the woman on the other side. 'But the only thing that kept me awake was Jeff's snoring. Have a toffee. I don't care for humbugs myself.'

'Thank you.' The toffee joined the humbug in her mouth.

Tell a group of complete strangers that she'd lost everything and that she wasn't sure how she was going to make it through the next hour, never mind the rest of her life? And that someone had tried to kill her and might try again if he found her? And that the crash had been her fault?

No, that wasn't right, was it? How could it have been her fault?

She was going home. These people would help her get home. That was all that mattered now.

They walked on, and she said nothing.

She found that she could keep up with the group easily. Most were in their late fifties or early sixties and their pace was slowed further by Jeff's insistence on regular stops to admire the view, to tell them stories from St Cuthbert's life, or to sing an impromptu hymn.

On the next rise, Jeff called them to a halt. 'A group coming the other way,' he said. 'That's unusual. A reverse pilgrimage.'

'Satanists,' muttered the woman with the humbugs, grinning gleefully at a group of six people heading up the path towards them. Unlike the pilgrims, they weren't walking in ones and twos but were spread out beyond the path for several metres on each side.

'They look like a search party,' said the man by Jeff's side.

'Funny sort of search party.'

The worst kind of search party. They were

searching for her.

The man at the head of the group wore a trilby and a loose leather jacket. His hair was dark, curling to his shoulders. In spite of the weather, his jacket was open, to reveal a low-necked white vest. Even without the distinctive clothes she would have known his short, squat shape, his lurching way of moving, the way his hands clenched into fists and then uncurled into grasping talons as he walked. He was here. This was him.

He'd found her.

His German shepherd trotted along unleashed at his side. It was a massive dog, even with fur clinging damply to its sides. As they drew closer, she could see that around the man's neck he wore a heavy gold cross on a chain. He carried what could have been a walking stick but, in the way he was swinging it, looked more like a club. Immediately behind him was a man with short hair and a dark beard. This one wore a padded coat, his hands thrust deep into his pockets. Apart from one woman, with very long blonde hair, they were all young men.

He had people. He wasn't alone.

She glanced back. Hiding was impossible. Running out of the question.

She closed her eyes and saw again the

carnage at the crash site, heard the sound of a woman's head being broken. Just by being with this group, she'd brought them into terrible danger. She'd seen what this man was capable of.

Oblivious to the peril he was in, Jeff led them down the hill, his head held high, maintaining a conversation with Nick. The others, though, had fallen silent; a nervousness had crept over them.

'*Who would true valour see, Let him come hither,*' she sang quietly.

She saw several glances turn her way, a couple of smiles. She'd always had a nice singing voice. The effort was robbing her of breath she badly needed, but something told her to keep singing.

The group coming up the hill were almost upon them.

'*One here will constant be,*' Jeff had joined in, followed quickly by Hannah, and all the others:

'*Come wind, come weather.*'

'Good afternoon.' Jeff stepped off the track, politely letting the others pass. The rest of his group followed. She did the same, pressing close to the humbug lady. She ran a finger around the rim of her hood to make sure her hair was hidden, and then tucked it quickly into her pocket, so no one would see how much her hand was shaking.

'Have you come from Holy Island?' Jeff asked the man in the trilby.

The man stared at him for a second. 'We're looking for some people,' he said, in a voice that was deep and coarse, as though his throat was sore. 'Couple of young women. You seen anyone lost? On their own? Maybe hurt?'

She waited for the group to turn towards her, to give her away with thoughtless glances. No one did.

And, a *couple* of young women? Someone else was alive? Or maybe it was a trick, to see how she reacted, make her think her sister had survived after all.

Was it even possible?

'I can't say that we have,' Jeff spoke loudly and decisively. 'We set off from Town Yetholm this morning with a church group from Liverpool, lovely people, but they walked a lot faster than we do and they left us behind. Apart from that, I can swear to the Lord I haven't seen a soul other than this group.'

It was not possible. She had seen her sister's dead face, felt her wrist for a glimmer of a pulse.

The man in the trilby stared at Jeff for a second, then walked past, scanning the faces

151

around him. 'Anyone see anything?' His accent was Scottish, but with a hint of something else. Something that made her think of hot, dusty countries, very far away. He seemed to be breathing deeply too, through his nose, as though trying to pick up a scent.

Her heart began to bang against the inside of her ribcage.

'These girls might be hurt,' he went on. 'Might need some help.' He was in the middle of the group now. A few seconds more and he'd be staring directly into her face. He'd know her then.

The dog was at her feet, more interested in her than anyone else, almost as though greeting an old friend. He would spot that. The dog raised its nose and nuzzled the pocket of her jacket. She longed to push it away, but knew any sort of movement would attract attention.

She wasn't sure how much longer she could stand up.

'We'll be sure to help anyone we come across,' said Jeff. 'Good luck to you.'

Jeff set off again, down the hill. Others followed. The search party was watching them go, scanning faces. She made herself keep her eyes and her head up. She passed within two feet of the man with the trilby and could have sworn she heard him sniff the air as she walked by.

'Can your dog have a biscuit?' The humbug lady was reaching inside her enormous pockets. The dog, either reacting to the word *biscuit,* or smelling something in the depths of the pocket, loped towards her.

'We don't feed him when he's working.' The man in the trilby had moved on, distracted by his dog. 'He's not a pet.'

'Oh, you're a good boy, aren't you, a very good boy?'

Out of the corner of her eye, she saw humbug lady bend bravely to pet the dog and its tail wag in response. The man with the padded coat passed by, then the woman with blonde hair. There was a resemblance amongst these people, a similarity, as though they were one family.

The pilgrims were all walking again now, past the group of searchers, back on the path. Still, she couldn't let herself breathe. It would only take one of them to say, *You know what, mate, there was something odd about the one in the blue anorak. Let's have another look at her.*

Keep walking. One foot in front of the other. Keep going.

'Don't like the look of that lot,' said the toffee lady, once they were safely out of earshot.

'Might be a good idea not to look back,' called Jeff, just loud enough for the walkers at the back to hear. 'It's usually taken as a sign of aggression, and we wouldn't want that now, would we?'

She didn't look back. But all the way down the hill and up the next rise, she could feel eyes upon her. He was looking for her. He knew she'd survived the crash. He would keep looking.

31

When Ajax pulled up at the gates of Wynding Priory they were closed and locked. There was no intercom, not even a bell. To either side of the gates, a tall stone wall stretched out as far as he could see along the road.

'And the gates of heaven shall be closed unto thee,' said MoJo.

'Let's not pretend you've ever opened a Bible.' Ajax sounded the horn.

'No one's going to hear that.'

He got out of the car. The wind was coming straight from the sea and the air seemed to swim with particles of sulphur and brine. He closed his eyes for a second, felt the damp on his face and licked salt off his lips. The convent building was less than a quarter of a mile from the coast; its grounds ran right up to the dunes.

In the most sparsely populated county in England, he couldn't imagine a more isolated spot. There were few trees and the dried-up, barren moorland around him seemed to stretch for ever.

The road he was parked on didn't even merit B status and was known to flood regularly during heavy rain. There were no other homes or buildings within five miles. According to the woman in the nearest post office, from whom he'd asked directions, the sisters kept one car that was rarely seen in the closest village. When the nuns appeared, they did so on bicycles.

Already the light was fading. He'd been kept later in the office than he'd have wanted and had got caught in rush-hour traffic on the way over. It was gone six in the evening and he had a feeling religious houses kept early hours.

He approached the gate. The main priory building was about two hundred metres away down a weed-ridden gravel drive. The building looked late Elizabethan, although he knew there had been a religious house on this site for over eight hundred years. It was dark-grey stone with a black slate roof. The adjoining chapel boasted a miniature tower topped with a statue of Christ. The windows were small and paned. Through the fading light, he could see a billowing black robe making its way towards him.

'Oh, ye of little faith,' he called back over his shoulder.

The nun, a tiny woman in her early sixties, had a gentle smile on her face as she pulled a large key from her pocket and unlocked the padlock. She didn't look directly at either Ajax or the car. Ajax went forward to help her pull open the gates but she stepped back and held up both hands, stopping him in his tracks. She shook her head. She still hadn't made eye contact.

'Silent order,' hissed MoJo from the car. 'I'll bet she's not allowed to speak.'

The nun pulled open one gate, then the other, and gestured that he should move forward. Ajax drove through and stopped again. He waited until she'd closed and locked the gates and then jumped out and held open the rear door of the car, wishing he'd thought to clear it of empty crisp packets and discarded papers.

The slight smile, less gentle and more creepy by the second, didn't falter but the nun shook her head and walked past him. She began to walk sedately back to the house, directly down the centre of the drive. There was no way he could drive past her — he would have to follow in her wake.

'You have got to be kidding me.'

MoJo was laughing quietly. 'I think we

157

play by their rules here. Just be grateful the drive isn't half a mile long.'

Ajax started the engine and released the handbrake. The nun was twenty metres away. 'This is absurd,' he said, running a hand through his hair.

'Give her a toot.'

'I can't toot a nun.'

'There's space to drive round her.'

'Over their grass? There'll be a special place in hell.'

Seeing no alternative, Ajax put the car into first gear and pulled forward.

MoJo sat upright. 'I'm going to get out and walk with her. Bet you I can get her to talk before we get to the house.'

'Please don't make me activate the child lock.'

He regretted saying it the second the words left his mouth. Even now, one couldn't mention children, the possibility of children in her life, to MoJo. She shrank down into her seat and he knew it would be some time before she spoke again.

The nun's steady pace never wavered and Ajax crawled along behind her. When they reached the house he stopped the car and jumped out. Not expecting the nun to speak, he allowed her to approach the large wooden-panelled front door and open it.

She disappeared inside, leaving it open behind her, just as a high-pitched, unearthly screeching sounded close by.

'What the hell was that?' MoJo muttered, shocked out of her sulk.

Ajax stepped back and looked around. Nothing. Except maybe . . .

There was a high stone wall to the right of the convent, some twenty metres away, and something large was perched on top of it. Not a statue, definitely not a statue; it was moving, sliding sideways along the top of the wall. The hideous cry sounded again, echoing around the turrets of the old building.

'Don't mind the peacocks,' said a low, mellow voice from inside the building. 'They'll be roosting soon. Please come in.'

The peacock spread its fabulous black and turquoise tail and jumped down from the wall. It began strutting towards them as the smell of stale cooking drifted out through the door, reminding Ajax of school dinners and of the time he'd been forced to eat parsnips, before vomiting on the dinner lady's shoes.

Another nun was waiting in the hallway. Ajax held up his warrant card and introduced himself. Behind him, unusually quietly, MoJo did the same. The nun pushed thick-rimmed spectacles further up her nose and examined his card. She did not offer to shake hands.

'I'm Mother Hildegard. Welcome to Wynding Priory.'

Mother Hildegard was tall and solidly built, possibly in her early seventies, although her barely lined face wasn't easy to read. Behind the spectacles, her eyes were a soft grey. A milky white cloth framed her face and her black clothes flowed almost to the flagged floor. The cross around her neck was gold, bigger and more elaborate than the one they'd found around the neck of Sister Maria Magdalena. She was looking at him curiously. He watched her frown, her mouth turn down, then she stepped forward. She raised her left hand and placed it gently on his forehead, making the sign of the cross with her other hand and muttering a blessing.

He was too surprised to speak.

'I hope you don't mind.' She stepped back and looked deep into his eyes. 'I was moved to do it. I'm not sure why. You seem in need.'

Ajax found himself oddly touched. 'I've not had the best of days. And I don't mind. I was raised a Catholic.'

'I know that.'

Hildegard turned on her heels and they

followed her across the hall to a wide wooden staircase with carved balusters. She went up, they followed. At the top of the first flight, she led them into a large room, furnished as an office. A wooden desk, old but not antique, was close to the window. Bookshelves lined the walls. A Bible stood on its own lectern to one side of the desk. There were four armchairs, covered in a floral fabric that might have been fashionable in the 1980s, and a small, patterned rug on an otherwise plain wooden floor. The room smelled like the houses of old people, and of an elderly lady's sweat.

Mother Hildegard gestured that her guests were to sit, then joined them.

'I expect you've come to tell me about Sister Maria Magdalena's death? It was kind of you to do so. I'm sure it must have been a very busy day for you.'

Well, that made things a bit easier. 'You must have seen it on the news?' Ajax said. 'About the balloon crash, I mean?'

She smiled again, a smile of endless patience. 'We do have a television set in the convent house. It's kept in the recreation room, but the sisters prefer to spend the hour or so of allotted time watching comedy shows. They're very fond of *Father Ted*. And *The Big Bang Theory* is a great favourite, because one of our sisters used to teach physics and the rest of us enjoy watching her roar with laughter at the science jokes. We don't see the news, though. We're at either vespers or compline when the news programme is broadcast.'

'Then how . . . ?'

'Sister Maria Magdalena was due to be back at twelve noon. Trips outside the convent are very rarely permitted and times have to be adhered to very strictly. Had there been an unavoidable delay, Sister would have telephoned my office. I have a telephone answering machine for when I'm not here.' She looked at her watch. 'That was nearly seven hours ago, during which time I've had several messages from your colleagues. I knew something terrible must have happened.'

'I'm sorry to tell you that you're right. The balloon came down unexpectedly. We found Sister Maria Magdalena's body at the crash site. I'm very sorry for your loss.'

Hildegard crossed herself and closed her eyes for a second. 'I was very uncomfortable about that trip, but I always hated saying no to Jessica.' Her eyes opened wide in alarm. 'Jessica?' she said. 'Her sister Jessica?'

'You knew Jessica too?'

'Of course. She's been visiting for years.

She comes most months, sometimes twice a month. I feel I've watched her grow up. Such a sweet girl. And so — oh my goodness.'

The nun dropped her face into her hands. Ajax could feel MoJo giving him that look, the one that always made him think she was about to bite something. Or someone.

With an obvious effort, Hildegard composed herself. Her hands, when she dropped them, were damp. 'Please excuse me,' she said. 'Human frailty never leaves us, however much we might try to dispel it. I was very fond of Jessica.'

'We haven't found Jessica's body,' said Ajax. 'So we don't know for certain. But it would be dishonest to tell you I'm hopeful. Of the thirteen people on board, nine have been confirmed dead. Another is critically ill in hospital.'

A tear rolled down the old nun's cheek.

Somewhere in the house, a bell began to toll. Ajax suppressed a shudder as Hildegard got to her feet.

'Vespers is about to begin. I never miss it. We will pray for the souls of everyone on that ill-fated balloon. God bless you, Superintendent. Sister Winifred will show you to the gate.' For a second, her eyes drifted to the chair on which MoJo was sitting. She frowned and then forced another smile. 'God bless you,' she repeated, her eyes wavering.

Ajax remained in his seat. 'Mother Hildegard, I'm very sorry to intrude on your sorrow but I'm afraid I do need a little more of your time.'

The nun pulled back her shoulders. 'The sisters will be expecting me.'

'Nevertheless. Please, sit back down.'

32

Towards the end of the afternoon they walked down the last of the hills, crossed one more field and climbed the final stile to reach Wooler. In spite of having walked up hills and over rough ground for several hours, she was feeling better. Her headache hadn't gone, but had gradually become more bearable in the cool, fresh air. Her body was stiff and sore, but the walking had helped, if anything.

As the group of pilgrims made their way down the high street, she spoke the words she'd been silently rehearsing for the past half-hour.

'I need to catch the post office before it closes,' she said to the woman who'd lent her the coat. 'Can I return your jacket at the Youth Hostel later?'

'Of course. Perhaps you can join us for dinner?'

'Thank you.' She turned away, was about

to hurry down the street, when she felt a hand on her shoulder.

Jeff asked, 'Is there anything we can do to help you?' in a voice unusually subdued for him.

His kindness was disarming and for a second she wanted nothing more than to tell him everything. But she was so close now. From Wooler, she could get a bus, a taxi, make phone calls. 'You already have,' she replied. 'I'll see you this evening.'

She waited for him to say that he would look forward to it, because that was the sort of thing he said. He didn't. He put a hand on her shoulder again. 'God bless you,' he said, before steering his group down the street. Watching them go felt like standing on ice, seeing the last crack form, and knowing the fall was inevitable.

In the post office she bought a single envelope. She ripped a page from a notepad on the counter and scribbled a few words. She sealed the envelope and then, carefully, in case she should meet anyone from the group of pilgrims, she made her way to the Youth Hostel. She left the envelope, addressed to Jeff, and went outside again.

A hundred metres down the street, beside a telephone box, the man wearing the loose leather jacket and the trilby was climbing out of a Land Rover. The man in the blue padded coat got out of the passenger seat.

She stepped back into the Youth Hostel doorway, out of sight, and watched the man in the trilby walk down the street. He stopped the first person he met and they spoke for a few seconds. She saw the person, an elderly woman, shake her head and the man moved on. Meanwhile, the man in the blue coat was heading her way. A woman with lots of blonde hair had climbed down from the back of the Land Rover and was crossing the street.

How stupid she'd been. There were so few towns and villages in this part of the county. They were bound to look in one of the biggest. She slipped out of the doorway and began walking away from the town centre.

St Cuthbert's Way left Wooler along the B6348. By the time she left the road to head north-east across open countryside, the light was fading. Her headache was back, she was trembling from lack of food, and the voices of the dead were gathering about her again.

Hildegard used the backs of her fingers to wipe away the last trace of her tears. Then she walked to her desk and rang a small, metal bell. Turning to face the window she fixed her gaze on something outside. Over her shoulders, Ajax could see nothing but the darkening sky.

He was about to resume the conversation when he heard footsteps approaching along the corridor. The door opened and only then did Hildegard turn.

'Tell the sisters not to wait,' she told whoever was in the doorway. 'I'll be along as soon as I can.'

The door closed, the footsteps receded. The elderly nun remained by the window, her face impassive.

'Mother Hildegard, the circumstances of the balloon's crash are unexplained,' Ajax began. 'The pilot was very experienced. The flight was one he'd done many times before.

The balloon itself was subjected to regular safety checks. The conditions were good. This crash should not have happened.'

Her face had softened, fractionally. 'How can I help?'

'Something happened during the flight. We can't rule out the possibility that the accident was caused by the actions of one or more of the passengers.'

Deep frown lines broke the smoothness of the nun's forehead.

'Do you have any reason to believe Sister Maria Magdalena was troubled at all? Did you notice anything unusual about her behaviour in recent weeks?'

The nun's face remained steady. 'You suspect our sister of causing the accident?'

Ajax quickly shook his head. 'I have no reason whatsoever to do that. I will be asking these same questions of all the families involved.'

The nun's eyes left Ajax and fixed on the ceiling. 'Her behaviour was the same as normal,' she said. 'I don't remember anything unusual or remarkable. If anything, there was an extra — I don't know — vigour about her. We'd planned a small celebration for her fortieth birthday; her sister was coming to visit, that always made her happy. She didn't know about the balloon trip, although the rest of us did. It was to be a surprise. All the sisters were excited on her behalf.' She sighed. 'Our mission here is to dispel earthly wants and considerations. I guess we can only ever suppress them.'

'Was Sister Maria Magdalena happy here?'

Hildegard fixed him with a look. 'She was a bride of Christ. We believe there is no higher calling for a woman.'

Ajax stood. 'Can I see her room?'

From the expression on Hildegard's face, you'd think he'd asked to see her underwear. 'Her room?'

'Yes, her private space. The place she kept her stuff.'

'We have no stuff, Superintendent. We eschew personal possessions when we commit to a religious life. And we don't have rooms of our own. The cells where the sisters sleep are rotated so that no one gets attached to any particular space.'

'Then I'd like to see the cell where she slept last night.'

'I can't permit that.'

Ajax told himself this was an elderly lady who knew nothing of the world, and who'd just received bad news. On the other hand, he'd had one pig of a day. 'Mother Hildegard, this is the beginning of what could become a very serious police investigation and I am more than capable of coming back with a warrant. It's up to you.'

There was a flash of fury in the nun's face. Then she suppressed it. 'Wait for me outside,' she told him.

In the corridor Ajax and MoJo looked at each other.

'Didn't seem too bothered about Mary Magdalene's death,' Mojo said. 'Did you notice that?'

'I did.'

The door opened and Mother Hildegard slipped out. Without a word, she set off along the corridor, away from the stairs. They followed and as the smell of dinner gave way to that of incense, Ajax realized they were approaching the chapel.

He felt MoJo's finger in his ribs.

'Mother, I'm sorry to be blunt,' he said, 'but I couldn't help noticing you seemed more upset by Jessica's death than by her sister's.'

The nun paused. 'Did I give that impression? I'm sorry. All deaths are equally to be mourned. And celebrated, because the ones we have lost are with the Lord.' She set off again.

'She's fucking with you,' mumbled MoJo.

'How long was Maria with you?'

Hildegard slowed her pace, allowing Ajax

171

to catch up. 'Sister Maria Magdalena joined us at the age of eighteen. We don't normally accept young women until they are twenty-one. The life of the bride of Christ is arduous and not for everyone. But the Mother Superior at the time felt her vocation was strong and so, against the advice of several of the senior sisters, she was admitted.'

'Twenty-two years,' said Ajax. 'You can't say she didn't stay the course.'

They'd reached the end of the corridor. In the wall ahead was a grilled window. The sound of the sisters singing came through it. Hildegard paused, allowing Ajax to look down.

The chapel below had huge, arched, stained-glass windows in three of the walls. The floor was chequered with black and white tiles and three rows of pews ran down each long side, facing inwards. The fading light outside cast coloured shadows around the room and candles danced in some invisible breeze.

The sisters, around four dozen in the pews closest to the altar, sang in Latin without accompaniment.

'It's beautiful,' said Ajax. 'You're very lucky to hear this every day.'

The nun said, 'To be frank with you, I was against Sister Maria Magdalena joining the order. I argued that she was very young for so great a commitment. The truth was, I doubted her vocation.'

'When did she convince you?'

The nun's eyes became cold again, before she turned and led them up another, narrower staircase. Ajax had to duck his head at the top. They were in the roof. Narrow doors lined the corridor on each side. The smell of undiluted femininity was stronger here. Laundry and unwashed bodies, the sweet, musty smell of female lavatories. They followed Hildegard to the middle of the corridor where she pushed open a door and allowed them to go inside.

The room beyond, not called a cell without reason, thought Ajax, measured ten feet by seven; which made it almost exactly the dimensions of the cells back at the station. The only furnishings were a narrow metal bed and a wooden cupboard beside it. The back wall followed the slope of the roof and the window looked out in the direction of the sea.

Above the bed hung a wooden cross.

'We lead simple lives,' said the nun, and it sounded like a boast.

'No personal possessions at all?'

'Family photographs are permitted but not displayed. I believe you will find a photograph of Sister and Jessica in the drawer.'

Taking that as permission, Ajax crossed the room and pulled open the top drawer of the small wooden cabinet. In it he found a box of value tissues, a toiletry bag, sanitary towels, a rosary and a framed photograph of two girls.

He carried the photograph to the light, feeling MoJo pushing up behind him.

Maria Magdalena, the older of the two sisters, couldn't have been more than seventeen in the picture. Her face still had the plump, uncreased gleam of the very young. Her dark hair shone and curled down past her shoulders. Her eyes were brown. Jessica was a little younger, a little fairer, very slightly less pretty. Only slightly. The two were exceptionally alike.

'They were beautiful,' said Ajax, feeling a stab of guilt at remembering that Jessica, officially, wasn't dead. The nun didn't pick up on it.

'Another reason why I felt Maria Magdalena was unsuited to convent life. Her face, even when she was veiled, had a way of drawing the eye. Nuns practise modesty at all times. In the old days, a beautiful nun would have had her face scarred to discourage vanity. I wouldn't advocate that, of course.'

'What was her name? Before she became Maria Magdalena? Do you remember?'

The nun's face said that she forgot very little, if anything. 'Her name was Isabel.'

'Isabel Lane?'

'No. Jessica was married briefly. She brought wedding photographs to show us years ago. She never told us she was divorced. We guessed.'

'So Isabel was . . .'

'Isabel Jones. And it's possible Jessica was known as Jones too, in the police force, although I'm not certain about that.'

Ajax stared. 'Jessica is a police officer?'

The nun looked amused. 'I assumed you knew.'

'We only have the balloon company's paperwork to go on. It lists home address and next of kin, not occupation. Do you know where? What force?'

'I'm afraid I don't. Not locally, I think, because she had to travel to get here. The address we have for her is in York.'

Ajax nodded. Someone from North Yorkshire Police would be on their way to Jessica Lane's home, to break the news to anyone they found there. She'd listed her next of kin as Sister Maria Magdalena.

'I really must go, Superintendent. I want to pray for the souls of our dear sisters. Of course, you are welcome to join us.'

'Thank you, but I'll be working for a few more hours yet. May I keep hold of this photograph? Just for a short while. I'll see you get it back.'

After Hildegard had nodded her permission, he allowed her to lead them out of the room, along the corridor, down the stairs, to the ground floor.

'Winifred will unlock the gates for you. Is it too soon to ask what will happen to Sister Maria Magdalena's remains? We have a small cemetery here. I'm not sure she had any family other than Jessica.'

He'd nearly forgotten. The main reason for coming here.

'They'll be released to her next of kin as soon as possible. In the event of no family members coming forward, the coroner is likely to conclude that that is the convent. There is one thing I do have to ask you though, Mother. It's a difficult task, but a necessary one.'

'You want me to identify the body?'

'It doesn't have to be you.'

She sighed. 'Of course it has to be me. Tonight?'

'Tomorrow will be fine. I'll pick you up

and drive you to the mortuary.'

'Thank you. Was she very badly —'

'Her face was a little damaged. But she should still be the woman you knew.'

'And Jessica? You'll keep looking?'

'Of course. Let's hope you won't have to mourn them both.'

34

'A serving police officer? Interesting.'

'Aren't you going to be late, sir?' said Ajax.

The chief glanced down at his dinner jacket and starched white dress shirt as though he'd forgotten what he was wearing. 'I'll only miss the prawn cocktail. Do we know which force?'

'Not yet,' Ajax said, 'although my guess would be North Yorkshire, given that she lived in York.'

'Not so, sir,' Chapman spoke up. 'I've heard back from North Yorks. She wasn't one of theirs. They did send someone round to her address, but there was no one there. They spoke to one of the neighbours who said she thought they were away for a few days.'

'They?'

'Lane lives with her fiancé, a bloke called Neil Fishburn, who is a serving officer with North Yorkshire. They own the house together.'

'He might be up here as well, I suppose,' Ajax said. 'Although I'm surprised he hasn't come forward.' He looked round. 'Has he?'

Stacey, who was in charge of dealing with next of kin, shook her head.

'The neighbour also said that Lane is away a lot,' Chapman went on. 'She often drives off first thing Monday morning, appearing again Friday evening. Suggests to me she's attached to a force some distance away.'

'We'd have heard by now,' said the chief, 'if she was still alive. She's had, what, ten hours to get in touch? Same with the kid.'

'It doesn't look good,' Ajax agreed. 'I think we have to be prepared for a couple more bodies in the morning.'

35

When Patrick arrived at Newcastle General, he parked in the furthest corner of the car park, where he already knew CCTV cameras didn't reach. He'd been to this hospital many times. He bought a parking ticket and carried his bag in through reception and into the nearest public lavatory.

In the cubicle he changed into medical scrubs and tied his long hair back into a ponytail. Before leaving home he'd scrubbed his hands clean, but he checked them again now. Medics' hands were always spotless. He hung a lanyard with hospital ID (fake, but convincing enough at a glance) around his neck and left the lavatories, carrying his holdall with him. He went via the male doctors' changing rooms, leaving the bag on a bench immediately inside the door.

The evening meal was being cleaned away and peak visiting time would start shortly. It was also shift-changeover time, when staffing levels temporarily slumped.

He made his way up to intensive care, punched in the key code that had been texted to him earlier and found Helen Carlton's room. He slipped inside, pulled the syringe from his pocket and injected 40 ml of insulin into a vein on her left wrist.

As he left the room, he figured it would be roughly ten to fifteen minutes before the convulsions began and alerted her attending medical staff. He'd be long gone by then.

36

Evening visiting hour was long over and there were several parking spaces in the hospital car park, but Ajax took his time. He found a spot some distance from the entrance. As he made his way inside he saw a vehicle he recognized; DC Steve Chapman was here, dealing with paperwork in the mortuary.

Helen Carlton was in a room off the main ward. He didn't attempt to enter, but stood instead at the large window. She was surrounded by machinery and breathing with the aid of a respirator.

'Excuse me?'

Ajax turned to see a slim, Asian nurse standing behind him.

'You're obviously with the police.' She let her eyes drift over the uniform he was still wearing. 'Are you involved with the balloon crash?'

'I'm the police officer in charge for the

time being.' He pulled out his warrant card and introduced himself. 'I don't think we've managed to contact Mrs Carlton's family yet. Her husband was killed in the same crash.'

'I know. It's terrible. Can you stay a minute? Our administrator would like to see you.'

'Actually, I was about to head out.'

'I believe it's very important.'

37

Back at Castle Faa, Patrick unfastened the padlocks, the one at the top of the farm-house door, then the one at the bottom, and drew the bolts. He turned the deadlock and kept hold of the key. Moving inside the house, he stepped aside to let William and Cat, their cousin, follow him in. William had the food, Cat carried the other stuff. Once they were clear of the door, he deadlocked it again and pocketed the key.

Taking no chances this time.

The boarded windows kept the house dark, even on the sunniest days. He heard Cat's hand sliding, insect-like, along the wall until she found the light switch. The single bulb in the hallway flicked on and they moved towards the stairs.

He had no idea when people, normal people, had last lived in the farmhouse. None of the family could remember that far back. Now, decades after it had been a habitable home, plaster had crumbled from the ceiling and covered everything in the house, like soiled snow. Paper peeled down walls and turned to mush on the damp carpets, which were so stained and worn their original colour and pattern were indiscernible.

They crunched over mice droppings, brushed their way through cobwebs, to the sound of the constant drip of a leaky tap in the kitchen. Criss-crossing the bare boards of the stairs were silvery snail trails.

At the front of the house, a bramble had forced its way in through the gap between door and frame. No one had pulled it up, and it had gained in strength and reach, its thorn-ridden tendrils stretching towards the stairs. Ivy had followed it and was climbing the walls.

Filthy, torn curtains hung at every window, in spite of the boarding that kept out all light. As the breeze they'd brought in with them made its way through the house, the curtains began to sway, the strips of wallpaper to rustle.

This house was never silent. When its human occupants settled, the others started up. Rats lived in the cavities, bats in the roof area, cockroaches and woodlice and beetles scuttled everywhere.

Right on cue, Patrick and the others heard movement on the floor above. They always began scurrying about when they heard the back door open.

As Cat turned to precede him up the steps he saw her nose wrinkle. The plumbing worked OK, as far as he knew, but a house that was never cleaned or aired was always going to stink.

Someone began banging on one of the locked upstairs doors.

'Here we go,' muttered Cat who, of all of them, hated this job the most.

The three occupants of the house were all in one room, the largest of the four bedrooms, with its own adjoining shower room. He went in first, Cat following, William bringing up the rear.

The oldest occupant, a woman of around thirty-five, stood in the centre of the room. The teenage brother and sister pressed themselves against the far wall.

'Where is she?' the older woman said, in heavily accented English. 'Where is my friend?'

Patrick ignored her, turning instead to watch his brother carry the food over to a tall chest of drawers in one corner.

'What the fuck?' William made an exasperated gesture. 'Look at this. They've left half of it.'

Cat joined him. 'Well, what twat bought pork pies and bacon sandwiches?' she asked in an undertone. 'You know they won't eat that stuff.'

William pulled a face. 'They'll eat it if they're hungry enough. I say we leave it here till they do.'

'Shut up, Will,' Patrick said. 'We'll take the old stuff with us. We don't need any crap today.'

'You need to come with us to the next room,' he told the woman. 'You first, then the others know there'll be nothing to worry about. Just an injection, a vaccine, you'll need it before you get your papers.'

She shook her head.

'Your friend was stupid,' he went on. 'We're looking for her. If we find her before the police do, we'll bring her back and everything will be fine. If the police find her, she'll be sent home. There's nothing we can do. Now come on, let's go next door, no one's going to hurt you.'

He'd learned to be polite and careful when he dealt with them. There was no point making them scared, or too hostile. They only fought harder. After the first few times, when things had gone wrong, there

187

was no point denying it, the people who'd stayed in the farmhouse had been treated well. They'd been fed, kept warm and safe. After what they'd been through on the journey, the farmhouse really wasn't that bad.

Warily, the woman stepped forward, allowing Cat to take her arm and lead her into the next room, the one where they kept the medical equipment and the records. He breathed an inaudible sigh of relief. He'd got quite good at keeping them calm and cooperative.

Of course, they all panicked when they saw the leather straps.

38

Evenings in late September are short and chill, and the sky turned quickly from dove grey to charcoal. Damp seemed to sit in the air. Trees she passed shook icy droplets down, bushes smeared her with cold. Even the mud beneath her feet seemed to covet her shoes, sucking and grasping with every step, trying to pull them off her feet.

Her head was aching badly again, and the voices had resumed after she'd left the pilgrims behind, becoming increasingly grim and threatening as the day had darkened. As the light left the sky, her spectral companions took form and out of the corner of her eye, she could see dark, sloping figures keeping pace. They spoke of sorrow sometimes, but mainly of guilt. The bolder ones pressed close until she could feel their breath, hot and rank, on the back of her neck.

Her fault. Everything bad that had ever

happened had been her fault. Her fault that her sister had been on the balloon. Worse, her fault that all those people had died. If not for her, they'd all be alive now.

Tiny hands pulled at her hair, and she let them, welcoming the sharp pain, until she realized her hair was simply getting caught in the overhanging branches of the hedges she passed.

Much of the trail from Wooler followed minor roads or farm tracks, but there came a time when she had to cross open countryside once more, and the full force of the wind hit her. When the moon was hidden, even the ground at her feet became a treacherous mass of invisible mud, rocks and puddles.

There was no light to be seen, not the tiniest pinprick on the horizon that might indicate habitation. In this darkness, she wouldn't see any of the shepherd's huts or ramblers' shelters that she knew to be along the trail. She might pass them by, feet away.

When the moon was high above her, she judged it was close to midnight. She began looking for somewhere to spend the next few hours.

39

'We're off now, Ma.'

Snip. Snip. Mary didn't turn round, didn't stop what she was doing, but Patrick knew she'd heard him. Cat and William, their arms full, walked ahead and made for the caravans.

'I had a call while we were in there,' he went on. 'The police dogs picked up a trail at the crash site.'

She raised her head, her secateurs hovering above the dead rose. She always pruned the roses after the sun had gone down. Less stressful for them, so she said.

'They tracked it out of the woods, lost it after a mile or so, on the border by that footpath. The one called after the saint.'

The secateurs danced in front of his mother as she crossed herself.

'Might be nothing to do with the crash. Could have been left days ago, but we're going out again, further along the path this time. Both directions. Will and Jez are taking the horses.'

Mary turned then, the shrivelled husk of a flower in her hand. The roses that grew in the small garden behind the house were the only flowers cultivated on the Faa land. Every other bloom that appeared, and in summer there were several, grew wild, but the roses were important to his mother. They were black, the only known variety of naturally occurring black rose in the world, and Mary told the story of how they grew only in Turkey, but when the Faa ancestors had travelled to Europe from India, they'd brought cuttings with them. Stolen, the legend had it, because the black roses were carefully guarded. For a reason that nobody understood, they'd thrived in the Scottish Borders and, to this day, every Faa bride carried them in her bouquet.

From inside the farmhouse came the sound of something banging, then a moan of pain. Patrick and Mary both looked up at the barred window directly above their heads. Then at each other.

'What happened here last night?' Mary nodded towards the rear door of the farmhouse. The bolts on the outside were drawn.

He shrugged. 'I don't fucking know, Ma. The dogs were kicking off. You know what

192

they're like when there's one of them bad-gers around. I let Shinto out, he ran off. I stood at the door trying to see what was bothering him.'

Mary's almost shapeless face twisted. 'You stood at the door? She got past you while you stood at the door?'

He kicked at a loose stone. 'I might have stepped outside for a couple of seconds. I lost sight of the blasted dog. He was over by the bottom corner.'

'You left the door open?'

'I was yards away. For less than a minute.'

'How did she get out of the compound, that's what I want to know. What the fuck did she do, climb?'

He looked at the fence. It was ten feet high, a tight-weave mesh of sharp, strong wire. No one could climb it. 'I haven't had a chance to walk around in daylight,' he said. 'There might be something, I don't know, a way underneath. A foxhole. She was a wee lass, it's possible.'

Mary glared at him for a second longer then turned her back and resumed her task.

'It has to stop.' Snip. Snip. More dead husks fell to the ground.

He'd been waiting for this. 'We've had some bad luck. We'll get through it.'

'It was never meant to go this far. She

would never have wanted this.'

The name she never said any more hovered in the air between them.

'We can't cancel tomorrow night,' he said. 'That's the last.'

She was upset. She'd calm down. He could argue later. 'Let's just get the crash sorted,' he said. 'Then we can talk.'

40

Without speaking, the administrator led Ajax to the locked doors of the theatre suite.

'Are you sure you can't tell me what this is about?' he asked.

She tapped in a key code. 'Better if Mr Wallace tells you himself.'

They walked through into a wide, functional corridor. Fluorescent lights flickered overhead. Empty trolleys lined one wall. The corridor wasn't busy, but energy seemed to emanate from one room at its far end.

Footsteps sounded and Ajax turned to see two green-clad medics striding towards them. They raced past without acknowledging either him or the administrator and burst through the crash doors into the busy room.

The administrator stopped at the double doors and used an internal telephone. Ajax tried to eavesdrop, caught only, 'He's here.'

There was a rattle behind as a cleaning

team arrived. The cleaners pushed past him, parked the trolley and one of them peered through the window. He shook his head. 'Still at it,' he said to the other. Leaving the trolley, they went back the way they'd come.

The big swing doors crashed open and two more medics strode out. Ajax hadn't got a good look at the pair who'd just entered, but he didn't think these could be the same. These two were covered in blood. Both carried large white bags, solid and rectangular in construction, like picnic cold-bags. Except that these had *HUMAN ORGAN for transplant* in bright red letters on the side. They strode off down the corridor.

The doors pushed open again. The man who stepped through this time was tall and very thin, possibly in late middle age, but the lower half of his face was covered by a surgical mask and his hair concealed beneath a cap. His scrubs were drenched in blood. So were his gloves, mask and cap.

Ajax resisted the temptation to back away.

The doctor stood in the doorway, looking around, as though not really sure why he was there. Then his eyes fixed on the administrator. He inclined his head and strode across the corridor to a side room, gesturing that they follow him.

Once they'd all entered the small, white-painted storage room, the door slammed behind them. The surgeon had his back to them, was pulling off his mask, then his gloves. He dropped them into a surgical waste bin and then froze, breathing heavily. His hands, clean and pale without the gloves, were clenched into fists.

Ajax raised his eyebrows at the administrator. She pursed her lips, her eyes flicking from one man to the next. Getting no answer there, Ajax looked round the room, bitterly missing MoJo in the sheer absurdity of it all, but she never came into hospitals.

'Superintendent Maldonado.'

Ajax turned back. 'That's me.'

The surgeon looked down at his blood-covered clothes. 'You probably won't want to shake hands.'

'Good call,' Ajax said. 'What's this about?'

'I'm Ralph Wallace. You've already met Susan Hammond, our hospital administrator. She's here because, if you agree to what I'm about to ask, there'll be paperwork to sort out urgently. I'm in the middle of a procedure and I have to get back to it right away. I shouldn't have left.'

'What's so important you're risking a patient's life?'

'The patient is dead. We're carrying out a complete organ transplant on a young

197

woman who died of serious head injuries in a climbing fall earlier today. Liver, kidneys, heart, lungs, corneas — everything it's possible to remove. She was young and very healthy. She was also from the Middle East and we get very few donors of that particular ethnicity. There are couriers on standby to take the organs to recipients throughout the north-east.'

Ajax thought of the doctors leaving the theatre, their drawn faces, bloodstained gowns, the bags they'd carried.

'I never normally see people, especially people I don't know, immediately after organ harvesting,' Wallace went on. 'I wouldn't usually dream of leaving theatre during a procedure. Today, though, it's unavoidable.'

'Excuse me for saying so,' Ajax said, 'but you don't look well.'

The man's nostrils pinched as he took a deep breath. 'I'm perfectly well. You had to deal with a serious incident today yourself, Superintendent. You saw terrible injuries. Quite possibly people in dreadful pain. You understand about trauma.'

'I guess.'

'People don't appreciate, because we don't — we can't — tell them, how traumatic transplant surgery is. We have a very short space of time to tear a body apart and rip out everything that made it functional. Physically, it's draining, it's extremely messy and, when the person is young, it's quite heartbreaking. And we do it because it saves lives. Out of an unavoidable death, good can come, if we act quickly.'

It might be the sight, even the smell, of all the blood, but Ajax was starting to feel light-headed. 'What can I do?'

'You're the police officer in charge of the balloon crash.'

Ajax inclined his head.

'The only passenger known to have survived, Helen Carlton, was admitted shortly after eleven o'clock this morning,' Wallace said. 'She was taken immediately into surgery. We did everything we could and for a while we were hopeful, but she deteriorated earlier this evening. I'm afraid there's no chance of her recovery.'

Impossible to prevent the thought that it was probably for the best. 'Her husband and son are both dead,' Ajax said. 'Possibly her daughter too, although we haven't found her yet.'

'So I understand. A terrible business.'

'I saw her a couple of minutes ago.' Ajax turned to the administrator. 'She's still on the ward.'

'We confirmed brain death forty minutes ago,' she told him. 'It's only the ventilator keeping her alive.'

'Do you need permission from next of kin to turn it off? Because I'm afraid —'

'No. We need the permission of her next of kin to harvest her organs.'

'I see.'

'She carried a donor card,' said the administrator. 'As did her husband, incidentally, but it was too late by the time he arrived. As you know, the law requires that we get confirmation from the next of kin before proceeding, even when the deceased person has made their wishes perfectly clear.'

'I think I see what you're getting at, but even if we do find Poppy Carlton, even if she's in a fit state to give permission, she's fifteen years old. She couldn't authorize you to turn the machines off and open her mother up.'

'You misunderstand,' said Wallace. 'I'm asking you to find Helen Carlton's new next of kin. Sibling, parent, cousin if necessary. If we can get their permission before the night's out, any number of lives could be saved.'

A wave of pure exhaustion washed over Ajax.

'There are currently seven thousand

people in the United Kingdom who are critically ill and whose lives could either be saved or improved immeasurably by a transplant,' said the surgeon.

'I'm aware of that.' Ajax felt his jaw tightening.

'I have a father of three young children on my list who is suffering from severe liver disease. Without a transplant, he has less than two years to live. I already know his HLA and blood group are a close match to Helen's. He lives less than an hour away. There is every chance he could be matched and in theatre before the night is out.'

Silence. There was a ticking clock somewhere in the room. The surgeon swayed and put a hand out to steady himself.

'I'll see what I can do,' said Ajax.

41

She drew closer to the tiny light, listening carefully. It would be a farm, and isolated farms had dogs. Usually chained, but not always. On the other hand, shelter of any sort would be better than spending the night in the open.

Closer up, the farmhouse looked large, with four windows facing the front on the upper storey and a double front door opening on to a small, railed garden. She could see lights in two of the upper windows.

A grass verge ran alongside the farm track. She kept to it, close to the hedge, knowing the chances of being seen, even by someone looking out of the window, were slim. There were no more lights that she could see and the wind was masking most of the sound she was making. When she reached the small semicircle of gravel in front of the house, she stopped. Two cars were parked outside.

There was no shelter from the wind here. It raced around the chimneys, sliding down the pitched roof, buffeting the trees that circled the farm. Against the dark night sky she could see them bending and swaying, almost as though reaching down towards her.

The farm buildings were all around the rear of the house and she had to tread on gravel to get there. Sudden movement in the field made her jump, but it was only a spooked horse, cantering away. An empty stable would be ideal. She could bury herself in straw.

Farm vehicles — a Land Rover, a tractor, a pull-along plough — were parked at the side of the house and beyond them she could see the enormous outline of a hay barn. It was open on four sides, only the roof offering protection from the elements. But the hay bales would screen her. She moved on, feeling specks of rain on her head again.

The hay inside the barn was piled high, a dozen bales or more in the highest point of the stack, but those lower down had formed a crude stairway, to allow the farmer to access the ones at the top. She went up, sensing instinctively that being off the ground would make her feel safer, until she reached a hollow in between two larger stacks. Surprised at how heavy hay bales were, she managed to move two more and jump into the hole they'd left behind. All around her now was thick-packed hay. Above, the roof of the barn kept the rain away. She wasn't going to die tonight; not of exposure anyway.

42

'Ajax, I'm in my dressing gown. You can't come now, people will talk.'

Ajax overtook a lorry and pulled into the inside lane. The road was busy, even at this hour, and this wasn't going to be an easy drive. He had to smile, though, at the picture of the elderly West Indian lady feigning modesty about her dressing gown. It was bright purple, quilted, with gold buttons. He'd seen her walk to the corner shop in it before now and God help anyone who dared stare or laugh.

'I'm sorry, Teresa. I should have called before,' he said. 'My nice quiet day didn't quite turn out as I'd planned.'

He heard the sound of a yawn being stifled, then, 'Have you been dealing with that balloon crash?' she asked. 'I was watching it on the news. Them poor folk, God bless their souls.'

'I'm going to try and make it tomorrow,

Teresa. But if I don't, it's not because I don't want to, it's because —'

'You work too hard. Where are you now? You're not at home, are you? I can hear traffic.'

He stepped on the brake to avoid a car approaching down the slip road. 'I've got something to do. Shouldn't take me long,' he lied.

'Come round anyway. Let those fools say what they like. I'll leave a key under the mat. You can sleep in Clark's old bed and I'll cook you a nice West Indian breakfast, how about that?'

He smiled at the thought of pork steaks with glazed pineapple, of spicy sweet-potato chips. 'My feet stick out six inches from the bottom of Clark's bed, and if you leave a key under your doormat in that part of town you'll be murdered in your sleep.'

'Hah! No one dare mess with me. What with you and Clark, I've got the best protection on the estate. I'm like the Godmother.'

Clark, Teresa's son and Ajax's best mate from school, had spent roughly half his adult life in prison. He had contacts Ajax didn't want to think about.

'Go to bed, lovely lady. I'll call you in the morning.'

206

He ended the call and pulled out into the fast lane.

43

She woke with a start. She'd been dreaming of eyes staring down at her, of hot breath on her face. The cloud cover must have passed, releasing the moon from its grip, because she could see the dark shadow of the barn roof, the crinkled texture of the hay, the dotted stars too far away to come to her aid. And the enormous German shepherd dog less than a foot from her face. She knew this dog. His dog had found her. He'd be seconds behind.

'Shinto!'

His voice. Deep and sore, his accent a peculiar mix of Scottish Borders and something foreign. He was in the barn, looking for the dog.

The dog dropped both front paws into the hollow that had been her nest. Distracted momentarily by a scent that wasn't hers, it dug its nose into a corner.

'Shinto! Get back here.' Footsteps and low

murmurs of conversation sounded from below. He wasn't alone.

The dog raised its head and she caught a glimpse of fang-like teeth in its open mouth. They wouldn't let a dog kill her, surely? The crash survivors had been killed quickly, with blows to the head, a sharp upward twist of the neck. They wouldn't be so cruel as to leave her to a vicious dog?

A dog couldn't be tried for murder.

Giving up on the rat, or whatever had saved her so far, the dog slunk back towards her, its brown eyes gleaming. She couldn't help the whimper slipping out as its head hung above her face and a droplet of saliva fell on to her cheek. She could hear a steady, thumping rhythm that could only be her own heartbeat.

'Shinto?' Another angry call from below.

The thumping grew faster but she could place it now. Not her heartbeat after all. The dog's tail was banging against the hay. Remembering that Shinto had allowed the toffee lady to pet him she reached out.

'Good dog.' The whisper melted into the hay as the dog pressed its head into her hand. She scratched behind one ear. Shinto pawed at her to carry on.

Then he stiffened. And sprang. His claws dug into her flesh before he leapt from the

209

hollow, just as she heard the frantic barking of another dog.

Shouting below. Several dogs barking. Running. Torch beams on the barn roof. Then a hideous din of snarling and growling. There was a dogfight taking place beneath her in the barn. She pressed tight into her hiding place as the voice she recognized yelled at his dog. Other men swore and shouted. A male voice, louder than the others, demanded to know what the hell was going on, did they have any idea of the bloody time and he'd have the law on them.

The noise of the fight subsided. She pictured the two animals, still snarling, being held by their collars as their claws scrambled on the barn floor.

'Get him away. Chain him up. And shut the others up.'

The barking faded.

'What do you want, Faa?'

The man hunting her spoke. 'Looking for someone. A kid. Had a row with her mam and dad. Ran off.'

'What makes you think she's here?'

'She was seen in Wooler, heading out along that pilgrims' trail. We're checking all the places just off it.'

'We've seen nothing.'

There was enmity between the two men. And fear also. The owner of the farm was afraid of the man looking for her. A man called Faa.

'Then you won't mind if we have a look around?'

'A kid wouldn't come here. A kid would head for the city. You're wasting your time.'

'Maybe, but it's my time to waste.'

She pictured them below. Faa with his hand on Shinto. The farmer squaring up to him, scared, but not wanting to lose face.

'Are the police looking for her?' the farmer said.

'We don't bother the police. We look after our own.' A different voice this time, similar to Faa's, same accent.

'Five minutes. Then I want you off my property.'

Silence for several long seconds. Then the sound of someone turning around and walking away, calling to someone.

'Pat, we're done,' said a voice below. 'There's no one here.'

'Yeah.' A third voice. 'It was a false alarm. They're both dead. We've looked everywhere they could have gone.'

'Give me a minute. I've just . . . I don't know, a feeling.' His voice again. His name was Pat. Patrick? Patrick Faa.

'Ma wants us home.'

'And you've got those phones to deal with just now.'

Three distinct voices. All with the same not-quite-Scottish accent. Similar in pitch and cadence. Three close relatives.

She could almost hear his sigh of frustration. 'OK, quick look round, then we're out of here. Off you go, buddy.'

She heard the scramble of paws as the dog was released again. They'd watch it this time, see it come bounding up the bales towards her.

She saw a beam dance around the barn roof. Felt the hay move as someone heavy began climbing the stack. A large, masculine hand appeared over the edge of the hollow. He was a split second from seeing her. The hand moved closer, until it was inches away. A left hand. She could see dark hairs, the edge of the jacket sleeve, and an odd bracelet, strands of plaited black hair held together by a carved silver clasp.

Then the stack shifted beneath her. She heard a muttered curse as the hand disappeared. He'd fallen. She heard the sound of someone heavy landing on the barn floor. Then footsteps.

She lay, not daring to move, listening to voices fading and then, finally, the sound of a vehicle starting.

It felt like a very long time before she was able to sleep again.

44

Six years earlier

The sisters sat in the chapel of Wynding Priory. It was empty, but for them, and cold, because the heating was only ever used during services. Isabel had found them cloaks, and they were both wrapped, head to foot, in black wool. It was dark, too, because Isabel hadn't thought, or wanted, to turn on the lights. From a distance, the two shrouded women might be indistinguishable, two nuns, talking in chapel about religious doctrine or the wonder of a life in Christ.

Jessica couldn't imagine anything more vile than what she'd just heard.

A short distance away across the tiled floor was the elaborately carved confessional, where the nuns knelt and confessed their sins before God and the visiting priest. How very appropriate.

'Why didn't you tell me before?' she said.

'Are you the better or happier for knowing?' asked Isabel.

'Of course not.'

'That's why I didn't tell you.'

'All the same, I had a right to know.'

Isabel sighed. 'You were too young when it happened. For a long time, you were too young. I couldn't burden you with it.'

'Auntie Brenda, Uncle Rob? They knew?'

Isabel inclined her head. 'Later on, when you probably were old enough, I asked myself what the point was. He's been out of our lives for so long now and you're a grown woman. He's no danger to you.'

Jessica reached out, fumbled beneath black wool and found her sister's hand. 'I don't get it,' she said. 'Why didn't Dad do something? Or was it after he —'

Isabel sighed. 'To be honest, Jess, I'm a bit confused about the timing of everything myself. There are big chunks of that time that I can't remember at all. But no, I think he'd already gone into the army when Dad . . . well, when he died.'

Jessica pulled away, sitting upright on the hard wooden seat. 'Dad knew,' she said. 'He sent him away to protect us. And then he couldn't live with himself, with losing Mum, with what Ned had done.'

'Jess, calm down.' Isabel reached out a

pale, cold hand. 'We can't know what was going on in Dad's head. We'll never know what drove him to do what he did.'

'I know,' Jessica said. 'I don't care what you say. I know.' She took a deep breath to steady her head and then took hold of her sister's hand again. 'And this is why you've been hiding away all these years.'

A moment's pause, then, 'That's an ungenerous interpretation of my calling, Jessica.'

'You were the strongest person I knew. There was nothing you couldn't do and now . . .' She stopped.

'And now?' prompted Isabel.

'Now you do nothing.'

'You were a child, Jess. Admit the possibility that your memory is flawed and that I never was the person you've created in your head. Besides, Mother Hildegard tells us regularly that we are the strongest women of all. When we're breaking the ice on water in order to wash our faces on winter mornings, or when we're carrying home firewood from the far corners of the grounds, I'm inclined to think she has a point.'

Jessica realized she was squeezing Isabel's hand. She had to stop. She would hurt her sister, who'd already dealt with so much. 'We should find him,' she said. 'He

216

shouldn't get away with it.'

'He'll answer to God, Jess,' Isabel said, her voice flat and hard. 'At least, that's what we tell ourselves every day, that sinners will answer to God.'

'Do you believe that?'

No answer.

'I still want to find him,' Jessica said. 'I want him to answer to me. And the law.'

Isabel got to her feet. 'There speaks the policewoman. The nun's duty is to forgive. I've spent years learning that lesson.' She walked forward towards the chancel rail. When she reached it, she sank to her knees and let her head drop into her hands.

Jessica stood too. Her high heels clicked on the tiles as she approached Isabel's kneeling figure.

'Maybe he's sorry,' she said to the back of her sister's veil. 'Maybe he wants to make it up to you.'

No reaction at all.

'Blood is thicker, Isabel.'

Her sister's face shot round. 'Don't you dare patronize me, Jess. It didn't happen to you, you don't get to tell me how to deal with it.'

Isabel got to her feet. 'You can track him down, if you want to,' she told a stunned Jessica. 'I can't and I won't stop you, but don't imagine for a moment that you can be some sort of peace envoy, brokering a reconciliation between the two of us. I will never see him, or speak to him, or hear of him again. And if you try to force him on me, I will never see you again.'

45

Thursday, 21 September
Patrick got back to Castle Faa at three in the morning. The fire directly outside his mother's caravan had been stoked until the flames were leaping four feet into the air. As he drew nearer, his lungs clenched in his chest, reacting to the smoke of the fire, the cigarettes, the joints.

The adult members of his family sat in a wide circle around the flames. Some of the seats were the cheap fold-up kind of hollow metal and plastic. Some were taken from car interiors. Some were car tyres balanced one on top of the other. There were no empty seats. No one offered to fetch him one.

'I dropped two between the pylons and the river,' he said. 'One in a bog near one of the bodies. The rest among the trees where it came down. They'll find them come daylight, kick themselves for missing them yesterday.'

Sneaking around the perimeter of the crash scene, placing all the mobile phones he'd stolen from the dead and dying passengers, had been his last chore of a very long day. When they were found, the police would assume they'd been in passengers' hands — natural enough — and dropped when the balloon came down.

'And Jimmy is sure they're clean?' Mary asked. She had the distrust of technology that comes of being older and a traveller to boot.

Fifteen-year-old Jimmy had a talent for technology. Since he'd arrived home from school he'd been using his own computer to hack into each of the passengers' phones, looking for evidence of text messages sent during the final few minutes, or photographs of Patrick. Two of the phones had grainy, indistinct pictures but they'd been wiped. The teenage boy had sent tweets and one text message, but hadn't specified how the accident had happened.

'As clean as they can be.' Jimmy's dad had his fag clutched between forefinger and thumb, the lit end tucked away in his palm to protect it from the wind. 'The traces are still there if anyone digs deep enough. We just have to hope they don't.'

'We've still only cleaned eight, though,' said Mary. 'The pilot's makes nine. Thirteen people in that balloon. There could be four more out there.'

'Not everyone has a phone, Ma,' said Charles.

'How'd you get on?' Patrick asked his brother. Charles and William had been tasked with getting rid of the pilot's body.

'Forty feet down in Hoselaw Loch,' said Charles. 'Spent two hours cleaning Mam's car.'

'So we're good?'

'No, we're not good,' snapped Mary. 'There's still two passengers not found.'

'They'll find them in the morning,' Patrick said. 'They had a helicopter over earlier tonight. Spotted two hot spots that they're pretty certain are bodies. They're going out first light to bring them in. They're dead, Ma; if they're not, we'd have found them by now. This time tomorrow, it'll all be over.'

'It'd better be.' His mother got up, dropped her cigarette and stamped it out. She turned without another word and walked to her caravan. Taking that as a signal that the day, finally, was over, the others got up too. Some said goodnight, some simply walked away, until Patrick was alone by the fire.

46

It wasn't far off dawn when Ajax got home. He went straight upstairs, took off his clothes on the landing and crept naked into bed. It was warm, sweet-scented, felt like bliss.

MoJo turned and wrapped her body around his with a soft, sleepy grunt. 'Any luck?' she mumbled into his left shoulder.

He lay staring at the ceiling, knowing he had to be up again in two hours.

'I found her parents in Yarm, drove them up to give them a chance to say goodbye and handed them over to a family liaison officer. Helen Carlton is being stripped of all spare parts as we speak.'

MoJo stretched up and kissed his ear. 'It was the right thing to do.'

'Will it count in my favour, do you think?'

'On Judgement Day? Oh, I should think so.'

'We had a helicopter with heat-seeking

equipment go over after dark. Boss's orders. They found a couple of sites of interest. We'll go straight to them in the morning. Touch wood we'll find Jessica Lane, Poppy Carlton and the pilot, and we can hand the whole scene over to the crash investigators.'

'You should sleep now,' she said.

'I never sleep, baby. You know that.'

She ran her hand across his chest. 'Then think about something nice.'

47

Six years earlier
The blues and twos were directly behind now and he could no longer pretend they were chasing someone else. Ajax pulled over, turned off the engine and got out. The traffic cop coming towards him was small and thin. Another, bigger bloke, the driver, remained in the police vehicle.

Then the copper heading his way stepped into the light of a streetlamp and he did a quick reappraisal. Tall for a woman, slim but strong. She looked like an athlete, a rower or a swimmer, broad in the shoulder, but with long slim legs. Her black trousers fitted perfectly. Regulation kit didn't often look like high fashion, but on this woman, oh yes.

'Step away from the car, please, sir.' She was several feet away, walking deliberately, not rushing. Her dark hair was fastened at the back of her neck in a bun. She could

have been a model, posing as a police officer in a glossy magazine.

'What's the problem, Officer?'

'Are you aware this is a thirty-mile-an-
hour zone, sir?'

Ajax made a point of looking round at the
wide road that would take three cars abreast
with ease, at the large houses set back
behind long front gardens. No one parked
on the street here, no one needed to. The
road was entirely clear. 'Can't see any signs,'
he said.

'I think you'll find there was one a quarter
of a mile back.' She pulled out a notebook
and looked at his registration number. 'And
the default speed limit on roads with lamp-
posts is thirty miles an hour. We clocked
you doing thirty-seven miles an hour along
a three-hundred-metre stretch. Keep your
hands where I can see them, sir.'

Ajax had been reaching for his inside
jacket pocket. Ignoring her, he pulled out
his warrant card but kept it tucked away in
his hand. She saw it, though, and her jaw
tightened as she stepped up to him. He
noticed her eyebrows, thick and black, and
her dark, almond-shaped eyes. Her lips were
wide and plump, her chin pointed and cleft.
In the lamplight, her skin looked as white as
paper.

'What's your name, love?' he asked.

She told him, making it sound like an insult, as she pulled out a warrant card. He bent closer to look at it.

'Do people call you MoJo?' he asked.

'Not if they're wise.'

'Mine's Detective Chief Inspector Ajax Maldonado.' He held out his own warrant card. The second officer, who'd heard the entire exchange through an open car window, dropped his eyes.

The PC looked at her feet. 'Sorry, sir, I didn't know.'

Ajax felt a stab of disappointment at her sudden capitulation. 'No problem, love. We all make mistakes.' He turned to get back into his car. 'You have a nice night.'

'Ajax?' She put out a hand to hold the car door in place. 'Like the cleaning fluid?'

He put his own hand on top of hers. He'd planned to lift hers away from the car, but kept both in place for a second. 'Like the legendary Greek hero.' He winked at her.

She gave him a speeding ticket. They were married six months later.

48

Thursday, 21 September

She woke before the sun appeared but even so, the farm beat her to it. She could hear the lowing of cows in the milking shed, the scrabble and bark of dogs, the steady grind of machinery. Her body had stiffened overnight. She rolled on to her back, pushing her legs out from the coffin-shaped nest. She raised her head and saw that the hay barn was empty but for her.

Painfully slowly she climbed down the bale mountain. The farmyard was still in darkness, with only slender beams of light stealing out from the house and the milking shed.

Her headache was better. Still there, but less intense, no longer pounding. She had a feeling she wouldn't be hearing the voices today and that felt right. For a time, yesterday, she'd walked with dead people, but had a sense of leaving them behind now.

She could smell the milk as she slipped from one shadow to the next. She'd eaten nothing yesterday except for the pack of Reese's Peanut Butter Cups and sweets the two lady pilgrims had offered her. There was a village, though, a short detour off the trail before it headed north towards Holy Island. There was money in her rucksack. She could eat. Today, she could face the living again.

Today she could be with people she loved, start to grieve properly.

Today would take her home.

49

Overnight, the autumn had turned cold. A chill wind was driving in from the west and the sky was the colour of wallpaper paste; the cloud formation, lumpy, heavy, looked to have something of its texture.

The absence of sunlight muted the colours of the National Park. Everywhere Ajax looked he saw dull browns, mud, the colours of a dying world. The damp seeped through his uniform, until he felt as though it was corroding his bones.

He was standing beneath a large beech tree, some thirty metres from the spot where the balloon had eventually come down. A police climber had minutes earlier disappeared into the leaves. Close to the trunk, another member of the line-access team — the specialist police unit brought in when climbing was called for — relayed rope up to his colleague. A few hundred metres away, another team with dry suits were searching a moorland bog.

'Every time someone jumped or fell out, the balloon would have shot up again,' said the line-access officer. 'That guy Richard was explaining to me yesterday. The ones left in must have been thinking it was never going to stop.'

It wasn't long after seven in the morning, but their attempts to get the grim job done without an audience had failed. Already a small crowd had gathered at the site's perimeter. Media people, mainly, but a few sightseers too, the sort of people who slowed down on motorways as they passed fatal traffic accidents.

Ajax knew some of the men and women in the crowd. A journalist from the local BBC news station, the lead reporter from the *Newcastle Times.* He spotted Richard Allan from the balloon company and several people in brightly coloured hiking clothes. Also, a dark-haired man in a trilby.

'I think I've got something.' The voice buzzed through the radio and Ajax stepped closer. He shared a look with the man on the ground.

'What is it, Paul?' said the line-access officer.

'Hold on.' The crackled reply told them nothing.

Ajax moved round the tree, trying to get a better angle. 'Is there someone up there?' His neck was beginning to ache. The climber's mate held up a finger to silence him.

The radio crackled again. 'I'm looking at the body of one juvenile female.'

'AJ,' said a soft voice behind him. Ajax rubbed his face. The adrenalin that had carried him through a sleepless night was running dangerously low.

'AJ,' repeated MoJo. 'The grandparents are here.'

Ajax looked back to the waiting crowd. He hadn't registered them properly the first time he'd looked. A quiet, unassuming couple in their seventies, who in the past twenty-four hours had lost almost everything and who had still allowed themselves to be dragged from their bed, without complaint, and driven forty miles north to give permission for their daughter's corpse to be cut apart. Now they were about to hear that 'almost everything' had been hopelessly optimistic. The last blow was about to fall.

Telling the line-access team to hold off for a few minutes, to get everything ready but delay bringing the body down, Ajax set off towards the waiting crowd. The grandparents were close to the man with dark hair and the trilby.

'Eileen, Tom, come with me.' Ajax beckoned them away from the others. 'We'll find somewhere for you to sit down.'

They came with him willingly enough. Eileen tottered over the grass in unsuitable shoes, but couldn't hold her nerve until they were out of earshot of the media. 'Is there any news? Have they found Poppy?' Her questions sparked an immediate flurry of activity.

'Are these the grandparents? Are you still hoping to find Poppy Carlton alive?'

'Ajax, is it true someone survived? That you've got people out looking for her?'

Keeping one arm around Eileen's shoulders, Ajax turned back. 'Press conference at ten, guys.'

'Is this it?' asked Tom, the grandfather. 'Is this where the balloon came down? I can't see anything.'

'It came to rest about thirty metres that way.' Ajax pointed. The balloon no longer draped the nearby trees like blown-away laundry. It had been retrieved late yesterday and taken away, along with the basket, for examination. 'We found Helen and Harry there. And Nathan.'

Stacey had seen Ajax beckoning and was hurrying over.

'I'm going to leave you with Constable McElvoy now,' he said. 'I have to get back to Newcastle for a press conference. Stacey will take you to a car where you can sit down.' He glanced over to where the team at the tree had ignored him. They were sending up more ropes. They had a stretcher. The sort that is attached to a body bag.

He put his body in between the grandparents and what was happening at the tree. 'Just until we have more news,' he said.

50

Patrick stayed until he knew for certain that the body lowered from the tree was the only one the police had found. He listened to the rumours, buzzing around the onlookers, that it had been the body of a child. He watched the body bag being loaded into a mortuary van and driven away. Then he watched the police team start to move out. There was nothing else here. The team in the nearby bog were continuing their search, but he knew there was no way she could have ended up in it. He'd seen the last few minutes of the balloon in the air. It hadn't gone anywhere near the bog.

Against all odds, one woman had walked away from the crash. Somewhere out there, she was still walking.

51

'Sir, I need a word.'

Steve Chapman had practically leapt into the corridor in front of Ajax, making him wonder, not for the first time, if glass-walled offices were entirely a good idea.

'I'm on my way to the boss,' Ajax told him. 'He wants a word too, and that usually means I'm in trouble. And the press conference starts in ten.'

Chapman wasn't taking no for an answer this morning. 'Thing is, sir, when I was in Newcastle General last night, I was asked to take a report of a fatal accident, and I think it needs looking into.'

The door at the end of the corridor opened and the chief appeared, looking pointedly at his watch.

'Got collared, sir,' Ajax said as they drew closer. 'Chappers here thinks we don't have enough work on at the moment.'

'Is it quick, Steve?' the chief asked. He

ushered them both into his office. The force's medical adviser, a reed-thin bloke called Standish, was sitting at the conference table, nervously fiddling with a pen.

'A young woman was brought into A & E midday yesterday.' Chapman leapt straight into it, as though afraid the chief might change his mind. 'In a bad way — morning, Dr Standish — name of Tahmina Farah. She'd been walking on the cliff path near Howick and fell on to rocks. Bad head injuries. Died shortly after arrival.'

He stopped for breath.

'We're listening,' Ajax encouraged, although the look on the chief's face suggested that might not be the case for long.

'She carried a donor card and the relatives gave permission, so she was taken into theatre. Newcastle have a very experienced organ surgeon. It was a bit of a lucky day for them, if you see what I mean.'

Standish's eyebrows rose.

'I was there,' Ajax said. 'I talked to him last night. Walker? Wallace? He was in the middle of a transplant procedure.'

'Wallace,' Chapman agreed. 'I haven't spoken to him, but a couple of the junior doctors, an anaesthetist and a registrar, weren't happy. When they heard I was in the building, they asked to see me.'

236

'In what way unhappy?' Ajax asked.

'It didn't feel right to them that she had such severe head injuries but no damage to the rest of her body apart from a few scratches and bruises. If she'd fallen any significant distance, they'd expect cracked ribs, broken limbs, fractured wrists, extensive lacerations. None of that. They wanted to convey their concerns to the coroner, but Wallace was the doctor in charge and he disagreed.'

'Anything to add, Paul?' the chief asked the medical adviser.

'These things are always open to interpretation,' Standish said. 'Presumably there'll be a post-mortem. If there's anything dodgy going on —'

'Yeah, but the really worrying thing is her two relatives, a couple of blokes, can't be contacted,' Chapman said. 'The numbers they gave aren't responding.'

A moment's silence, while the chief and Standish frowned at each other.

'Open up a file,' said Ajax, 'although you've probably done that already. And get someone down to the hospital to take statements. Check CCTV, make sure the post-mortem is marked urgent. You may need to find someone else to take it forward, though, Chappers. I need you on the balloon inquiry for now.'

Nodding his thanks, the constable left the room.

'We probably should go downstairs,' Ajax said. 'Morning, Paul, how you doing?'

'They'll wait five minutes,' the chief said. 'I've been hearing about your midnight race to Yarm and back.'

Ajax said nothing.

'Well?'

'With respect, sir, that wasn't a question.'

The boss gave an exaggerated sigh. 'We have a very busy week. We would have had a busy week even without this balloon business. You, in particular, will be very thinly stretched and yet you choose to sacrifice a night's sleep at the random request of a member of the medical profession whom you don't even know. Have I got anything wrong so far?'

'No, you're pretty much bang on.'

Paul Standish stood up. 'Do you want me to wait outside?'

'Perhaps that would be —' the chief began.

'No,' Ajax interrupted.

'You're bloody lucky Helen Carlton's parents didn't put in a complaint about insensitive behaviour,' the chief said. 'As if they haven't been through enough.'

'Ralph Wallace called me first thing this

morning,' Ajax said. 'He thinks seven lives will have been saved, or immeasurably improved, as a result of Eileen and Tom agreeing to release their daughter's body.'

'I don't doubt it.' The boss moved to the corner of the room and pulled his jacket from a hanger. 'Look, Ajax, I know this sort of thing is always going to be an issue for you, but personal crusades have no place in the police service.'

'I was only trying to help. And, again with respect, we have three minutes.'

'Yeah, that's why Paul's here. Sit down a minute.'

Ajax sat.

'I'm not sure about this press conference, Ajax,' the chief said. 'I've been talking to Paul about the likelihood of Jessica Lane and Sean Allan surviving the crash and what sort of state they might be in. Tell him what you just told me, Paul.'

'A pretty bad state, frankly, given the severity of the injuries the other passengers suffered,' Standish said. 'No one leaps out of a hot-air balloon unscathed. The chances are they're still in the National Park, dead or very badly injured.'

'I don't disagree, but that's no reason to postpone the press conference,' said Ajax. 'We've already put it off twenty-four hours.

We're going to take some serious flak if we cancel now.'

'And when they want to know what a serving police officer was doing on the flight and why she was in Northumberland?' the chief said. 'For God's sake, stop looking at the clock. I can tell the bloody time.'

Ajax sighed. 'We haven't released details of Jessica Lane's profession, so I doubt it will come up, but as far as we're aware she was here visiting her sister and the balloon trip was a birthday surprise. I don't see the problem, sir.'

'If Jessica Lane survived that crash, why hasn't she been in touch? Any police officer with anything about them would have stayed at the scene, tried to administer first aid, got in touch with the emergency services. Why didn't she do any of that?'

'All good questions, sir, which suggests to me she didn't survive.'

'Or there's more going on than we know about.'

Once again, Ajax thought of the spatters of brain tissue on the basket. No, he was not letting that cat out of the bag. Not until he knew something for certain.

'Thanks for your time, Paul, I'll be in touch.' The boss fastened his jacket and found his hat from the cupboard. He could make a simple action like putting on a hat convey disapproval.

Ajax followed him along the corridor. He was taller than his boss, by a couple of inches, and heavier. His colouring, he knew, made him stand out, especially in the north-east of England. And yet the acting chief constable had a presence Ajax knew he'd never have. Even the way he walked into the press conference room, looking round before carefully removing his hat, would convey precisely the right blend of authority and courtesy. A short distance from the door, he slowed, letting Ajax catch up.

'Ajax, I've been meaning to talk to you about tonight,' he said, in a low voice, because on this floor anyone could be listening. 'We've had another tip-off from the lads on the coast about a possible boat of migrants coming in.'

'Coming in tonight?'

'Apparently so. Guy on the dock has been told to clock off early and go home. His pay won't be docked. Says his boss is a tight-arsed bastard who wouldn't pay him for nothing unless there was something going down.'

'And you want me to release officers from St James's Park?'

'I'm asking if we can do it with no risk.'

241

'We can do it, and we'll almost certainly get away with it. No one really believes that warning was serious. But . . .'

He left the 'but' hanging.

The boss glanced towards the press room, where the Head of Communications, a stern-faced young woman in a grey suit, was waiting to usher them inside. 'If anything does happen, and it gets out we directed officers away from the stadium to chase asylum seekers — and they'll be asylum seekers in the world's press that morning, not illegal immigrants — we're up shit creek?'

'Beautifully put, sir.'

The Head of Communications pushed open the door and led the way inside. The boss paused in the doorway, looked around the room and took off his hat.

'Good morning, ladies and gentlemen,' he said. 'Thank you for coming.'

The room seemed to settle, to give a collective sigh of satisfaction and anticipation. The boss had that effect.

52

She used a corner of toast to wipe grease from her plate and swallowed the last mouthful of tea. She was still hungry, but having polished off the full English breakfast with all the trimmings and extra toast, she knew that to order more food now would be to draw attention to herself.

There was a phone behind the counter. Maybe the café owner would let her use it, if she offered to pay.

The café owner had already asked an uncomfortable number of questions about where she'd come from, was it the first time she'd walked St Cuthbert's Way, and was she hoping to get to Lindisfarne by the end of the day, because it was going to be another wet one. Oh, and was she sure she was OK travelling alone, because pilgrims were all very well but they saw some dodgy types coming through the village and she wouldn't want any daughter of hers walking those lonely footpaths by herself.

Three mothers with toddlers had listened to every word.

Maybe she'd find a public phone.

Others had come into the café. A foreign-looking truck driver, an elderly man who rarely looked up from his newspaper. The owner's attention had been forced away and she'd taken her food to the furthest table from the counter.

'Turn it up, Madge.'

High on the wall in the corner of the room a television set had been playing quietly, tuned to the BBC news channel. A woman in a blue coat, with a flawless face and perfect hair, was standing in front of a copse of beech trees, talking about how the trip of a lifetime had turned into a journey from hell for thirteen very unlucky people.

'At least ten people died when the balloon came down and the death toll may rise higher yet.' The reporter's hair was being blown around her face and every few seconds she had to brush it out of her eyes or mouth. 'Police have so far not confirmed that an eleventh body has been found this morning, but the signs are increasing that no one came out of this tragic accident alive. The pilot, forty-year-old Sean Allan, is one of the missing.'

A photograph of the pilot in company livery appeared on the TV screen.

'We may never know what happened on this pleasure trip, or how a routine flight could have gone so terribly wrong.'

The picture changed to a large, modern room. People were sitting, theatre style, facing a long table. A voiceover announced that they were going live now to a press conference at Northumbria Police headquarters in Newcastle.

A young woman entered the room, followed by two tall men. The one at the back was massive, six foot three or four at least, and wide at the shoulders. His skin was very dark, his hair black and curly. He looked Mediterranean, possibly North African. He sat down behind a sign that read Superintendent Ajax Maldonado. The man in front, the acting chief constable, wore a uniform that gleamed with polished metal and insignia. His hair was short and not quite completely grey. His face was finely cut, handsome, his eyes dark brown. He sat, thanked everyone for coming and glanced down at some notes.

The sound of her mug landing heavily on the tabletop momentarily caught the café's attention.

'I regret to inform you that at first light

this morning, my team recovered the body of fifteen-year-old Poppy Carlton from the crash site,' the acting chief constable began, as people around her turned back to the TV screen. 'An initial examination suggests that she died instantly. That brings to eleven the total number of fatalities arising from yesterday's tragic crash. Our thoughts are with the families of the victims, all of whom have been informed.'

'Are you still hopeful of finding survivors?'

'Of course we're hoping for survivors. But the severity of the crash, and the injuries sustained by the eleven people who lost their lives, means that we have to be cautious and realistic.'

'Are you widening the search area?'

This time the senior officer indicated that his superintendent should speak.

'We're tracking the likely course of the balloon from its take-off site near St Boswells to where it eventually came down,' Maldonado said. 'The company are helping us do this. It's an imprecise science, though, because the exact movement of the wind is difficult to predict and to reconstruct.'

A man in a grey suit at the back of the room bobbed to his feet. 'Is it true that someone else was strapped into the pilot's seat when the balloon came down, suggesting that the pilot was no longer on board?'

'There is no pilot's seat, as such,' Maldonado told him, 'but we are considering the possibility that the pilot left the balloon some time before it crashed and that lack of an experienced pilot was a primary factor in the disaster.'

A woman at the front raised her hand. 'Can you suggest why the pilot would leap out of a hot-air balloon?'

Maldonado stared directly back at her. 'No, I can't.'

'So you've no clue as to why this happened?'

Maldonado frowned. 'It's too early to say and I'm not about to speculate.'

A man in the second row raised a microphone. 'What about the other missing passenger?'

Maldonado glanced at the acting chief constable and paused a beat before taking the question himself. 'The other missing passenger is thirty-six-year-old Jessica Lane, of York. She was on board the balloon with her sister.'

In the café, she slid lower in the seat.

The man at the back was up on his feet again. 'If these two — Jessica Lane and Sean Allan — survived the flight, why haven't they contacted the authorities? Why haven't you found them?'

Maldonado sat back, visibly relaxing into the task. 'Two very good questions, both of which stop us from being too optimistic. It is possible, though, that either or both of these individuals were concussed. Able to walk away from the site, but confused and weak. Head injuries can have all sorts of unpredictable effects. They may have walked only a short distance before having to stop, but far enough to have taken themselves out of our search area. It started to rain very heavily yesterday, shortly after the balloon came down. They may have headed for shelter but been too weak to go on.'

'I think we have to remember,' the acting chief interrupted, 'that the Northumberland National Park covers an area of nearly four hundred square miles. And that it's surrounded by a much larger area of open countryside. There are no towns, very few roads and villages. We're talking about a big and challenging area to search, even with the very sophisticated equipment that we have at our disposal.'

The large flat screen on the wall behind the two men came to life, showing two portrait photographs. The one on the right was that already shown of the pilot in his company uniform. The second was of a woman with curly dark hair, held back from her face with glittering pins, who looked younger than thirty-six. In the photograph, Jessica Lane was smiling confidently. She was wearing make-up, earrings and an emerald green jacket.

She could not have looked more different to the cold, wet, pitiful creature trying to sink further down beneath the café table. Except for the bright green jacket.

'We're asking anyone out and about in the National Park today to keep their eyes peeled and their ears open,' Maldonado went on. 'Similarly, if anyone noticed any-thing unusual yesterday afternoon, then please get in touch with us. We urgently need to speak to the pilot, and both these people may need medical attention.'

She had to get out. She grabbed the bor-rowed (stolen) blue coat from the back of her chair and pulled it on over the green jacket. Tugging the hood up around her face, she slipped out of the café. As the door slammed shut, she looked back through the glass.

All six occupants of the café were staring at her.

53

'They're bound to run with the pilot-leaping-out angle,' said the Head of Communications as she, Ajax and the acting chief huddled in the corridor for the usual press conference debrief. 'After the Germanwings incident, and the mystery of what happened to the Malaysian plane, suicide by pilot is becoming a big story.'

'Upsetting for his parents, but I can't see how that could rebound on us,' said the boss.

'Neither can I, at the moment,' she replied. 'Mind you, it's only a matter of time before we have to come clean and admit that Jessica Lane was a police officer. If we don't even know what force she was attached to by that time, we're going to look pretty daft. And then there's the mystery of the missing mobile phones.'

'Ah, sorry,' Ajax said. 'Meant to tell you. I had a call from the site before we went into the conference room. Six phones found this morning, scattered around the site like I said they'd be. Several failed calls to the emergency services on each. Nothing else obvious so far. Look, you're both going to have to excuse me. I'm due to take Mother Hildegard to the mortuary and I'm already running late.'

'Does that need to be you?'

Ajax ran a hand through his hair. 'I said I'd pick her up. I'll be on the other end of a phone if anyone needs me.'

'Superintendent!'

Ajax turned to see Stacey's head poking out of the main office.

'Café owner on the phone from a place called Belford,' she called. 'Tiny town a few miles from the coast.'

He nodded. 'I know it.'

'She says Jessica Lane was in her café eating breakfast. Saw herself on the news and rushed out.'

'How long ago?'

'Less than five minutes.'

Ajax set off for the main office, the others close behind.

54

The kids were playing with one of the old wooden wheels. It lay on the cinders, its once garish paintwork now faded and peeling. They were chasing each other, jumping between spokes. Patrick had to step around them to get to his van. He'd been hoping to avoid seeing his mother, but she came into view as he approached the driver's door. She and a couple of other women were braiding the hair of one of his younger cousins.

'Where you off to?' She didn't look up. A trail of red ribbon drooped from her teeth.

'She's been spotted. The woman who walked. I've got to go.'

'Spotted where?' She pulled the ribbon from her mouth and started weaving it in and out of the long black hair of the girl sitting on the upturned barrel. He looked away. He could never watch this hair-braiding ritual.

'Belford,' he said.

'That's miles away. The police will get there first.'

'No, they won't. There's no patrol cars anywhere near.'

'Do you even know who you're looking for?' Mary asked. 'Have you got a picture?'

'Jimmy's going to find one and send it through to me.'

She let the braid fall and took a step towards him. In the presence of the youngsters, she lowered her voice. 'Pat, you're taking too big a risk. Even if she saw you, she can't identify you. She doesn't know who you are. It's better to stay away from her now. Too many people looking. And it's broad daylight. What can you do in broad daylight?'

'I'll see you later, Ma.' He climbed into his van and started the engine.

'And this is the fucking problem.' His mother strode up to the driver's door. She tried to pull the handle but he'd locked it.

'You're not after her because you need to be,' she called after him as he pulled away. 'You're doing it because you enjoy it.'

She didn't intend him to hear what she said next. At least, he didn't think she meant for him to hear it. She'd lowered her voice, and half turned away. He did hear it though, he had ears like a fucking bat and he didn't miss a thing.

'The boy's not right,' she said to one of the other women. 'Never has been. Never will be.'

55

She could not run. She could not run. They would chase her for sure if she ran. She could feel the food she'd eaten churning in her stomach. She had to get out of sight, give herself a moment to think. She turned down the first street she came to, walking as quickly as she dared. It was raining again, which would help. People would be keeping their heads down.

Jessica Lane of York. The only survivor of the balloon crash. Everyone in the country was looking for her. He was looking for her.

He would find her.

The road she'd turned into was a dead end. Why hadn't she seen that? At the end of the road was the church.

'Confused and weak', Maldonado had said. She was weak, certainly, but was she confused? She remembered the dead voices she'd heard the day before, the shadowy hallucinations, her inability to think clearly, to properly remember what had happened. She'd been concussed, it was obvious now.

She passed through the church porch and along the path, knowing she was about to heave. The breakfast she'd eaten was going to pour out of her. She stopped, leaning on a headstone for support.

'Can I help you in some way?'

The man standing in the church doorway was the priest. He wore black trousers and a padded black coat, but his clerical collar was visible beneath. His hair was short, sandy, looked as though it might curl if grown a little longer. 'Are you ill?' he said. 'Can I get you a glass of water?'

He was a young man, not much more than thirty-five, and he had one hand on the church door. 'Would you like to come inside for a few minutes? It's doing the proverbial cats and dogs out here.'

There was something about his simple, friendly smile that drew her to him. She stepped forward. 'I'm Catholic.'

His smiled widened. 'I'm not proud. Course, a lot of people, most of your lot, in fact, would say that's exactly our problem, but it's too late for me to change now. So, come inside, pet, put your feet up.'

She glanced around — saw no one in sight — and followed him into the church.

'It's brass monkeys in here. Come on through to the vestry.' He led the way up the side aisle.

Halfway up she stopped walking. 'You don't have time for this,' she said. 'I'm fine, really.'

He glanced at his watch. 'I have a meeting with the churchwardens in thirty minutes. Until then, I'm twiddling my thumbs. You're doing me a favour.'

The vestry was already warm but the priest switched on an electric fan heater before disappearing through another door. 'Kettle's just boiled,' he called back. 'Coffee all right for you?'

The room was small. A large wooden wardrobe stood against one wall, a mirror on the wall opposite. A window looked out over the churchyard and the fields beyond. She should be crossing them, making her way back towards St Cuthbert's Way.

There were photographs on the desk. One, a large silver-framed portrait of a young woman with dark hair and a pale, heart-shaped face. Another showed a baby boy, just old enough to sit upright, with bright ginger hair, grinning at the camera. She caught a sour smell a second before she spotted a pair of muddy trainers in the corner. And an open gym bag.

The priest came back, carrying two mugs, a plate of biscuits balanced on one of them.

'Sit down, loosen your coat, sip hot liquid. You'll be right as rain in a few minutes.' Putting the tray down on the desk, he unfastened his own coat and pulled it off. He wore a waxed wool sweater beneath. 'Tell me if it gets too hot in here. Ginger nut?'

She stared back at him. He put the biscuits down and handed over a box of tissues.

She cried silently for a while, pressing tissues to her face to stifle any sob that threatened to slip through. When she was calmer, he swapped the tissue box for the coffee mug and watched her drink.

'Better?' he asked.

She shook her head. 'My sister died yesterday.'

It was real then. Finally, she'd said it, and made it real.

He was silent for a second, then said, 'I'm sorry to hear that.'

'I don't think I can go on without her in my life.' She started sobbing again, and made no effort to keep silent.

He let her cry for a while longer. She stopped when, above the noise she was making, she thought she heard something in the church. She blew her nose and took several deep breaths. She glanced round at the door.

'Would you say you're a woman of faith?' the priest asked.

She sniffed. 'I told you, I'm Catholic.'

Creases appeared at the corner of his mouth. 'Lots of people would describe themselves as such. It doesn't mean they believe in God.'

'My sister did. And she was the smartest, most sensible person I've ever known.'

He had to realize she hadn't answered, but he didn't push it. 'What can I do to help?' he asked.

She shook her head. 'I don't know. Nothing. I shouldn't even be here. I should go.'

'Can I call a relative for you? Parent? Another sibling? When families are grieving, they should be together.'

She couldn't suppress the shudder, had to wait for it to pass. 'There's no one,' she said. 'My parents died years ago. I have no other family.'

He looked towards the door. 'Are you in danger?'

'What makes you say that?'

'You're sitting bolt upright. You can't keep still. You keep glancing over your shoulder at the door or over mine out of the window. I've seen grief many times, and I've seen fear too. You're showing classic signs of both.'

She took a deep breath. 'I saw a terrible crime committed yesterday. I'm the only person left who knows what really happened.'

'Then we should call the police?' He glanced round, to where a phone sat on the desk behind him. When he looked back, he held a hand up, his voice raised in alarm. 'No, don't panic. I won't, I promise. Sit down, take it easy.'

She stopped at the door.

'You don't want to call the police?' he asked.

She shook her head so sharply it started hurting again. 'It would be the very worst thing I could do,' she told him.

PART TWO

56

Two years, eight months earlier

Close to the water's edge at Tilbury docks, Jessica drove across the wide expanse of tarmac and pulled up just short of the police van. A yawn slipped out as she opened the car door but the dark chill of the January night shook her awake. Even at this hour, the docks were busy with people and vehicles, milling around in never-ending lines and circles. Massive ships seemed unnaturally close, the water shone oily-black in the darkness and cranes soared to the sky like predatory animals.

The back doors of the police van were open and a soft pool of light was spilling out. Several uniformed and plain-clothed officers stood around. From a surrounding scatter of cars came the illuminating flicker of blue lights. Jessica held up her warrant card for the sergeant in charge.

Fourteen people were in the van, some

staring at her, others keeping their eyes down. Their origins were unknown. None of them, so far, was showing any signs of understanding the English language. They'd been found an hour ago in the hold of a cargo ship. The master of the vessel was currently claiming to have no knowledge of them being on board.

'*Braucht jemand ärztliche Hilfe?* Does anyone need medical attention?' She looked from one pair of black eyes to the next. The people were filthy, looked half-starved. No young children, thank God.

'*Es besteht keine Notwendigkeit, Angst zu haben. Wir können helfen.* There is no need to be afraid. We can help.'

Again, no response.

She switched languages. '*Skond wy pochodzicie? Czy ktos potrzebuje lekarza?*'

Nothing.

'Well, that's me done,' she muttered, and got ready to climb down. 'I tried German and Polish,' she told the sergeant. 'I asked where they'd come from, whether they needed a doctor. I told them not to be afraid.'

As he put up a hand to help her, she heard a low moan from behind. She turned, and caught the eye of one of the youngest. A boy. Not a child exactly, but not adult

264

either. Fifteen, maybe? He was paler than the others, a thin sheen of sweat covering his face.

Jessica stepped back into the van and approached the boy. She raised a hand and, when he didn't flinch, put the back of it on his forehead.

'Sergeant, this one looks very sick.' She turned back to the watching officer. 'He's running a hell of a temperature.' She put out a hand, beckoning the boy forward. He didn't move so much as fall towards her. Immediately the woman on his right pulled him back.

'Are you his mother?' Jessica asked. '*Sind Sie die Mutter?* You can come with him, if you're his mother, but we need to get him to hospital.'

'*Ja,*' said the woman. '*Ich bin seine Mutter.*'

Jessica and the boy's mother sat side by side in the reception area of Basildon Hospital's Accident and Emergency Department. In the forty minutes since the ambulance had pulled up and the sick boy had been rushed inside, she'd managed to glean a few facts about the immigrant group.

She'd started by asking the boy's name and been told it, because mothers are programmed to tell the names of their

265

children. The name, Muhamed, told her something else. The immigrants were Muslims.

The people she remembered from the van had had a Middle Eastern look about them — dark hair, skin, eyes — but few people in the Middle Eastern or Arab world speak German, so she'd guessed Bosnia and been rewarded with a startled look and then a single confirmatory nod.

'How long has Muhamed been sick?' she'd asked.

His mother held up ten fingers. 'Ten days.'

Footsteps came towards them. Jessica looked up to see a man in green scrubs approaching.

'Detective Constable Lane?'

'That's me.' Jessica stood up. 'This is Dula, Muhamed's mother.'

'Come this way, please.'

They followed him along the corridor and into a small treatment room. Muhamed lay on his side on the narrow metal bed, his eyes closed.

'Can you tell her that her son is comfortable and that we're waiting for a bed to become free. She can stay with him tonight if she wishes.'

Jessica translated the first part. She was far from sure Dula would be allowed to stay in the hospital. The other immigrants had been taken to Basildon police station, and from there would probably be transferred to a detention centre in Middlesex.

'What's the matter with him?' Jessica asked the doctor. 'He seemed to be running a temperature.'

'Serious infection.' The doctor's face was grave. 'We've given him antibiotics — hopefully we'll have caught it in time. He's also on a lot of painkillers so he's going to be very groggy for the next few hours. We can get him cleaned up when we get him up to the ward.'

'But he's going to be OK?' Jessica caught Dula staring at her.

In response, the doctor stepped towards the bed and gently raised the cover from Muhamed. In the small of the boy's back, to the right of his spine, was a large, fresh surgical dressing. The skin around it was red and inflamed.

'What happened to him?' Jessica asked.

'We haven't had a chance to X-ray and scan him yet but I'd put money on him having recently had a kidney removed.'

Dula was holding her son's hands tight. Her head had fallen forward.

'Dula?' said Jessica.

In response, Muhamed's mother stood up.

She shrugged off her jacket and then the large sweater she was wearing under it. She raised her shirt to let them see the dirty surgical dressing on her own back.

'These people have been selling their kidneys,' said the doctor. 'You'll probably find similar scars on the whole lot.'

Late in the winter afternoon, the laurels were gleaming with a silver frosting and un-swept leaves carpeted the path. The sunlight had become a dull, yellow pool in the sky. The trees that grew around the perimeter wall of Wynding Priory stood in stark outline against the grey sky, and were skeletal black where the late sunlight couldn't reach them. The two sisters passed through the creaking, paint-peeling, iron gate and left the convent grounds.

'They sold their kidneys to fund their trip to the UK?' Isabel's usually pale face was white with shock.

'It really doesn't bear thinking about,' Jessica agreed. 'That boy was only fourteen.'

The wind around them was rough and noisy, even for early February, tossing gulls high into the sky and hurling sand into their faces. As the sisters moved out of the shelter of the wall, Isabel's robes began to flap around her body. She caught hold of the edges of her black, serge cloak and pulled them close.

They reached the dunes and began to climb, sinking deeper into the sand with every step. Great strides made little progress and both women were breathing faster by the time they reached the top. The wind hit them with renewed strength.

'Is he OK?' Isabel asked.

'He's fine. His parents and his two older brothers are all OK too. Despite having only one kidney each. And the good news is they'll probably be given permission to stay here.'

'They paid a very high price for the privilege.'

Before them, the cloud was low and threatening, the sea turbulent, a mass of churning grey and white. It was hard to pinpoint, exactly, where one ended and the other began. Even Holy Island, out across the water, and its hilltop castle were blurred, sometimes visible, sometimes not. Often, when the sisters walked along the beach, they could see sailing yachts, fishing boats, passenger ferries. Today, a single grey container ship moved across the water.

Isabel began to step down, finding clumps of tussock grass to steady her feet. She had to shout, to keep turning her head back, so that Jessica could hear her. 'So what can you do?'

'Very little,' Jessica yelled back. 'We can patrol the docks, but when your country is an island there are a lot of small harbours to keep an eye on. We can try to find out who these gangs are, who their contacts are in this country, but the people we rescue, the smugglers we catch, often know very little about the chain of command. Take this one group, for example. The people moving them changed several times on the journey. Bosnians drove them up through Croatia, but then the gang who took them across Italy spoke French with North African accents. Then others got involved in Spain and a Spanish crew brought them to Tilbury.'

Isabel stopped halfway down to shake something from her boot. 'It sounds like a long and very ugly chain.'

'Tell me about it. We have the crew of the ship detained, and we'll be sharing what they tell us with Interpol, but it's a big problem. So many desperate people in the world, wanting to come to the rich countries, prepared to do anything they can to get here. And lots of unscrupulous types willing to take whatever they can get their hands on.'

Once on the beach, the two women

crossed from soft, springy sand to a swathe that was firm-packed and damp. As they turned to walk along the waves' edge, Isabel had to hold her veil back from her face.

'And people can survive with only one kidney?' she asked.

'Yes. Donation within families isn't uncommon, even here. If you were ill, I'd probably find one I could spare.'

Isabel's face tightened. 'That's good of you, but I can't help thinking organs are a little wasted on me.'

Jessica stopped walking. 'What's that supposed to mean?'

'Nothing,' said Isabel. 'I spoke without thinking. Come on, keep up.'

They walked for a minute in silence.

'I don't know how you resist swimming here,' Jessica said. 'In the summer, I mean. Not now.'

'There are few temptations at Wynding Priory,' replied Isabel. 'I rarely bother resisting those that present themselves.'

Jessica looked at her sister, at her beautiful, impassive face surrounded by the white veil, and then back at the churning, frothing sea. 'Really?' she said.

'The water can look very inviting on moonlit nights,' Isabel said. 'And we're still only allowed one bath a week. Whoa!'

A sudden gust had hit the two women hard, ripping Isabel's veil from her head, taking the cap she wore beneath with it. It had been years since Jessica had seen her sister's hair. There were strands of grey in it, but it wasn't as short as she remembered. The tight curls were still the same. In the wind they danced around her head, getting into her eyes.

Jessica set off after the veil but Isabel was faster. She overtook her sister and, in spite of the constricting gown and cloak, she soon pulled ahead. The veil landed on a patch of damp sand, close to the surf. Isabel grabbed it and then came jogging back up the beach.

'Does the Vatican enter an Olympic team?' Jessica said.

Isabel was barely breathing heavily. She tucked the veil into her sleeve. 'I could always whip your arse in a sprint,' she said.

'So it's out of your hands? You can go back to tracing stolen cars?'

'Yep. They've found another, better interpreter. They don't need me any more. One thing did puzzle me, though. Something Dula said when I went back to see them a week later in the detention centre.'

'What's that?'

'She said no one wants to go to the northern ports.'

'Nobody wants to go to the northern ports?' Isabel's face had screwed up, partly because of the wind, partly as a result of what she'd just heard.

'There was a place in northern Spain where they were held for several days,' said Jessica. 'There were a lot of people waiting there, apparently, lots of different routes into the UK. It was a sort of . . . Do you know what I mean by "hub"?'

'I'm a nun, not an idiot.'

'Sorry, well, while they were waiting for transport to become available, they got talking to others. One of the young women Muhamed got to know was very pretty. I dread to think what she had to offer these people to get passage, but anyway, one of the smugglers had told her that, whatever happened, she had to avoid going to the northern ports. London, Kent, Essex, even East Anglia, but not the north. The north is a bad place.'

'What does that mean?' Isabel asked.

'We don't know. They didn't know. Just that nobody wants to end up in the north of England.'

'We should get back,' Isabel said. 'Mother Hildegard will have little patience, even with you, if you keep the others waiting for their tea.'

The women began to walk back along the beach.

'I was going to join you for compline,' Jessica said. 'Will that be all right?'

'Of course, but I won't be able to say goodbye to you afterwards.'

'I know.'

After the last service of the day, the nuns would retire for the night, flowing back to their private rooms, surrounded by silence until the next hour of recreation.

At the bottom of the dunes was a short sandy track that took them back to the convent gate.

'Hang on a minute.' Jessica's hand froze on the heavy iron frame. 'This gate is padlocked at dusk. How do you get out for your moonlight skinny-dipping?'

Isabel passed inside and closed the gate carefully. 'I said nothing about skinny-dipping, or dipping in any sort of apparel. You're letting your imagination run away with you again.' She stopped, facing the wall. 'But if, for the sake of argument, someone needed to get out of the convent grounds at night, the mortar in the wall here is quite worn. And there are several places, see there, and there, where a foot can get a hold.'

Jessica looked at the wall. It was probably

as old as the convent itself, built of great stone pieces. There wasn't the money any more to keep it in perfect repair. She had a sudden flashback to the two of them as children, scaling a wall to get into a neighbour's garden, Isabel going first as always, moving with a strength and speed that the younger Jessica never dreamed she'd have. And always, once she'd made it to the top, seeing her big sister on the ground at the other side, arms held wide, ready to catch her.

'And how do you get out of the house? I can't believe the doors aren't locked.'

Isabel's feet began to crunch along the path towards the convent building. 'Look directly ahead. See the flat roof at the back of the kitchen? The place we call the lower outer.'

Jessica followed her. 'Hmmn.'

'Now see the narrow ledge running around the building at first-floor level? Well, it's not as narrow as it looks from here. And it's quite solid. It leads round to a bathroom window with a very dodgy lock. I'm still speaking hypothetically, you understand.'

Jessica stepped ahead and turned, blocking the path. 'Bella, why do you not just leave? This place served its purpose years ago. Come with me now.'

Bella's brown eyes stared back at her, as though she didn't quite understand what her sister was saying.

'You can live with me. I can help you get settled. It's not too late. It can't be.'

Isabel's eyes dropped and when she spoke, her voice was as hard as ice. 'Don't be silly. I'm very happy here.'

'Your life has no purpose.'

Isabel looked up, condemnation in her eyes. 'That you, of all people, should say that. You have always had faith.'

Jessica knew she wasn't going to win this. Not now.

Maybe not ever.

She stepped out of her sister's way and the two women set off towards the shadow of the convent. As they walked, Jessica had a sense of the silence creeping over her sister once again. She always fought it, if she could. 'Anything you want me to bring you when I come next?'

Isabel gave a grateful smile. 'My trainers are getting a bit worse for wear, but save it for my birthday.'

'That's six months away.'

'Mother Hildegard doesn't approve of gifts. One a year you might get away with.'

They walked on towards the rear door of the priory.

'What are you going to do?'

Isabel wasn't talking about birthday gifts. 'Nothing,' Jessica said. 'I'm based in London. When we come across more illegal immigrants we can ask them about this business of the north being a bad place. I've already sent a bulletin to northern constabularies. But you know, "north" could be anywhere from Whitby to Aberdeen, so unless something else comes up, there really is nothing to be done.'

The chapel bell began ringing. Recreation time was over. Isabel replaced her veil, tucking her dark curls out of sight. As they drew closer to the building, her head drooped, her hands slipped behind her large sleeves. Out of reach of the wind, her robes settled themselves around her. Her footsteps slowed and Jessica felt the familiar sense of loss. Her sister was turning back into a nun.

57

It was two months before 'something else' came up.

The Diana Memorial Playground in London's Kensington Gardens was swarming with pre-school children and their mothers and nannies. Jessica had to step around a prone, weeping mermaid and a Spider-Man peeing in the shrubbery as she made her way towards the giant, replica pirate ship. She left the path twice to avoid racing toddlers.

As she drew closer to the centre, the cold crept into her pockets and nipped at her fingers. She should have worn gloves, a hat. Around her, the playground had been planted with evergreen shrubs, but elsewhere in the park, most of the trees still had their spindly winter look. On her way here she'd passed daffodils on the path edge, but their flowers had yet to bloom, were still tight and green, not wanting to face the late-

278

spring chill.

On the edge of the sandy beach that surrounded the ship, she spotted a woman in a red coat. In her mid-thirties, of Indian origin, her face had a pinched, nervy look. Her eyes were fixed on the deck of the pirate ship. As Jessica watched, she waved at it, before raising her phone and taking a picture.

Jessica walked over and sat down beside her on a bench that felt cold even through her clothes. Neither woman spoke. Jessica pulled her oversized bag on to her lap and took out a blue teddy. She put the bag back on the ground and pulled an unopened pack of nappies over the rolled-up newspaper that was padding out the rest of it.

'I was a bit worried you wouldn't be allowed in.' Jasmine Sharma glanced over with large, amber eyes. 'I forgot about the rule. The one about no unaccompanied adults.'

'I blagged it,' Jessica said. 'I looked stressed, pretended to be on my phone, and looking for someone.'

'No one can see us talking in here.' Jasmine's eyes flicked up to the deck of the pirate ship. 'The planting was deliberate, to prevent the wrong sort of people watching the children.'

Up on the mast of the ship, a skinny brown-skinned boy waved. Jasmine waved back. Jessica did too. Then she made the blue bear wave.

'When we spoke on the phone, you said you were concerned about a doctor on Harley Street that your father had consulted,' Jessica said. 'That you thought he might be behaving unethically, even illegally.'

Jasmine said nothing. Jessica tucked the bear back in the bag. It had served its purpose. 'I'm listening,' she urged.

'A little over a year ago, my father was diagnosed with advanced heart disease,' Jasmine said. 'He was fitted with a pacemaker, put on a special diet, prescribed drugs, but his condition worsened. Doctors started to talk about months, not years, and that the only possible long-term treatment was a heart transplant.'

'I'm sorry to hear that.'

'Unfortunately, or so he was told, there are very few hearts available in any given year. Most people in this country die before a transplant becomes a real possibility and hardly any hearts are suitable for people from Asia and the Indian subcontinent.'

A scream nearby caught Jessica's attention. She turned, instantly on alert. It was only a child.

'He was still quite a young man,' Jasmine said. 'Sixty-four. He didn't want to die. He began asking around his friends and business colleagues. After a few months, someone recommended a transplant surgeon on Harley Street. A Mr Ralph Wallace. Dad made an appointment.'

Jessica committed the name to memory. 'Did you go with him?'

'No, but he talked about it afterwards. He said that Mr Wallace had been very encouraging.'

'In what way?'

'He told my father that in other countries the laws aren't so strict and people are less squeamish. He said that overseas, people are more willing to donate organs because there's financial compensation that is illegal here,' said Jasmine. 'Say, for example, a young man was killed in a road accident. The hospital would pay his family well for his organs, knowing they could sell them on to several people who were waiting. The family are pragmatic. They've lost a loved one, but the money can help those who are still living.'

'Well, I have to see the logic,' said Jessica. 'But this would have meant your father travelling to somewhere like India for his

281

heart operation.'

'No, not so. He would stay here. The heart would be brought to him.'

Jessica had a picture of air ambulances, of medics running across rooftops, clutching precious white boxes. Except — 'How could that be? Don't organs have to be transplanted within a few hours? Surely you can't fly a heart over from India and it still be viable?'

'No, you can't. I checked. A heart can survive for ten hours, maximum, after harvesting. There is no way it can be flown over from India.'

'So how?'

'The donor is flown over.'

'The dead donor?'

Jasmine gave a tiny shudder. 'No, not dead. Not properly anyway. He would be brain-dead, or donation would be out of the question, obviously, but the machines keeping him alive would be kept switched on. He'd be flown, with a medical team, in a specially adapted aeroplane, to the UK, so that the harvest could take place in the same hospital as the transplant.'

'OK, that does sound a bit grim,' said Jessica.

'Grim? It can't be legal, surely?'

'Did your father ask any difficult

questions?'

'Of course. My father wasn't a villain. Mr Wallace told him that because the financial transaction took place in India, the matter was perfectly legal. And because the transplant was carried out privately, in this country, it was a matter between surgeon and patient.'

'But you weren't happy with that?'

'No, and neither was my father. He wanted to live, but not at any price.'

'Why didn't he go to the police?'

'He was thinking about it. Being strictly honest, I think he was keeping his options open. And then his condition worsened. He died two weeks ago.'

'I'm sorry.'

Silence. Jessica looked around again, at the trees and bushes, at the railings, at the blue bear in her bag.

'So, why are you frightened?' she asked.

No reply.

'Why did you want to meet me here, where no one will think we're anything other than two mothers?'

For the first time, Jasmine took her eyes off her son and dropped them to the sand. 'I went to see Mr Wallace, a few days ago. I was troubled by what my father had told me. I didn't feel that I could just let it rest.'

'Ah.'

'He told me it was nonsense. He claimed it had been my father who'd asked about the availability of organs overseas. And that he — Mr Wallace I'm talking about now — had advised against it, because the surgery would be unsafe. He said my father must have been confused, that people often become desperate in the final days of their life.'

'That may actually be true.'

Jasmine opened the clasp of her bag and reached inside. 'Yesterday morning I got this in the post.'

She handed over a stiff brown envelope. Jessica upturned it and looked at the photograph that had fallen out. A boy of about five years old, wearing school uniform, in a playground, taken through the bars of a railing.

'That's Raffy,' said Jasmine. 'My older son. Taken at his school and sent anonymously. Coming so soon after my meeting with Mr Wallace, I couldn't help making a connection, seeing it as a threat. Am I being stupid?'

Jessica slid the photograph back into the envelope. She could have it checked for prints, although she had a feeling she wouldn't find anything. 'Not necessarily,' she said.

58

'And what is the name of this surgeon?' The director of the National Transplant Database held her pen poised above her notebook.

Jessica let her eyes fall. 'I'd prefer not to say for now. My informant was very nervous about speaking to me at all, and I promised her complete confidentiality.'

The director closed her notebook and made a point of finishing her coffee. 'She wasn't actually present in any of these meetings, if I understand you correctly? She may have misunderstood what her father was telling her.'

'That's entirely possible, but before I close the case, can you tell me whether what she was saying is at all credible?'

The director shook her head and put her cup on to its saucer with an air of business concluded. 'Oh, the problem as she's described it is accurate enough. There is a crisis of solid organs in the UK, particularly among people from the Middle East, India, the Asian subcontinent.'

'Because donation is frowned upon in these cultures?'

The director glanced through the glass partitioning of her office and held up a finger to someone outside. 'Partly,' she said. 'Although donation is a difficult issue in every culture. Mainly the shortage occurs simply because there is a broader population of Caucasian people here in the UK. Another reason is that people from these ethnic groups are more prone to certain diseases that impact upon the major organs.'

'And ethnic background is a factor?' Jessica said. 'You can't put — sorry to be crude — a black heart in a white body?'

'It's a little more complicated than that. You said you'd looked at our website?'

Jessica nodded. She'd been up early to avoid rush-hour traffic on the M4 and had arrived at the Bristol headquarters an hour ahead of schedule. She'd had plenty of time to mug up.

'So, you'll know that in the UK, there is one central database of everyone who needs a transplant and everyone who has chosen to be an organ donor. We manage that database here.'

'And you coordinate matches? A sort of organ-centred dating agency?'

The director showed no sign of finding that amusing. 'When organs become available —'

'Following a fatal accident?'

'Or sometimes a natural illness that doesn't compromise the organs. When that happens, as long as the next of kin doesn't withhold consent, the hospital where the potential donor is situated will alert us and we will identify the best matches.'

Such huge power over people's lives. 'How is that done? Just whoever's been waiting the longest?'

'Length of time waiting is a factor. Most importantly of all, the blood group and HLA — the human leukocyte antigen — have to be compatible. Then we have a matrix system that takes into account factors such as the recipient's age, their circumstances, their chances of reasonable quality of life, their location.'

'Location?'

'Yes, indeed. If we have a heart in Glasgow and two potential recipients, one in Edinburgh, one in Truro, then, all other things being equal, we'll favour the one in Edinburgh.'

'Thank you, that's useful to know.'

288

'So you see, no transplants take place in the UK that we don't know about, that we don't manage, that we don't authorize. No hospital, no medical team would work on a transplant that hadn't been coordinated through us. The system is foolproof.'

As the director spoke, Jessica's eyes flowed round to the framed images on the wall behind her desk. In one of the photographs she was posing with the Prime Minister.

'And as for the idea of smuggling still-living but brain-dead donors in via a major UK airport, well, it's simply absurd.'

The lowering sun was painting the clouds and the sea a soft shell pink and the dunes gleamed with warm colour. Jessica raised one bare foot and watched a sparkling trail fall from it, back into the water.

'Absurd, huh? And yet you have an intelligent, educated woman, who believed that her intelligent, educated father was told exactly that,' said Isabel.

Jessica sighed. 'The busy director told me that if I was prepared to give her the names involved, the surgeon and the patient, she could look into it. Otherwise, she could only conclude this was about nothing more than an elderly and frightened man getting confused.'

Isabel said, 'So that's it? End of investigation?'

From further down the beach came the sound of excited squealing. One of the noisier nuns had dropped the hem of her robe and was flapping her arms, on the point of falling over. Another strode over quickly, grabbing the arm of her panicking sister and pulling her back towards the shore. At the water's edge, seven more black-clad figures waded, splashed, or stood in the surf, gazing out to sea. Behind them, the low hills of Holy Island glowed golden in the early evening light.

'I think Sister Belinda waded out further than she intended,' Isabel said. 'There's a shelf there. It gets deep quite quickly. Oops, there she goes.'

Jessica smiled as Sister Belinda, losing her balance again, sank to her chest in the water and howled her shock to the sky.

'There never was an investigation,' she said, answering Isabel's question. 'There was a complaint, of sorts, but the woman concerned was too scared to make it official and the authorities have told me that what she alleges is impossible.'

Isabel said nothing.

'This really is quite surreal.' Jessica let her eyes travel the length of the beach. Twenty of the sisters, nearly half the convent's population, had come out for the evening's recreation hour. All but two had removed shoes and stockings to wade in the water. 'How did you persuade Mother Hildegard to agree?'

'Every sister in the convent apart from me is plagued with foot infections. Verrucas, athlete's foot, yellowing crumbly toenails. They take off their shoes during recreation hour and compare ailments.'

Jessica pulled a face. 'You realize I may never eat again.'

'I managed to convince Mother that regular exposure to sea-water would cure ninety per cent of the problems. She's limited us to paddling. For now.' Isabel grinned. 'I'm slowly introducing the benefits of full salt-water immersion. That lot are riddled with yeast infections.'

'No, please. No more.'

'Is there really nothing else you can do?'

'About the convent's health problems?'

'About this doctor on Harley Street. Can you not send someone in, you know, undercover?'

'We call it covert surveillance these days. Have someone join the cleaning or administrative team is the usual route, but it could take months to uncover something, if there's anything there.'

'But you'll keep an eye on it?' Isabel said. 'You won't let it drop?'

Jessica smiled. 'I have two consciences. My own, and that of my sister, the Carmelite nun.'

'You should be grateful, really. You have your own brain, and free use of mine, whenever you need it. Goodness knows, it has little enough to do most of the time.'

'Bella, do you never feel the urge to get out more? I know, you've told me dozens of times, you don't want to leave. But lots of nuns work in the community. They teach, they nurse.'

Isabel's face had fallen again. 'I am neither teacher nor nurse.'

'You can run an office. Work a computer.'

'I operate a computer that would be classed as antique by anyone in the outside world and run an office that belongs in the pages of a Dickens novel. All I can do is pray, and think.'

Jessica stopped walking. 'And hide?'

Isabel glanced back up the beach, to where most of the nuns had left the water. 'We should get back,' she said. 'I'm on peacock duty.'

They left the water and walked back to where they'd left their shoes in the shelter of the dunes.

'I've been thinking,' Isabel said as she sat on the sand to dust off her feet. 'Are there statistics you can check? I mean, the actual numbers of transplants taking place according to different ethnic groups. If the number of black and Asian transplants has increased substantially, or if there's a particular cluster in a given area, that might point to something going on.'

Their shoes back on, both women stood up. Jessica gestured for her sister to go first up the dune. The other nuns had left the beach now and their chatter trailed behind them like litter. 'Do you think about this stuff a lot?' she said.

'Of course not. A nun's thoughts are trained at all times upon her relationship with God.'

'Just when I'm here then?'

'Yes, just when you're here. So, could you?'

'I tried. And I did see some fluctuation, year on year. The trouble is, the overall numbers involved are too small to draw any meaningful conclusions. And illegal operations, if they're even happening, wouldn't be on official figures anyway, would they?'

'I guess not.'

'One thing I did learn was that this Mr

Wallace has consulting rooms in the north-east as well as Harley Street.'

Isabel looked back. 'Near here?'

'Not far. Newcastle. He divides his time between here and London.'

'And is that — sinister?'

'Not really. I did compare transplant figures in London and in the north-east to the UK average and, actually, they were up a bit. But given the ethnic populations in cities like Newcastle and London, you'd probably expect that. It certainly wasn't enough to set alarm bells ringing.'

'Except with you?'

'Yes, except with me. I can't really explain it, Bella. I know Jasmine was telling me the truth.'

They reached the top of the dune. The other sisters were already back in the convent grounds. 'Yes, but maybe Wallace wasn't,' Isabel said.

'What do you mean?'

'Maybe he makes big promises, takes the money and then lets the patients die while they're waiting for the life-saving organ to miraculously appear.'

Jessica pretended to frown. 'Should nuns bandy that word about?'

'Organ?'

'Miraculously.'

'If she, or rather her father, was telling the truth and remembering accurately, there must be other patients he said the same thing to. Can you get hold of a list of his patients?'

'Not without a court order, and I don't have nearly enough to even broach the subject with the boss.' Jessica sighed. 'It's going nowhere, Bella. I should give it up. I will. I will give it up.'

Isabel laughed out loud. 'No, you won't.'

59

She was still on her feet, halfway to the door. 'I can't contact the police,' she told the priest. 'Not here. Not in Northumberland.'

Frown lines contracted his brow. 'I don't understand.'

'I can't trust them.'

'The police?' He looked mystified.

'I can't tell you why, but I have good reason not to.'

He took a deep breath and blew it out again through pursed lips. 'Is it about why the balloon crashed?'

The start of her head told him everything he needed to know.

'I was watching the news on my iPad before you arrived. I'm very glad to see that you're all right, Jessica.'

She sat back down again.

'Have you considered that you're probably in shock? There's a nasty bruise on your temple, you could be concussed. You might even be suffering some sort of post-traumatic stress or something. You may be exaggerating the danger you're in. Maybe misinterpreting events.'

'There's more,' she said. 'I made a terrible mistake. I did something, and I didn't realize the consequences until now. I have to put things right.'

'I understand,' he said, although his face said clearly that he didn't.

They both jumped at the sound of the church door opening again.

'It'll be my churchwardens.' He stood up. 'Wait here.'

He poked his head through the vestry door. 'Morning, Stan. Good morning, Olive. Can you give me a second?'

He leaned back in. 'I've got to see these two, but if you wait in the church, I can drive you somewhere immediately afterwards. I have to be back in Bamburgh by four to pick up my son, but until then I'm at your disposal.'

She got to her feet. 'I can't ask it.'

'It's really no problem. Where do you want to get to?'

She thought about it for a second. Only a second.

'York,' she said. 'There are things I need to find, and someone I have to see. I have to go to York.'

'Do you have money?'

'Of course.'

'There's a railway station here in Belford but, to be honest, I don't recommend you use it. If the police are looking for you, they'll have people there. I can drive you up the road to Berwick-upon-Tweed. You'll be on the direct line to York and trains will be more frequent from there.'

'Thank you.'

'Also, and I'm not sure when I became an expert in avoiding the police, but if you use a mobile phone or a credit card, or get money out of the bank, they can trace you very quickly. You might like to bear that in mind.'

She smiled. 'You're very kind.'

He pulled open the vestry door. 'There's a room at the back of the nave, to one side of the main door, where a mothers and toddlers group meet. They've got easy chairs and a heater you can put on. Wait for me in there.'

'You didn't tell me your name.'

'Harry,' he said, and smiled again. 'Harry Laycock, vicar of the parish of St Mary, Belford, at your service.'

Keeping her head down, avoiding eye contact with the two churchwardens, she made her way down the aisle and found the mother and baby room. It had three narrow windows, one of which looked out towards the church porch.

A stocky, dark-haïred man wearing a leather trilby was walking up the church path. Patrick Faa had found her.

60

Resisting the temptation to kick open the church door — an act he knew would piss his mother off big time — Patrick turned the handle and pushed. It had been well oiled. It didn't make a sound as he stepped inside.

Out of habit, he took hold of the cross on his rosary and made the sign.

Before him, separating the chancel from the nave, was a high stone arch. To his left, a white-painted wall held a viewing gallery. There was a tower, too. Lots of hiding places.

She was in here. There was a smell in the air that he knew instinctively belonged to her. It was the smell of fresh, cheap soap with a suggestion of fried food. According to the bozos in the café, who'd actually believed he was a detective, she'd spent a long time in the toilets getting cleaned up before eating breakfast.

Voices. She wasn't alone. That made a difference.

At the back of the church, either side of where he was standing, were two doors. He could see from the shape of the walls that there were internal rooms beyond. The voices, though — faint and anonymous, hard to tell whether male or female — were coming from the front, from behind the organ, maybe, or that room where the priest kept his robes.

He went left and glanced round a small kitchen and lavatory. There was an external door in here, but it was bolted on the inside. The room to the other side of the entrance was a playroom with bright, childish posters on the walls and a box of toys in the corner. The cheap floral smell was stronger in here.

The room had a window that overlooked the church porch.

Uneasy now, he left the playroom and made his way up the centre aisle. He checked in all the pews and came to a halt in front of the vestry door.

'So, if you can do worship together next week here, Stan,' said a man's voice, 'and Olive the week after, I think we're covered until George gets back.'

He heard low murmurs of assent. Then

301

something about the following week's flower rota.

'OK, if that's it? I'm sorry to rush you guys out, but I've got someone waiting to see me.'

The sound of people getting to their feet, pushing back chairs. 'Sorry, Vicar, you should have said.'

'No, no. This was completely unexpected. Someone who turned up out of the blue. A bit troubled, though, so I don't want to keep her waiting long.'

The vestry door opened and Patrick stepped back, out of sight behind the organ. He watched a man and a woman — not the one he was looking for — walk to the rear of the church, pull open the door and leave. The priest was moving around noisily in the vestry.

Without making a sound, Patrick stepped down the chancel steps, and then down the nave until he reached the front door. He pulled the bolt at the top, then the one at the bottom. Wherever she was hiding, she wasn't going to make a quick getaway.

He pulled aside his jacket, found the knife he always kept there, and walked back towards the vestry.

He'd never killed a priest before.

61

'Say when you're ready, mother Hildegard.'

Ajax stood to one side of the elderly nun. He always made sure he could see a person's face when they identified the dead. The first glimpse, either the confirmation of their worst fears or a shocked reluctance to hope, invariably told him all he needed to know.

She was inches away from the curtained window of the mortuary viewing room, closer than most people stood. Her eyes were closed, her lips twitching. She was breathing heavily, her hands clenched into fists.

He waited. She crossed herself and her eyes opened.

'I'm ready,' she said.

The heavy purple velvet curtains opened. The slender form of a young woman lay shrouded a couple of feet from the glass. The mortuary assistant folded back the sheet to reveal the head.

Ajax kept his eyes on Hildegard, waiting for the reaction.

It didn't come. He'd never seen this before. The complete absence of any sort of response. The nun stared. Blinked. Stared some more. Finally, she took a step that brought her almost into contact with the glass. She raised her hands, put her fingertips on the glass and leaned in.

She might have been looking at a snake in the zoo, fascinated but repelled at the same time. Finally, Ajax let himself look at the corpse.

Her dark hair had been washed clean of the blood that had stained it the day before. It curled around the sheet beneath her, spreading out from her head like a dark cloud. The skin of her face, neck and shoulders was like the inside of a shell, except where it had been scorched.

He turned back to Hildegard. 'You can go inside, if you prefer,' he said, offering an option not usually available to the more emotional visitors. There seemed little danger of Hildegard losing control.

'No, thank you, I can see perfectly well. That's a terrible injury to her face.'

'Mother Hildegard, can you confirm that this is the woman you knew as Sister Maria Magdalena?'

Finally, the nun showed some emotion, but Ajax could only describe it as weariness. She allowed her eyes to close, her face to relax.

'Yes, of course,' she said. 'This is our beloved sister. We shall pray for her soul.'

'Thank you,' said Ajax. 'I'll take you home now.'

Her eyes snapped open. 'What about Jessica? Is she here too?'

62

The A1 was like a giant, angry monster, roaring just out of sight. She'd found it easily enough, had heard it from the back of the church. She'd crossed the fields and was beneath it now, following its course north.

But the field she was trying to cross had been ploughed and was thick with mud. Within minutes her shoes had more than doubled their weight as earth clung to them. She was forced to stop frequently. And yet hardly had she cleaned them before they clogged up again. She pressed on, knowing it could be nearly fifteen miles to Berwick-upon-Tweed.

The road was too close. Each time a large lorry went by, she was showered with fine drops of oily water, mud and even small stones. The hedge was protecting her to some extent, holding back the splashes from the cars, but the lorries were too big.

It took for ever to cross the first field. She

fell to her knees more than once, soon filthy. It was starting to feel hopeless.

'Jessica!'

Her heart thudding, she turned. On the bank above her, having climbed over the metal barrier and pushed through the spindly plantation of young trees, stood the vicar from St Mary's.

What did this mean? Had he called the police? Was Faa with him?

Harry began to scramble down the bank. 'My car's up top,' he called when he was close enough. 'I pulled over as soon as I could.'

'How did you find me?'

'I saw you run past the vestry window heading for open countryside.' He looked down at his own shoes and pulled a face. 'When my churchwardens left, I saw a bloke in the church and I really didn't like the cut of his jib. He bolted the front door, for one thing. I decided discretion was the better part of valour and left through the vestry. Come on, I'll drive you to Berwick.'

63

'Do you mind my asking a question?' Ajax said as he pulled out of the car park.

'Not at all,' Hildegard told him. 'Whether I choose to answer it is another matter.'

'Why was Jessica so obviously your favourite of the two sisters?'

'All souls are precious to our Father, Superintendent Maldonado. Favourites would be inappropriate.'

He tried again. 'Would it be fair to say you had more of a bond with Jessica?'

For a few seconds he thought he wasn't going to get an answer. Then she sighed. 'I suppose I always felt, if this doesn't sound too foolish, that we got the wrong sister. Jessica was the one with the simple, unquestioning faith. I saw her joy in chapel, her pleasure in the simple rituals. She understood the nun's calling, without really having to think about it. And yet, she had such a love of life. She raised people's spirits.

She was a joy.'

'And Maria Magdalena wasn't?'

'No one ever really knew what was going on in Sister Maria Magdalena's head. She was a strong woman. The early years in the convent would have broken her, if she hadn't been.'

'Sounds brutal.'

She glanced at him sharply. 'The life of an enclosed order isn't all swanning about in black robes, praying by candlelight, Superintendent. It's a life of endless, rigorous discipline. Few are cut out for it. I would never have believed that Sister Maria Magdalena was. And yet . . .' Her shoulders shrugged beneath the black coat.

'And yet she stayed.'

The phone rang. It was Stacey. He pulled over, asked Hildegard to excuse him and got out of the car. As he listened to what the constable had to say, he watched the elderly nun sitting motionless in the passenger seat.

'Thanks, Stace,' he said, and climbed back into the car. 'I may have some good news for you, Mother Hildegard.'

She turned to him then. 'How so?'

'We've already had a positive sighting of Jessica in Belford this morning. I didn't say anything because we didn't manage to pick her up and I didn't want to give you false hope. Now, though, it seems there was another one in Wooler yesterday. And a group of walkers from Buckinghamshire are pretty certain they spent some time with her on the St Cuthbert's Way.'

The nun's face transformed. 'Jessica is alive? Definitely alive?'

'It would appear so. Not only alive, but it looks like she's heading for the priory. Let's go and see if she's turned up, shall we?'

64

The train made its way south towards York. People got into the carriage and left it. She kept her head turned to the window, taking no notice of people who sat down on the seat beside her.

When the train stopped at Durham, her carriage pulled up alongside a café. Through its large picture windows she could see a television screen. The recording of that morning's press conference was being shown again.

Could there be a single person in the country not looking for her?

65

'Ok, this is the situation,' said Ajax. 'On the basis —' he stopped as the door to the conference room opened and the acting chief constable slipped inside. 'On the basis of no body being found at the crash site, nor any personal possessions, including no mobile phone, and with three different but equally reliable sightings, Jessica Lane has now been designated a vulnerable missing person.'

He paused and let his eyes travel to the other photograph pinned to the noticeboard. 'Sean Allan is similarly still missing. On the other hand, his kit bag was found inside the balloon, and we've had no sightings whatsoever of him.'

'Ajax, I'm sorry to ask you to go over old ground, but can you quickly update me on the sighting of Jessica Lane this morning?' The chief's eyes were fixed on the tabletop.

Ajax looked over at Stacey and gave her a nod.

'It was in the Birdcage Café in Belford,' said Stacey. 'She came in looking like *Keep Death Off the Roads* — the café owner's words, not mine — spent a long time in the toilets, apparently getting cleaned up, and then ordered and ate a massive breakfast. When the press conference was screened on the café TV, she got up and left. Someone followed her out but lost her. They called us immediately. As luck would have it, though, the nearest car was forty minutes away. By the time it got there, she'd vanished.'

The acting chief frowned. 'So she knows we're looking for her, she knows people will be worried, and she's deliberately avoiding being picked up?'

'Difficult to assume anything else,' said Ajax. 'At this point, we thought she might be heading for the convent. St Cuthbert's Way doesn't go through Belford as such, but another well-known track, the Northumberland Coast Path, does, and then meets St Cuthbert's Way a couple of miles north. From there, both paths head northeast, towards Fenwick and Holy Island. I went to Wynding Priory myself, but no sign of her. A couple of our guys are walking that part of the trail now in both directions. We've also put a car at the convent.'

'Why would she go to the convent?' the

chief asked.

'Good question,' said Stacey. 'I've had a quick chat with Paul Standish. His best theory is that she's in shock, possibly with a head injury, and instinctively heading for a place where she feels safe. She's been visiting the convent for twenty years. Her only family member lived there and she was very close to Mother Hildegard.'

'Pure conjecture, of course,' said Ajax, 'but we know her car is still in the balloon company's car park. And that no one appears to have returned to the house in York.'

'So she's confused, out of her mind with grief, wandering about more or less aimlessly but in the general direction of the convent?' the boss said.

'That's the theory we were working on,' said Ajax. 'Until young Chappers heard back from the National Police Federation.'

'We're all ears, Steve,' said the chief.

'So, I contacted the NPF yesterday evening, after the super asked me to try and trace Jessica Lane,' said Chapman. 'As it wasn't urgent, they said it would have to wait till the morning. I had to chase three times, but they finally gave me an answer of sorts half an hour ago.'

'You'll like this,' said Ajax.

'Jessica Lane has been attached to the

National Crime Agency for over a year now,' said Chapman. 'When I asked for more details — what station, any of the special units, what rank, uniform or CID — I was told she worked out of Scotland Yard, although the nature of her work involved being posted all over the UK. And that she had the rank of sergeant. No further information would be immediately forthcoming.'

The chief did a pantomime double take. 'Come again?'

'They thanked me for letting them know and asked me to keep them informed of progress.'

'She hasn't been in touch with them?'

'Not that they were admitting to.'

'She still has her phone?'

'Her phone hasn't been found. We have to assume she still has it.'

'Based at Scotland Yard, the NCA playing secret squirrels with us — I'm betting she was some sort of covert operative,' said Ajax. 'Question is, did whatever she was working on have anything to do with the balloon accident?' 'I'm not happy about this,' said the chief. 'A covert police operation taking place under our noses that we know nothing about, and one of the officers concerned is involved in a freak fatal accident that is some way from being explained. I don't suppose we've heard anything from the lab yet?'

No one answered. It hadn't really been a question.

Ajax sighed. 'I've been holding this back because I didn't want to set any hares running, but one of the CSIs who attended the crash thought she might have spotted brain tissue on the basket. She wasn't certain.'

He waited.

'Brain tissue that probably didn't come from any of the dead passengers,' he added. 'All the bodies we found had skulls that were still reasonably intact.'

'So, given that Jessica is alive and walking, it must have been Sean Allan the pilot,' said Stacey.

'If it *was* brain tissue,' said Ajax.

'Injured or killed before the crash,' said Chappers. 'Or his body would still be in the basket.'

'If it *was* brain tissue,' repeated Ajax.

'What could possibly happen in a hot-air balloon to break open a skull to that extent?' asked Stacey. 'A bang on the head wouldn't do it.'

'Gunshot?' said Chapman.

'I knew this would happen.' Ajax shook his head. 'We really need to wait for the lab.'

'One more thing,' Chapman spoke up. 'As

we know, Jessica Lane's fiancé, Neil Fish-burn, is also a serving officer. He's been away on leave for a couple of days and not contactable, but he's expected back tonight.'

'I think she's heading for York,' said Sta-cey. 'Most women would go home, in her position. Especially if her fiancé's due back.'

The chief stood up. 'I'm going to give the NCA a ring. See if they'll be any more forthcoming with me.'

'If this woman's involved in something,' said Ajax, 'she could be going anywhere.'

'Exactly. And while we believe she's still on our patch, we're well within our rights to look for her,' the chief said. 'I want to know about it if she uses her phone or any of her credit cards, and I want the guys in the CCTV room watching out for her. Pay special attention to the train and bus stations.'

'If she's deliberately trying to stay under the radar, she'll know all those tricks, sir,' said Stacey. 'I think we should concentrate our efforts on York.'

'Fair enough,' the chief said. 'Get on to North Yorkshire. Ask them to keep a close eye on her house. If they're stretched, we'll send someone down.'

'All our spare officers are at St James's Park tonight,' said Ajax.

The chief looked weary. 'I'd forgotten that. OK, we rely on North Yorkshire. I think you're right, Stacey. I think she will be heading for York.'

66

His mother's voice always sounded older on the phone. Patrick could hear the tar that lined her lungs scrabbling up towards her throat.

'I don't like it, Pat. None of it makes any sense,' she was saying. 'If she's a police officer, why hasn't she been in touch with them? Even if she didn't have a phone — because some thieving git nicked 'em all — she could have walked to the nearest house.'

'I don't know, Ma,' he said, because he knew he had to say something. 'Nobody does.' He looked at his watch. Well past midday already.

'What was she doing in the balloon? Surveillance? God bless us and save us, the things she might have seen from that balloon.'

'Get a grip, Ma. No one uses balloons for surveillance. You can't steer 'em.'

'Why hasn't she phoned someone, said,

"Oi, I'm in a bit of a fix, can you give me a lift?" '

He was tapping his fingers on the steering wheel now. 'Good question, Ma. If I can ever get going, maybe I'll ask her.'

He wouldn't. Conversation didn't play a major part in his plan for Jessica Bloody Lane.

'So where's she going?'

He sighed and swallowed his first response. 'York, they think.' He revved the engine, but quietly. No point asking for it.

'You don't have time to go to York. Have you forgotten what's happening tonight?'

'I'll be back.'

'What if you get held up?'

'I won't.'

'And they're asking questions about that girl we took in yesterday morning. I told you this would happen. We should have stopped when —'

'Ma, I've really got to get going.'

'Just bloody make sure you're back.'

He killed the call, pulled away and turned on to the A1. Heading south.

67

Two years, three months earlier

'Jess, are you mad? You went into that dreadful place by yourself? You could have been killed.'

Isabel was some feet away in the convent's peacock enclosure, Jessica waiting in the entrance. In nearly twenty years of visiting, she'd never got used to being so close to the admittedly beautiful but huge and sometimes downright aggressive birds. Isabel, right now, was surrounded by them. Males, females, chicks, all clamouring for their food.

'I would never have got permission to go, so who could I take with me? And it's not so bad. There's crime there, of course. And abuse. But killing an English woman really wouldn't help their cause and they know that. And you can talk. You're about to get bitten.'

Isabel looked down. One of the peahens

was inches away from her right hand. She threw the handful of pellets and the birds moved away. 'Their cause being to get to England?' she said, throwing more.

'Yep. I was gambling on my nationality working for me. They all want a friend in England.'

'English? You English?'

The youngsters approached her first, as she'd expected. She had small packets of sweets and crayons to bribe them. The adults watched from behind their tent curtains and lopsided doors, curious, suspicious, ready to act if she posed the least threat. Or showed any weakness.

When she watched TV footage of the Jungle in Calais, the people who lived there always looked as though they were wading through mud. Because they were, she realized now, as her feet got stuck and she nearly lost her boots again.

There was a main street, of sorts, a ribbon clearing in the tents, shacks and shelters, along which travelled stolen bicycles and four-wheel-drive news vehicles. Narrower paths forked off from it, like branches from a diseased tree, sprouting homes on either side. In the distance, she could see the cheap wooden cross of a church. There was a mosque here too, and shops, and a school was being built. Here, in this dreadful place, an infrastructure of sorts had formed.

'I want to talk to your mother,' she said, to young face after young face. 'Does your mother speak English? Or German? *Sprechen sie Deutsch? Polska?* I want to ask your mothers some questions.'

One of the older children was poking at her rucksack, trying to see what was inside. She turned and faced him, shaking her head.

'I speak good English. Where in England you live?' He was about sixteen, his eyes red-rimmed, one of them with a swollen, angry sty.

'I live in York. In the north.' She waited for a reaction. None came. 'Also in London.'

'London, London.' It became a chorus around them. 'We want to go to London.' More people joined them, mainly teenagers, some young men. Jessica reached into the large pocket of her coat and pulled out the photographs. She turned the pile so that her new friend could see the top one. His eyes narrowed and he took a step back.

'Do you know anyone who has done this?' She looked from one set of brown eyes to the next, letting them all see the photograph of Muhamed's angry, infected wound.

'You?' She spoke directly to the boy, who was backing away now. She pointed at his back. 'Have you done this?'

'You want buy kidney?' Another voice this time. A young man.

'No.' She thought for a second, decided it was worth the risk, and pulled out her warrant card. 'I'm an English police officer.' She waited for them to scatter, to behave the way crowds invariably did when confronted by the police, but none of them moved. She could do nothing to harm them. The French police they might fear, but she was still an English citizen, one who might hold the key to the promised land. 'Someone is hurting people like you. Someone is stealing from you. I want to find who.'

The man beckoned. He wanted her to follow him.

They left the track, weaving between tents, ducking beneath lines strewn with dirty clothes, stepping over rubbish, sensing eyes watching them at every turn. She passed dark huts from which Arabic rock music blared, and pools of filth that nearly made her retch.

When she looked back, she could no longer see the main street. Just a crooked line of blue tents and precarious huts, and the crowd, bigger now, that was following her. For the first time, the people in her wake weren't mainly children.

Her guide stopped suddenly, beside a shelter made from wooden pallets covered with waterproof sheeting and wide strips of clear plastic. He called in a language she didn't recognize.

From inside came a grunt, then a rustling. A face appeared. A black man, his tight black curls streaked with grey. There were deep wrinkles at his temples and on his forehead. He was thin, dressed for winter, rather than a rainy day in June.

The conversation continued. One man was pointing at the other's body, then tapping his own, roughly where a kidney scar might be.

Jessica held up her photograph, saw the older man's eyes narrow.

'This for him too,' said her guide. 'He speak no English. I help.'

Jessica pulled her rucksack from her shoulders. She found two packets of paracetamol and held them out. She'd brought sweets for the children, over-the-counter medical supplies for the adults. 'He has a scar, like this?' she asked.

The older man took the packets, the younger one said, 'Yes. Scar like that.'

'I need to know who took it. Where, and when.'

The to and fro of rapid conversation went on for several minutes. Then her guide turned back. 'He is from Eritrea. You know this place?'

Jessica nodded. 'I do.'

'He was travelling with his family. Wife, three children. Two brothers. Brother's wife. His mother. They came across the sea, then by land. Very expensive trip. Many thousands of dollars.'

'How did he pay for it?'

Her guide pointed at the photograph still in Jessica's hand. 'That way.'

'His family too?' She tried to see inside the gloom of the Eritrean man's home. 'Are they here?'

'No. Just him. And his mother.'

He pointed inside the shelter and Jessica bent to peer into the darkness. Sitting on an upturned box at the back, wrapped in shawls and blankets, was a figure topped with a brown wrinkled face.

'They travelled to Belgium. The family went on ship. Not him. Not his mother.'

'Why?'

'He was sick. The . . . the . . .' He struggled for the word, pointed to the photographs again.

'The operation?' suggested Jessica. 'To remove his kidney?'

'It make him sick. Fever. Weak. They say he too sick. They not let him on boat. They leave him behind. And mother. They come here.'

The older man interrupted with a flurry of words.

'He say all he want to do now is get to England and find his family.'

'I'll look for them,' Jessica said. 'If he tells me their names, maybe shows me a photograph, I promise I'll look for them.'

'He say, you must look in the north. His family were taken to the north and this makes him very afraid. Because he knows the north is a terrible place.'

'The north again,' said Isabel. She was surrounded by the birds now as she emptied the tub of pellets into the feeders.

'Not just the north, a place called Yellow House. This man believes his family have been taken to a place called Yellow House in the north of England.'

'Yellow House? What is that?' Standing upright again, she put the lid on the feeder.

'No idea. I assumed it was a town or city name that he'd misheard.'

'Or an actual yellow house?'

Jessica rubbed a hand over her face. 'Wish me luck tracking that down.'

Isabel moved out of the pen, leaving the door wedged open. Behind her, the peafowl were intent upon their food. Soon though, their meal would be over and they'd start roaming the convent grounds again. 'I can't believe you never lose these things,' Jessica said. 'Don't foxes get them?'

'We do lose them. Peafowl have a tendency to run wild, if allowed, even if they're born in captivity. And they can fend for themselves quite well. They eat just about anything and roost in trees. We lost Pea-soup for three months once, then she turned up one afternoon in chapel, right as rain.'

'Why don't you keep them locked up?'

'We lock ourselves up. Why should they suffer too?'

Jessica said nothing. Isabel, as usual when she let slip what Jessica believed were her real feelings about the convent, would not meet her eyes. Then she looked up and seemed to force a smile. 'And now for once, I have something to tell you. I've been in big trouble with Hilda.'

'Sister, what are you doing in here?'

The desktop computer gave a last ping as it closed down. Its feeble light disappeared and the room was cloaked in shadows.

Isabel, behind Mother Hildegard's desk, considered her options. They were few. Hildegard was standing in the doorway. Short of leaping from the window, there was no way out of the room without physical violence. She walked around to the front of the desk. 'I admit my fault, Mother Hildegard. I will willingly do penance.'

Hildegard's brows flicked upwards. 'I don't doubt it, but you haven't answered my question.'

Isabel tried again. 'I have allowed my thoughts to be diverted from God. I will pray He forgives my weakness.' She dropped her eyes to the carpet and began counting threads.

'I'm not going to let this go, Sister. What were you doing in my office in the middle of the night?'

As if on cue, the chapel bell began to ring and two low musical sounds sped around the convent building. It was two o'clock in the morning.

'I was searching for something on the Internet,' Isabel said.

'I'm all ears.'

Isabel risked looking up. Mother Hildegard hadn't bothered dressing. She was wearing an old brown dressing gown and a thin cotton cap over her hair. Without the flowing black robe, the bumps, knobbles and angles of an elderly woman were much more visible. This would be her, Isabel realized, in thirty years' time. Old and lumpy, grey and dry.

'Excuse me, Mother,' she said. 'I would prefer not to say.'

'Sister, do I have to remind you — again — that you took a vow of obedience?'

Isabel sighed. 'I was curious about something that Jessica is investigating. I wanted to know more about it. I found a report and printed it off to read later.'

Hildegard leaned back, nodding gently. 'Ah, Jessica. I sometimes think we'd all be much better off without that young woman's frequent visits. And yet we'd miss her so much.'

Isabel waited. It helped, sometimes, having a relative who was such an obvious favourite with the convent leader. Hildegard shook her head. 'Well, I am unlikely to sleep again now, and I feel an unusual thirst,' she said. 'Sister, I suggest we go quietly to the kitchens and put the kettle on. You can tell me all about it.'

'I wanted to find out what happens in other countries,' Isabel said to Hildegard once they were sitting at the small kitchen table, two mugs of steaming tea in front of them. 'I thought it might help Jessica. She has so little time. This isn't something she's working on officially. I thought I —'

'You thought you, with so much time, could help the woman who has none? Do I need to remind you, Sister, that time here is given for a purpose? Your time, and mine, and that of all the sisters, belongs to God?'

'I'm sorry.'

'You know this, and yet the hours hang heavy on you, don't they? I often ask myself if God is enough for you.'

Isabel looked up from her mug. 'I can't leave here.'

Elderly eyes stared. 'Why? Because you belong, or because you've been here so long you've lost track of where you might go?'

Isabel said nothing. Hildegard sighed.

'And there are really parts of the world where the poor will sell their kidneys to feed their families?'

'Kidneys and parts of the liver,' replied Isabel. 'The liver can grow back, apparently, if you cut it in two. And yes, it may be to feed their families, it may be to settle debt, or even, as Jessica suspects, to pay people-smugglers the cost of a trip to the West. And I know that sounds horrible, but if the stuff

I found is right, it's not only kidneys that are traded. Organs are taken that people can't survive without. The heart, for example.'

Hildegard crossed herself.

'In some countries, doctors have special authority to remove organs from unclaimed bodies and, conveniently, a lot of unclaimed bodies turn up at the hospitals where these doctors work. In others, political prisoners are used as live donors. I found stories about people still breathing after their organs were removed, but being thrown into the incinerators anyway.'

'Sister, I'm not sure either of us will sleep soundly for some time to come. But did you find anything that may actually help Jessica?'

'I don't think so. I suppose I was hoping that I might have a brainwave about how it could be happening in the UK. But everything here seems so tightly regulated. I can't see how it's possible.'

'We should hope and pray that it isn't.' Hildegard drained her mug and put it down. 'I think it's time for me to get ready for lauds, Sister.' She stood and looked around. 'I've thought for a few days now that the windows in here are looking grimy. Perhaps you'd like to spend the rest of the dark hours letting in a bit more light.'

■ ■ ■ ■

'And that was it?' Jessica said. 'She made you clean the windows?'

As they'd finished feeding the peacocks, rain had started to fall, and the two women had found refuge in the convent greenhouses. Huge, long and elaborate Victorian constructions, the greenhouses ran almost the full length of the rear of the convent building. In the past, they'd been used exclusively for growing food. While some foodstuffs — tomatoes, peppers, cucumbers — were still grown, seeds from outside had found their way in and flourished. Huge, unruly plants in the beds and larger tubs gave a rainforest feel to the greenhouses on warm, wet days.

'If only.' Isabel gave a mock sigh. 'I had to make a public confession where I explained everything I'd learned to the sisters and asked them to join my prayers that the cruel and ungodly practice can be ended. We prayed for the victims, for the forgiveness of those who exploit their fellow men, and for the courage and strength of all those who were working to protect the vulnerable. Special prayers were said for you, of course. We've done a great deal of praying on the subject.'

'Well, I'm rather surprised we still have a problem. But good to know I've got a convent of crime-fighting nuns on my side.'

'Not to mention God.'

Jessica gave her sister a sideways look, but Isabel looked perfectly serious.

A rustling from behind made them both jump. Jessica got up from the iron bench to see a bunch of large, tropical leaves shivering. Something or someone was close by, listening to their conversation. 'Hello?' she said.

'I'm not sure which of us will be most surprised if you get an answer,' Isabel said. 'That'll be Pea-nut.'

The leaves moved again. Something seemed to be making its way out of the leaves towards them.

'Possibly Pea-brain,' Isabel went on. 'But Pea-nut is the one we find in here most often. Especially when it's raining.'

The foliage parted and a small, sharp head appeared a foot from the soil. A bird's head, the most perfect shade of blue imaginable, a regal tuft of blue, flower-like feathers standing up from its crown. Deep brown eyes looked into Jessica's for a second, before the peacock emerged completely and walked past her down the path. The tur-

quoise feathers of its tail, adorned w
hundred unblinking eyes, trailed behi
as its feet tapped on the stone flags.

'Pea-nut,' confirmed Isabel.

'Don't tell me you can tell them apa
Jessica said.

'Of course. We all can. Even Sister Se
pis, and she's practically blind. She says th
each have a different cry.'

The peacock looked back, briefly, before
leaving the path again and disappearing
behind a row of tomato plants. Its tail
remained visible, a shimmering mass of blue
and turquoise feathers, twitching occasionally.

'I tell you what, though,' Isabel said. 'If
Hilda had realized how interested that lot
were going to be, she'd have made me burn
that report and never mention a word to
anyone. They can't talk about anything else.
We don't watch American sitcoms any more
at recreation, we search for documentaries
about organ trafficking. Sister Serapis
wanted chapter and verse on how much
various organs cost on the black market and
actually argued with me for ten minutes that
a liver should be worth more than a heart
because a liver clears the body of all the ill
humours. Sister Alfreda has offered her
kidney to pay for repairs to the chapel roof

and Sister Tabitha insists I tell you that you have to — her words now — stake out Whitby because there's always been something dodgy about Whitby since Dracula landed.'

Jessica sat back down on the bench. 'I'm living in a budget sequel to *Sister Act.*'

'Oh, and Sister Eugenia has asked me to speak to you specifically. She seems to think there's some sort of national police computer system that records all crimes.'

Jessica sighed. 'She's probably thinking of HOLMES. The Home Office Large Major Enquiry System.'

'She thought you could search it. Type in black people and organ trafficking, with a plus symbol, she was very clear about that. Apparently, her nephew is studying computer science at university.'

'I know what she means. I did actually run a search when this first came up. Nothing.'

'But maybe you need to keep doing it. Do it every week. Sooner or later, you might get something. Bide your time. Be patient.'

Jessica was smiling. 'Funny, you were never the patient one of the family.'

Isabel looked through the glass at the walls of the convent building. 'I've had nearly two

decades in this place. What else was I supposed to learn?'

68

'Ok, people,' Ajax said. 'We're talking about the accidental death, in possibly suspicious circumstances, of a young woman known as Tahmina Farah who was admitted to Newcastle General yesterday morning. Round about the time the first fatalities from the balloon crash were arriving, although I'm sure that's coincidence. DC Chapman, you've got our attention.'

Steve Chapman, at the front of the meeting room, rose to his feet.

'So, I've spoken to Northern Area who dealt with the accident initially. Tahmina was found lying at the foot of some small cliffs just off Howick.'

'Found by who?' Ajax asked.

'Early morning jogger. Couple of dog walkers were soon on scene too. No one saw her fall and they weren't sure at first whether she was alive or dead. They called an ambulance and local uniform attended as a matter of routine. She was rushed to Newcastle. Shortly after she arrived, a couple of male relatives pitched up.'

Chapman glanced down at his notes.

'A Mohammed Farah, no relation to the athlete that I know of, and an Abdul Bari,' he went on. 'Farah was her next of kin, and he gave permission for the machines to be turned off and her organs to be used.'

Around the room, a couple of officers were making notes. Most, though, were watching Chapman, slightly puzzled frowns on their faces.

'This is where it gets interesting.' Chapman had obviously sensed the waning attention. 'Mo and Abdul left the hospital, having collected all the necessary details about arranging the funeral, and vanished. When I tried to contact them following the concern expressed by the two doctors, the phone numbers were unobtainable.

'There is a Farah family living at the address they gave, and it does include a young woman called Tahmina, but she was looking pretty hale and hearty when I showed up. None of them knew anything at all about the accident yesterday, and no young women belonging to the family are missing.'

'Identity theft,' someone said.

'Did they kill her?' another asked. 'Honour killing? Or a bad accident?'

'Maybe,' said Chapman, 'but why turn up at the hospital, why go through the rigmarole of organ donation, and why with fake identities?'

'Chappers, presumably this Mo and Abdul will be coming back to Newcastle General to collect the body?' Ajax said. 'They won't know anything about our involvement yet. When are they expected?'

'Sometime today.'

'Get some plain-clothed officers in there,' said Ajax. 'When they show up, nab 'em. Not you, though, Chappers. In fact, I want you to hand it over to Charlie and let him take it forward. I need you on the hunt for Jessica Lane.'

As Chapman sat down, Ajax got to his feet.

'This woman — Jessica Lane — should have died,' he said. 'Eleven people were killed in that crash. Not only did Lane survive, she walked away. She's still walking.

'So, I want to know where she's going. I want to know why she hasn't been in touch. Why she isn't seeking help. Why she's deliberately avoiding the police.

'I want to know who she's running from.

'Most of all, I want her found.'

69

The Tudor-fronted, narrow cobbled streets of the old city of York were busy, its shops gaudy and rich, like a trail of discarded Christmas presents. Everywhere she went it seemed that bells rang out, people called to each other, traffic roared past. From every open doorway came a new smell: tropical perfumes, roasting meat, burning sugar. After the isolation of the National Park, the quiet, steady purpose of the small Northumbrian towns, the size and speed and sound of York came as a shock to the senses.

She crossed the River Ouse at Micklegate Bridge, glad of the double coat now, because York was cold. Further inland than Berwick-upon-Tweed and the warming effect of the sea, the city held chill winds around every corner.

With the hood of the blue coat around her head, keeping to the narrow old streets where there would be fewer cameras, knowing that a woman alone would be more conspicuous because that's who the police were looking for, she moved from one group of tourists to the next, even following a guided tour for a few hundred metres.

Paranoid about being seen, she hadn't taken the direct route from the station, heading instead into the city, wandering the old streets, as though trying to shake off a tail she knew couldn't possibly be there. The sense of being followed, of being hunted, was growing stronger by the second.

As a nearby church was striking four o'clock, she reached the street that faced the south-western stretch of the old city wall. She stood on the corner for several minutes, knowing that police vehicles came in all shapes and sizes.

After ten minutes she slipped into the alley that ran between two terraces. At the eleventh door along she stopped and looked around. No one out. She ran at the wall, finding footholds, scrambling up and then over. The bin on the other side broke her fall.

The space at the back was half garden, half empty dog pen. The two German shepherds that shared the house with its human occupants were in boarding kennels. She made her way past the statue of the weeping nun, over a tiny lawn, and unlocked the back door.

'Neil?' she called. 'Hello?' Although she already felt sure the house was empty. She took off her shoes, removed and hung up both jackets, drank water straight from the tap and nearly a pint of milk from the fridge. She would have eaten and drunk more, but found nothing fresh, only a square of cheese that had dried and cracked, some bacon, a few limp vegetables. The fridge said, as clearly as did the silent house, that no one was home. No one had been home for several days now.

Dishes and cutlery on the draining board were bone dry. A large kitchen knife had been used to open a brown envelope but the postmark was several days ago. The knife was perilously close to the edge of the counter. A strong breeze might send it spinning to the floor. She picked it up and put it down again on top of the envelope.

On the worktop, by the bread bin, was a wholesale pack of Reese's Peanut Butter Cups. At the sight of them, she caught hold of the kitchen counter to steady herself and laid her head against the cool melamine of the cupboard. It was odd, the stuff that she could deal with, and the things that might just break her.

The curtains in the living room were open. Touching nothing, moving nothing, keeping hold of the rucksack, she moved through the ground floor to the hallway and then upstairs. She needed a bath, clean clothes and some time to rest in a warm place. Before they came looking.

At the top of the stairs, she walked past three closed doors into the main bedroom and then the en suite bathroom. The bathroom was faux Victorian, the walls lined with tongue-and-groove panelling, painted a soft creamy pink. A huge roll-top bath with clawed feet took up most of the space.

On the shelf between the hand basin and the mirror was a thin stick of white plastic, on which two tiny windows each showed a thin blue line. She picked it up, couldn't see it properly because she was crying again. Clutching it tight, she walked back into the bedroom, lay down on the bed and pressed the remote control that would turn on the small TV. It took her a few minutes to find the BBC news channel.

The man she'd seen on TV that morning, Superintendent Ajax Maldonado, was standing outside the police station in Newcastle.

'We now have reason to believe that Jessica Lane survived the balloon crash and could be in urgent need of medical assistance.' Maldonado was good at speaking to the camera, with none of the over-formal delivery that most self-conscious police officers fall into. 'She may be suffering from a condition called Acute Stress Disorder. She may not even have any clear recollection of what happened.' He paused and glanced down at something in his hands. 'Any member of the public seeing Jessica shouldn't approach her — in her confused state of mind, she could be a danger to herself and others — but should contact the police immediately.'

A photograph appeared on the screen. The same one she'd been seeing all day on TV screens. A young woman, with dark hair, wearing a bright green jacket. Then Maldonado was back. Running along the bottom of the screen was a telephone number for the public to call.

'Where do you think she is?' called a reporter, out of shot, as a big furry microphone was pushed closer towards Maldonado.

'Why hasn't she contacted the police?' called another.

Maldonado nodded his thanks and headed back into the building.

She lay back on the pillow, and caught a whiff of a musky, masculine scent. Neil.

70

Two years earlier

'You don't think you're getting a bit — I don't know — obsessed?'

Jessica spun her chair round to see Neil in the doorway, naked but for his boxers, red in the face and damp around the chest hair. Neil always turned into an inferno at night. She still wasn't used to waking up in sheets wet from his sweat.

'Sorry,' she said. 'Go back to bed.'

He didn't. He came further into the room, and turned her back to face the screen. She reached up, found his hands on her shoulders and they looked together at the map of the north of England.

'There was a story on the radio, when I was driving up,' she said. 'A young woman in Newcastle is dying of liver disease. She's got days to live without a transplant. None of her close family is a match. She needs a donor. Probably tonight.'

His fingers strayed towards her neck. 'It was on the local news as well. She had a big family. Colourful bunch. Catholics. Said they were praying for a miracle.'

'But a miracle for them is a tragedy for someone else. It just felt so creepy. As though someone had to die tonight so that she could live, and it could have been me. The M1 was busy. You know what those lorries can be like. All the way up, I was half waiting for something to happen.'

'OK, now I know you're taking this too far.'

A dark shape crept into the room, a huge German shepherd bitch, one of two that lived in the house with them. She moved across the carpet and pressed close to Neil's side. He took one hand off Jessica's shoulder to reach down and scratch behind the dog's ear.

'There's no good news with organ donation,' Jessica said. 'Every time an organ becomes available, someone has died. A family somewhere is grieving.'

'But these people are dying anyway. The two aren't connected.'

'What if they are?'

Neil gave an exaggerated sigh. 'Jess, you've got the half-remembered anecdote of a dying man and some rumours about immigrants being frightened of the northern ports. That's it.' He leaned over and shut the computer down. 'You've combed through statistics and found nothing. You've talked to the authorities and they've all told you it's impossible. There is nothing there.'

'I know.'

'And here was me thinking you'd be worried about the new job.'

She reached across for her wine glass and drained it. 'I'm worried about that too.'

'Or about moving in with me and the girls.'

She glanced down and met a pair of brown canine eyes. 'I'm not worried about that.'

'Really? Because they get pretty jealous.'

'So long as they don't expect to share the bed.'

He pulled her up, turned her to face the door. 'Speaking of bed.' Gently, he pushed her from the room. The dog tried to follow and was turned back at the bedroom door.

71

Thursday, 21 September

Patrick sat back down, his heart still thumping. He didn't like aggro, well, not unless he'd started it in the first place.

Over at the bar, the couple of lads who'd tried to switch the TV to Channel 4 for the racing were muttering to each other. The bloke behind it was polishing a glass, his eyes fixed on the bar. No one was looking directly at Patrick, but he knew he was being watched all the same.

Don't get yourself noticed, you idiot! He could hear his mother's voice as clearly as if she'd been in the room.

It had been wasted effort anyway. The news item was finishing and Maldonado walking back into the station.

Jessica Lane of York. A woman confused. A danger to herself and others. A woman in a bright green jacket.

His hand was shaking. He picked up his

drink and let the smell of it wash into him. Sometimes, this was enough. Not this time. The pint of beer on the table in front of him was untouched. He didn't like beer. The beer was for show, and to discourage any hints from the staff that he might leave. It was the double whisky chaser he needed. More than ever now.

On his phone he opened up the photograph of Jessica Lane that Jimmy had found for him earlier on the Internet. A different shot to the one the police were using. In the photograph he'd been looking at all day, she wasn't wearing the green jacket.

Something was seriously fucked up.

He tried making a phone call. Got number busy. He even thought about phoning his mother.

He finished his whisky. And then drank the beer.

72

'Sir, something you need to see.'

No sleep in twenty-four hours was catching up with Ajax. He picked his head up off the desk and focused on Chappers in the doorway. 'What is it?' he asked.

'Finley called me a couple of minutes ago. I think he's right, but you need to look as well.'

Finley from IT stepped forward and both men came into the room. 'I ran Jessica Lane's photograph through the facial recognition system, like you said,' he told Ajax. 'It's thrown up something very interesting. I've sent you an email.'

He leaned over Ajax's computer and opened his inbox. 'There you go: image captured three days ago at eighteen-thirty hours.'

The still picture showed HQ's reception area — sergeant's desk, noticeboards, visitors' chairs. Three people were coming in through the revolving doors.

'The one in the middle,' Finley said. 'I've blown it up as much as I can.'

Ajax leaned forward. The three people in the shot wore tabard aprons over their clothes. They were employees of the contract cleaning company that came into the building every evening as the day shift ended.

'The one in the middle,' Chappers repeated.

Ajax rubbed his eyes. The cleaner in the middle of the group was a slim woman in her thirties, about five foot seven and a hundred and ten pounds. Her dark hair was scraped back into a high ponytail.

'We've found her a few times,' said Finley, 'but she nearly always keeps her head down, as though she's checked out where the cameras are and is avoiding them. This is the only time she looks up.'

Ajax shook his head. 'I'm not sure.'

'Thought you might say that. So compare this image taken earlier this afternoon at Berwick railway station.'

Another image flashed up. This time, the woman's hair was loose, dark and curly, flying out around her face in an unruly mess. The face, though, was the same.

Ajax looked at Chappers. 'Have you shown anyone else this?'

'No, sir, we brought it straight to you. Do you think it's Jessica Lane?'

'Oh, I'm sure it is,' said Ajax. 'The question is, who and what in this building was she investigating?'

73

A dog barking in the street woke her. She sat upright on the bed, hot and breathless, but the bark was high-pitched, suggesting a small dog, not the one that was looking for her. The house had grown dark while she'd been sleeping.

Still holding the thin white strip, she got up, straightened the duvet out of habit, and then replaced the plastic strip on the bathroom shelf before turning on the bath taps.

Back in the bedroom, it took her a few minutes to find hiking trousers, a cotton sweater and a larger fleece, underwear and socks. Her filthy clothes went into the linen basket. A few more seconds of searching and she found Neil's mobile phone, in his top drawer, where he'd said it would be. Leaving it on top of the cabinet, where she'd see it when she left the room, she found a robe behind the bathroom door, picked up the rucksack and then walked back along the landing.

The smallest spare bedroom had been converted into a home office. In the bottom drawer of the desk cabinet she knew she'd find more cash. Three hundred pounds. It went into the rucksack.

On the desk was a laptop.

I'm sending Neil the password for my laptop. Lots of important stuff on there.

An entire investigation, one that had taken so much time and energy these past two years, was detailed on this laptop. And only on this laptop.

She tucked the thin computer into her rucksack, looked around for a power lead and took that too. Back in the bathroom she took off her robe.

The bath was surrounded by heavy shower curtains, creating a capsule of sweet-scented steam that she stepped into. There had to be a dozen or more scratches and bruises on her body, some of them caked in dried blood, and she cried out as the water made them sting. She sat down, clenched her teeth and picked up the soap. After a while, her wounds stopped hurting.

The warm water, the steam, the darkness, were making her drowsy even before she'd soaped her skin and washed her hair. She dozed off while the soap bubbles were still glistening on the water in front of her.

The sound of the front door opening woke her. It slammed, shaking the entire house. She heard footsteps striding along the tiled hall. Heavy steps. The thud of low heels.

Neil was home.

This was not how she wanted to be found. She pushed herself up, trying not to disturb the water, not to make any sound. She swung one leg over the side before the water began to drip from her body and grabbed a towel.

The sound of a second set of footsteps — this time shrill and clipped — stopped her. Someone with high heels was following Neil along the hall. With the bathroom door open a fraction she could hear the rustling of coats being removed, of shoes being pulled off, then voices, confirming what she'd already guessed. Neil was downstairs, talking to a woman. And that woman was not a policewoman, because police officers did not remove their shoes when they entered people's houses.

She heard the suction of the fridge door, the chink of glasses, the sound of liquid being poured, and became acutely conscious of her own nakedness. She pulled on underwear, the trousers and cotton top, the thick socks, and had barely made herself presentable when they reached the top of the stairs. She put her hand on the bathroom door.

'I shouldn't be here,' said the female voice. 'She could turn up any time.'

As though the steam in the bathroom were amplifying sound, she heard the clink of a glass on a hard surface, a wardrobe door being opened.

'If she turns up, she turns up,' Neil said. 'I'm done sneaking around. Can we not talk about this for the rest of the evening?'

The sound of him drawing the curtains.

'Seems a bit brutal,' said the female. 'She's just lost her sister. Not to mention —'

'Yeah, I know.'

Silence in the bedroom.

'I should go,' said the female.

The bedsprings creaked.

'She won't come here,' said Neil. 'She'll head for that convent. That's obviously where she was going when they saw her in Wooler. She's always been close to those nuns. I wouldn't be surprised if she joins them herself one of these days.'

The bedsprings creaked again.

'Neil, we can't. Not now. No, I'm serious.'

Even behind the bathroom door, she could hear clothing being pulled off, and the quiet whimpers people make when they are kissing. She heard the bed protest again as they moved on it.

Holding her breath, she stepped to the door and through its gap caught a glimpse of the two people on the bed. Neil was still in his jeans, his torso and feet bare. The female was in red underwear. Clothes lay strewn across the carpet. On the cabinet by the door was a bottle of red wine and a glass. The phone was behind the bottle. If the woman had put the bottle down, Neil might not have seen his phone immediately behind it. He wouldn't have seen that she'd moved it.

The woman in the red underwear, who was slim with curly dark hair, had stopped moving. 'What was that?' she said.

Neil was kissing the side of her neck. 'What was what?'

'I heard something.'

Neil's head tilted upwards to reach the woman's ear. She half pushed him away. 'Neil, I think there's someone downstairs.'

He pushed back. 'Not possible.'

No, it wasn't possible. The intruder, the Peeping Tom, was upstairs, in the en suite bathroom, trying to pluck up enough courage to come out and say what needed to be said. There couldn't be another one downstairs. Could there? Suddenly very afraid, she stepped back, away from the bathroom door.

'I thought I heard the back door,' the woman on the bed insisted. 'Shit, it's Jessica.'

She hadn't locked the back door.

'I think you should check.'

'I can't walk downstairs, I'm so frigging hard. Feel this.'

A soft giggle, more subdued moaning.

The police, if they'd traced her, wouldn't enter a house surreptitiously, through the back door. They'd knock, loud and insistent, at the front. And she could hear something too, now. A quiet step as someone climbed the stairs.

A gasp, from the woman in the bedroom, sharp and shrill. Not quite a scream.

'What?' Neil said. 'What've I done? Aargh!'

A choking sound from Neil. Low, terrified wailing from his partner.

The sense of being removed from reality grew with every step she took. From the bedroom came more sounds, none of them reassuring. She stretched her neck, to see into the room through the inch-wide gap.

In the bedroom, not two metres from where she stood, was Patrick Faa. He'd taken off his leather jacket, his trilby, and

361

wore instead a simple white T-shirt. A rosary had been pushed around on his neck so that the cross hung down his back. There was a Celtic cross tattooed on his right bicep. The plaited-hair bracelet she'd noticed in the hay barn last night was on his left wrist where most men would wear a watch. In his gloved right hand he held a knife, with a gleaming red blade. At his feet lay the green jacket that half the country was on the lookout for, the one he'd found downstairs.

She couldn't see much beyond him, just the edges of the bed, and for that she was grateful. She could hear, though. The terrified wailing of the woman and a silence, from Neil, that was so much worse.

Faa moved, not taking his eyes off the bed, but edging closer to the bedroom door, as though to head off the woman's potential escape.

Neil was lying face down, motionless. He had to be dead. No one could lose that much blood and not be dead. It covered the bed, covered the half-naked woman huddled up against the pillows, had leapt high into the air, to reach the walls, the ceiling, even the curtains. Faa had cut through the main artery in Neil's neck, nothing else could explain how much blood he'd lost so quickly. He'd sneaked into the bedroom while the two of them were distracted, grasped Neil by the hair and sliced his throat almost in two. And now he was taking his time, staring at the rear view of the woman who was scrambling away, across the bed, down on to the carpet. Her legs wouldn't hold her up, she was clutching at the curtains, as though about to fling herself through the glass of the window.

Faa left the doorway, strode around the bed, carefully avoiding the blood that was already pooling on the carpet. Screams rang out as he caught hold of the woman by her hair. She fell to her knees, twisting away from him.

He thought the woman in the bedroom was her. He thought he was killing her.

She felt hard enamel pressing against the back of her knees as the screams stopped suddenly. She edged around the back of the tub to the sound of the woman keening, 'No, no, please God, no.'

The roll-top bath was freestanding, some six inches from the adjacent wall. By the time the last choking sound broke out, she'd stolen into the tiny space between them and was counting on the voluminous shower curtain to hide her. Closing her eyes tight, she willed herself to stay upright, to breathe steadily, not to ruffle the curtain.

People would have heard. There were houses either side, the walls couldn't be thick enough to disguise the sound of so much screaming. Neighbours would be looking at each other in surprise. In alarm.

Silence from the bedroom.

In the bathroom, a shrill, tiny splash as a drop of moisture fell from the curtain into the bathwater. The bathroom door was pulled open. The bedroom light framed his silhouette in the doorway. She could make out his head, his shoulders, even the knife. He seemed to be looking directly at her.

She heard his step on the tiles, the rustle of the curtains at the other side of the bath as he pushed them aside. She heard the water move as he dipped his hand into the bath, checking its temperature.

She heard him inhale a long, deep breath.

He turned. She heard him cross the bedroom, step heavily downstairs and then leave the house through the back door.

74

The steam-filled room, already dark, seemed to be losing light.

From the bedroom came a soft, low sound. On hearing it, she squeezed out from behind the bath. She would call an ambulance, use basic first aid, if it could be of any help at all. In the distance, sirens sounded. They might be nothing to do with her. They might be heading this way. She had to be sure. She would find a phone.

The bedroom was still dimly lit. Neil was lying face down on the bed. The woman was at its foot, collapsed over the green jacket, the wound on her throat gaping open like a hungry mouth. Neither looked alive.

That sound again. She watched a bubble of blood form in the woman's wound. It grew bigger, and burst. This woman wasn't alive. It was her dead body making these noises.

The knife Faa had used lay on the pale

grey carpet like a Hallowe'en prop, although it had probably once been a normal kitchen knife.

It *was* a normal kitchen knife. It had opened a brown envelope downstairs and then been left close to the worktop edge. She'd touched it herself, never dreaming the use to which it would soon be put.

How did he keep finding her? How did he always know where she was?

Another sound from behind. The wine bottle had been knocked over, was spilling out from the chest of drawers to the carpet. The glass Neil had been drinking from was blood spattered. So was his watch. His mobile phone was gone.

She looked back, at the dead people, the bloodstained room, the knife on the carpet.

A knife with her fingerprints on it.

She saw the green jacket, half hidden beneath the dead woman. She'd worn that jacket practically non-stop since early yesterday morning and now it was covered in another woman's blood.

The siren was drawing closer.

She grabbed the rucksack, heavier now that it contained the laptop. Downstairs, she pulled on hiking boots and a large jacket of Neil's. On impulse, she snatched up a packet of the Peanut Butter Cups and shoved them into a pocket. The torch beam caught her as she stepped into the alleyway. 'Police. Stay where you are.'

75

Patrick sat in his van, spraying antiseptic on his hands and wiping them with tissues. He'd found a Lidl carrier bag in his glove compartment and he dropped the soiled tissues and his bloodstained T-shirt inside it. He'd have liked to dump it in the street, even find a waste bin, but knew he was still too close to the house. It would be found.

He reached behind and found a sweater he'd brought from home when he'd had a feeling the day might get messy.

He'd barely started the engine when he heard the siren. Fifty metres away, a police car — lights flashing, siren blaring — crossed the top of the street. Then another. He opened his window a couple of inches and heard footsteps approaching fast.

A woman appeared from a nearby alley, running flat out. He recognized the hair straight away, the face a second later. This was Jessica Lane. How the hell? She paused for a second, then ran right, across the street, leaping up a wall and climbing a grassed bank. She was heading for the path that ran around the top of the city wall.

A third police car passed him and turned into the street ahead.

A few more seconds and a police officer, yelling into a radio, ran out of the alley. He stopped, hands on knees, to get his breath, then jogged to the street corner and shone his torch around. He found the woman, already almost at the top of the bank, and set off after her.

Lane reached the wall at the top of the bank and set off along the perimeter path, heading north towards the city.

Patrick knew the city of York. He knew the walls, he knew the limited official exits and entrances, and he knew that when Lane reached Station Road she'd almost certainly have to come down. He'd wait for her there. He started his engine, turned round slowly in the road as though he hadn't a care in the world, and then gradually picked up speed as he drove towards the river, wondering who the fuck he'd just killed in the house.

76

She ran without thinking, away from the torchlight, along the back of the terraced row.

'Police!'

She didn't stop. Across the street she saw a large white Transit van with a man in the driver's seat. Patrick Faa. She switched direction, ran across the street, over the low wall and on to the steep, grassed bank. Shouts below told her to stop. Instead, she scrambled up and pulled herself to the top.

Breathless, she reached the flagged footpath that ran along the upper reaches of the medieval stone wall. On one side was the grass bank she'd just scaled. On the other, a sheer drop.

Not far to the station. She could jump on a train, any train. Gulping in air, she set off. Past the house. Blue lights flashing in the corner of her eye. Indistinct figures in high-vis jackets gathering, banging on the door.

Neighbouring houses spilling cold, curious occupants into the street.

She risked a quick look back to see two men in uniform had scaled the bank. She ran faster. Over Micklegate Bar. On towards the western corner. She spun around it and could see the grand brick station. No way down.

Shouts from behind. Her pursuers weren't catching her up, but sooner or later she'd come to a dead end. After sunset, the wall was punctuated by locked gates. The police would radio ahead, have people waiting at the next gate. She had no choice but to get off the wall. She got ready to leap down and, at the last second, in the street directly below, saw the police car.

She set off again, conscious of the police car keeping pace as the floodlit towers of the Minster came into sight. All she could do was run on. And yet, ahead, blocking the path, was a black wrought-iron gate, nearly six feet high, with the white rose of York embossed on a red plaque. No way past.

Except for those with nothing to lose. She reached the gate and took a hold of it, put her left foot on the old iron lock and jumped. Her right foot found the cross rail on the railings. Keeping hold of the gate for balance, she swung her body around and dropped down on the other side. She set off again. Downhill this time. Easier.

77

The phone rang while Ajax was watching the last few minutes of the ten o'clock news. He had a glass of Scotch in his hand, the remains of a microwave dinner by his elbow. He'd been on the point of nodding off.

The voice was unfamiliar. A woman, late forties, Yorkshire accent. 'Superintendent Maldonado? DI Dickinson from North Yorkshire. I understand you've been looking for a Jessica Lane.'

He was instantly awake again. 'We have, yes.'

'She's here. In York. I'm standing outside her house now.'

'I thought we had a car outside that house?' MoJo had been lying on the sofa, her feet on Ajax's lap.

He held one finger to his lips. 'Is she in custody?' he asked.

'Not exactly. I'm sorry to tell you that she's dead.'

'Interesting. I thought she'd last longer than that,' said MoJo.

'Stabbed to death in her house,' Dickinson was saying. 'Along with her fiancé, Neil Fishburn. Neighbour heard screams and called us out. The bodies were still warm when we arrived.'

'So she went back home after all,' said MoJo.

'Superintendent Maldonado?' DI Dickinson was impatient, had other things to do.

'No, no, no, you cannot go out again,' said MoJo.

'I'm on my way,' said Ajax.

78

Under the shadow of Station Road bridge, Patrick trained his binoculars on the path. He thought he could see movement, a second later he was sure of it. She'd made good time. She was both fit and fast. She seemed on the point of breaking off the high path, making for the street, but she turned and ran on.

For a moment he felt sure she'd seen him. Then he spotted the police car cruising alongside the grassed bank. If she came down now, they'd pick her up. With some awe, he watched her scale the gate and realized there was actually a chance she'd get away. The police couldn't tail her any more in their car because ahead of this point the wall moved away from the road. Their next chance to pick her up would be at the river. Obviously aware of this, the police car pulled on to Station Road and turned right towards the Minster.

He'd be faster on foot. He jumped down, left the van where it was and ran for the bridge. The path ended at the river. She'd have to come down then. After a few metres he was breathing heavily. Unlike Jessica Lane, he wasn't used to running.

There was no sign of her on the bridge. The Ouse was high after all the recent rain and the squat, round Barker Tower with its cone-shaped slate roof was barely out of the water. Waves were lapping at the steps leading up to its raised door. The city wall at this point was turreted, elaborate. There were steps leading to the river, tiny alleys and dead ends. On the far side of the bridge, down near the water line, was a series of covered arches. Too many frigging hiding places. A police car passed him, pausing for a second in the traffic, before moving on.

The city ahead of him was busy with tourists, locals out for the evening, students, and the town centre bridges were always crowded. He tried to freeze out the people walking towards and away from him, looking for movement that stood out. She wouldn't be walking, she'd never have the nerve, not with the police after her. She'd be going faster than everyone else.

Seeing nothing, he made his way across

the river, checking quickly around the foundations of the Lendal Tower, continuing along Museum Street, as the railing of the bridge gave way to a stone wall.

Then he spotted a young couple on his side of the road staring over the wall into the museum gardens. They looked at each other. The girl shrugged. They'd seen something.

He heard heavy footsteps behind and stepped to one side to let the police run past. When they were out of sight at the opposite end of the bridge, he swung his legs over the park wall and dropped down.

Instantly the city changed for him. Sounds were softened, the smell of petrol fumes and wet tarmac was replaced by that of vegetation and earth. Much of the light was gone. He was conscious of the river, very close, the huge medieval arches of the Abbey ruins ahead, the Georgian splendour of the museum gardens. This wasn't a large park. So much the better.

The hunt was on.

He dropped to a crouch and took stock. There was still too much noise coming from the city for his hearing to be of much use. He'd have to rely upon spotting her. When fugitives knew the hunters were close, they hid, waiting for the danger to pass, giving themselves time to recover from the chase. Then they ran again. She was somewhere in here, not too far away, hiding, waiting for her chance.

He took a deep breath, willing his heartbeat to slow down, then breathed in deeply again, trying to catch a whiff of the floral scent he remembered from the bathroom. He couldn't track people using scent, not like Shinto, but it helped him become familiar with his surroundings and that was always useful.

He had to keep out of sight too, though, in case the police came back. A double hunt. Leaving the shadow of the wall he ran quickly, avoiding the path, knowing the crunch of gravel would give him away. He ran to a large tree and stood behind it so no one would see him from the road and his dark clothes would blend in from the park side. He waited.

She appeared after ten minutes, when he was beginning to think he'd missed her. Fifty metres further down the hill he caught sight of a slim figure dashing from a clump of bushes to round the back of the old building on the river's edge.

He jogged down the hill after her and stopped in the shadow of the building. It was Tudor style, rectangular, with a high-pitched roof. The lower storey was constructed of stone, the upper painted white with black beams. To his left, adjoining the main building, were much older ruins.

Heading left, he passed through an archway in the ruined wall to find the river only metres in front of him. No sign of her. Staying close to the walls, he crept towards the water, peering around the corner. Nothing. He leaned back against the wall, staring up at the night sky, thinking about his next move. Trying to predict hers.

Coming in here was an odd thing to do. Unexpected. Losing pursuers would have been easier in the old streets of the city. Maybe she was intending to double back, head for the station or the bus terminal, and had leapt into the gardens because she knew about all the trees, the bushes, the hiding places, figuring this was the best place to lose someone, without actually going very far.

And she'd already thrown off the police.

Smart girl. He liked hunting the smart ones.

Then his smile widened. He knew where she was. A few metres from where he stood, no longer serving any useful purpose but kept because of their historic value, were several heavy stone coffins. Some still had lids. She was lying in the darkness of one of them, gambling he wouldn't see her in the shadows, would be in too much of a hurry to check.

They were so close to the river here. He could hear it whispering to him. He could drag her to it, hold her head under the surface. She wasn't big enough to struggle hard, especially if he put his entire weight on her and pressed down. Then he'd let the river take her body.

There were five coffins. Two had lids, and she wouldn't be strong enough to have raised and lowered a stone lid. One was too shallow. That left two. He stepped closer and felt the warm glow in his belly grow cold as he realized he was hunting for his quarry in a coffin.

She'd already cheated death twice. Maybe there was something not quite natural about this girl. He crept closer still.

'Jessica,' he called. He couldn't resist it. They always freaked when he called their names like that, soft and low.

He looked around at the high white walls and pitched roof, at the ruined wall of the old building, the nearby trees, the slick black river. He didn't want to get too close to those coffins. And yet he had no choice.

He took a step. And another.

'Police! Stay where you are.'

A light shone in his face. Then another from the opposite direction.

'Put your hands up, put them where we can see them.'

Two police officers, both in high-vis jackets, were approaching from both sides.

'What's going on?' He did as he was told, thanking his lucky stars he'd changed his T-shirt in the van and cleaned his hands.

'Who are you and what are you doing here?' One of the officers was frisking him, running his hands down his body, his legs, around his waist.

'I'm meeting someone. That a frigging crime now?'

'This park's closed after dark.'

'Which is why I'm here. I thought I wouldn't be disturbed. You guys got any real villains to chase?'

Both officers stood facing him. 'What's your name? Got any ID on you?'

'Wallet in inner jacket pocket.' He raised both arms again to let them reach in and find his wallet.

'Mr Patrick Faa, of Kirk Yetholm.' The police officer read his driving licence with his torch. 'What's your business in York, Mr Faa?'

'Came to see a man about a horse.'

The officer looked around. 'I can't see a horse.'

'It was only good for the knacker's yard. I'm not a mug.'

'Who were you meeting here?'

'A gentleman doesn't kiss and tell.'

Stalemate. The two stepped to one side and talked to each other in low voices. Then a third copper appeared from the park, a fourth walked along the river. The park was lousy with the filth.

'OK, I'm guilty of hoping for an illicit shag with a married woman. Arrest me and let's get on with it, I'm fucking freezing.' He stuck his hand in his jeans pocket and pulled out the condom he always kept there. 'Either of you guys got a use for this, because I sure as hell don't any more.'

One of the officers stepped back, the other shone his torch around the building, the ruins, towards the river.

'Have you seen anyone else since you've been here?' the copper asked him.

'Not a soul. I heard your footsteps and I thought my luck was in. Just goes to show.'

His wallet was handed back. 'Seeing as how your date hasn't shown up, I don't think you'll mind coming down to the station to answer a few questions.'

He threw up his hands. 'You are fucking kidding me.'

'Walk this way, if you would, sir.'

One constable took hold of Patrick's upper arm. For a second, he was tempted to fight back. Then he realized what a mistake that would be. He was going to have to go quietly.

His mother would kill him.

79

She waited a long time. Even after Patrick Faa was led away, she stayed where she was. She kept her eyes closed and her body very still while the police officers wandered around the old Tudor building, shining one end of their torches into corners, poking the other into bushes. They spent ages peering into the Ouse as though she might be beneath its surface, breathing through a reed, waiting to emerge.

They didn't really look up. They didn't shine their torches into the tops of trees, into the high places. If they had done, they might have seen her.

By the time she was sure they'd gone, she had to force herself to move, to push away from the stone lining of the medieval window, to get down on to her haunches on the uneven and uncomfortable window ledge. To climb the fifteen feet down to the ground.

Three times now, he'd made the same mistake. He hadn't looked up. Not properly.

She didn't go back the same way she'd entered the gardens. She wasn't that stupid. Instead, she took the long route, past the Abbey ruins, behind the museum and over the wall into St Leonard's Place. Back in the city, she set off towards the bridge.

Faa had really, really pissed her off now.

She was done running.

80

Ajax gave his name to the uniformed officer controlling the crime scene and was allowed to walk down the street.

It was a row of terraced houses, once considered quite modest, now desirable city-centre residences. Each house was brick-built, with a porticoed front door and two tall, narrow windows. Tiny gardens at the front were edged in black railings. As he approached the house, several faces watched him from nearby properties.

A tall woman, her white Tyvek suit noticeably short on her ankles, strode out through the front door. Her hair was short and dark, her face heavy and plain. She looked at his warrant card.

'Did you know Jessica Lane?' she asked him. 'Had you met her?'

'I've been looking at photographs for two days now. And I saw the body of her sister earlier. By all accounts they were very alike.'

She looked him up and down. 'Better get suited up.'

He followed DI Dickinson down the narrow front hallway, past photographers and crime scene investigators, through the living room and into the kitchen. A small cloakroom stood off to one side of the back door.

'That's her coat,' said Ajax, as his eyes fell on the blue anorak hanging in the cloakroom. 'She borrowed it from a hiker.'

'Yeah, we thought so. OK, Alan, bag it. And the shoes.'

Beneath the blue coat were a pair of brogues. Covered in mud. Ruined.

'I was told someone would be watching this house, in case she returned,' Ajax said.

'We had cars doing drive-bys. We don't have the officers to keep someone outside twenty-four seven. Not for a missing persons case, which was all this was, up until now.'

'So what happened?'

'You'd better come upstairs.'

Ajax followed Dickinson back through the house, up the stairs and into the bedroom at the front. It looked, and smelled, like an abattoir. One of the bodies, the male, was already being moved into a body bag. The other lay face up on the carpet.

'This is how we found her,' said Dickson.

For a few seconds, Ajax could see nothing but blood. Then he forced himself to look past the gore to the features beneath. A woman in her mid-thirties, an attractive face, if perhaps a little horsey. The nose was prominent, the chin quite long. Her cheek-bones were thin, but her eyes had been large and blue. Her hair was dark brown, chin-length, curly, which had probably caused the confusion. She lay half covering a bloodstained green jacket.

'The coat looks familiar,' said Ajax. 'And there is definitely a superficial resemblance. But that's not Jessica.'

'No, we didn't think so,' said Dickinson. 'I didn't want to influence you one way or the other, but after I called you we found a woman's handbag downstairs with a number of credit cards belonging to a Zara Jenning. If you ask me to guess, I'd say your Ms Lane got home, bit stressed after her experience, found her fiancé having sex with another woman and flipped.'

'Well,' said Ajax, 'at least I know why she ran this time.'

81

Patrick couldn't stay in York any longer. Already he'd be cutting it fine. He left the police station and half jogged, half walked to his van.

They'd detained him for longer than they should, but not as long as they could have done. Small mercies. Coppers were always looking for a chance to pin one on the pikey bastards, but in the end they had no reason not to believe his story about being in the park to meet a girlfriend. And as for what had happened in the south-western corner of the city this evening, they were looking for someone slim and fast, almost certainly female, not a short stocky bloke.

He got back to the van to find he hadn't locked it. He climbed in, started the engine and headed out of the city. In less than two hours he was on the outskirts of Newcastle. Another hour and he was turning into the small harbour south of Berwick-upon-

Tweed. He drove all the way down to the sea wall.

The tide was up, sending black waves high into the air, filling the world with oily salt-water droplets. A cold wind was coming in off the North Sea and the sky was a swirling mass of black clouds.

His Uncle Tommy was waiting for him. A few men hung around in the shadows. The boat had already docked. He put the van into reverse, backed down the slipway and then watched in the wing mirror as a group of six people left the cabin of the boat, stepped to shore, and climbed into the back of his van. He felt the vehicle rock as each clambered inside, heard the shuffling and the grunts as they tried to find somewhere verging on comfortable for the journey ahead. He kept his eyes on the slipway as his uncle closed the doors and vanished into the night. Not a word had been said. Patrick started the engine and pulled away, thinking the van felt heavy, even allowing for the six extra bodies it was now carrying.

Actually, there were seven people in the back of the van. One of whom had slipped inside the unlocked doors while Patrick had been detained by the police in York, and who lay now, curved around the front right wheel arch, out of sight beneath a dirt-encrusted horse blanket.

As one of the others in the van, a woman, began to croon in a low-pitched voice, she closed her eyes.

82

Two months earlier

The cluster of singing nuns moved out of the garden of reflection and repose at Wynding Priory and made their way back towards the convent building, their voices fading as they gained greater distance from the group they'd left behind.

In the garden, placed around the central shrine to the Holy Mother, were two semi-circular stone seats that allowed several sisters at once to sit and pray. The garden was also a favourite spot for the convent's peacocks, although they preferred to perch on the walls, still as statues, staring unblinkingly down at those who walked and sat below.

Jessica had never been in the garden without an audience of the birds and never failed to find it unnerving. On the other hand, the colours and the scents, especially on a summer evening, made it one of her favourite places in the convent. On the central stone seats, she and eight of the sisters were huddled together. Sister Serapis was stroking the head of a large peacock that she'd previously introduced as Peacoat.

'So, Sister Eugenia was bang on the money with her suggestion about a computer search combining the terms black people and organ donation,' Jessica said. 'Because, thanks to her, I found a little girl called Aayat Akel.'

A couple of the sisters' lips moved, as though they were trying the foreign name out for themselves.

'Aayat died in a car accident on the outskirts of Liverpool,' Jessica went on. 'She was with her parents, in the family convertible, top down, on the way home from Chester Zoo. This all happened late last year, although I didn't find out about it until March. Anyway, Aayat released her seat belt. Her parents didn't notice. When the father had to brake hard to avoid an animal on the road, a cat I think, although that was never confirmed or the animal found, Aayat — well, I'm sure you can imagine. She was thrown some distance and fatally wounded.'

Distress was visible on every face around

her. Except that of Isabel.

'The police were called, the road was closed, Aayat and her mother were flown by air ambulance to the nearest hospital, but the little girl was pronounced dead on arrival,' Jessica finished the story.

'And how was this of interest to you?' Sister Tabitha asked.

'Her parents offered to donate her organs,' said Isabel. 'Just offered them up, as in, "Anybody want these?" Sorry to interrupt, but I've heard this before.'

'Goodness,' said Tabitha.

'That's actually quite rare,' Jessica said. 'And they didn't seem to be showing much emotion. So the Senior Registrar acted on his instincts and phoned the police. Unfortunately, while he was still waiting for them, he made the mistake of asking Aayat's parents for identification.'

'They didn't have any?' guessed Sister Belinda, a small, rotund nun in her fifties.

'They had plenty. The father offered a driving licence, the mother a passport, according to which she was a British citizen, born in Jordan. The father showed the doctor photographs of his family taken on his phone. The mother produced the child's donor card. It all looked above board but felt a bit too —'

'Easy?' suggested Tabitha. 'Planned?'

'Exactly. The registrar left the parents in the family room and took their ID to his office. When the police arrived and he took them to the parents, they were gone. The driving licence and passport turned out to be fake. A different family entirely lived at the address the couple had given. A twelve-year-old girl called Aayat Akel was on the transplant database, but the police could find no evidence of her birth or life prior to the accident. Her so-called parents still haven't been found.'

'Could it perhaps have been a family of illegal immigrants who panicked when the doctor started checking ID?' Sister Florentina, one of the keenest gardeners, had been gathering fat pink roses. She waved them around when she spoke, and Jessica, sitting close, kept catching their rich, musky scent.

'So they left their daughter behind?' Belinda looked shocked.

'Their dead daughter,' Isabel reminded them. 'Maybe sentiment doesn't last too long when you're desperate. What happened to the child? To her body, I mean?'

'Still in the mortuary,' said Jessica. 'At some point she'll have to be cremated, if she isn't claimed.'

'But we have no idea who this child really

was, or whether the couple with her were actually her parents?' Florentina asked.

'No, it's still an open case,' Jessica replied.

Sister Belinda leaned forward. 'But the child could have been already dead or, technically, brain-dead, when her so-called parents put her in the car. Whatever killed her originally, let's say it was a head wound, would have been disguised by the more recent injury.'

'Not so,' Sister Eugenia jumped in. 'A pathologist can differentiate fresh wounds from less recent ones. The body starts healing itself immediately and signs of the healing process are manifest during post-mortems.'

All heads turned to Eugenia. She gave an exaggerated shrug. 'I watched five episodes of *Silent Witness* on catch-up when you all had the flu last winter.'

'I did wonder that myself,' said Jessica. 'But, first up, Sister Eugenia is right, and second, people who are brain-dead are kept alive artificially. If there'd been life-support machines in the back of that convertible, I think the motorway police would have spotted them.'

'They didn't spot the cat,' said Sister Tabitha.

Up on the walls, one of the peacocks gave

a sharp cry and spread its tail. All nine women looked towards it, the nuns with smiles of pride. Jessica suppressed a shudder.

Isabel was sitting opposite Jessica. 'How long would someone live after being taken off life support?' she asked.

Jessica shook her head. 'You'd have to ask a doctor that, not a detective.'

'My mother lasted three days,' said Sister Alfreda. 'And she was ninety-eight.'

Sister Belinda had been staring down at her feet. 'There could have been signs that would prove the brain had been inactive for several days before the child's death, but the — what do they call those doctors who cut open dead bodies?'

'Pathologists,' said Sister Eugenia.

'Yes, thank you. Well, the pathologist wouldn't think to look for them. Why would he? Jessica, you say the child is still at the hospital. He could carry out a second post-mortem, couldn't he?'

'I'm sure he could, but I don't have the authority to request one.'

Sister Basilia had been silent up to now. She raised a hand. 'Illegal immigrants driving a convertible?'

Jessica turned to her. 'Yes, I thought that too. And guess what, the police haven't been able to trace the car.'

'But what would be the point?' said Isabel. 'Even if the accident was staged, if the so-called parents deliberately killed the child so that they could offer up her organs, even if there was someone seriously ill in a nearby hospital more than willing to pay a fortune, that child's organs would still go into the system. They could end up anywhere.'

'Not necessarily,' said Jessica.

'What do you mean?'

Jessica looked round at eight eager, worried faces. And the curious reptilian stare of the peacocks. 'I think these people are playing the system, making it work for them. I think —'

'Good evening, Sisters.'

More than one of the nuns jumped. Three of the younger ones got to their feet.

'You missed a highly entertaining episode of *The Big Bang Theory* when Sheldon and Howard got into an altercation about a parking spot at the university. Sheldon was reluctant to cede one of the perks of office, in spite of having no interest in driving or owning a car. Amy left her own car there to deter Howard, and Bernardette had it towed. Penny sustained an accidental injury to her nose.'

These women had a remarkable ability to

close their faces, thought Jessica. Each of the nuns appeared to be lost in thought. Only Isabel held eye contact with her superior.

'Also, I thought you might appreciate a reminder that recreation hour finishes in five minutes. That it usually takes at least that time to get the peacocks to bed. And that a state of considerable excitement is an unwise preparation for a return to the great silence.'

With mutterings of 'Yes, Mother', 'Of course, Mother', the sisters all got to their feet and turned to leave the garden.

'One moment, Sister Maria Magdalena, and Jessica. Stay behind, if you please.'

The three women waited until the other nuns had left the garden, until they heard the chirruping sound Sister Serapis made when she was calling the peacocks home to roost.

Hildegard said, 'This case of yours is disturbing the sisters, Jessica.'

'In Jessie's defence, they followed us in here. They asked her about it,' said Isabel.

'Jessica has no need of a defence, Sister. I am accusing her of nothing.'

Isabel's voice was clipped. 'My apologies.'

'We live apart from the outside world for a reason,' said Hildegard. 'Our minds are free, unfettered by the constraints of what is going on around us, to bring us closer to God. Jessica, I cannot expect you to understand this, but Sister Maria Magdalena has been part of our community for over twenty years now. She knew, as few others would, of the disturbing impact that talk of such matters can have.'

'Begging your pardon, Mother —'

Hildegard held up a hand. 'Don't bother, Sister. I know exactly what you're about to say. I am at fault for encouraging you to share the news of Jessica's work with the other sisters. I hardly expected they would take to it with such relish. But now I'm bringing it to a close. Jessica, it would be better if you didn't visit here again for some time.'

'Mother Hildegard, is that really necessary? I completely understand your concerns. I won't talk about my work any more. Not even with Bella — I mean, with Sister Maria Magdalena.'

'My dear, my fondness for you has left me blind to the distraction you present. You will always be welcome here, but it would be a kindness on your part to leave Sister Maria Magdalena to her reflections for a while.'

Isabel's eyes were on the ground. Her face set tight.

'Sister has a birthday at the end of the summer,' Hildegard said. 'An important one. I'm sure by then she will be ready to welcome you back.'

Isabel's birthday was in September. Nearly eight weeks away.

'That little matter you discussed with me last time you were here.' Hildegard stopped on the path and turned back to Jessica. 'That surprise you had in mind to celebrate our sister's birthday?'

'You said you'd think about it,' Jessica said, as Isabel gave her a puzzled frown.

'Well, I've thought about it, and I think it would be a good idea. Something to look forward to.'

The bell began to toll. 'And silence comes for us again,' said Hildegard. 'You can see yourself out, dear, can't you? Goodbye, until September.'

83

Thursday, 21 September
The people sharing her space in the back of the van were mainly women, she thought, but occasionally she caught the lower tones of a man, or the squeak of a very young child. The soundtrack for the journey became one of heavy breathing, coughing, clearing of throats, the occasional word or two in a language she didn't recognize.

She could smell them — sweat, urine, vomit, soiled nappies — stale smells that spoke of captivity and degradation. Not so very long ago she'd soaked in a floral-scented bath. It was possible that they could smell her too, that they'd already spotted the odd-shaped lump under the blanket and were on the point of pulling it up and exposing her.

A child cried. His mother crooned. Faa banged on the cab and yelled for quiet. The child cried on and on, until it seemed that her head had always been filled with the sound of a young child crying.

84

Seventeen months earlier
Sister Belinda spotted Jessica and Isabel in the window seat of the recreation room and marched across. She stopped directly in front of Jessica and pushed forward her ample bosom. There was a badge pinned to her right breast that read *Ask Me About My New Grandson.*

'Hey, Sister Belinda, what's new with you?' Jessica teased.

'Max Lionel Hartnell, seven pounds, three ounces, born at ten fifty-five in the morning on the fifth of May.'

'I expect you have a picture or two?' Jessica said.

Belinda fished inside her habit — Jessica was never entirely sure how nuns' clothes were put together — and handed the photograph over.

'Oh, he's beautiful. Isabel, look at his little fists. And his nose. How can that nose be real? Bella, look.' Jessica held the picture out to her sister.

'I've seen it.' Isabel didn't move, didn't even look.

'Have you been to see him yet?' Jessica asked Belinda.

'I'm sure his parents will bring him when he's old enough to travel.' Sister Belinda's voice had flattened. Her smile faded as Isabel stood up, silently, and moved across the room.

'Bella!' Jessica caught up with her sister in the vegetable garden of the priory. 'What's up?'

'Nothing.' Isabel bent to snap a dried flower-head off its stalk. 'But you have to remember that child is four days old now and the rest of us have heard of nothing else since he pushed his way out into the world. And it wasn't very tactful to ask about visiting. You know we don't leave here except in exceptional circumstances.' She straightened up and set off down the narrow gravel path.

Jessica followed close behind. 'Sister Belinda has left two children and several grandchildren for the sake of her faith,' she told the back of her sister's head. 'It can't be easy for her.'

'Belinda's children are adults.' Isabel seemed weary of the conversation. 'And she probably sees more of them than lots of mothers do their grownup families. I assure you, no one need feel sorry for her.'

'This isn't like you.'

Isabel paused on the gravel. 'I've lived here since I was eighteen, Jessica. Maybe you don't know the real me any more.'

'I don't believe that.'

Her sister carried on walking. 'Suit yourself.'

Jessica let Isabel get half the path ahead, then set off after her again. Her heart was beating fast. She was going to do it before she chickened out again. She was going to ask her.

'When you were sixteen, you went away and I didn't see you for months.' Nervousness made her voice louder than necessary. 'Where did you go? I know you didn't come here. Not then.'

Isabel had reached the corner and swivelled on the spot ninety degrees to head back to the house. 'It was a very long time ago, I hardly remember those days.'

'Rubbish. Were you pregnant?'

Isabel kept on walking.

'Is that why you can't bear even to talk about babies? Were you pregnant with his child?' Jessica stopped, taken aback by the enormity of what had occurred to her. 'Jesus wept, I can't even begin — Bella, did you have an abortion?'

When Isabel turned again, her eyes were shining and her face clenched tight. Jessica had never seen such a look on her sister's face before. For a second, she thought Isabel might hit her. Then her face relaxed and Jessica caught a glimpse of how her sister might look as an old woman.

'No, Jessica.' Isabel gave a long, heavy sigh. 'I did not have an abortion. I'm a devout Catholic, remember?'

85

Friday, 22 September
The van travelled on. The baby allowed itself to be soothed. Someone leaned against her. Another child, she thought, someone light. She felt his warmth through the blanket, felt him wriggle into a comfortable position. Then his head settled down on her hip and he gave a sleepy little sigh. Now she couldn't move at all, because he would feel her beneath him.

They drove for what she guessed was another twenty minutes, and she could tell from the speed of the vehicle and the smoothness of the ride that they were still on the A1. Then the van slowed and turned in a wide, sweeping bend as they left the main road behind.

She'd known when she climbed into the van that Patrick Faa would almost certainly drive back north, and so it had proven. They would be heading inland now, towards the

National Park and the Scottish border. Towards where the balloon had taken off and come down. She closed her eyes, tried to zone out the pain of being pressed against ridged metal. She tried not to think about the growing nausea and told herself it wouldn't be long now. Not long now.

The vehicle slowed almost to a crawl as the road deteriorated. They bounced over potholes and, had it not been for the alarmed cries from the other passengers, someone would surely have heard her whimper in pain as her shoulder banged hard against metal.

They stopped. The murmuring hushed. She heard voices outside the van, in English, but too fast to catch any of the words, and then the grinding of metal over tarmac as gates opened. The van pulled forward, turned, travelled on a few more metres and stopped.

People were waiting for them. She heard more voices, footsteps drawing closer, the barking of a dog. This was where it could all go terribly, terribly wrong.

The van doors were pulled open. Passengers began to get up. They'd fallen silent again, sullen and scared. The baby cried. Beneath the horse blanket she held her breath.

When the last passenger had jumped down, the doors were slammed shut.

She pushed herself up, ignoring the shooting pains that ran up her legs, and, keeping hold of the blanket, crawled towards the doors. When she risked lifting her eyes above the lower rim of the rear window she saw a junkyard. Bare electric bulbs had been strung around the site, creating dirty pools of light in the darkness. There were piles of rubbish everywhere.

The passengers from the van were being herded towards a large old farmhouse about fifty metres away. Dark-haired men and women surrounded them. At least two of the men held the leads of German shepherds. The dogs barked. Several of the bystanders followed the van's passengers into the farmhouse. Others hung around, talking quietly together.

The yard they were in was enclosed by a high wire fence and a towering wall of old cars. Junk was everywhere: old fridges, washing machines, stuff overflowing from huge metal skips. In a semicircle around the house, like wagons from the Wild West, stood several caravans. There were lights in most of them, some had garish fairy lights strung around the windows. One had been completely burned out.

They didn't lock the van. They probably figured they didn't need to, seeing that the compound they were in was fenced and they had guard dogs. In twos and threes, the people of this odd community returned to their caravans. Lights went out. Quiet fell over the site. She waited as long as she dared, and some more. Then she opened the van door.

Nothing happened. No one yelled. No dog barked. She closed the door, and slipped round to the driver's door.

Before the vehicle left York, she'd already checked beneath the front seats and in the glove compartments. She checked again, but found nothing. Neil's phone, if it was still in Faa's possession, was probably in the pocket of his leather jacket and she'd taken a huge risk for nothing.

On the other hand, she was a whole lot closer to where she needed to be.

Leaving the van, she crept across the gravel. Amidst the rubbish, she could see echoes of the community's Romany past. A painted wooden chest here, an enormous caravan wheel there. Hanging from a cast-iron lamppost was the carcass of a deer, its dead eyes gleaming in the moonlight as she walked past.

She passed a massive cairn of stones that formed a shrine for the Holy Mother. A statue of Mary stood patient and sad before it, a scattering of plastic flowers at her feet. The plaster had chipped from her face below one eye, making it look as though the statue were weeping.

In the shadow of the farmhouse, feeling less exposed, she let herself look around. The site was bigger than she'd pictured from the limited visibility of the van. It stretched back, away from the road, filled with the dying shells of cars. They lay in rows, piled high, reaching back towards the woods in the distance. There were dozens, maybe hundreds, of old cars on this site and every pair of headlights looked like eyes.

She set off again, this time following the line of the fence that ran along the road, keeping to the shelter of the hollowed-out cars. After a few metres, her heart sank. Directly ahead, she could see the close weave of the wire fence. It had turned a corner. She pressed on, needing to be sure.

Twenty metres further, by a skip pushed close to the road, was a collection of discarded bicycles. Some were missing wheels, some had no handlebars, but a few looked to be in working order. A bike would cut her journey time in more than half.

She chose one that looked about her size and dragged it with her, until she reached the corner and saw that the fence did, indeed, encircle the site. She was trapped.

Her options were fast running out. If she stayed where she was, she'd be found by the dogs in the morning. She could climb back in the van and wait for it to be driven out of the site. Or keep walking along the line of the fence, hoping to find a gap. Maybe even tunnel underneath.

The last seemed the only sensible option. She set off again, pushing the bike when she could, carrying it when she couldn't. A night bird screeched and then an answering scream, that sounded more human than animal, seemed to come from the farmhouse.

Ahead, there was a car pushed right up against the fence, one she couldn't walk around. She picked up the bike and put it on the roof of the car before climbing through. On the other side, something caught her eye.

A piece of fabric, about four feet from the ground, had snagged on the fence. In the daylight it would probably be a bright emerald green, possibly the exact colour of the jacket she'd been wearing all yesterday. It was a scrunchie, the sort of thing women used to keep long hair back from their faces. When she touched the material it felt soft and damp. She tucked it into the pocket of her coat and saw a way out.

There was a way out.

The fence had been clipped through, from the ground to about four feet up, at the exact point she'd found the scrunchie, and then fastened back together again with a length of wire. From a distance, especially at night, no one would spot it. She'd have missed it herself if the scrunchie, with its old memories, hadn't caught her attention.

Ten minutes later she was through. Then she only had to push the bike through the mud of the nearby field, lift it over a gate and she was on the road. An hour later she was at the pub car park where she and her sister had left their car, two mornings ago. The keys were still in her rucksack.

86

She left the car a mile from the convent and travelled the last part of the journey by bike, riding past the gated main entrance and on down the road to the farm that, centuries ago, had belonged to the Carmelites. She cycled up the farm track, not worrying about the dogs, who might bark initially, but who knew her scent. They only looked at her with mild curiosity as she went past, their eyes closing again before she was out of sight.

To the rear of the farmhouse was an old path that led directly to the priory. She parked the bike in the sheds by the convent's one and only car. It was nearly three in the morning, and all the nuns would be asleep, or trying to sleep. Shortly after four they would be up for morning prayers.

To the rear of the kitchens was a lean-to shed where the nuns kept their outdoor boots and gardening aprons. By moving a waste bin right up to it, she could climb on to the window ledge and then its flat roof. From there, it was a matter of using the crenellated stonework as a ladder, to take her up to a ledge that ran around the second storey.

The ledge was wide enough to stroll around, although she didn't quite have the nerve to do that. She stepped sideways, her back to the wall, her hands feeling and counting each window frame. The ninth was the sisters' bathroom and the old window hadn't been repaired in years. It opened easily and the familiar smell of sour, wasted femininity hit her. She lowered the rucksack to the floor and climbed in after it.

The room, or cell, in which a nun known as Sister Maria Magdalena had slept the night before the balloon crash was on the opposite side of the corridor, two doors down. She pushed the door open carefully.

It was empty. Completely empty. All trace of its former occupant had been removed. Even the bed was bare of its sheets and blankets.

It didn't matter. All she needed was time and privacy. She sat down on the bed, put her feet up and opened the laptop.

87

Two months earlier

Adar Nasser's body was thin, twisted out of its true line, as though someone had pulled tight her internal strings, distorting limbs, bending the spine, crooking the neck. She was staring up at the ceiling of the hospital room and each blink of the lashless lids seemed to make her eyes less lustrous. She looked like a corpse that death had over-looked. Jessica approached slowly.

Adar's care was low tech. She could breathe unaided. She had a tube connected to her stomach that dripped nutrition in and another plumbed into her bladder. The bed was raised to prevent fluids gathering in her lungs.

Five months ago, Adar had tried to take her own life. She'd climbed to the roof of a four-storey apartment block in Derby and jumped. Landing among rubbish bags, she'd broken her neck and spine in two places and suffered a significant head injury. Her left fibula and tibia were fractured, her wrist broken and eight ribs cracked. Internal injuries included a ruptured spleen, traumatic contusions to her heart and lungs, and traumatic tearing of her bowel.

Footsteps alerted Jessica to the presence of a nurse.

'You can go and sit with her,' he said. 'She responds to visitors.'

'The report said she'd suffered brain damage,' Jessica said.

'We don't know how bad the damage is because the tests we can do are limited,' the nurse replied. 'She talks, just doesn't make much sense.'

'And no memory of the accident? She hasn't told anyone why she did it?'

'Not that I'm aware of.'

'Any sign of her family?'

He shook his head.

Shortly after Adar's arrival in A&E, her father and brother had pitched up. They'd stayed with her for twenty-four hours. When they'd been told their relative was out of danger for the time being, they'd left to go home, shower and eat. They'd never returned.

'Did she carry a donor card?'

The nurse looked shocked. 'There's no

question of that, I'm afraid. She may be very badly injured but —'

'I understand. I have a particular reason for asking. Do you know if she carried a card?'

'I can check.' He walked behind the desk at the nurses' station and peered at the computer. A moment later, he looked up. 'She did.'

A beeping sounded. The nurse pulled a monitor out of his pocket. 'I'm wanted.'

Jessica walked across and took a seat by Adar's bed. 'Adar.' She held up her warrant card. 'I'm a police officer.'

Adar flinched but didn't even look at Jessica or the card.

'Can you tell me your name?'

No response.

'Is it Adar? Or something else entirely?'

'No police. Going to Yellow House.'

'Yellow House?' Jessica leaned forward. 'Adar, where's the Yellow House?'

'Any luck?'

Jessica turned to see the nurse had reappeared. 'She seemed agitated when I mentioned the police.'

'Yes, we had an incident when some uniformed officers came to talk to her. We think she might be here illegally.'

'She doesn't have any documents?'

'Nope. Her relatives disappeared and haven't been seen since. There's no one to ask.'

'Any possessions? A phone?'

'Actually, that does ring a bell.' The nurse spun on his heel. 'Give me a second.'

Jessica watched him stride back to the nurses' station and lean behind it. He tapped away on the computer keyboard for a few seconds.

'Thought so,' he said when he returned. 'One of her relatives left a phone behind. It slipped down behind the bed. We hung on to it for a while, then we handed it over to the police.'

'Has she ever mentioned the Yellow House to you?'

He shook his head. 'Yellow what?'

The detective constable with Derbyshire Constabulary CID leaned back on his chair and scratched the side of his head. 'Yep, I took it from the ward. Handed it over to the technical guys to see if they could get anything off it.'

'And did they?'

'No idea. I got moved on to another case.'

'Can you find out?' Jessica asked.

His eyes narrowed, then he sighed. 'I suppose I can make a couple of phone calls.'

She resisted the temptation to hand him his desk phone. 'I'd appreciate it.'

While the detective was on the phone, Jessica looked out of the window, waiting for the banter to be concluded, for the nods and grunts and fixed stares in her direction to be done with. Finally, he put the phone down and turned to face the other side of the room.

'Jez. Seven twenty on the fifteenth. Bring the gear. Yeah, right.'

Jessica was on the point of clearing her throat when he seemed to remember her presence. He turned back to his desk and picked the phone up again. 'It's gone.'

'Gone where?'

'Northumbria Police claimed it. They signed it out a couple of weeks ago.'

Northumbria? *The north is a bad place.* Northumbria was hours away. She couldn't possibly get there today and one day was all she'd been given. 'Why would Northumbria want it?'

He gave her a *How should I know* look. 'Something to do with a case they had that sounded similar. They thought she might be from their neck of the woods.'

'Who? Who in Northumbria?'

'I think there must be some mistake,' said

the voice down the phone line. 'I haven't been anywhere near Derby this year.'

Jessica sat in her car watching the rain on the windows blot out the outside world. 'I'm at Derbyshire Constabulary HQ now,' she said. 'They told me you collected a mobile phone left behind by a suspected illegal immigrant. That you were dealing with a similar case.'

'When was this?'

Jessica gave the date.

'Nope, definitely not me. I was on a training course that day. I'm looking at my diary now. A dozen people can vouch for me.'

'You're definitely Paul Roderigues?'

'Last time I checked.'

'Anyone there with a similar name? Of the same rank?'

'Not that I know of.'

The sisters lay side by side on the coarse beach towels that Jessica had thrown over the damp sand. Isabel's cloak covered their naked bodies. Above them, the night sky was clear. The tide was high, the waves whispered gently a few feet away.

'So who's lying?' Isabel said. 'Roderigues or Derbyshire Constabulary?'

Jessica pressed closer to her sister's cold skin, felt the crustiness of the sea salt scratching between them. 'I'm inclined to think neither. It's too easy to check up on both of them.'

'So how can a piece of evidence disappear?'

'Oh, you'd be surprised. But if you want my best guess, I'd say someone borrowed Roderigues's warrant card that day. Or faked something up to look like his, counting on the evidence handler at Derbyshire Constabulary not checking too thoroughly.'

'So, definitely someone from Northumbria, but not Roderigues.'

'Looks like it. There's another reason I think there's something going on up here.'

'Nobody wants to go to the northern ports? The Eritrean family supposedly being sent to the north?'

'Well, that too, but as I was sitting in my car outside Derbyshire HQ, trying not to break something I was that mad, I started flicking back through my notes.'

Jessica glanced sideways to make sure that Isabel was still listening. She was.

'When someone is admitted to hospital, basic information is taken: name, address, age, history of allergies, name and address of general practitioner. So, Adar Nasser's GP is a Dr Brown of New Chapel Surgery, High Street, Banbury.'

'A GP in the south-east? Even though Adar was supposed to live in Derby?'

'It's not that uncommon. People move, and then don't change their GP until they get sick. So the hospital staff didn't question it.'

'Well, that's it then. You contact the GP, they'll have patient records. You can find out who she really is.'

Jessica smiled. 'I thought of that. Even Derbyshire police thought of that. Turns out there is no such GP's practice. There was a Roger Brown, who retired in 1996, but he's never practised in Banbury. According to Google, there is no doctor's surgery on the High Street of Banbury.'

'So Adar's relatives lied. Just invented a GP, choosing a common English name?'

'That's what Derbyshire have concluded.'

'Not you, though?'

'Not me, though, because I remembered seeing Aayat Akel's hospital records too, and I was pretty certain John Brown in Banbury rang a bell.'

'Both cases claimed the same non-existent GP?'

'Exactly.'

Isabel pushed herself upright and cold air blew on Jessica's skin. 'But that's what you've been looking for. Proof that something is going on. And at least a strong suggestion that something isn't right at Northumbria Police.'

Jessica sat up too and reached for her coat. She pulled it around her shoulders. 'Oh, we've got more than that,' she said. 'Adar's GP details included an email address, because communication between hospitals and GP surgeries is electronic these days. So, I had a word with our IT people, and we sent an email, making it look as though it had come from a Derby hospital, to Dr Brown of Banbury. Nothing to raise suspicions. Just a request for allergy information. We got a *Surgery Is Closed* notice pinged back five seconds later.'

'End of line?'

'Not at all. Do you know what an IP address is?'

'Should I?'

'It's a number that's unique to every computer, basically every device that connects to the Internet. The computer in Hilda's office will have one. If we need to trace a particular computer, under the Regulation of Investigatory Powers Act we can request the Internet Service Provider to give us the actual address of the IP address. Are you following me?'

Isabel nodded.

'The computer that responded to us on Dr Brown's behalf is somewhere in the head office of Northumbria Police.'

'Wow.'

'The ISP can't tell us which computer, out of the several hundred that are in there, but the force's internal IT department will be able to.'

'So what are you going to do?'

'Well, to use a police cliché, there are several lines of inquiry that we can now follow. We're going to be working with the Transplant Database to check that every organ donor in the last three years was a real person and not someone like Aayat and Adar who were admitted under rather weak fake identities.'

'That could take a while.'

'We'll start with donors from Asia, India and the Middle East. There won't be that many of those.'

'That will just prove there's a problem, though, won't it? It won't find who's responsible.'

'True. We could issue a formal request to Northumbria's IT department to trace the actual machine that sent the email. The problem with that is, if it fails, we've let the cat out of the bag.'

'How could it fail?'

'Our guy could work in the IT department, in which case he'll be able to cover his tracks. Or whoever's doing it could be using more than one computer, in case of exactly this eventuality.'

'What else?'

'We've begun a low-key operation. Someone has started work at Northumbria Police headquarters. Just to see how the land lies.'

'That someone being you?'

Jessica said nothing.

'Is it dangerous?'

'No, of course not.'

Isabel's lips clamped tight. She turned away, gazing out across the sea to where the moon had appeared from behind a cloud. It was a few seconds before she spoke again. 'Do you ever think, Jess, that we swapped places?'

'What on earth do you mean?'

The moon cast a silver path across the water, and its light glowed on Isabel's white face. 'You were always the timid one,' she said, without turning round. 'The one who struggled to keep up, who'd barely say boo to a goose.' She glanced at Jessica and smiled. 'Now look at you.'

It was on the tip of Jessica's tongue to say, *And look at you too, Bella. What happened to you?* 'Actually, what I wonder is what the two of us could achieve if we worked together,' she said instead.

'I thought we did.' Isabel's brows contracted. She sounded hurt.

'We do, of course, you're a great help, but that kind of makes it worse. I look at you and I see so much waste.'

Isabel looked back across the sea. 'That's because you're seeing the situation from an entirely worldly point of view. We believe that there is no more worthwhile way of spending a life than in growing closer to God.'

Isabel could have been reading from a textbook.

'Well, that would be fine, Bella, if you believed in God. But I know for an absolute fact that you don't and you never did.'

Isabel closed her eyes and breathed in deeply. Then she threw back her cloak and began looking around for her clothes.

Jessica knew she'd gone too far. She opened her mouth to apologize, when Isabel turned back, her black habit clutched against her. 'So, what's my surprise?' she asked, in a voice so full of fun that the last few minutes might not have happened.

'You do understand the meaning of the word surprise, don't you?'

'The sisters are running a sweepstake.

Sister Belinda thinks you've got tickets to the *Sound of Music* at Newcastle's Theatre Royal. She's willing to share the entire pot with me if I can talk my way on to the stage during a crowd scene.'

'They're winding you up. They know exactly what I have planned. You need to be ready at four a.m. on the twentieth.'

Isabel gave a soft laugh. 'Four in the morning? Where are we going?'

'Not far.'

'What do I wear?'

'Seriously?' Jessica looked at her watch. 'Come on. You need to get back. If Hilda catches you out skinny-dipping, and me on the premises after being expressly forbidden, you'll be eighty before we can talk about a birthday celebration again.'

They stood and began pulling on clothes.

'Jess,' said Isabel, when her black habit took away her form, making her white face seem to be floating in the moonlight. 'You will be careful, won't you?'

'I'll be invisible,' said Jessica. 'Just like the old days.'

88

Tuesday, 19 September (three days earlier)
Cleaners were invisible, thought Jessica, as she ticked the chart on the wall of the second-floor ladies' and carried her bucket back on to the corridor. People paid no more attention to the cleaners than they did to the colour of the walls, or the placement of the light switches, or the times the central heating clicked on. They were background noise. They'd be missed, soon enough, when the waste-paper baskets spilled over and the sticky circles on desks started to gather dust, but as long as the carpets got swept and the bins emptied, they went unnoticed.

Fooling the other cleaners was far harder than fooling the police officers she was supposed to have under surveillance. Some of the other cleaners were Polish and only by pretending to be a bit simple these last two weeks had she kept their suspicions at bay. Jessica's command of the Polish language was enough to fool a non-Pole, a native was another matter entirely.

She kept her head and her eyes down when she was anywhere near the others. She cleaned well and thoroughly, so that no one would have any cause to grumble about her, and she already knew which officers sat where on the second floor, which had families (photographs on desks, late afternoon calls to confirm school pick-up and dinner arrangements) and which were having affairs (furtive calls when they thought no one else was around). She knew which were smokers, which had drink problems and, thanks to the bins full of chocolate wrappers and diet snacks, which had trouble controlling their weight.

She'd already spotted the terminals that were the most likely to have been used to send the email from the fake GP's surgery. At one end of the floor was a suite of three incident rooms, each with six terminals. None were used on a daily basis, but everyone in the building would have access to them. All the time she was working on the second floor she kept one eye on the incident rooms for people going in at odd times.

She had learned nothing of use. The building was too big. There were too many people in it. It was never empty. Between the hours of six and nine it quietened down, when those who worked normal hours went home, but there were always people covering the shifts. Were she to spend weeks coming in, she might begin to spot odd departures from the patterns but for now, nothing.

She would not have the luxury of weeks here.

She made her way down the corridor, heading for the men's toilets at the other end of the floor. To her left were the lifts, stairs, utility cupboards. To her right a glass partition beyond which were the main offices and incident rooms. As she passed the lifts something caught her eye.

Tucked against the wall in the void between the two lifts was a glass-fronted display cabinet. Three shelves inside held cups, shields and photographs of sports teams and award ceremonies. She'd polished the glass yesterday, but there was a mark on it again.

She stopped and reached up with a duster in her hand. A faint mark that would probably be invisible in some lights, it had been made by breath when someone had stood close to the glass, staring in.

She'd cleaned exactly the same mark away yesterday. Possibly before as well, she wasn't sure. She just had a feeling, now, that she cleaned this glass more than she might expect to.

The mark was above her eyeline, had been made by someone well over six feet tall. She polished it away, looking inside to see what someone stood here and stared at so often.

Directly opposite the mark was a framed cutting from a newspaper, a half-page taken from the *Northumbrian Herald,* containing a story and three photographs. The first picture was a headshot of a young, pretty woman with dark hair and eyes, the second, a group of uniformed police officers holding up certificates of commendation. Jessica peered closer. The same young woman, hair tied back this time, was one of the police officers. The third picture had been taken at a very elaborate funeral, with black horses pulling a glass hearse, and a crowd of people following behind. A crowd of very distinctive-looking people.

Brave Moira loses fight with liver disease. Beneath the headline was a date. Then the story. Moira Faa had died in September, two years ago.

Jessica spun slowly on the spot. She already knew there were no cameras focused on this stretch of the corridor. By the time she was facing the display case again she had her phone in her hand. She took one

433

photograph then moved away.

At the end of the corridor she knocked on the door of the men's toilets. 'Hello, cleaning team. Excuse me.'

No response. She pushed the door open, waited a second, and then left the *Cleaning in Progress* sign outside the door.

Moira Faa. She knew that name. She'd known it instantly.

She pushed open the cubicle door and wedged it in place.

She remembered a late-night drive up the M1 to Neil's house, being exhausted after a busy week. She remembered cranking up the air conditioning to full whack and having the radio on at volume, to stay awake. There'd been a story about a young woman dying of liver disease, her only chance being to find a donor within the next few days.

She remembered talking to Neil about it when she couldn't sleep. He'd seen the same story on television. That woman's name had been Moira. It had stuck, because she'd thought it an old-fashioned name for a young woman. Neil had thought she was from a travelling family and that would fit, because Faa was a gypsy name. She hadn't known what had happened to Moira Faa. Hadn't wanted to find out. The case had spooked her.

The toilet bowl was encrusted. She squirted cleaning fluid around the bowl, aiming up and under the rim, then leaned over, picked up the brush and got to work.

So, the appeal had failed. No one had died that night after all and no liver had become available. Had she known Moira Faa was a police officer? She didn't think so. Certainly not a police officer who'd worked in this building.

Behind her, the door opened. She didn't bother looking up. Whoever it was would see the equipment she'd left in the middle of the floor, see her backside bent over a bowl and finally allow the *Cleaning in Progress* sign outside to register.

Whoever it was didn't. Instead, he unzipped his trousers.

Jessica shook the brush, replaced it in its holder and flushed the loo.

'Sorry,' said a male voice. 'Been holding it for a while.'

'Is OK.' Jessica got down on her knees and began wiping the outside of the bowl. She heard the zipping again. The sound of a tap being run. Then a loud clatter.

'Aw, shit and corruption!'

She moved without thinking, jumping up and stepping out. The officer, the chief constable of all people, had knocked over her bucket, sending dirty, soap-flecked liquid spilling out across the floor. Jessica caught a glimpse of the man's face in the mirror, mainly side on, but enough.

Oh dear God.

She fixed her eyes on the floor again, wishing her hair was loose, so that it could fall over her face and hide it. 'Is OK. I fix. Is no problem.'

He was standing right by her. She could see his highly polished shoes with drops of water on them. 'Look, can't I just . . . ?'

'Please no. Is no problem.' She held up both hands, fending him off.

'Well, if you're sure. I'm really sorry. I'll get out of your way, shall I?'

Yes. Yes. Go.

He left.

She straightened up when the door slammed, leaning back against the cool wall in relief. He couldn't have seen her properly, he'd have said something. Fighting back the temptation to pick up her things and leave the building, she forced herself to do enough to make it look as though the room had been cleaned.

When she creaked open the door he was nowhere to be seen. The chief constable's office was at the end of the corridor. There was still another hour of her shift to go, but it couldn't be helped. She had to get out of here now.

She took the lift down and put her equipment back in the cleaning cupboard. She was supposed to sign out with her supervisor but it didn't matter. She wouldn't be coming back again.

She had to cross the car park and then the road to get to the bus stop. Her own car was parked two stops away. She dodged the traffic and managed to squeeze into a place beneath the shelter roof.

Across the road, people were still leaving the station building. She glanced up at the electronic sign. The bus was still seven minutes away.

She pressed as close as she could to the people standing next to her, unable to dismiss the uncomfortable sensation that she was being watched.

Six minutes. Cars drove out of the police station car park, forging their way through the rivers of rain on the road. Five minutes. The traffic slowed as something out of sight caused a hold-up. Headlights shone steadily into the car park, illuminating several of the parked vehicles. One of them had an occupant.

Nothing unusual in that. Lots of people had partners pick them up after work, although this particular vehicle, a steel-grey Land Rover Defender, old, mud-spattered, with a bull-bar on the front and a sturdy luggage rack on the roof, looked out of place in a car park full of hatchbacks and family-sized saloons.

Four minutes.

The occupant got out. A man. Five foot eight, stocky build, dark hair that fell in straggly curls to his shoulders. An oversized black leather jacket. White T-shirt. Feeling the rain, he leaned back into the vehicle and pulled out a black trilby. Fixing it firmly on his head, he set off across the car park. She lost sight of him when he disappeared behind a row of police vans.

She took out her phone again, pretended to check messages for a few seconds and then, a second before the bus blocked her from view, she took a picture of the Defender's registration number.

89

Friday, 22 September

It was still dark outside when Ajax pulled into the senior staff car park and switched off his engine. The framed photograph of Sister Maria Magdalena and Jessica Lane lay on the passenger seat of his car. It would have to go back to the convent soon. He wasn't even sure what impulse had prompted him to take it away in the first place. The picture was over twenty years old, it would be no use at all in trying to identify Jessica now.

Something about it had called to him, he just wasn't sure what. Whatever it was, though, it was still calling. He slipped it into his case.

The message requesting his immediate presence arrived as he was going through security. He didn't bother going to his own office, but made his way to the end of the corridor.

The chief looked worse than he felt. 'What time did you get back?' he asked Ajax.

'Lost track,' Ajax replied.

'I had an email from North Yorkshire waiting when I got in.' He motioned for Ajax to help himself to coffee. 'A woman answering the description of Jessica Lane was pursued around the old city walls in York for several hundred metres before the pursuing officers lost sight of her near the river. They think she headed into the city.'

Ajax knew this already. He hadn't left York until the police there had given up hope of picking up Lane quickly. He carried his coffee to the table and sat down.

'They had people at the station until all the trains stopped running,' said the chief. 'Same at the bus station. They've combed through security footage. She hasn't left York. Nor has she been seen on any of the cameras around the city. She's vanished.'

'An accomplice?' Ajax drained his cup and stood up to get a refill. 'Someone picked her up?'

'I've got someone from the NCA coming up this morning. Going to fill us in on what she was doing up here. As much as they can, anyway. I rather got the impression that wouldn't be much.'

A wave of exhaustion washed over Ajax.

'She was in this ruddy building, John. She was investigating us.'

'Something else,' the chief said. 'I had an early report over from the lab. It's looking like they have found brain tissue on the basket. And, while they're not one hundred per cent certain, they think damage to one of the guide ropes is consistent with gunshot.'

'Is Jessica Lane firearms trained?' Ajax asked.

The chief inclined his head. Outside, the blackness of the pre-dawn was beginning to splinter.

Back behind his own desk, Ajax opened his case and saw the photograph, face up, the two girls staring at him.

The frame was wood, cheap, had warped with age, and the picture, now that he was looking at it properly, skewed. He turned it over to see four metal clips holding the various parts together.

If he were in a place that permitted only one family photograph, what would he do? He slid back the clips one by one and let the backing card fall away.

There was something else. Ajax gave a little triumphant smile. He knew he'd brought this picture away for a reason.

Another photograph. A four-inch square sheet of glossy white paper. An old photograph, gone a little yellow around the edges. The image was facing inward.

'OK, Sister Maria, let's find out your secret, shall we?' He used the tip of a fingernail to ease the smaller picture away. It tumbled on to his lap, face up.

'Christ.'

The picture had been taken in a hospital, a maternity unit to be exact, the only place he'd ever seen small, transparent, plastic cots. Tucked under a blue blanket was a tiny form, his minuscule head showing the crustiness characteristic of newborns.

Sister Maria was hiding a photograph of a baby boy.

90

'Shinto, come out.'

The dog ignored him. Patrick called again. Nothing, and raising his voice this morning hurt too much, given what he'd drunk last night. It was too goddamned early, the morning light still cold and blue. He walked up to the open rear doors of the van. Towards the front, he could just about see a twitching canine tail. The dog's head was down. He'd found food, most likely. Hopefully not vomit or, God forbid, human shit, although it wouldn't be the first time for either.

'I'm done, Pat. Want me to leave it running?'

Patrick looked over to the far corner of the yard, where William had been rinsing out waste bins.

'Nah, I'll be a couple of minutes.' He jumped into the van, immediately regretting the sudden movement. He took a deep breath, then another. He'd have to clear out the back of the van before he could wash it. There was a horse blanket over the wheel arch that had to come out, for one thing. And whatever Shinto had found.

Shinto was half under the blanket, had one paw pinning something to the van floor, was tearing whatever it was apart with his teeth. Patrick gave the dog a gentle kick with his foot and saw chocolate in a bright orange wrapper. Reese's Peanut Butter Cups. He was suddenly conscious of his heartbeat.

This was the same brand of candy he'd seen in Jessica Lane's house in York. That bunch of immigrants he'd picked up last night would not have been in any European shops for over a week. The chances of them bringing in the chocolate were slim.

He leaned down and pressed his face close to the horse blanket. Not just horse. Not just fetid smells of captive humanity. Something fresh. Floral. A scent he distinctly remembered from the bathroom in York.

'Jesus. Fucking. Wept.' He ran both hands over his face.

'What?'

Trust his mother to be in earshot the second he blasphemed.

'Nothing.' He got to his feet.

444

'Pat?'

'Give me a frigging minute.'

Pushing past her, knowing he'd pay for it later, he jumped down and set off towards the wire fence. He followed it around the compound, trailing his fingers over the steel mesh when he could, as though if he lost physical contact with it, even for a second, he could miss something. Only when he reached the Ford Mondeo, the one pushed right up against the fence, did he break away. He opened the door, climbed inside and saw the blue headscarf.

Not a headscarf. A hijab. Nothing to do with the woman who might, or might not, have hidden in the back of his van last night, but almost certainly once owned by the girl who'd escaped the compound in the very early hours of Wednesday morning. The one who'd started this whole frigging fiasco.

He climbed out of the other side of the car and stood looking at the fence. It ran all the way around the compound. How the hell had they got out?

Then he saw the gap.

How the hell had that got there?

91

Tuesday, 19 September (Three days earlier)
A pinging sound told Jessica that an email had arrived in her inbox. The one she'd been waiting for. Thank God for night shifts. She opened it.

Sorry to keep you, Lane. Needed fifteen minutes to myself before I could run the search. Anyway, the vehicle in question isn't registered but I did find a police interest report on it. Seems it's been spotted more than once entering a property in Kirk Yetholm in Scotland. Known address of a notorious family of gypsies. Name of Faa. Best, Bazza.

Jessica felt something — energy, adrenalin — draining from her body. For a few seconds she mistook the feeling for exhaustion, then recognized it as relief. She'd known there was something familiar about that trilby. The newspaper photograph of Moira Faa's funeral had shown family members following behind the hearse. Two men and an older woman had been at the front of the grim parade; one of the men had been wearing a black trilby.

Faa. She accessed the Police National Computer and searched for the Faa family of Kirk Yetholm.

The Faa family have been living at Kirk Yetholm for a long time. According to them, since the fifteenth century. Whilst there is no way of verifying such a claim, there are no records of the property being owned by anyone other than the family.

The property consists of two acres of land, much of it fenced and kept secure, and a large, farmhouse-style building. According to social services and police reports, the family do not live in the house, but prefer to inhabit a number of caravans (typically between eight and a dozen) that encircle the house. Their income, ostensibly, comes from the scrap-metal business that is run from the land.

The family have strong ties and a huge sense of loyalty. Their willingness to give each other alibis has been a major stumbling block in more than one case brought

447

against them.

Cautions and convictions:

1997: Official caution given to Patrick Faa in respect of alleged theft of two bicycles.

2004: Official caution to Charles Faa for driving with broken right tail-light.

2005: Official caution to Rebecca Faa, aged fifteen, for attempted shoplifting.

2010: Arrest of Patrick Faa, William Faa and Jeremy Faa for drunken and disorderly conduct in a public place. Bound over by magistrates to keep the peace.

The black (or possibly white) sheep of the family is Moira Faa, the youngest child and only daughter of Mary Faa. Moira went to Hendon Police College and later joined Northumbria Police. Whilst her unconventional family must surely have been cause for embarrassment or unease over the years there has never been any suggestion of Constable Faa acting improperly. On the contrary, she has received three commendations in her time at Northumbria Police.

Closing down the PNC, she went back to Google searches she'd done earlier, just to read through them one last time, to make sure.

She was tired at last. She could sleep for a couple of hours. Tomorrow, after dropping off Isabel, she'd double-check everything she'd learned and tidy up the paperwork. On Thursday she would go to London and update the rest of the team. Then she'd have the weekend with Neil. Finally, they might be able to start looking for wedding venues, make some firm plans. She closed down her laptop and went back into the bedroom. She climbed into bed, closed her eyes and forced a smile on to her face.

It didn't work. After a couple of minutes, the muscles in her face were aching. Then she sat upright. In front of her closed eyes a vision had appeared. One of the photographs she'd found on the Internet had been of the Faa family home and the business they owned in Kirk Yetholm. Right in the middle of the scrapyard was a large farmhouse. Painted yellow.

92

Friday, 22 September

'Ajax. This is Detective Inspector Frank Boscombe of the National Crime Agency.'

Ajax let the door close on the chief's office.

Only a couple of years old, the NCA was the government body responsible for investigating serious organized crime: cybercrime, economic crime that crossed international borders, weapon and drug smuggling, and human trafficking.

'DI Boscombe.' Ajax nodded politely.

'Superintendent.' Boscombe was nervous. His hand, when he picked up his coffee cup, was trembling. When he put it down, he started picking at a rough cuticle. The door opened and the chief's PA stuck her head in. 'Sir, call for you. Says it's urgent. And personal. Wouldn't leave a name.'

'Fifteen minutes,' he told her. 'Sooner, if I can.'

When the door closed again, the chief said, 'DI Boscombe is about to explain to us why an officer from the NCA was coming into our building posing as a Polish cleaner.'

'Can I ask what you know about Project Kraken?' Boscombe said.

Ajax pulled a face, shook his head, noticed the boss looking equally mystified. 'Why don't you help us out?'

'Basically, it's a joint initiative with the UK Border Force and certain regional police authorities to increase vigilance along the UK's coastline.'

'Actually, that is ringing a bell,' the chief said. 'We had some literature through a few months back. Posters, leaflets, that sort of thing. We sent it to the stations that have coastal responsibility.'

'Project Kraken encourages local people to be more vigilant around the water,' said Boscombe. 'We've got nearly twenty thousand miles of coastline in the UK, we can't watch it all ourselves. Kraken is aimed at people who work in the maritime industries, or anywhere near a harbour. Fishermen. Sailors. Divers. Even walkers. Anyone who comes into contact with the water on a regular basis is encouraged to keep their eyes open and report anything unusual to

451

us. Jessica is part of a team that follows up reports we think have merit.'

'Yeah, well tell me if I'm missing something, but I can't see the sea from where we are,' said Ajax. He caught the boss raising an eyebrow and gave him a half shrug. One of them had to play bad cop.

'Jessica has a particular interest in people trafficking,' said Boscombe. 'She has language skills and, back when she was with the Met, she was often called upon to help out with the vulnerable if they couldn't get an interpreter out of bed. She came across a few boatloads. Saw how people were suffering. Wanted to do something about it.'

'People trafficking has never been an issue on my patch,' said the chief. 'Not while I've been here, anyway.'

'That you know of,' replied Boscombe. 'We've been getting intelligence that the increased security around Kent and London, the south in general, is forcing these gangs to move further afield. We've got signs of possible trafficking activity around East Anglia, Lincolnshire, even parts of Yorkshire.'

'Possible activity?' asked Ajax. 'Any actual arrests?'

'I don't need to tell you these people are sharp. We've been working with the regional police forces to increase surveillance, but we're talking about a lot of water and a lot of coastline, even before you take the rivers, canals and sea-water lakes into account. And let's be honest now, the British are very good at smuggling. We've been doing it for hundreds of years.'

'Bringing people into Northumberland would require a very long sea voyage,' said Ajax. 'Where are they coming from?'

'We're not sure. The Netherlands. Possibly even Denmark. And you're right, bringing them in up here would require a lot of time spent at sea. And would only be worthwhile if the chances of getting in undetected were substantially higher than in the south.'

'And if the local constabulary were deliberately looking the other way?' asked Ajax. 'I assume that's the reason she was working in this building. She thought someone in here was aiding and abetting people-smugglers.'

'That's a bit of a leap, Ajax,' said the boss.

'So tell me I'm wrong,' Ajax said.

'I'm not at liberty to disclose the nature of Jessica's investigation,' said Boscombe.

The chief's cup clattered in its saucer.

'What I can tell you is that it had come to an end,' Boscombe went on. 'She left this building for the last time three days ago.

Tuesday. A decision she made herself, for good reasons, although I can't tell you what they were.'

The chief got up, walked away from the table and stood with his back to them, looking out of the window. 'And had she found what she was looking for?'

'Yes, I believe she had. She was reluctant to say too much via email, and also wanted a day or so to think it over. She had a day's leave and had family plans. The balloon trip, I guess. She was going to drive down to London on Thursday to brief the team.'

'Except the balloon went down on Wednesday, and she went on the run,' said Ajax.

'That, I admit, does puzzle us. I can think of no reason why Jessica didn't contact us as soon as she could.'

'Her sister had been killed,' said the chief. 'She might not have been thinking straight.'

'I understand that. But Jessica is not the sort to lose it, even in the event of a tragedy. Something made her run. Something has prevented her from getting in touch.'

'Given that same something has also led to her murdering two people, one of them her own fiancé, I think it's time you were more frank with us,' said Ajax.

'She's simply wanted in connection with

those crimes at present,' said the chief. 'There's no warrant out for her arrest.'

'Jessica didn't kill anyone,' said Boscombe. 'It's inconceivable.'

'Was she licensed to carry firearms? The lab team have found traces of gunpowder in the balloon.'

Boscombe frowned. 'She was firearms trained, but she certainly wouldn't be carrying a weapon in the normal course of her duties.'

'How about a knife?'

'Ajax,' warned the chief.

'OK, help us out now,' said Ajax. 'Let's assume she's not in league with the bad guys. Let's assume she's running from them. She's out there on her own somewhere, she's scared, exhausted, running out of money. Where would she go?'

Boscombe gave Ajax a hard stare. 'I'd expect her to come to me. To make contact with me.'

'Yeah, well she's had forty-eight hours to do that, so I reckon you can stop holding your breath.'

'Failing that?' asked the chief.

'She'd go to York,' said Boscombe. 'We know she did that, but it's no longer a safe space for her.'

'Not bloody safe for anyone else while

she's around.'

'Ajax, get it together or leave us to it,' snapped the chief. 'Where else?'

'One possibility is that Jessica went to York for her laptop,' said Boscombe. 'All the details of the case were on it. I doubt she'd risk taking it up in the balloon, and we know it's not in her car. North Yorkshire have confirmed that no laptop was found in the house.'

'So she has it with her,' said the chief.

'That's what I'm assuming,' said Boscombe. 'Given the investigation she was involved in, she may not have felt comfortable contacting the local police. She may have actively wanted to avoid doing so. I wouldn't be surprised if she's making her way south. She'll know about phones being traced. She'll know about cameras at bus and train stations. If I were Jessica, and I wanted to get to the office without being picked up, I'd be hitch-hiking my way south.' He looked at his watch. 'So I really should be getting back.'

The chief stood up. 'I have a call to make myself,' he said. 'I appreciate your time, Frank.'

Ajax's phone began buzzing. He picked it up, meaning to hold the call, and saw who wanted to speak to him.

'The mortuary,' he said. The chief nodded at him to take it.

'Ajax,' said the voice on the line. 'I think you should get down here right away. There's something you need to see.'

93

'What do you mean, she's here?'

Patrick stepped further from the farm-house. Mobile signal wasn't great in the compound, but there was a ridge of higher ground a little way beyond the shrine to Our Lady where it was slightly better. 'She was in the van last night,' he admitted. 'Must have sneaked in while I was in police custody. I brought her all the way back here.'

'How the fuck —'

The voice broke off. Patrick could hear footsteps striding along a hard floor, then, 'You've got to get those people out of there. Get them into the caravans. Drive north. Get off the roads as soon as you can.'

'Already on it.' He glanced back to where the entire family were moving about the site. The gates were open and, as he watched, a caravan pulled out and disappeared along the road. His mother, alone, wasn't moving, just glaring over at him. He turned his back on her, focused on the voice on the phone.

'There'll be time to clean the house and the site completely,' said that voice. 'I can tell you how to do that. For now, make sure there's nothing to arouse suspicion if anyone comes looking. And clean the van.'

'She'll have gone for her car,' Patrick said. 'The one in the pub car park. William's out there now.'

'We've got people watching that car. Hang on a sec —'

His mother was still looking. When he made eye contact, she took a step towards him. He shook his head.

'You still there?'

'Go on,' he said into the phone, holding up a hand to stop his mother.

'The watch was taken off the car when we got the news she'd been killed in York. Putting it back on has been overlooked. I'm going to remind people now, but Will should get there ahead of them. Phone me as soon as you know.'

'You can trace the car, can't you, with that, what do you call it, number plate —'

'Automatic Number Plate Recognition system. Yes, but once I set that in motion, we'll know officially she's back in the north and we'll pick her up, instead of —'

The thought was left hanging.

'Instead of me?' Patrick said.

No reply. Not to his surprise, the line went dead. Patrick turned to see his young cousin, a sneaky little bastard at the best of times, had crept up on him.

'You've got a problem, Pat.' Jimmy had a mobile phone in his hand, the same one that Patrick had lifted from the house in York last night.

'What?'

'This phone got three pictures of you sent through to it on Wednesday.' Jimmy pushed the phone almost into Patrick's face to make a point. 'You at the old house with that girl on the ground. Two more of you chasing the balloon. It's obviously you, your hat, Shinto, everything.'

Patrick stared at his cousin and wondered if he'd get away with swiping him one.

'The good news is, no one's seen them,' Jimmy went on. 'The messages weren't opened.'

Patrick's heartbeat, which had been racing away, calmed a little. 'So we're good?'

'One of the pictures here is captioned,' Jimmy said. 'It says, "This man is involved in my current investigation." '

Patrick said nothing.

'They were sent from a phone we haven't

found yet,' Jimmy said. 'The one belonging to that police officer, Jessica Lane.'

'So?'

'So, she has pictures of you on her phone. And another thing. She sent a message, to this phone, giving the password for a laptop. Said it was important. Did you see a laptop when you were in the house?'

Patrick spat on the ground. 'I wasn't looking for information technology.'

'No, but she would have been. If she went back to that house, it will have been to find that laptop. So she's a police officer, investigating us, with pictures of you on her phone and who knows what on her laptop. I tell you what, mate, if you don't find her, it's all over for you.'

94

'Curiouser and curiouser,' said MoJo as they pushed open the doors to the mortuary building.

The pathologist came to meet them as they walked down the corridor and led them to the giant fridge where the bodies were kept.

'I've finished the post-mortems on the balloon-crash victims,' he said, as the door closed behind them. 'Nothing I wouldn't expect. All injuries consistent with blunt-force trauma caused by falling from a great height. I'll be sending my report over later today.'

'Thank you.' Ajax waited.

At a nod from the pathologist, an assistant pulled out one of the large steel drawers. She unzipped the bag and they saw the Carmelite nun, Sister Maria Magdalena; her face beautiful and calm in death on one side, on the other burned beyond recognition.

'This woman spent twenty years in a convent,' the pathologist said. 'Closed order, very strict.'

'So I understand,' Ajax confirmed.

'So you wouldn't expect her to be pregnant?'

'Pregnant?' Ajax repeated stupidly.

'Twelve to fourteen weeks, at a guess.'

'Are you sure?'

'I can show you the foetus, if you want.'

'No,' said MoJo.

'I'll take your word for it,' said Ajax. 'What the hell are we talking about? Visiting curate stepping out of line?'

'Nope.' The pathologist reached to a counter and lifted a clear bag. 'I was a bit puzzled by these, to be honest, but I didn't want to say anything until I'd had the chance to have a good look at her.'

'What is it?' Ajax was looking at fabric, black lace, scrunched into a heap.

'It's underwear,' said MoJo.

'Black lacy briefs and a size 32D under-wired bra,' said the pathologist. 'Didn't strike me as standard convent-issue.'

Ajax walked closer to the corpse. He looked at the face, naked of make-up, the dark curly hair. Did nuns still shave their heads? No, not for a century or more.

'This is a nun with some serious issues,' he said.

'This isn't a nun at all,' said the pathologist. 'Sister Maria Magdalena had never had her fingerprints taken, so I couldn't check them. Jessica Lane, though, as a serving police officer, had hers on file.' He looked down at the dead woman, and lifted her hand where her fingers still showed traces of black powder. 'This is Jessica. Sister Maria is the one you're looking for.'

■ ■ ■ ■

PART THREE

■ ■ ■ ■

95

The chiming of the hour bell was always the loudest sound heard in the convent of Wynding Priory. Sister Maria Magdalena, who forty years and two days earlier had been born Isabel Jones, opened her eyes and saw the familiar cracked and yellowing ceiling. She'd often, in the past, thought the stains on the plaster were caused by the souls of the incarcerated women, slowly leeching out through boredom and despair. Nuns, she'd decided years ago, were like cruelly broken ponies, stripped of all self, emptied of humanity in a never-ending quest to become vassals of a non-existent God.

She was cold, but that was nothing new of late. And a mattress, even one old and worn out like this one, was the most comfortable place she'd slept for several nights. She sat up, and became conscious that she was no longer alone in the room. In the solitary wooden chair in the corner sat the stiff, solid figure of Mother Hildegard.

'Good afternoon, Sister,' she said. 'Welcome home.'

96

'Isabel,' said the chief. 'Isabel is alive? Are we sure?'

'Sister Maria Magdalena,' said Ajax. 'And yes, there's no doubt. The body in the mortuary is definitely Jessica.'

'How? How the hell could we get that wrong?'

'The body we recovered was dressed in a habit, although I can't tell you right now how that happened. And the two sisters were very alike.'

The chief pulled out a chair and sat down. 'This throws a completely new light on everything. Jessica is the one who's dead?'

Ajax suppressed a sigh. 'Most significantly, sir, I think we can forget about her hitch-hiking towards London. Jessica might have done that, but someone who's spent the last twenty years as a nun wouldn't have the nerve. And no reason to either.'

'She's spent the last forty-eight hours getting the better of two police forces,' said Chapman. 'I don't think we should under-estimate this woman, whoever she is.'

'More to the point,' said Stacey, 'she's still the prime suspect in two murders. And we have even less idea why she was on the run in the first place.'

'So, where do we think she is?' asked the chief. 'Still in York?'

Chapman said, 'She could be. We've been watching the train and bus stations since she was spotted on Station Road. She hasn't left the city.'

'Unless she hitched,' said the chief.

'Sir, I can't see a woman like that hitching a lift, at night, from a stranger,' said Stacey. 'And if she had, there's every chance who-ever picked her up will have realized and called us by now.'

The chief was nodding. 'She's going to go where she feels safe. What is it those reli-gious types call it? Sanctuary? I'll bet she's in a church in York. Get on to North York-shire, will you, Ajax? Start with the Minster. Someone will be sheltering her.'

'I think you're right, sir,' said Ajax. 'I think she'll be with her own kind.'

97

'She's a nun? What do you mean, she's a nun?'

'She was in the tree,' Patrick said, more to himself than anyone else. 'Waiting for me to leave. She must have swapped clothes after I'd gone.'

'I can't believe you've been given the run-around by a nun,' said Jimmy. 'The female cop was bad enough, but a fucking nun!'

'Don't you dare touch your cousin.' Mary pushed her way in between the two of them. 'He's only telling God's truth.'

She pushed a finger into his face. 'So let me get this straight. You saw a woman in a green jacket lying dead on the ground, and then all yesterday the entire fucking country was looking for a woman in a green jacket, and you didn't think to say, "Hang on, there's been a frigging mix-up"?'

Patrick took a step back. He'd never seen his mother quite like this before. 'I didn't see that picture till I was in York.' He stabbed his own finger at his cousin. 'The one that daft arse sent me was different. No green jacket. How was I to know?'

'Is it better, or worse, that she's not the filth?' said Jimmy.

They were all distracted by the sound of the gates opening. William trotted in on one of the piebald ponies.

'She could still have the laptop,' said Jimmy. 'She could know everything her sister knew.'

William swung himself down and led the horse to a trough. Leaving it there, he came over, shaking his head, first at Mary, then at Patrick.

'Are we sure?' she said.

'Pale green Fiat?' William said. 'Not there. Rode past twice.'

'I mean, are we sure she's a nun? She's been running around the country like a blue-arsed fly.'

'Cops there?' said Patrick.

'Not that I saw,' said William.

'If she's in a vehicle, she could be anywhere,' said Mary. 'Do nuns drive cars now?'

'If she's in a vehicle the coppers know about, she won't get far,' said Patrick. 'They'll pick her up in a couple of hours.'

'Then we have to let them do that,' Mary said. 'You can't be killing a nun, Pat.'

'She'll be at that convent place,' Patrick said. 'What's its name? Wynding Priory.' He threw the end of his cigarette into the fire.

'Pat, where you going? You're not going to that holy place — Pat!'

'It's all on here.' The two women paused by the refectory door and Isabel held up the thin, light laptop she'd carried downstairs. 'The whole investigation. I finished reading it just before I fell asleep. And there was a letter to me that she wrote a couple of hours before she picked me up. She wrote lots of letters to me over the years that she never bothered to send. I found a whole file of them. I think it must have been her way of working things out for herself.'

Hildegard gave a tired smile. 'I imagine they'll be a great source of solace in time.'

'She didn't sleep that last night. Before she picked me up for the balloon trip. I thought she looked tired. She hadn't slept a wink.'

'What on earth was she doing?'

'Quite a lot, as it turns out.'

Wednesday, 20 September (Two days earlier)
Shortly after two in the morning, Jessica drove past the entrance to Castle Faa. A very high wire fence, at least ten feet tall and topped with a coronet of barbed wire, encircled the compound. Huge double gates were chained and padlocked. The fence stretched a good thirty metres along the roadside, before curving back into the woodland.

Beyond the fence, a string of bare electric bulbs allowed her to see an area of gravel yard, a semicircle of caravans, assorted cars, trucks and vans and, beyond, a pile of vehicle carcasses that seemed to go on for ever.

Right in the middle of the yard, facing the road, stood the Yellow House. Two storeys, five narrow windows and a front door. There were no lights visible. It was hard to tell from a drive-past, but the windows appeared to be boarded.

She drove on, past the property, several hundred metres down the road, until she came to a field entrance where she could pull over.

She wasn't authorized to search the property. Anything she found on an unofficial search wouldn't be admissible. What she was considering was probably very dangerous. If she was right about people being held here, she might even be putting lives at risk. On the other hand, if people were being held here, she had to act now. She slipped a pair of pliers and some heavy-duty wire into her pocket, climbed out of the car, locked it, and clambered over the gate into the field.

She crossed the field, squeezed through a hedge; another field and she was up against the high steel-mesh of the perimeter fence. The house was fifty metres away. Two windows at the side, one on the upper storey, one on the lower. There were probably eight rooms in the house, maybe a couple of smaller bathrooms and utility areas. Perhaps one central staircase. The yellow render was in poor repair. It had chipped away beneath the eaves, was damp-stained close to the ground. This was not a treasured family home.

The wind blew softly in her face, bringing

her the smell of campfires, burning oil, septic tanks.

She moved on, away from the road, following the line of the fence. As she left the shelter of the house, the caravans came into view. She counted nine. Smoke was trickling from more than one. Lights shone in at least two. She saw the shrine, the huge, stone-rimmed fire with its orange glowing embers, the stockpile of Calor-gas bottles.

She went on, leaving the light from the site behind as the mountains of wrecked cars loomed above her. The wind whistled through them, making eerie, almost human, sounds. Occasionally, the creak and groan of shifting metal made her jump. She walked on. The fence couldn't encircle the entire perimeter. That would be complete overkill.

Unless the fence wasn't about keeping thieves out.

She was nearing the corner. Already she could see the fence did indeed turn the corner and rim the back boundary of the site. There was no way in. She couldn't climb it. Tunnelling under didn't seem like an option.

She set off back towards the house. Why didn't the family live in it?

When she got to the halfway point, she reached into the inner pocket of her coat and pulled out the pliers she'd brought from the car. She tried them on a strand of wire, by way of an experiment. It sprang apart with one sharp squeeze. If she cut through twenty strands, she could peel back part of the fence and get through.

It was the work of a few minutes. She crouched down and made her way through, feeling edges of wire pull at her hair. She felt resistance, and a second later heard the fabric of her jacket tear, but she was on the other side of the fence.

The wire had pulled the green scrunchie from her hair, the one that was a perfect match to her favourite green jacket, and it was dangling in the fence, about four feet from the ground. Knowing it would act as a marker if she had to find her way out in a hurry, she left it in place.

The cars would shield her from view. She could get almost to the caravans without anyone having a chance of seeing her. First, though, she'd have to climb through a car that had been pushed right up to the fence. She squeezed in through the missing window, noted that the car was a Ford Mondeo, and then out through the empty doorway on the other side.

She moved quickly, back the way she'd come, stopping every few seconds to look around, to listen. She could see the roof of the Yellow House. Now the upper windows. She was getting close. The roofs of the caravans were coming into view.

From somewhere very close, she heard a dog barking.

She crouched low. She should have anticipated this. Scrapyards always had dogs. She risked lifting her head, checking the wind. It was coming towards her, she was still getting whiffs of oil and sewage.

A door opened. A man's voice, speaking low, but audible enough from where she was.

'What is it? Go see.'

She heard the scampering of a sizeable dog. It wouldn't come straight for her, not with the wind on her side, but would find her eventually.

'Shinto.'

A door at the back of the house was open. She could see light shining out.

'Pat?' Another voice. 'What the fuck's going on?'

'Nothing. Go back to bed.'

She could see the huge silhouette of the dog now. It was following the line of the fence, able to detect her scent from earlier. It was a German shepherd.

And that was good.

German shepherds weren't the fierce attack dogs of popular belief. Neil had taught her that. It took months of hard work and patience to turn a good-natured, people-loving animal into a creature that would hunt and attack on command. Most people outside the police dog units simply didn't bother. German shepherds were used as guard dogs because their sheer size was intimidating. Most were perfectly friendly if approached in the right way.

'Here, boy.' She whispered the call. The dog would hear it. 'Shinto, here, boy.'

She saw the dog's head turn her way. Saw its nose lift. It had her.

It moved towards her at a steady trot rather than a full-out run, which was good, because it implied less than one hundred per cent confidence. It wasn't sure about what it was going to find.

'What a good boy. Such a good boy.' She was channelling Neil, trying to copy the way she'd seen him working with the youngest, least predictable dogs. They always gave him the difficult ones. He was one of the best trainers the unit had ever had. The trick, he always said, was never to be afraid.

The dog was close now. She stayed low, reaching into her pockets for the dog treats she and Neil were never without.

It was close enough for her to see the light in its eyes.

'Good boy.' She held out her hand, clutched around a treat, and saw the dog's nose twitch. She tossed it towards him. He snatched it up in seconds.

'Good boy.' She threw another. She had one more, then she'd have to rely on sweet words and confidence.

Oh, this really wasn't the best time to take a gamble with an unpredictable canine.

The dog was upon her now, nosing towards her face, then lower, seeking out the last treat. She made him hunt for it.

'Hey, beautiful.' She reached up and scratched his head behind the ears, the exact place that all long-haired dogs loved to be scratched. He carried on sniffing into the pockets of her jacket. 'You'll know me next time, won't you, boy?'

'Shinto. Heel.'

The dog turned and ran back to its owner, but she'd made a friend. She was safe, from the dog, at least.

'Pat, what the hell's going on? Why's the fucking door open?'

'Chill out. Dog was restless, is all.'

She heard the slamming of the back door and waited for things to settle down again. Then suddenly it was flung open.

'Get the frigging lights on. Everyone! Get up, now!'

Instantly, lights started to appear around the site.

Jessica turned and scurried back towards the entrance she'd cut in the wire. At the Ford Mondeo she paused for a second, hidden within the car's dark interior, to look back. Torches were being shone around the site. People were calling to each other. Shinto was barking excitedly. They couldn't be looking for her, but they were clearly looking for something and, sooner or later, their search would widen. She squeezed out through the window.

Her green scrunchie made it easy to find her escape route. She forced her way through the gap in the fence and found the length of wire from her pocket. Starting at the top, she wound it through the gap, plaiting it together so that when she got to the bottom and fastened it off, anyone would have to look very closely to see the fence had been cut at all. She reached up for her scrunchie and froze.

The Ford Mondeo she'd just climbed through was moving.

She stared, willing it to have been a trick of the light, the moon slipping out from behind a cloud, giving the illusion of movement.

Nothing. The car was still.

'I'll take the north fence.'

She was on the north side of the compound. And that voice was close. She had to go now. She turned, ready to crouch and run.

From feet away came the sound of someone landing lightly on soft ground.

She turned back. Nothing. Lights couldn't reach this corner of the yard. The moon had gone again. Nothing to see. Nothing to hear. And yet the sense of a presence was very strong. She could almost believe that that glimmer, two metres the other side of the fence, wasn't metal on the old car but the gleam of a pair of eyes.

Freaked now, Jessica turned and ran.

When she got back to the car she sat for several minutes. She'd seen nothing at all to justify bringing a team out here ahead of giving her full report on Thursday. And she'd carried out an illegal search. For now, there was nothing to be done. She turned on the engine. It was barely more than an hour before she had to pick up Isabel.

100

Without warning, Jessica braked hard and pulled over to the side of the road. She made sure the road was clear, jumped out of the car, ran to the ditch and bent over it, just as her stomach clenched painfully and threw up its contents. The Peanut Butter Cups she'd eaten in the early hours came first. Then a whole load of liquid. She'd got to the point of dry-heaving when she heard the car door slam.

'We should go back.' Isabel stayed behind her. 'Whatever you've got planned, we can't do it if you're ill.'

'I'm not ill.' Another heave bent her double. There really was nothing left to come out. 'There's some water in my rucksack, would you mind?'

She wiped her mouth and spat while she waited for Isabel to hunt in the rucksack and then hand her the bottle. She rinsed and spat again, then drank.

'If this is what you're eating for breakfast these days, I'm not surprised you're throwing up.' Isabel was holding up an orange wrapper. 'What even are Reese's Peanut Butter Cups, anyway?' Her stern face softened. 'I can drive us back,' she said. 'I'm safe enough this time of day.'

The convent rules stipulated that at least three of the sisters had to maintain current driving licences to operate the convent-owned vehicle, an elderly silver Ford Focus. Isabel had passed her test ten years earlier. One time, she and Jessica had worked out how many miles in total she'd driven. Three hundred and eighty-six was the closest they could get.

'We're not going back, you're not driving and I'm not ill.' One last spit and she was done. Jessica turned to face her anxious sister. 'I'm pregnant,' she added. 'The Peanut Butter Cups are a craving. I'm going through them by the vanload.'

Isabel didn't speak but her mouth pursed into a small circle. Her eyes widened.

'Fourteen weeks. Due late March. We're not planning to find out the sex, but I'm not sure I'll be able to resist.'

Isabel stepped back until she was leaning against the car. Her face, always pale, had whitened. 'Are you OK?' Jessica asked, not without a hint of irony.

No answer, just her sister's brown eyes looking back at her.

'Bella?' Jessica said, when the staring contest was verging on creepy. 'Seriously, what is it?'

A lorry sped past, honking at the sight of the two women, one of them a nun, at the side of the road. Isabel seemed to pull herself together. She gave a broad smile. 'It's wonderful news,' she said. 'Congratulations.'

'We're going to be late.' Jessica stepped out into the road and climbed back into the car. She started the engine as Isabel got in.

'Neil must be thrilled?' Isabel said.

Jessica looked in her mirror and pulled out.

'That pause was longer than I'd have liked,' said Isabel.

Jessica thought about making some conventional excuse. *He's got a lot on his mind at the moment. I'm not sure he's really taken it in yet. You know men, rather struck dumb by the enormity of parenthood.* On the other hand, this was Isabel.

'As was the silence in between my giving him the news and him saying, "That's wonderful",' said Jessica.

Isabel thought for a second. 'You've been

waiting a long time for this. Maybe it takes a while to sink in. He'll probably turn up tomorrow with a teddy.'

They drove on for another mile.

'He left his phone behind,' Jessica said. 'In his top drawer, he said. He called me last night from a landline to say I shouldn't expect to hear from him until he gets back. Which, of course, means I can't reach him.'

'And is that a problem? He's only away two days.'

'No, of course it's not a problem,' Jessica said. 'Take no notice of me.'

They drove for a minute or two in silence. Ahead of them, the sky was lightening, becoming the soft grey of dove's wings.

'The sun will be up soon,' said Isabel. 'Are we doing something — pagan?'

Jessica smiled. 'Be patient.'

The road turned west and against the still, dark horizon, the women saw a burst of flame.

'Did you see that?' Isabel was bolt upright in her seat.

Jessica smiled again. 'I saw it.'

Isabel leaned forward, practically pressing her nose against the windscreen. Her seat belt pulled her back and she unfastened it. 'Again. What is it? What's on fire?'

'That, my dear, would be your ride.'

They'd reached the pub where they were meeting the balloon company and the other passengers. As Isabel read the sign on the company Land Rover she gave an audible sigh and then bounced in her seat like an excited toddler. 'Oh!' was all she could manage.

'Happy birthday, Bella,' said Jessica.

101

Friday, 22 September

Patrick heaved himself over the convent wall. The ground on the other side was soft after heavy rain and a few spindly conifer trees screened him from the house. He'd have to sprint across three hundred metres of parkland to get to it.

He'd been watching the convent for a while now. Around half a dozen nuns, white aprons over their black clothes, had been working in a vegetable garden at the rear. Another was sweeping out a chicken coup. Yet another was cleaning external windows.

It was creepy, the way they worked in absolute silence, almost as though none of them were aware of the others. And yet when one cut her finger on a thorn, the rest seemed to know instantly, even though the hurt nun had said nothing. They had an animal-like instinct of what was going on in the pack.

That was it exactly, he realized. They were a pack. They moved and acted as one.

He'd have to watch that.

A bell began to toll and the sisters reacted. They began gathering their equipment. Still no words were exchanged. They picked up buckets, hoes, forks and watering cans. The one in the chicken coop pulled off yellow rubber gloves and tucked them away in a lidded bucket. They began moving back towards the house and disappeared inside.

When he got closer, the door through which the nuns had disappeared blew open in front of him and he almost lost his nerve. Its swinging gape was like a grin on the face of a scary clown. He had a vision of a dark-clad figure hiding behind it, luring him in. Of the whole collection of them, lying in wait.

He approached carefully, standing to one side of the open door, listening, testing the air the way his dog did. They were just women. Mainly old, almost certainly weak. They were nothing to be afraid of.

A sudden memory flashed into his head. His dog, Shinto, not much more than a puppy, being surrounded by a flock of angry, jabbering magpies. They'd flown around the young dog, swooping down,

490

cawing and cackling like witches, always staying out of reach. Not one of the birds, alone, would have been a match for the dog, but the dozen or so of them together? He'd had to run at them with a stick, beating and swiping, before they'd flown off, and not before Shinto had taken a nasty peck above one eye. He didn't like to think about what would have happened to the puppy had he not been there. He'd seen what the birds did to newborn lambs.

The nuns were not magpies, for all their outward appearance. He had no need to be afraid.

Sure, at last, that no one was in the room immediately behind the door, he stepped inside and the smell of the convent hit the back of his throat like smoke from a chemical fire. It was the smell of the caravans in which elderly women lived, the smell of the lavatory after his mother had spent some time in it, but also the smell of cooking food and the church of his childhood. The smell of the convent made him feel like a child again.

He felt suddenly dizzy, as though the walls around him were growing, *Alice in Wonderland* style, getting taller, pushing the ceiling out of sight, as he shrunk in size. He was afraid to look up.

On one Formica worktop, a knife had been left. It was large, about seven inches long, used for cutting meat rather than fruit or vegetables. He picked it up, and felt himself again.

102

'When the balloon went down, when I knew that Jessica was dead, and that man was looking for me, my first instinct was to come home. I swear to you, Sisters, this is where I was coming.'

Past noon, the sun in the convent refectory was shining through the old, flawed glass of the windows. Dust particles danced in the golden light. The smell of the meat stew and of cooking oil wafted around the room every time the door to the kitchen opened. Florentina had brought a vase of freshly cut roses in from the garden. When she thought no one was looking, she pushed it fractionally closer to Isabel.

Some of the nuns were sitting at the great oak table. Hildegard at its head, Isabel alone on her left-hand side. Other sisters drifted around the room, their feet making soft scuffing sounds on the polished floor. They kept bringing her food: milk, bread, oat

493

biscuits, cheese. There was something vaguely biblical about the stuff they brought, as though their choice of sustenance might help bring her back to God. Or maybe just back to them.

'It never occurred to me that people would assume Jessica was alive and I was dead.' Isabel looked from one face to another. 'I know it was stupid of me to change clothes, I simply didn't think.'

'You could not have travelled all that way in a habit, Sister,' Eugenia spoke up. 'Changing clothes was entirely sensible, and Jessica would have been the first to agree. What I don't understand is why you didn't contact the police when you had the chance?'

'Yes,' said Belinda. 'Once you met the other pilgrims you were safe, surely? You should eat something, Sister. Try honey on that bread. Or I can bring you some of the apricot jam?'

'I was going to contact them from here. I felt I could deal with them, with all of it, if I was here, with all of you.' For a second, Isabel was tempted to reach out her hand. She'd always been fond of Belinda. But something held her back. These women were looking at her with a mixture of pity and curiosity but with something else too.

Maybe a hint of alarm. She might have returned to them, but she wasn't one of them again. Not yet.

'But then, in a café early on the second day, I saw the news,' she went on. 'I realized what I'd done and that Neil would believe his fiancée was alive when she wasn't and —' There was something stuck in her throat. She shouldn't have tried to eat anything. Except, she didn't think she had. The bread on her plate was untouched. 'She was pregnant,' she managed. 'Jessie was having a baby, Sisters.'

A low-pitched moan, almost musical, seemed to hum around the room. Hildegard dropped her face into her hands.

'I identified her body,' Hildegard said through her fingers. 'I told the police she was you. If anyone's to blame, it's me. You'd think, after all these years, I'd be able to tell the two of you apart.'

'From what you told us, her face was very badly damaged, Mother,' said Florentina.

'And let's be honest now,' Tabitha piped up, 'it's been quite some time since you had an eye test.' She pushed her chair back. 'Excuse me a moment, Mother. I can hear the kitchen door banging. It's blown open again.'

Hildegard nodded sadly as Tabitha left the room.

'I felt I should be the one to tell Neil the truth, to explain,' Isabel said. 'And so I set off for York, but on the way, I had a lot of time to think. Jessie recognized the man we saw attacking the girl on the ground. The man I've learned since is called Patrick Faa. And she was investigating the police in Northumberland. She knew they were involved in people trafficking. She'd been working undercover, posing as a Polish cleaner in their office. You know how good she was with languages?'

Hildegard gave a single nod of assent. Around her, black-clad heads bounced and veils swayed.

'Not just the usual people trafficking, though,' said Isabel. 'Patrick Faa and his family are smuggling illegal immigrants into the country to order; to provide healthy organs for sick rich people.'

The nuns across the table seemed to press closer. The ones still moving around the room paused.

'That we should live to see so much evil in the world,' said Hildegard.

'And the police are involved too?' asked Serapis.

'Someone in the police is. Jessica had her

suspicions about who, but she wasn't sure. There's a doctor, too — this Mr Wallace whom she mentioned before. He's the one who finds the . . . I'm not really sure what you'd call them.'

'Customers?' suggested Belinda.

'Let's just call them patients,' said Isabel. 'They come to his clinics in Harley Street or Newcastle and he spins them a story about brain-dead donors being flown in from overseas, about the money they'll pay going to help poor families.'

'But the donors are alive and healthy when they arrive?' said Eugenia.

Isabel nodded. 'Do you remember that last time Jessie came to see us in the summer?' she said. 'We were talking in the garden of repose about how we couldn't see any way organs could be bought and sold because the system in the UK is so rigorous?'

The sisters' faces creased in concentration.

'I remember,' said Basilia. 'We were talking about that little foreign girl who'd been killed in a car accident, and I said that, even if she'd been killed deliberately, even if the accident had been . . . what's the word?'

'Staged?' suggested Eugenia.

'Yes, exactly, so that her organs could be

497

made available,' Basilia said. 'Even if that was the case, they'd still go into the system, along with those of all the genuine donors, and be allocated according to the rules. I said that. I said they could end up anywhere.'

'Unless the system was being manipulated,' said Isabel. 'Jess was about to tell us how she thought it could be done, when —'

'When I happened upon the scene and reminded you all of your primary duties here?' With a creaking of bones and a rustling of fabric, Hildegard stood and arched her back. 'Prayer and contemplation, not *CSI: Northumberland*?'

As one, the nuns across the table bowed their heads and clasped their hands together. Then, one at a time, the boldest first, their eyes darted back up, to fix again on Isabel. Standing at the head of the table, Hildegard didn't move away. She nodded once, a signal that the conversation could continue.

'Do you remember Jessica explaining that location is one of the factors taken into account when organs become available and a recipient is sought?' Isabel said. 'A heart, for example, wouldn't be flown from here to Kent if a suitable recipient lived locally.'

'Yes, I remember her saying that,' said Serapis.

'Well, take that little girl, Aayat. There would be a lot of people waiting for her organs, but only a few of them would be physically compatible. Of those few, how many do you think would have been in Liverpool, near the hospital where she was dying?'

'Maybe just one,' said Eugenia. 'The one that counts.'

'So, what are you suggesting?' asked Hildegard. 'That —'

'The system would actually work in favour of the traffickers,' interrupted Sister Belinda. 'They wouldn't have to get round it at all. Just make sure the donor died in the right place.'

'And if there was more than one recipient in Liverpool?' said Eugenia. 'If the organ needed was assigned to the "wrong" person?'

'Then they'd kill someone else,' said Isabel. 'They're bringing in people by the vanload, keeping them at the Faa family home until they're needed. Maybe the next one would drown in the Mersey, to save anyone getting too suspicious. Sometimes the accidents go wrong. The little girl, for example. And another woman Jessica found, called Adar. She's still in hospital in Derby. It doesn't matter to these people, because there are always plenty more where they came from.'

Shocked silence seemed to settle over the room like a damp towel. More than one woman started moving her lips. Several pale hands reached up for the crosses they all wore around their necks. Isabel could feel the prayers floating around the room like the humming of trapped bees.

'And Jessica told you all this?' asked Hildegard.

'Some of it. Right before the crash, though, she did one last thing. I knew it must be important, for her to think of it when we were all so scared. She sent a text to Neil, telling him the password for her laptop.' Isabel dropped her eyes to the thin, silver computer on the refectory table. 'All the details of the case, including things she hadn't had time to share with the rest of her team, were on the laptop that she'd left at home. I think she wanted to make sure Neil could access it before anyone else could get their hands on it and, I don't know . . .' She looked round, helplessly.

'Wipe it clean?' suggested Basilia.

'Take a sledgehammer to it?' said Belinda.

'Has someone moved the cheese knife?'

Tabitha came back into the room, carrying a covered dish. 'I remembered the new Cheddar. I'm sure we can tempt Sister with a small piece.'

'Yes,' said Isabel. 'I think Jessica was worried about the laptop going astray. But Neil didn't have his phone. She must have forgotten in the heat of the moment. She'd told me that morning when we were driving to meet the balloon that he'd left it at home. So I knew I had to find the phone, and the laptop, and make sure they were safe.'

'And Jessica thought the police were involved?' asked Eugenia.

'She was sure of it. She went undercover to find out who.'

'Hold on a cotton-picking —' Sister Belinda caught Hildegard's eye. 'I mean, forgive my interrupting, Sister, but whilst I understand your engagement in Jessica's work, at some point in the last three days you must have thought, *This has gone too far, I have to go to the police.*' She looked round, almost guiltily. 'I mean, they can't all be bent?'

'When should I have done that?' Isabel asked. 'When Patrick Faa followed me to Belford and then to York, and I realized only the police could have told him where I was or was likely to be?'

Belinda dropped her eyes.

Isabel went on. 'When they nearly caught me in York, fleeing a murder scene, at which I'd left behind a knife with my fingerprints on it and a jacket covered in blood? They'll probably try to blame me for the balloon crash as well.'

'They can't do that,' said Sister Florentina.

'Has there been anything on the news about finding the pilot's body?' asked Isabel. 'What about the poor woman we saw Faa attacking from the balloon? Has she been found? I am the only person left alive who knows what happened.'

'You're also the perfect fall guy,' said Sister Belinda. 'A grief-stricken, emotionally unstable, religious nut.'

'Sister!' Hildegard's face was a picture of shocked disappointment.

'Belinda is right,' said Isabel. 'Once the police find me, I'm likely to be charged with murder. If Patrick Faa gets to me first, he'll save them the trouble. And yes, Sisters, in case you were wondering, I am completely terrified.'

Hildegard walked to the window and looked out. Isabel could see her reflection frown in the glass. 'Sister Winifred,' Hildegard said. 'Would you please take four of the other sisters and check that the convent gates are locked?'

Without looking round, Winifred put down the candlestick she'd been polishing and stepped gracefully towards the door.

'Mother, if he's followed me here, he can climb that wall. I've done —' Isabel stopped herself. 'He can climb over the wall. We should lock the doors. Make sure there are no windows open. I'll be going in a few minutes. You'll be safe once I've gone.'

'Hmmn.' Hildegard's frown deepened. 'Doors and windows, please, Sister Winifred. Please take care. And tell the other sisters that nobody goes outside. In fact, I think it's better that they all come and join us here.'

Belinda bounced to her feet. 'Mother, may I have permission to go to the bell tower? It's possible to see a long way from up there. I can take the peacock binoculars. If anyone tries to steal a march on us, well, I'll see them coming.'

Hildegard bowed her head in agreement, then waited for the refectory door to close behind Winifred and Belinda.

Eugenia said, 'But why on earth would you get into his van in York? You already had Jessica's computer? Surely that was taking the most terrible risk.'

'Faa had Neil's mobile phone, the one with the password. I had to find the password before the police found me. I thought perhaps I could get it back when he stopped for petrol or something.'

'Did you?' asked Tabitha.

Isabel shook her head. 'It must have been in his jacket pocket and he never took it off. But it turns out I didn't need it after all. I guessed Jessica's password first time.'

Hildegard resumed her seat with a waft of incense and body odour.

'It was Magdalena, after me.'

The first sign of a smile broke Hildegard's face. 'Well, that at least doesn't surprise me,' she said.

'So, have you read her files?' asked Tabitha.

'Yes,' said Isabel. 'I know everything. I know what she knew or suspected. I know about the people being smuggled across Europe into Northumberland and then taken to the Yellow House, where they're tested for blood type and the other thing that's relevant. I know that a consultant called Ralph Wallace handles the medical side of it all, that someone in the police is helping the Faa family create fake identities for these people and get them on the donor register. He or she probably arranges the accidents too, wherever it is they're needed. The Faa family pose as next of kin and sign the consent forms. The police keep people away from the ports when the people are smuggled in.'

'Do you know why?' asked Hildegard. 'Do you know why they are doing such a terrible thing?'

'I think so,' Isabel replied. 'I think it all started with a young police officer called Moira Faa.'

103

Three years earlier

Sometimes Patrick looked at the scrapyard and found the wall of wrecked cars unnerving. The headlights, or gaping holes where headlights used to be, all looked inwards at the row of caravans, at the yellow farmhouse, at the people who moved around the cinder-gravel site, giving him a sense of constant vigilance. Other times, he found it reassuring. The cars were the walls of the family citadel, guarding them against the outside world, shielding them from the worst of the weather, providing the income that kept them all fed.

The cars arrived, no longer roadworthy but largely intact, and were nibbled away. Petrol was drained into a tank that supplied the family's own cars, batteries were removed and sold on, followed quickly by sound systems, tyres, seats, steering wheels, then body panels. The cars grew lesser, until only the shells remained.

And still they watched him.

Sometimes he woke in the night when the moon was full and imagined the glow around his caravan was the light of hundreds of ghostly headlamps, and that if he went outside — he never did on such nights — he'd see them all turned on, shining brightly, showing the world what he really was.

Two weeks into August, on a night as warm as ever occurred this far north, all but the very young members of the family were up, playing cards, drinking, watching the smoke rise from the oil-drum fires. Rock music was playing in one of the caravans, but by the time it reached Patrick it was tinny and distorted.

He heard the clanging and scraping of the big gates being opened and recognized the black estate car. Through the fog of cigarette and fire smoke, it seemed to glide into the yard. As the driver door opened, he grabbed the bottle at his feet and poured another drink, bigger than he'd intended. When he raised his head, his mother was watching him.

He could smell Moira before she came into his eyeline. Her perfume wound its way through the smoke and the cooking smells,

507

through the cannabis and the whisky fumes, and he actually put a hand up to his face to shut it out. Too late, that peculiar mix of jasmine and lemons was seeping its way inside him. More than once, he'd stood at perfume counters in big stores, trying to identify the scent she used. He never could. No other woman ever smelled the way she did.

'Moira, is it you, girl?' said their mother. 'Come and sit beside me. Patrick, get a drink for your sister.'

Her accent had long been softer, more English, than that of the rest of them, but even so he knew from the low, flat pitch of her voice that something was wrong. 'not for me, thanks, Mam,' she said. 'I'll make myself a coffee later.'

He heard the springs of the plastic chair as she sat. His sister was wearing black, as usual. Her jeans were tight, her boots knee-high, her vest top cut away to show off the muscles of her shoulders and upper arms. She'd demand his jacket later, like she always did, and then he'd be stuck with the smell of her all night.

'Not drinking? What are you, ill or pregnant?'

His mother laughed, but the laugh turned into a cough and she bent forward, her

508

shoulders rising and falling as she hacked the blockage out of her throat.

'Well, I'm not pregnant, that's for sure.' She caught Patrick's eye as she leaned over to pat their mother on the back. 'How are you, Pat?'

'Sound.' He let his eyes drink her in. The mass of black curls around her head, the eyes that seemed to bounce back light, skin like dark cream. He always won these staring competitions. She always looked away first.

As she turned back to their mother, her face flinched in a tiny contraction of muscles that nobody but he could have seen. She leaned back, as though in pain, and with the fingers of her right hand began rubbing at her upper left arm.

A burst of laughter sounded. The poker game had finished. Money was changing hands.

'How's that fella of yours?' Their mother had finished her coughing and was lighting another fag.

'He's sound. Sends his apologies.'

There were muffled titters around the group. For the most part, Moira's husband avoided her family. 'He thinks it's better not to know,' she'd explained once.

'We had a visit from your lot last week,'

one of Patrick's uncles called over. 'Here for an hour. Poking in everywhere. Found nothing.'

'Not my lot.' Moira slipped a hand beneath her vest and rubbed at her stomach.

'All the fucking same.'

'Are you ill?' Patrick put his glass down. The light wasn't good enough to look properly at his sister. The cheap electric bulbs distorted everything. Even his mother had a sickly yellow tint to her skin.

'What are you talking about?' She frowned at him and dropped her eyes.

'If you're not pregnant, what's up with you?'

'Who says something's up with me? I've got to drive back. I've got to be up at six. We don't all need half a bottle down our necks to sleep at night.'

'You don't look yourself.' Their mam had noticed now. She'd take it from here. She was peering closer. 'Will, fetch me that lamp.'

'Don't bother.' Moira held up both hands in surrender and slumped a little in the chair, as though she'd given up the effort to look normal. 'I came here to tell you.'

Patrick had a sense of the others drawing nearer. The new card game paused. His cousin shushed the baby.

'I'm not well, Mam.' Moira spoke to their mother, but her voice was loud enough to carry to them all. 'I've been having tests. I didn't want to say anything until I was sure.'

Patrick had a sense of the very cars leaning closer, their skeleton bodies quivering in disbelief. *Not Moira. Anyone but Moira.*

Nobody spoke. Nobody asked her for details. No one wanted to know the worst.

'What?' Their mam cracked first.

'My liver. Turns out the liver is fairly crucial to ongoing life.'

'Liver?' Mam's eyes dropped to the bottle by Patrick's chair, to the glass in her own hand. 'You've never been a drinker.'

'I know. For fuck's sake, if I'm going to pay the price, you'd think I'd have had the benefit first. But it turns out not all liver problems are drink-related.'

'What then?' one of the cousins asked.

Moira took a deep breath. 'I have something called Primary Sclerosing Cholangitis,' she said. 'It's quite rare. No one knows what causes it, and for a long time there are no symptoms. I've had it for several years, and didn't know a thing.'

'God bless you and save you,' said Mam, as though God hadn't given up on Moira, on the whole damned bunch of them, a long time ago. 'What can be done?'

511

'There is no treatment.'

Four simple words that told him his world was about to end. Patrick got up and walked away, stopping when he reached the low wall that surrounded the yellow house.

'I know you can hear me, dumbass, and I'm not about to repeat myself.' Her voice reached him, like the pictures he couldn't shut out of his head. 'I'm going to tell you once, we can all have a bloody good moan, and then we get on with the rest of our lives. At least, you lot do.'

'Don't joke.'

Moira dead. Moira's corpse lying in one of the ridiculously over-elaborate coffins the family always chose when one of them passed. Moira, reduced to a headstone, and memories.

'I'm not joking, Mam. I can expect cirrhosis of the liver — or rather, for what I've got already to get worse — quite possibly cancer of the liver, and then liver failure. I won't be making plans beyond the next couple of years and we've been advised that trying for a baby right now would be very irresponsible.'

One of the women began to cry.

'I don't believe there's nothing they can do.' Charles had come to stand behind their mother, had put his hands on her shoulders

as though forcibly keeping her in her s

'My only chance is a transplant. Som(
in the next twelve months, ideally, bef
get much worse. With a new liver, I c
live as long as the rest of you.'

'Well, then that's what has to happen.

'Out of our control, Mam. I join the v
ing list, which is long, and I have a gen
make-up that is not common. The char
aren't good.'

Patrick walked away from the camp.

104

A week after his sister's confession to the family, Patrick pushed open the door of the pub and stepped inside. It was early in the evening and he could still see the bar, could still make his way across the carpet without having to push people out of the way. In a couple of hours, the place would be crammed with hot, sweating bodies.

The man waiting had a pint in front of him and a double Scotch. He slid the whisky over to Patrick. 'There's a Breathalyser unit on the A1 tonight,' he said. 'I'd make that your only one, if I were you.'

He led the way to a table by the window. Patrick pulled out a chair and sat down first. A mistake. His brother-in-law stayed upright, looking down at him, making him feel like a kid taken to the pub for a treat by an uncle.

'What?' Patrick said. 'What is it you want?'

'I want to talk about Moira. I'm assuming

you give a fuck, in spite of the impression you give most of the time.'

'She told us.'

'She didn't tell you everything.'

'I'm listening.'

His brother-in-law pulled out a chair. 'She needs a transplant,' he said. The chair groaned as he sat on it. 'But the chance of one is less than five per cent. One in five people on the transplant list will die before a liver becomes available. With her genetic make-up —'

'Am I supposed to know what that is?'

'You know the legend about how you lot came from India originally?'

Patrick shrugged. The Romani people, or gypsies, were believed to have migrated throughout Europe from Northern India. It was supposed to explain their dark hair and eyes.

'Well, turns out it could be true. Either that, or you have Asian ancestors somewhere not too far back. And the constant inbreeding over the years hasn't helped, either. Your sister needs a donor from that part of the world to reduce the chance of her body rejecting the new organ. Trouble is, there are almost no donors from there.'

'Why are you telling me this?'

'Because there's such a thing as living

515

donors. The liver is a weird organ. It can grow back. Someone physically compatible can donate half their organ to my wife and suffer no ill effects other than being a bit tired and sore for a few weeks. I'm not a match. We already checked.'

'But I might be?'

His brother-in-law inclined his head. 'Given how close you lot are, there could be several potential donors in that scrapyard you call home. And that's before you approach the wider family.'

'I'll do it.'

'Appreciate it. But you might not be a match either.'

'I'm her fucking brother. Why didn't she tell us?'

'Because there are always risks with surgery and she didn't want to put anyone in that position. I figured you'd want to know.'

Patrick felt something burning in his chest. Something that had nothing to do with the Scotch. He could save her. He'd rip his own liver out here and now if it could save Moira. There was nothing he would not do to save Moira.

105

'Right, OK, yes.' The doctor looked nervous. Patrick doubted he'd ever before seen fifteen people crammed into his consulting room at once, including a six-month-old baby in a buggy.

'Nobody wanted the bad news second-hand.' Moira, in spite of visibly weakening every time he saw her now, had refused to sit down, insisting instead that her mother and cousin take the only two seats. 'If they're going under the knife, they want to hear it from you.'

She was standing next to her husband on one side of the room. She'd have gone to the back if she'd been allowed. It was like she was trying to pretend this wasn't all about her, that she was an onlooker like the rest of them, worried, of course, but not directly involved.

'So, come on, lad. Which of us is it?' Their mother was directly in front of the young, anxious doctor, her arms folded.

'I'm sorry, but I'm afraid it isn't good news.' The git couldn't look at them. Patrick had known from the minute he'd set foot in the room that it wasn't going to be good. 'None of you is a match.' The doctor looked up then, timidly, like a young deer in the rifle sights.

'That's fucking impossible.' Ma waved her arm around, as though he might not have noticed the sheer number of them. 'I brought you fifteen donors, one of us must be suitable.'

The doctor picked a pen up from the desk and began twirling it. 'I certainly would have hoped so, but no. We can't operate on any of you. The chances of organ rejection are too great for us to risk surgery.'

'Good.' Finally, Moira looked up. 'I wouldn't have agreed anyway. It just saves an argument.'

'We didn't test Rebecca,' Patrick said.

'No.' Moira's eyes shot round to meet his. 'She's fifteen.'

The doctor shook his head. 'We couldn't use a minor,' he said. 'It wouldn't be ethical.'

'She hasn't moved up the list at all.' Patrick's brother-in-law lifted his eyes from the back of his wife's head. 'She's been on the transplant list for three months now, and she hasn't moved. I can't believe there have been no liver transplants in that time.'

'Almost certainly there will have been. But I did explain to you that Moira's requirements are uncommon. She may have to wait a little longer than most.'

'What if we go abroad?' Patrick spoke up. 'If our genetic whatsit is Indian, it's simple. We go to India and wait for a donor there. We pay someone. It's not illegal there, I checked.'

'I'm not flying to India to buy a poor person's liver,' said Moira. 'Forget it, Pat.'

He snapped. He didn't mean to. But misery and worry and frustration meant he spent his life pissed-off these days. 'What, you're just going to give up?'

Moira's face contracted and she leaned back against her husband. She put on such a front it was easy to forget how ill she was. And then you caught a glimpse of the colour of her skin in the daylight, of the yellowing of her eyes, or her too-thin frame, and you realized that time was running out.

'I don't recommend going to India,' said the doctor. 'Even if livers are available, I couldn't guarantee the safety of the procedures. Most ethical surgeons, I imagine, will steer clear of commercial operations. There would be a high risk of infection, of something going wrong. And don't forget, while you're out in India waiting, you could miss the chance of a transplant here.'

'Not while she's way down the list.' Moira's husband had wrapped his arms around his wife. She'd pulled against him once, then given in, leaning back and closing her eyes.

'That list isn't set in stone. If an organ became available that was a good match for Moira, if it was available close by geographically, there is every chance a match would be made and she'd be bumped straight to the top of the list.'

'I hate that someone has to die for me to live,' said Moira, her eyes still shut.

'That's a common reaction,' said the doctor. 'But what you have to remember is that you haven't caused someone else's misfortune. They would have died anyway.'

'We want a second opinion.' Their mother had folded her arms and planted them on top of her bosom. Her kids had learned long ago that you didn't argue with Ma in that mood. Luckily for him, the doctor didn't either.

106

Mr Ralph Wallace, one of the country's pre-eminent transplant surgeons, was taking no nonsense from the mob-handed family of gypsies in his waiting room. 'I'll see Ms Faa herself, her husband and her mother.' He strode ahead of them into his consulting room.

Patrick held open the door for the others then slipped inside after them. 'I'm her twin,' he announced to the surprised surgeon, knowing none of the family would correct him. He and Moira were only ten months apart. It was close enough.

Wallace was a Scot, from somewhere around Edinburgh. He was in his early sixties, slender and pale-skinned.

'I've had a chance to look through your notes.' He took his seat and removed a pair of glasses from a case on the desk. 'And the good news is that, should a donor organ become available in the near future, there is every reason for optimism. There are no signs of tumour yet and minimal damage to the kidneys. On the other hand, I'm afraid I can't disagree with my colleague. None of the family are suitable donors and I really don't recommend travelling to India. While you are as ill as you are, Ms Faa, home is the best place for you. And your situation could change overnight.'

'We haven't been given any reason to be optimistic about a donor,' said Patrick's brother-in-law.

'Well, there I don't quite share my colleague's view,' said Wallace. 'Twenty years ago, he'd have had a point, but the population of the UK is changing all the time. The birth rate among the Asian population is higher than among native British people. We've seen increasing numbers of immigrants from Southern Europe in recent years. A lot of asylum seekers are from the Middle East and North Africa. All of these people are potential donors.'

'Great,' said Patrick. 'We just need a few of them to die.'

107

Friday, 22 September

As the kitchen door closed behind the elderly, bespectacled nun, Patrick stepped out of the store cupboard. Through a gap in the door, he'd watched her stare down at the countertop, registering the disappearance of the knife. The one that was currently tucked into his belt. He'd seen her pull up the back of her skirt to scratch at her arse, before stepping to a door next to the cupboard he was hiding in and taking out a covered dish.

He couldn't risk someone coming back.

Following an inbuilt sense of direction, reliable as the magnetic north in a compass, he slipped back outside and then into a long, narrow greenhouse that ran most of the length of the back wall of the building. Instantly, the temperature rose by several degrees, and there was a scented dampness in the air that made him think of thunderstorms in the forest. A scrabbling in the knee-high foliage made him jump, but he put it down to rats and carried on. There was another door leading back into the convent at the far end.

This time, he found himself in a library, a large room lined by wooden bookshelves. Built into one wall was a slate fireplace. The rug beneath his feet was Turkish, red and highly patterned, but so thin the dull floorboards beneath could be seen in places.

His tinker's instincts took him on a detour around the side of the room, pausing to stare into glass-topped cabinets, on the lookout for anything of value. What he saw were papers written in a faded, incomprehensible script, the odd small box, even what looked like a shrivelled finger. No gold, silver, jewellery or coins.

The tropical-scented damp of the greenhouse had given way to a smell of mould and rodent droppings. When he looked more carefully at the books, he saw that some of the shelves carried great water stains. These books hadn't been touched in years; they'd turn to mush if someone tried to pull one off the shelves.

The decrepit books, though, were solid enough to insulate sound and Patrick could hear nothing but his own footsteps. Then a high-pitched screech from behind made him leap like a whipped dog. There was something in the greenhouse.

Black-clad women, sharp-taloned, teeth-like fangs, bearing down on him. These weren't nuns, they were witches! He was actually crossing himself, like his mother did, something he hadn't done in years, as he strode back to check out what was in there.

It was a bird. A peacock. It was strutting the length of the greenhouse like it owned the frigging place and if he didn't have bigger fish to fry he'd wring the fucker's neck right now. He wiped the back of his hand over both temples.

Ashamed of his nerves, of how this place with its odd mix of religious and feminine mystery was making him feel, he left the room. The hallway beyond was empty, the great front doors closed. Voices were coming from the right, from the room beyond the staircase. He walked over and waited outside. He had no idea what the woman he was hunting sounded like. Only that he would know her voice when he heard it.

108

'So, it was about love then, not money?' Said Hildegard. 'In the beginning, anyway?'

'Yes,' said Isabel. 'A young woman, dying before her time, and a family who simply couldn't bear to let her go.'

'What is it they say about the road to hell?' said Serapis.

The sound of running footsteps made them all start. Then the refectory door opened and the round, freckled face of Sister Belinda appeared. She was breathing heavily, and her veil was crooked, showing short tufts of red hair sprouting around her glowing face like unruly weeds in a parched garden.

'Excuse me, Mother, Sisters,' she said. 'But there is a police car waiting at the gate and what looks like the Black Maria behind it. Also, another car approaching from the farm and a uniformed constable coming in via the beach path. It would appear that the filth have us surrounded.'

109

This time, Ajax didn't follow the nun up the convent drive. He steered his car around her, over the grass and on towards the house. So did the police van behind him. On the car radio, he heard that the car approaching via the farm was at the back of the property. The officers on foot were already at the convent building. There were four doors that he knew of. In a couple of minutes, they'd all be covered.

At the imposing front entrance, he pulled on the handbrake and got out, his Kevlar vest uncomfortably tight around his chest. They really didn't make them in his size. The van pulled up alongside and he caught a glimpse of the officers in the back, fastening helmet straps, checking their weapons. The sergeant from the armed response unit who would be in charge of the operation jumped down.

'Stand back, sir, please,' he said to Ajax,

as he strode to the huge double doors and banged hard. 'Armed police, open up.'

'God, I hope someone's videoing this,' said MoJo. 'A bunch of middle-aged nuns being told to get down and spread 'em.'

The sergeant in charge tried the door. It was locked. He banged again. Louder this time. 'Armed police.'

No response. An officer carried the steel enforcer over and held it ready.

'I'm sure Sister-Approaching-Swiftly has a key.' MoJo pointed back towards the nun who'd opened the gates. She was about twenty metres away, still continuing at the same, unruffled pace. 'Seems a shame to damage those lovely oak doors.'

Ajax thought about intervening and decided against it. He kept quiet as the steel enforcer was pushed against the old doors. The lock broke instantly. The black-clad, armour-plated, helmeted officers poured inside and spread out like busy black insects in search of a honey spill.

'Can't hear any returned fire,' said MoJo. 'It's probably safe to venture in.'

The sergeant was in the hallway, still and wary, his eyes moving in large slow circles around the room. Two police officers, their backs to each other, were making their way up the stairs. Another stood guard to one side of the door. The rest had moved into the house. No sign of any of the nuns.

'They're all in chapel, Sarge,' a voice shouted from somewhere in the building.

Ajax and the sergeant turned together, went through a set of doors and down a short corridor. On the radios he could hear the search going on throughout the rest of the house, doors being slammed and a series of short, sharp orders.

'Police!'

'Clear!'

As they approached the chapel, they could hear singing, the same Latin plainsong Ajax had heard on his last visit. Two officers stood guard either side of the doors.

'Not locked, Sarge,' said one.

The sergeant nodded at them to proceed. As the officers pulled back both doors he strode through into the small, high, medieval space. 'Armed police,' he shouted. 'Nobody move.'

Nobody did.

110

Ajax stepped into the convent's chapel behind the armed response sergeant. The chapel was cream, with a latticework of gold-painted wood decorating the central dome. A raised wooden platform held the altar, whilst the rear wall was panelled in a rich dark wood. A lectern stood to one side of the altar, an elaborate wooden chair for a visiting priest on the other. The stone flags were smooth beneath his feet. The pews were carved wood, high and densely packed. When full, the chapel might seat over a hundred.

The light was subdued. Some hours past noon, no direct sunlight was coming through the stained-glass windows. In walled recesses, on the chancel steps, in ornate candelabra, great wax candles flickered.

The forty or so nuns were in the front pews, their black flowing robes gleaming in the soft light.

'That's a lot of nuns,' muttered MoJo.

'Everybody, hands up,' ordered the sergeant from halfway down the aisle.

The nuns carried on singing. Not a single hand moved.

The sergeant reached the front pew and kept going, pivoting, taking the last couple of steps backwards to bring him up against the chancel. Reflections of the altar candles danced on either side of his black helmet.

'This is Northumbria Armed Police,' he said. 'Can you all put your hands in the air?'

The nuns showed no sign of having heard. At the back of the chapel, immediately behind Ajax, several armed officers had spread out, weapons pointed inwards at the sisters.

'God help us,' Ajax muttered as he walked forward.

'Bit late for that,' said MoJo.

One of the nuns, Mother Hildegard he saw as she stepped into the light, raised her right hand and the singing stopped. As one, the nuns lowered their heads, so that nothing of their faces could be seen. At one signal, they had become serried ranks of shapeless black figures.

Ajax had reached the front.

'For what reason do you disturb our devotions, Superintendent Maldonado?' said Mother Hildegard.

The armed sergeant kept his face blank, his stare into the middle distance.

'I've got a warrant for the arrest of Isabel Jones, also known as Sister Maria Magdalena. Do you know where she is?' As Ajax spoke, he looked along the lines of black, veiled figures. Barring a couple of very short ones, she could be any of them.

'Given that we have been mourning the loss of our sister for two days now, I imagine she is with our Father in heaven,' said Mother Hildegard. 'Although I admit there were moments in our relationship when I had my doubts as to her ultimate destination. Please continue with your prayers, Sisters. I have no doubt this interruption will be soon concluded.'

Ajax saw the gleam in the old nun's eyes and knew it wasn't caused by candlelight.

'Her sister's car has been moved from where it was left on Wednesday morning. It was caught on camera heading in this direction and we've just spotted it parked a mile away,' he said.

'Then perhaps you should look for Sister Maria Magdalena a mile away.'

'You identified her body two days ago. Were you lying?'

Hildegard's eyebrows twitched upwards. 'Truth is a virtue that is much prized here,' she said. 'If I made a mistake, I imagine it would be down to misleading information, on your part, and distress, on mine.'

'Do you know where she is?' Ajax repeated.

Hildegard set off across the chapel floor, speaking as she did so. 'I'm going to save some time, Superintendent. For our benefit, not yours.' She reached the lectern and stretched out a hand to touch the huge, leather-covered Bible. 'I swear on this most beloved book that, to the very best of my knowledge, every living member of our community is here with us, in this chapel. If Sister Maria Magdalena is in the building, she must be here too. You'll forgive me for being less definitive, but I have already been caught out in a lie this week, where she is concerned.'

Ajax glanced round. There were no other doors. No cupboards. 'Ask the sisters to raise their heads, please,' he said to Hildegard.

'Certainly not. Modesty is another virtue we value. And some of them are quite elderly, with very bad shoulders.'

Ajax took a sharp breath. 'Sergeant, have your officers escort the sisters one by one to

534

Mother Hildegard's office. I'll interview them there.'

'They will not speak to you. This is a silent order.'

He took a step closer to her. Hildegard was a tall woman, but few people, of either sex, came close to his height.

'I will have the whole lot of you arrested and held in custody overnight,' he said.

The nun stared at him, unabashed. 'Seriously?' she said.

Ajax turned to the sergeant. 'I need two female officers, now.'

The women police officers were brought forward.

'I need to see their faces,' Ajax told them, trying not to be distracted by the smirks of the armed officers around him. 'As gently as you can, because I do not want accusations of police brutality from the Vatican, can you raise their heads so that I can get a look at each of them?'

As he spoke, Mother Hildegard slipped back into line and lowered her own head. She was now indistinguishable from the rest. Ajax walked to the end of the front row. 'Excuse me, Sister,' he said. 'I won't keep you long.' One female officer held the nun tentatively by the shoulders, the other raised her head by pushing up under the chin. The nun, with a round, freckled, red face, lifted her head but kept her eyes down. Definitely not Maria Magdalena. 'Thank you.' He moved on to the next.

It took nearly ten minutes to examine all of the nuns, but at the end of it, he was as sure as it was possible to be that Isabel Jones wasn't amongst them.

111

Hildegard stepped across the stone floor to the far right side of the chancel. 'You can come out now, Sister,' she said to the chapel wall.

The huge, carved-oak chair began to move forward and then slide sideways. Its high, arched back became a door in the wall, revealing, as it opened, a small, stone-lined space with a wooden chair and a tiny, inset altar. It was a priest's hole, dating back to the days when Catholicism was outlawed in England, and the great Catholic houses kept hidey-holes to guard their priests from harassment, even death.

Isabel, still dressed in Jessica's clothes, stepped out. At that moment, they heard running footsteps, and the chapel doors opened again.

'They've all left the house, but they're still in the grounds,' said Sister Belinda from the open doorway. 'I think they're pulling back to the perimeter, but we have to expect they're going to keep a watching brief, probably into the small hours.'

Hildegard rolled her eyes. 'Five hundred metres down the south dune path, at the point where the bridleway runs into the woods, you'll find a bicycle,' she told Isabel. 'If you get as far as Haggerston, go to the post office. Maisie and Fred's Vauxhall will be in the drive and the keys in the ignition. Fred says you might need a bit of choke but to be careful not to flood it. And the gearbox is getting a bit rubbery, but it's sound.'

'Mother, the police will have some sort of listening device on our phone,' said Isabel. 'They'll have heard you make the phone call.'

'Way ahead of you, Sister.' Eugenia dug deep into her habit and pulled out a mobile phone, which she held out to Isabel. 'We used this. Bought for cash, pay-as-you-go. My nephew got it for me in Newcastle. For emergencies. You should have it, Sister. Begging your pardon again, Mother.'

Hildegard shook her head. 'In the greater scheme of things . . .'

Isabel took the phone and slipped it into her own pocket. Her rucksack was still in the priest's hole.

'I'm leaving Jessica's computer with you,'

she told Hildegard. 'If anything happens to me —'

'Nothing will happen to you,' interrupted Sister Florentina.

'If anything happens to me, take it to the newspapers. Don't trust the local police. You know the password?'

'Then let's do that now.' Florentina was becoming agitated. 'There's no need for you to take any more foolish risks. We call the papers now, on Sister Eugenia's phone, and we tell them what Jessica found out.'

'Jessica had no proof.' Isabel looked around, trying to meet each sister's eyes in turn. They were so dear to her, these women, and she might never see them all together like this again. 'The people I saw brought to the Yellow House last night will have been moved by now. All trace of them has probably been scrubbed away. The pilot's body and the body of that poor girl I saw killed will never be found. The surgeon, that Wallace man, will deny any involvement. There's nothing to definitely link any police officer with what's been going on. Without proof, Jessica died for nothing.'

Nobody spoke.

'And besides, I'm wanted on two counts of murder, which really isn't good for the convent's reputation.'

Belinda grinned for a split second, then burst into tears.

Hildegard leaned forward and kissed Isabel on the forehead. 'God be with you, my dear.' She sniffed once, before turning to the others. 'Sisters, you all know what you have to do.'

112

'Ajax, they're coming out.'

Ajax picked up his radio and tapped the car brakes. 'Who's coming out? How many?'

'All of them.'

Cursing, Ajax pulled over and looked back. The road was clear. He turned the car, tricky on such a narrow road, and set off back towards the convent. He shouldn't have left. He'd damn well known there was something going on.

'Talk to me,' he barked into the radio.

'There's a white van approaching from the farm. It didn't turn off the road, so it must be a farm vehicle. It's pulling up at the back door. And the nuns' own car is being driven out of the garage. It's coming round the front. You should be able to see it soon.'

'I've got it,' another voice picked up. 'It's heading down the drive now. I can see two people inside. Sir, we've also got a group coming down the front steps, on foot. I can count seven — no, eight.'

'More at the back too, Sarge. At least ten. And some leaving via the side door.'

Ajax pressed his foot down. 'What the hell are they doing?'

'Just walking, sir. They're all setting off in different directions. Some in groups, some on their own.'

'The car's at the gate now. Do we let them out?'

'The Transit van's reversed right up to the back door. We can't see who's getting in and out.'

'Check everyone who leaves the grounds,' Ajax said. 'If she's between the ages of thirty and fifty, detain her until she can prove who she is. And someone count those frigging nuns. There were forty-two in chapel. If forty-three have appeared, we've got her.'

'Transit van's pulling away. Heading back towards the farm. There could be anyone or anything in the back.'

'I've got a bloke here with a peacock in his arms, Sarge. Want me to detain him? Thing looks vicious. Shit, watch it!'

'I've got two sisters at the beach gate, on bikes, sir. Neither answers to the description. One of them is in her seventies. The other's black.'

Ajax turned off the road and pulled up at

the convent gates again. The police van was still there. The sergeant was talking to the driver of the convent's old Ford Focus. As Ajax got out of his car, he could see two nuns in the front seats.

'Where are you going, ladies?' the sergeant asked them.

'Visiting the sick,' replied the elder of the two. 'Eileen Richards was discharged from Berwick Infirmary last night. We're going to read to her from the scriptures and have an hour's uplifting conversation.'

'You won't mind if we check in the boot?'

The boot was opened and closed. It was empty but for a travel rug and a spare wheel.

'Penguins everywhere,' said the armed response sergeant as he and Ajax pushed the gates closed again. He handed over a pair of binoculars. 'It's like watching *Happy Feet.*'

'They're distracting us.' Ajax trained the binoculars on a group of three nuns who were following a narrow path towards a wooded area at the furthest corner of the convent grounds. One of them looked round and very stooped. The others . . . he was going to lose sight of them among the trees.

'How many people have we got on the dunes side of the wall?' he asked.

The sergeant held up one hand to hush Ajax as he listened to his radio. 'We've stopped the white Transit van,' he said when he looked up again. 'Four nuns in the back who say they're going to the whist drive in Haggerston. One of them looks about the right age. I think you should go up there, sir.'

Ajax set off back to his car. 'Get some more people to the dunes. North-eastern corner,' he said. 'Quick as you can.'

'What about the peacock?'

'Jesus, I am not interested in frigging peacocks!'

He jumped into his car and set off towards the farm.

113

Hildegard, Florentina and Isabel reached the north-east corner of the convent grounds under cover of the trees. Isabel took off the borrowed veil and habit, and handed them to Florentina.

'You're surely not going to climb that wall?' Florentina was tucking the borrowed robes into her bodice. 'It looks awfully high.'

'She's done it many times,' Hildegard said. 'Take very good care for the next thirty minutes, Sister.'

'Why only thirty minutes?' asked Isabel as she looked for somewhere to put her foot.

'It will take us that long to get back into chapel,' Hildegard replied. 'Then we can start praying.'

114

Patrick spent fifteen minutes in the peacock cage before making his escape. The officer who'd stopped him as he left the greenhouse, the peacock tucked beneath his arm, had accepted his explanation that he was employed by the convent to look after the birds. He'd watched Patrick carry the bird into the cage, and then seen the others appear and surround him, presumably expecting food. Patrick had found grains in a plastic bucket and had scattered them around, hopping out of the way as the birds got too close to his feet. When he'd looked up, the police officer had gone. Once again, they weren't looking for a man.

He saw several of the sisters moving around the grounds, but none of them looked his way. When no one seemed to be in sight, he left the cage and sauntered over to the wall. A quick glance around and he was up and landing on the sandy wasteland on the other side.

115

The Vauxhall belonging to Maisie and Fred, who ran the post office, was an easier drive than Jessica's Fiat, with fewer confusing switches and lights. Isabel started the engine without difficulty, and pulled away from the house in Haggerston as the curtains to the front-room window twitched behind her. She travelled directly west until she reached the A698 between Berwick-upon-Tweed and Coldstream and then turned south. The distance she had to travel was less than twenty miles, but most of the roads that would take her there were narrow, winding and very slow.

She expected roadblocks at every turn, but saw very few other vehicles, and none of them police cars. At Coldstream, she left the main road, continuing south until she reached the National Park. She drove as far as she could, and then pulled over.

With some time to kill, she ate the food

the sisters had hurriedly packed for her. The rather odd combination of bread and honey and chocolate biscuits made her suspect that Sister Belinda had been on kitchen duty.

A police vehicle was parked close to the spot where the balloon and its basket had finally come to a standstill, and she could see at least two uniformed officers. There were several bystanders too, staring in at the copse of trees. All the burned and scattered debris of the crash had been removed, but still they stared at the place where a murdering nun had begun her killing spree.

Isabel found an outcrop of rocks and settled down, hoping dusk would come quickly and that the rain would hold off. Sister Serapis had lent her the binoculars the nuns used for spotting escaped peacocks and she trained them on the trees, trying to find the place where her fall had been broken by the branches of a large beech tree. Once, she looked at the faces of the people at the site, dreading to see a man with long curly hair and a leather trilby, that Patrick Faa would somehow know her plans, as he'd known them for the past three days, and that he would be here, waiting.

He wasn't. The group of four stood and stared for fifteen more minutes and then moved on. Another group arrived within the half-hour. They stayed for five minutes, but took a lot of photographs. At six o'clock another police vehicle arrived, this one with a solitary constable at the wheel. The officers on the day shift stood talking to him for a few minutes, before climbing into their own car and driving off.

There was going to be a guard overnight.

The day darkened. No one else came to the site. For a while, the constable on watch kept his engine running and the interior light on. At seven o'clock, he turned the engine off and the vehicle slipped into darkness. At half past seven, she could no longer see his face in the driver's seat. At eight, she risked moving.

She took an indirect route, keeping close to a stone wall, so that when she entered the copse of trees she could no longer see the police vehicle. Even so, she crept forward, slipping from one shadow to the next, welcoming the screeching, the hooting, the sounds of the night that would deaden any noise she might be making.

When she could see the gleam of white, yellow and blue bodywork again, she knew she was close. When she could hear music, she knew she was safe. He would never hear her.

Climbing up was easier than climbing down had been. Easier to spot the knots and ridges in the first length of the trunk, for one thing, that helped her up high enough to reach the first branch. Easier to see where she was going, for another, even in the almost complete darkness. Easier to bend and twist through the ever-closer branches as she moved higher and the tree became more dense. Several times her coat caught but she eased it free and pressed on.

When she reached the point where several branches seemed to have broken, she knew she was at the right spot. Looking up, she could almost see the trail she'd made as she'd tumbled earthwards. She pulled herself on to the one that had been thick and strong enough to break her fall and looked up.

For several, long minutes, she didn't see it. She swayed left and right, ducked down and stretched up, and was on the point of deciding the journey here had been worthless, that she wouldn't get the proof she needed after all, when she leaned forward and looked up again.

There. Just out of reach, she could see a tiny corner of turquoise leather. Jessica's mobile phone was still here. Steadying herself with one hand, she stretched for it.

The phone was dead.

She turned it round in her hand, pressing buttons randomly. Nothing happened. The phone had broken in the fall. It was worthless. Then she heard Jessica's voice, loud in her head.

It's a dead battery, you idiot. The phone's fine.

Of course, mobile phones ran on batteries. This one had been in a tree for nearly three days. The photographs Jessica had taken, of the dead pilot, of Patrick Faa pursuing them, would still be on it. So would her last message to Neil. Isabel slipped the phone into her pocket and began the slow, careful climb back down the tree.

Leaving the copse the way she'd entered it she hurried back to the car. She drove until she could see a signal on Sister Eugenia's mobile phone and then pulled over and took out the card that Mother Hildegard had given her.

'Superintendent Maldonado,' she said, when the deep male voice answered. 'This is Isabel.'

116

Not far from the church, Isabel found a small car park. With Jessica's mobile locked in the glove compartment, she made her way on foot to the church. The gate's hinges creaked, announcing her presence to anyone who might be waiting.

The path led directly to the church door. St Ninian's Catholic Church, Wooler, said the blue inlaid sign to the right of the doors. Most of the graves would be around the back.

She kept to the grass, conscious that others would know these grounds better than she did. At the rear, where trees kept most of the streetlight at bay, she risked turning on the torch. If they were waiting, they would know she was here anyway.

She scanned the churchyard with the torch beam, looking for raised graves. Fresh graves. Tucked away in the bottom corner, in the narrow strip of land between the back of the church and the churchyard wall, was one with fresh-looking flowers.

The turf laid over the grave had had time to thicken, and for the first weeds to sprout. Isabel's torch picked up the spiral of a daisy, the zigzag leaf of a dandelion. The roses in the clay vase, though, appeared less than a week old, and the marble of the headstone gleamed. The roses looked dark, almost black, in the torchlight. She aimed the beam on to the headstone's wording as footsteps crunched on the gravel behind her. A single set of footsteps.

He'd come alone. That meant she was in trouble.

117

Two and a half years earlier

Ajax found the accident easily enough. Crime scene tape was stretched across the entire width of the road. A hundred metres away he could see an ambulance. A dozen or more officers surrounded the scene, their screamingly yellow jackets seeming to leech colour from the streetlights overhead. CSIs were here too.

'Ajax.' The officer in charge greeted him.

'How's it going?' Ajax said. Three paramedics were huddled over a form on the tarmac.

'Just been pronounced dead at the scene. They're about to zip her up.'

Ajax kept walking towards the ambulance. 'Female, right?'

'Asian female, early thirties.'

'On her own?' At nine o'clock in February, the evening had long been dark.

'She had a kid with her. He's in one of

the cars, waiting for relatives to arrive. From what he's told us, he and his mum were crossing the road when a car approached at some speed. Really fast, is what the kid said. His mum pushed him on to the pavement but the car caught her. Her head struck the kerb.'

The car had not stopped. The incident was now a fatal hit-and-run. Hence Ajax's presence.

'From the position we found her in, and from what we can get out of the kid, we're pretty certain the car was travelling south towards the A1148. No skid marks that we can see,' the officer said. 'The car braked very briefly after it hit her. Then accelerated away.'

'Witnesses?' Ajax didn't hold out much hope. The night was filthy.

'Only the kid.'

They'd reached the paramedics. 'May I?' Ajax crouched low, not waiting for permission. He lifted the plastic sheet. Someone leaned over with an umbrella.

The woman was lying half on, half off the pavement. Her face above her eyebrows had been cut apart. The skin was loose and hanging. There wasn't much blood to be seen, but it could have been absorbed by the black cloth of the hijab. She looked

Arabic, rather than Indian or Pakistani.

'Has she got ID? Did she have a bag?' Ajax glanced up at the nearest officer.

'I'm not sure.'

'Find it. Make sure it goes with her to the hospital. In fact, can you personally take charge of that? Can you make sure all her personal effects, especially any wallet and documentation, goes with her?'

'Of course, sir.' The officer walked away.

Ajax got to his feet. 'How we doing, tracing her next of kin?'

'She lives a few streets away. We've sent someone round.'

'Good. Make sure they get a lift to the hospital if they need one.' He ignored the puzzled frowns. 'I need to talk to the kid.'

The child was huddled in a blanket in the back of a police car. He'd been weeping, but was quiet now.

'Name's Jarfa,' the female constable with him told Ajax.

'Jarfa, I need to ask you some questions.' Ajax never played softly-softly with kids, especially traumatized ones. It didn't help them, and it got him nowhere. 'What can you tell me about the car that hit your mother?'

Round black eyes stared back at him.

'We've already taken a statement from

him,' the constable whispered.

Ajax ignored her. 'What colour was it?'

'Silver.'

'Good lad. Are you interested in cars? Do you know what kind it was?'

A blank stare.

'Do you know what a registration number is?'

An audible tutting sound from the constable.

'Did you see the driver?'

'No driver.'

Ajax leaned closer. 'I'm sorry, Jarfa, what did you say?'

'No driver. There was no driver.'

Ajax glanced across the street at the parked cars. Drivers and passengers in cars at night were difficult to spot, but not usually invisible. A runaway car would still be here.

'He was bending down,' he muttered to himself. 'Trying to reach something on the seat, or something that had slipped to the carpet. He didn't see them.'

'Circle on front.'

Ajax turned back to the child.

'Circle on front of car.' His little finger traced a circle shape in mid-air, about three inches in diameter.

Ajax glanced at the car. 'I tell you what,

Jarfa, could you get out for a second, and draw it for me.' He held out his hand, helped the child down, then turned him to face the rear side panel of the police car. It was damp with rain. 'Like this?' Ajax traced a circle.

'Bigger.' Jarfa repeated the circle, then traced a diagonal cross in the middle of it. He stared at it, as though not quite sure.

'Was it like this?' Ajax drew another circle. This time, instead of a cross inside it, he drew a three-pointed star.

Jarfa nodded.

'On the front of the car, in the middle of the bonnet?'

Another nod.

'Good lad, Jarfa.'

He was looking for a silver Mercedes.

118

The slender, grey-haired man who opened the door of the mock-Tudor house was in his early sixties. His irritated frown at being disturbed so late turned to genuine puzzlement when he saw the large black man on his doorstep.

'What can I —'

Ajax held up his warrant card. 'Detective Chief Inspector Ajax Maldonado, Northumbria Police,' he said. 'Can I have a moment of your time?'

The Tudor theme continued in the spacious, marble-tiled hallway. Wooden beams, too straight and perfect ever to have come from a tree, stretched the length of the ceiling. The walls were panelled in what passed for wood until you got close. A miniature suit of armour stood to one side of some double doors.

Ajax followed the man across the hall and into a study. He took the seat that was offered him — walnut, with a striped silk cushion — and waited for his host to sit likewise. He didn't. Instead he stopped in front of the desk and turned to face Ajax.

Ajax took out his notebook. Purely for show. There was nothing in it. He hadn't even brought a pen from the car. 'Can I ask where you were two nights ago, sir, between the hours of eight o'clock and ten o'clock?' he said.

The man turned, opened a leather-bound desk diary and studied it for a few seconds.

'Here,' he said. 'I was working at the hospital until seven, then I had a drink at the golf club. I'm pretty certain I was home by eight thirty, though.'

The hit-and-run accident in which a small boy's mother had been killed had happened closer to nine o'clock.

'You drive an E-Class silver Mercedes, is that right?' Ajax asked.

'It is.'

'Can I see it?'

A polite smile. 'I'm afraid it's with my wife. She's at the theatre this evening.'

'What time do you expect her home?'

'She's staying with friends. I can try to call her, but she's notoriously bad about leaving her mobile on. Especially when she's in the theatre.'

'A car similar to yours was involved in a fatal hit-and-run on Wednesday night on Woodstone Drive.'

The man frowned, allowed his eyes to drift, as though the name sounded familiar, but he couldn't quite . . . 'I see. And you're checking all registered owners in the area? Very thorough. Well, I can bring it to the station tomorrow when she gets back. Around two p.m. probably, will that suit?'

'The car involved in the hit-and-run would have sustained some damage to the front left wing.'

'I imagine so. Broken headlight. Shards of glass in the road. I watch *Crimewatch,* Detective. You know, you look very familiar. I'm sure I've seen you somewhere before. Golf club?'

'Can't afford the fees,' Ajax said. 'The headlight was intact when the car left the scene but some paint chippings were found on the victim's shoulder bag. They'll help us identify the model. Even the factory it came from.'

The man nodded, as though interested. 'It's really quite remarkable what you can do these days.'

'Actually, our success in solving hit-and-run cases is abysmally poor.'

'You don't say.'

'Without witnesses, and there were none in this case, without CCTV footage — and how much of that is there on a residential street? — we rely upon the conscience of the driver. We have to hope he can't live with himself. That he gets to the point where he has to give himself up.'

'And how often does that happen?'

'Hardly ever. People's instincts for self-preservation will nearly always outweigh their social conscience.'

'Pity.'

'You're right, you know, you and I have met before.'

'I thought so. Drink?' He glanced towards a table of decanters. 'Or is that not allowed?'

'My wife is a patient of yours. We came to see you a few weeks ago.'

'Really.' He frowned. 'Maldonado is an unusual name. I'm sure I —'

'She uses her maiden name still. She comes from a very old family. She promises me she'll change to mine if we ever have children.'

'Yes, families should have a name in common. Detective Maldonado, is there —'

'We came en masse. About twelve of us. It's the way they are. Drove me mad at first, now I'm used to it.'

'Oh good lord. Moira Faa. I remember

now. How is she?'

'Moira Joanne Faa Maldonado. I call her MoJo. And she's worse. We can expect her to decline rapidly now.' Ajax got up and crossed to the decanter table. 'You know, I think I will have that drink.' He found a glass from the shelf, took the top off a decanter and poured. He had no idea what it was. He sat back down.

'The woman who was killed in the road traffic accident on Wednesday, Mr Wallace, was thirty-two and in very good health. Her head was a mess but the rest of her was fine. She was from the Middle East. Could have been a match for my wife.' He raised the glass to his lips and swallowed. It was Scotch. 'My wife could be lying in a hospital bed now, recovering from a transplant operation and reading a book of baby names. Instead, she's in bed at home, turning a more vivid shade of yellow every time I look at her.'

Wallace leaned back against the desk. 'I understand how you feel, and it does seem like a terrible waste, but —'

'The woman had a donor card and her family went against her wishes. Her wishes counted for nothing, because they were squeamish and selfish.'

'I understand, but it's the law. If the family don't consent —'

Ajax reached inside his coat and pulled out his iPad. He opened up an app and turned it to face Wallace. 'Play it,' he said.

'What?'

'Play it.' He pushed the iPad at the doctor, giving him little choice. Wallace touched the screen. Ajax watched his face. The two-second clip was without sound.

Earlier that day, he'd visited a shop on the corner of Woodstone Drive and the A1148, not three hundred metres from where the accident happened. The shop had suffered a series of burglaries and vandalism in recent months and the shop owner had installed a surveillance camera on the outside wall. It was focused on the shop window rather than the road, but on the rain-soaked Wednesday night, it had captured reflections of cars driving past.

'You'll see the rear registration number of that silver Mercedes is just about visible,' said Ajax. 'I've frozen it and blown it up, to be certain. To have passed the shop at that hour, a car would have had to drive past the scene of the accident pretty much at the time it happened. If the paint chippings on the victim's handbag match the bodywork of your car, I'd say we have a pretty strong case, wouldn't you, Mr Wallace?'

Wallace didn't speak. His hands on the iPad, though, were noticeably shaking.

'On the other hand, this is a two-second clip of footage that would be wiped clean soon anyway. Nobody's seen it but me and, if it went missing, which could happen easily, no one would ever know. The case, like so many hit-and-runs, would remain unsolved.'

'What is it you want?'

Ajax drained his glass. 'I want to talk about my wife.'

119

St Cuthbert's golf club stood on high ground and on clear days the sea was a slender ribbon of cobalt-blue on the horizon. The wind was never still. Ajax watched the silver Mercedes curl its way up the long, winding drive and pull into the car park beside his own vehicle. The left front panel was pristine, perfect. From across the car park he saw Patrick climb down out of his Defender and walk towards them. Of everyone in his wife's big, eccentric family, Patrick was the one he'd found hardest to get used to. Going forward, though, he was going to be the most valuable.

Wallace sat staring straight ahead, as though he hadn't seen Ajax, as though the gypsy bloke heading towards him were invisible. Ajax got out of the car as Patrick put his hand on the Mercedes' passenger door.

'In the back,' Ajax told him.

A moment's stand-off.

Ajax kept his voice low. 'There'll be a time to unleash the inner psycho. Just not now. Get in the back.'

With his trademark sullen glare, Patrick did as he was told. At the same time, Ajax opened the passenger door and climbed inside.

Wallace didn't bother with social niceties. 'I've manipulated your wife's data so that she appears to be much more ill than she really is,' he said.

'She really is ill,' Ajax said. Moira was on extended sick leave from her job in CID. Without a transplant, she'd never go back.

'According to her notes, she's unlikely to live beyond another three months,' Wallace went on. 'That will put her very close to the top of the list in terms of urgency. Her youth will count in her favour, as will her previous good health. It's a pity you don't have children, but we have to work with what we've got.'

'Make it one month,' said Patrick, in the back seat.

Wallace shook his head. 'That would be counterproductive. The database administrators won't believe that someone within weeks of dying will recover sufficiently to make the operation worthwhile. Three months is best. The television appeal will help too.'

Ajax had been prepared to call in favours to get *BBC Look North* to run a TV appeal for more donors from ethnic minorities, but in the event, the programme makers had been surprisingly keen. Moira's colourful family, all of whom were to be involved, would make for good television. Only his wife was reluctant, but the broadcast could hardly go ahead without her.

'We always get a flurry of sign-ups after a TV appeal,' Wallace said. 'There's really every reason to be optimistic. I'm cutting back my London clinics for the foreseeable future so that I can be on hand.'

'It's not enough,' Ajax said.

'There really is nothing else —'

'Let's talk hypothetically. What does my wife need to live?'

'I'm not sure I —'

'She needs someone from a compatible ethnic group and blood group, someone who's registered as a donor and whose family will support his or her choice, to die within the next six months.'

'Yes, but it may need more than one. Even with the very particular HLA of Ms Faa, she may not be at the top of the list.'

'You said before, geography is a factor. A donor in the north-east would be more likely to benefit Moira than someone in, London, say.'

'That's true.'

'So how many?'

'Impossible to say. And, frankly, I really don't —'

'Two? Ten? How many do we have to bring here? How many people have to die before my wife can live?'

120

Friday, 22 September
'Busted,' said MoJo when Ajax turned the corner and saw the slim figure with the curly dark hair standing at the foot of the grave. Isabel didn't move as they approached. They stopped, a foot or so behind her, and saw her raise her torch beam to the wording on the headstone.

Moira Joanne Maldonado, née Faa
Beloved wife, treasured daughter,
adored sister

MoJo left his side then and slipped ahead, as though to get a closer look at the woman whom Ajax had been hunting for days. When she turned back to face them both, her hands were resting lightly on the headstone of her own grave. She glanced down, as though to check the wording remained the same, and when she met his eyes again, the spark in them had faded.

'I'm sorry about your wife,' said Isabel, without turning round.

'I'm sorry about your sister,' Ajax replied.

MoJo gave a long, heavy sigh and, for a second, her outline seemed to blur. Ajax took another pace forward and he and Isabel stood side by side. Neither looked at the other. He was looking at his wife while he still could. He neither knew nor cared what Isabel was looking at.

'I understand why you did it in the first place,' said Isabel. 'I might do much the same, for someone I loved. But Moira died two years ago. Why are you still doing it?'

It was a very good question, one his mother-in-law had been asking repeatedly of late. The money was useful, of course, but to suggest any amount of money could make up for what they'd lost was to do MoJo's memory serious disservice.

'There was some debt,' he said. 'Private medical bills. And I guess we were just angry.'

Yes, that was it. So angry, when she'd finally slipped away, her body wracked with pain and shrivelled with disease, that when the boatload of refugees arrived that same night, it was all he could do to stop Patrick ripping them apart with his own hands, because they'd arrived too late. Because in amongst this bunch of filthy, frightened people could be the healthy organ that would have saved his sister.

It had taken every ounce of self-control Ajax had not to join in himself. To tear limb from limb, to rip open stomachs, to crush bones beneath his fists. Of course, ultimately, they'd done exactly that. They'd merely contracted the job out to surgeons.

'So what happens now?' Isabel said. 'I'm guessing you won't want to take the risk of me testifying against you and your wife's family, even if you think I don't have any proof.'

'Did you find Jessica's phone?' Ajax said. 'I imagine you didn't have it to begin with, or we'd have heard from you before now.'

Directly in front of him — he still hadn't taken his eyes off her — MoJo seemed to be letting the headstone support her weight, as though she were suddenly weary. For the first time, his wife's ghost seemed to bear a keen resemblance to his wife in the last few weeks of life.

'Is the plan to stage an accident for me?' Isabel went on. 'Feed my organs into the system, add the cash to the Ajax Maldonado retirement fund?'

MoJo's eyes were still fixed on his face,

but her body had taken on a translucence. The wall of the churchyard, the line of yew trees, the tall headstones, all things he knew to be behind her, seemed to be traced across her body.

'I've had twenty years of very clean living,' Isabel went on, and he wanted to snap at her to shut up, that he had other, more important things on his mind right now. 'My organs must be worth something to someone. And it's not as though I care that much. Jessie was the only reason I —'

'No worries.' Patrick, unable to keep quiet any longer, appeared from behind the church wall. 'It'll be my pleasure.'

'Pat,' pleaded MoJo, but the effort seemed to take a lot out of her. She was fading quickly now.

Isabel watched Patrick draw closer. 'You must have loved your sister very much. Did you ever think that maybe you loved her too much?'

Ajax couldn't see Isabel's face but Patrick could and whatever his brother-in-law saw there made him stop, keep his distance.

'I had a brother once,' Isabel told Patrick. 'I still have, although I haven't spoken to him for years. He hurt me, a long time ago. He loved me, but he hurt me. Maybe he hurt me because he loved me, in his own

aware of uniforms surrounding Patrick, patting him down, reading him his rights. He saw a female officer take hold of Isabel gently around the shoulders and lead her away. All this was on the periphery of his vision. As the chief droned his way to the end of the customary words, Ajax couldn't take his eyes off his wife.

She wasn't really there at all any more, was nothing more than an impression, like the ripple a stone makes when dropped into water, fading imperceptibly, but irreversibly, until there came a moment when it was gone.

121

Wednesday, 25 October

John Jones

From Wikipedia, the free encyclopedia

John Edward Jones is a British police officer who is currently Acting Chief Constable of Northumbria Police. Jones was born in 1974 in Stanhope, County Durham. He joined the army at seventeen and was attached to the Royal Regiment of Fusiliers until age twenty, when the army sponsored him to attended the University of Durham. He gained a BA in Philosophy and Politics and, later, a diploma in Criminology from the Cambridge Institute of Criminology. Jones's policing career began when he left the army to join Leicestershire Police in the mid 1990s. He spent ten years as a detective, rising to the rank of detective inspector, before returning to uniform in 2008 and carrying out a number of operational roles with West Yorkshire and Northamptonshire. At Northamptonshire Police he was Assistant Chief Constable for Specialist Operations and was appointed Deputy Chief Constable in 2012. His position as Chief Constable is expected to be confirmed shortly.

In June 2013 he was awarded the Queen's Police Medal. He is married to Sarah, and has two teenage daughters.

Mother Hildegard removed her spectacles, rubbed her eyes and leaned back from the desktop computer. 'And you didn't know? Neither of you knew? I don't quite understand it. Jessica was a police officer too.'

Sitting across the desk in Mother Hildegard's study, Isabel said, 'There are nearly a hundred and thirty thousand police officers in England and Wales, and forty-three forces. Who can know everyone? John Jones is a common name, and we always called him Ned anyway, because our father was John. No, I don't think Jessica had any idea until she saw him in the police station that night.'

Hildegard nodded absently. She stared down for a few seconds and when she looked up again, her eyes were unusually bright.

'When you joined us, Sister, all those years ago, your aunt told us that she thought you'd been harmed. She claimed to have no idea who or how, but I remember distinctly her saying that she thought you were hiding.'

Isabel looked back at the wise grey eyes, then over the elderly woman's shoulder to where rain was beating against the window. Moments passed. And then she knew the time had come.

'I've been hiding for over twenty years, Mother,' Isabel said. 'I'm sorry I couldn't tell you the truth before.'

Hildegard put her spectacles back on, and seemed to be reading the Wikipedia page again. When she glanced back up, she said, 'And now you feel you have to meet with him again? To confront him?'

'Not exactly. Maybe.' Isabel stopped. She couldn't explain this to herself, never mind anyone else. 'I don't know, maybe to prove to myself that I'm not afraid any more. Or maybe I'm doing it for Jessie. *Blood is thicker,* she said. She knew he'd come through for me. Whatever he did in the past, I wouldn't be here now if he hadn't.'

'Well, thank heaven she was right about that.' Hildegard got to her feet. 'Will you be all right, Sister?'

Would she be all right? She was the sole

580

beneficiary of Jessica's will. She had a car, enough money to tide her over until she'd had a chance to make some decisions. But Hildegard wasn't talking about money.

'I guess there's only one way to find out,' Isabel said.

'There'll always be a refuge for you here. Even if you do, ultimately, ask to be released from your vows.'

'Thank you.'

Hildegard turned abruptly to face the window. The glass was streaked with tiny streams of water, so it was impossible to tell, especially from across the room, whether the trickles running down the reflection of Hildegard's face were really rain, or something else.

'You'll forgive my not showing you out, Sister,' she said. 'Somewhat to my surprise, I admit, I think that watching you of all people drive away might just break my heart.'

122

The rain had become a torrent by the time Isabel reached Berwick-upon-Tweed, pouring like a punishment from the heaven she'd never believed in. Trees seemed to slump, as though barely strong enough to hold up under the deluge, while the hard road surface beneath the tyres of Jessica's car had dissolved into a rush of water.

She spotted the restaurant and pulled up. The rain was now an endless drumbeat. Beating down on the roof of the car, on the street outside, it was drowning out even the roar of her engine, the swish of the wipers, the thumping of her heart.

She switched off the ignition, let the water cloud her windscreen, and sat listening. She was twenty minutes early. Indistinctly, through the almost-opaque car windows, she watched a family run towards the restaurant and race inside.

Still the rain came down, as if there were

no end to the darkness it had to wash away, until it seemed the flimsy shell of the car around her couldn't possibly hold it off for ever.

So many rainy nights in her past; she'd lain awake during heavy rain, wondering if the windows would hold up. Or if her heart would. Sometimes she'd wondered if he deliberately chose rainy nights, because the incessant battering against the side of the house would cloak what was going on inside it: his groans of pleasure, the silence of her despair.

The windows were misting. She wiped a streak clean in time to see a man, his build and speed of movement marking him out as young, stride through the streaming mass of water on the pavement to reach the restaurant. He didn't rush inside, like the family, but stood for several seconds, peering in through the window, looking up and down the street. He checked his watch. He pulled out his phone, seemed to make up his mind, then tugged open the glass door and disappeared.

More minutes went by. The news came on the radio, a story about a preliminary court hearing in Newcastle that day. Isabel recognized several of the names and turned it off.

A car pulled up outside the restaurant. A blue sedan, an unfamiliar make and model, but something about its sleek presence on the street set her heart beating faster. When its driver door opened, she crouched lower in her seat.

Ned wasn't wearing uniform. She'd been expecting that he would. Had prepared herself for the man in full dress regalia that she'd seen on television that morning in the café. Instead, he had a blue coat over jeans and thick hiking boots. His hair was the same though. Steel grey, with a few hints of the dark brown that she remembered.

She watched him glance up and down the street, rest his eyes for a second on her car and then go inside.

On winter nights at the priory, the rain had thundered down on to the roof, streaming in mini torrents along the guttering, pouring like tiny ferocious waterfalls to the ground. She'd spent long nights awake there too, staring at a succession of doors that wouldn't lock, with a cold nugget in her heart that told her, in spite of everything, that one night he would walk through. That she hadn't escaped after all, that five years, ten years, twenty, weren't enough, that there was no escape and that the day would come when he would find her.

When she opened the car door, the puddles on the pavement had merged, forming a shallow lake that she had no choice but to step into.

He was waiting for her in that restaurant. He'd found her.

She was becoming part of the rain. It had soaked through her coat. Her hair was dripping, she could feel rivulets running down the back of her neck. If she stayed out here much longer, she'd dissolve. She stepped forward into cold water that soaked her shoes, splashed her way across the road and pulled open the restaurant door.

A group of young women, obviously work colleagues, because they were all in smart suits, were sitting at the bar. The family she'd watched enter were still arguing about which seats the children were going to take. One of them, the youngest, had actually crawled beneath a central table.

The eyes that met hers when the door closed weren't those of her brother, who was sitting at a table towards the back of the room, but instead eyes of a deep chocolate brown. The young man at a table by the window had a thin glass of beer in front of him. Most of it was gone already. His hair was dark and curled almost to his shoulders. He looked nineteen, maybe twenty. He was thin, pale-skinned and long-limbed. He was a beautiful boy and, with a stab of pain, she saw how much like her sister he was.

'Bella?'

The deep voice, still with its north-eastern accent, made her start. She hadn't been expecting him to call her that, even though he always used to. She turned away from the young man in the window and faced her brother.

He was standing. She took a step towards him. They'd spoken briefly on the night it had all come to an end, but only about immediate events and only in the presence of witnesses. He'd used words like *procedure* and *regularity,* insisting she have a family liaison officer with her, and she'd gone along with it all because the last thing she wanted was to talk about anything important, or to be alone with him.

There was a bottle of wine on the table and two glasses. He was taller than she'd expected, taller than she remembered, and so much broader in the shoulder. But he'd only been eighteen when she'd seen him last.

'Can I take your coat?' he said.

Her coat was soaking wet, twice its usual weight and dripping on to the tiled floor.

She shook her head.

He looked uncertain for a moment, before gesturing to the seat opposite his own. She remained standing. Only when he sat down himself did she copy his example. He poured her wine. Red. She didn't touch it.

'I'm sorry about Jess,' he said. 'She was the best of us.'

Just hearing the name was like a stab in the heart. It was so easy to tell herself it would get better in time, so hard to see her way through the next hour.

'The first hearing was today,' her brother said, changing tack. 'You may have heard. Magistrates' court. Maldonado and five members of the Faa family were remanded in custody pending a trial at the Crown Court. Bail denied.'

He was buying time. Giving her details of the case.

'Ralph Wallace?' she said. It was a good idea. She would do the same.

'Next couple of days. He'll probably be tried separately. The evidence trail in his case is very different.'

She already knew the pilot's body had been found, pulled out of a lake not far from where the Faa family lived. 'The girl we saw being killed,' she said. 'On that first morning. Have you —'

He interrupted her. 'A young woman was taken to Newcastle General that same morning. Her family claimed she'd been involved in a climbing accident. Wallace was the harvesting surgeon and her ID does not stack up.'

'She was still alive? While I was running, she was still alive?'

He leaned forward, only fractionally, and only for a second. When he saw her pull back he straightened up again. 'Bella, you couldn't have saved her. Even if you'd reported what you'd seen, we would never have thought to look in the Accident and Emergency ward of the local hospital. She was lost once she fell into the hands of those people.'

She reached out, picked up the glass and put it down again. It had been years since she'd drunk alcohol. It was water she needed, she'd never known her throat to feel so dry, but she didn't want to ask him for anything.

'Think of it as Communion wine, if it helps.' Ned was trying to smile at her. 'Although I have to advise you that drink-driving laws have probably tightened up a lot in the last twenty years.'

She picked the glass up again and watched the dark red liquid swirl around in it.

Communion wine was sipped delicately from a solid silver chalice that always felt ice cold. She could feel the warmth of this wine through the glass.

'We have though, this week, rescued a group of people from two locked caravans on a site outside Stirling,' her brother told her. 'They were starving, ill, exhausted, but they'll be OK. They were probably destined for the same fate.'

'That's good. Not that they're ill and starving. That you've found them. And they're OK.'

His lips widened. 'Yes, it is.'

She brought the glass to her mouth. It was nothing like the sweet, watered-down wine the nuns drank at Communion. This was rich and smoky, with a texture that seemed to cling to her teeth. She felt its warmth glow in her chest.

'I know what you think I did,' Ned announced.

Her hand was trembling as she put the glass down. So they were going to do it now, here, tonight. She wasn't sure she could.

'I went to see Aunt Brenda when I came out of the army,' he went on. 'She didn't want anything to do with me, refused to tell me where you or Jessica were. I couldn't understand it.'

Aunt Brenda, that stout, rough-voiced woman, who'd stepped in and saved her and Jessica when their whole world had fallen apart. She should not have had to deal with —

He couldn't understand it?

Ned picked up his glass and drank. In spite of what he'd told her about drink-driving laws, it wasn't his first. The bottle was nearly half empty.

'I hung around and that night I saw Uncle Rob in the pub,' he told her. 'He'd had a few and he picked a fight. He told me what I was supposed to have done, said he'd string me up if I ever showed my face again. Called me the worst names I could think of and quite a few I'd never heard before, even after four years in the army.'

Ned's colour had risen. His hands were shaking. He was struggling with this too. Even so . . .

Supposed to have done?

Rain pouring down in the pre-dawn. Unbearable pain. A tiny, slime-smeared, solid little body, whisked away from her before she could even ask what sex it was.

'I tracked Jess down a couple of years later,' he said. 'It wasn't hard, once I'd joined the force. I knew she was in the Met. I stood at the back of the church when she got married. I couldn't find a trace of you, though. After a while, I stopped torturing myself.'

She wasn't listening.

Supposed to have done?

'I had a child,' she told him, and felt a surge of emotion that might, just might, be relief at having voiced those words for the very first time.

Across the table, her brother scowled and, for a second, his eyes left hers, to look at something behind her.

'Sixteen years old and pregnant,' she said. 'I don't believe in immaculate conception. Not two thousand years ago and not twenty-four years ago. You did that to me, Ned, and you are not going to pretend it didn't happen.'

'It wasn't me. It was Dad.'

Nothing. There was nothing in her head. She had nothing to say. She wasn't even sure she'd heard him right. Then —

'How dare —'

He held up both hands, as though to ward her off, leaned across the table and spoke low and urgently. She could smell wine on his breath.

'I didn't know,' he said. 'I swear I didn't. If I'd known, I'd have done something, I don't know what, but I wouldn't have let

591

him do that to you.'

She leaned forward too, until their faces were inches apart. 'It was not Dad, it was you.'

'Think about it, Bella. We were all grieving for Mum. We were all shattered. And then, the one person you thought you could rely on started doing that. It was a defence mechanism. You didn't want to believe Dad was capable of something so vile, so you projected what he was doing on to someone else. Not much better, admittedly, but slightly.'

'I was sixteen, fifteen when it started. I knew the difference between my brother and my father.'

'Really? We were the same height, same build, same colouring. A dark room. A terrified girl. Really?'

'No.'

'Why do you think the poor bastard topped himself, Bella? He couldn't live with what he'd done.'

He was not going to do this to her. Nothing he could say would make a difference.

'I can prove it,' he said.

'How?'

Ned turned to reach into his coat. He pulled a slim, white envelope from an inside pocket. She took it and removed the single strip of paper.

Personal Paternity Test Certificate

The first line was short, in bold, a case reference number. The second listed a sample number, then the name of the Alleged Father: *John Edward Jones.* The third line contained another sample number, then the name of the —

Her eyes shot up to meet those of her brother.

'I know,' he told her. 'Read it.'

Name of the child. Adam Rupert Townsend, born 15/10/1993

The paper fell from her hands. 'You've — He —'

'Bella, you need to read it.'

Most of the page was taken up with a table. Three columns. Letters and numbers. Some sort of comparison going on. It meant nothing.

'The conclusion will do it,' Ned told her. 'Read the conclusion.'

Mr Jones, whilst bearing some similarity of DNA systems, is excluded from being the biological father of Adam Rupert Townsend. The exclusion is based on the fact that he does not show the genetic markers which have to be present for the biological father of the child Adam Rupert Townsend at multiple DNA systems. Whilst there is likely to be a close family relationship, it is practically proven that Mr Jones is not the biological father of Adam Rupert Townsend.

The certificate had been signed by two doctors

Everything had changed. The grim certainty she'd carried in her heart for over twenty years had been crushed like black ice beneath a speeding car. And yet there was only one thing that was important.

'You've seen him? You've met him? You must have done, for this to have happened.'

'Bella, do you understand what it says? We did a second test, only on Adam this time. His DNA is particular. Enough to show that he was almost certainly the child of a close — there's no easy way of saying this — incestuous relationship. His biological father was also his maternal biological grandfather.'

'Adam. His name is Adam?'

Ned ran a hand through his hair. 'I did worry about how he'd take the news. Not an easy thing to saddle a kid with, but he's pretty switched on. He said himself, when you're adopted, you know there's something not quite right in your past.'

Isabel was no longer listening to her brother. She was staring at the name on the paper. Adam Rupert Townsend. Born on the fifteenth of October. It had been pouring with rain, she remembered. Just like today. Water had lashed against the hospital windows, streamed along guttering and out through overflow pipes. The world had been full of rushing water the day her son had come into her world. For less than an hour.

Behind her, the restaurant door opened and for a few seconds the sound of the storm outside was amplified.

'I contacted the adoption agency when I knew he was coming up to eighteen,' Ned was saying. 'I had my details listed on their system, in case he wanted to trace his biological family. There was no one else. Brenda and Rob were dead. Jessica never knew, and they had no idea where you'd gone.'

Adam. Her baby's name was Adam.

'He got in touch with me,' Ned told her. 'He's been part of my family for four years now. But you're the one he's been waiting for.'

She swallowed. 'Does he know? Does he

know that you've found me?'

'Yes,' said a voice behind her. A voice she'd never heard before in her life and yet knew instantly.

She turned her head and looked up. The young man from the table by the window, the one with Jessica's eyes, was standing by her side.

ACKNOWLEDGEMENTS

My loving thanks to:

My son, Hal, for staying calm when the two of us got horribly lost in Northumberland National Park. My parents, Pat and Vinny, for staying calm on Holy Island, when the tide was coming in fast. My mother-in-law, Jeanette, for staying calm in York when forced to wade through floodwaters, and again when trapped on the city walls. My husband, Andrew, for staying calm at all times. If I could be calm, I might not need any of them. But I can't, and so I do.

My grateful thanks to:

Richard Allan, for advice on how hot-air balloons fly and crash. Adrian Summons (again) for the police stuff. Denise Stott and Mary Frew for the medical detail. (Fabulously gory this time, ladies, well done!) Rosie Buckman for the German translation (and for selling my books overseas), and Jacqui Socrates (and her mum) for ensuring Jessica's Polish is credible. Kate and Jill of Kick Marketing, who have certainly kicked me into shape this year.

My cheery thanks to:
My friend Belinda Bauer, who makes me feel normal on a daily basis. Those who habitually visit the scene of the crime.

My eternal thanks to:
Anne-Marie Doulton of The Ampersand Agency. Transworld Publishers.

ABOUT THE AUTHOR

Sharon Bolton is a Mary Higgins Clark Award winner and an ITW Thriller Award, CWA Gold Dagger and Barry Award nominee. She lives near London, England. Sharon Bolton was previously published as S.J. Bolton.